JOHN PAUL JONES

The Stars and Stripes

The seamstress who made them:
Betsy Ross—a Scots American

First recognized by a foreign power (France) on Planet Earth, when John Paul Jones was on the USS Ranger.

First raised in Outer Space, by a Scots American—Neil Armstrong on the Moon!

John Paul Jones

Father of the United States Navy

U.S.S. Ranger—U.S.S. Bon Homme Richard—U.S.S. America

by Wallace Bruce

Writers Club Press
San Jose New York Lincoln Shanghai

John Paul Jones
Father of the United States Navy

Writers Club Press
an imprint of iUniverse, Inc.

For information address:
iUniverse, Inc.
5220 S. 16th St., Suite 200
Lincoln, NE 68512
www.iuniverse.com

Apart from *Gloria* and *Don Juan*, all ships and people mentioned at the beginning of each chapter did exist historically. All other names are purely fictitious to help illustrate the character of John Paul Jones and some of the major incidents in his life.

ISBN: 0-595-24232-4

Printed in the United States of America

This book is dedicated to all good sailors and marines, both past and present.

"I have not yet begun to fight!"

—John Paul Jones

Contents

FOREWORD

The background to this book started when the author took a group of students from Springburn College, Scotland, out to the U.S.A., as the guests of Neil Armstrong who, apart from other things, served in the United States Navy. Apart from a letter of thanks from Her Majesty the Queen, the author received a very complimentary letter from that gracious lady of happy memories, Her Majesty the Queen Mother, who relished every word of it and appreciated the first class research that was done into a very complex subject. From the presidential aspect, letters of thanks were received from Presidents Reagen, Bush Snr, and Clinton. From the astronautical point of view, Neil Armstrong was "delighted to add it to [his] library," and Captain "Rick" Hauck, U.S.N., who took the space shuttle *Discovery* up after the *Challenger* exploded killing all crew aboard, said he would be delighted to take a copy of *John Paul Jones: the Father of the United States Navy* into space, but was unable to do so as NASA had done the logistics down to the last ounce.

Coincidentally, the opening shots of the war against international terrorism were two Tomohawk cruise missiles, simultaneously fired from the state of the art destroyer, the U.S.S. *John Paul Jones,* and the Royal Navy nuclear submarine, H.M.S. *Triumph*; while the former is the subject of this book, the predecessor of the latter is also mentioned in this book.

Wallace Bruce

Further information may be found at **www.diadembooks.com/ pauljones.htm**

JOHN PAUL JONES

John Paul, before he became internationally famous as John Paul Jones, was born July 6, 1747, at Kirkbean, Arbigland, Scotland. His father worked as a gardener to the local squire, a Mr. Craik by name, whose illegitimate son was George Washington's personal physician and lifelong friend. As a barefooted boy, young John Paul assisted his father in his garden, doing such mundane things as weeding, leaf sweeping, *et cetera*.

At an early age he went to sea as a cabin boy, becoming a captain in his own right at the age of twenty-one in the British merchant service. However, his career came to a sharp end when he was master of the *Betsy* when, off the coast of Tobago, he killed the leader of a mutinous group in self-defense. Adding *Jones to* his name, he ended up in Philadelphia and offered his services to the infant American navy, becoming its ablest and most dashing commander, raising "Old Glory" for the first time ever to the jackstaff of the USS *Alfred,* then attacking British ports on the original USS *Ranger.* His hour of glory, however, was on the USS *Bon Homme Richard* when he engaged the Royal Navy off Flamborough Head. When all the odds were against him, and the skipper of the HMS *Serapis,* Captain Pearson, demanded his surrender, his immortal reply was, "I have not yet begun to fight!" On return to the United States, he ended up supervising and launching his flagship, the USS *Amenca.*

When the War of Independence was over, he found himself serving one of the greatest despots in history, Catherine the Great of Russia, as Admiral of her Black Sea fleet in her war against Turkey. Being a professional among amateurs, he left Russia in disgrace on a trumped-up charge of rape, to die in Paris at the early age of forty-five, on July 13, 1792.

On the instructions of President Teddy Roosevelt, his preserved mortal remains were escorted back to the United States on the USS *Brooklyn,* surrounded by warships of the U.S. Navy, in 1905. They now rest in a vast shrine, guarded by the United States Marines, in the crypt of the Cathedral of the Navy at the United States Naval Academy.

Considering that every president since and including Kennedy, save three, served in the U.S. Navy and, of the twelve astronauts on the moon, nine started their careers in the same navy, not forgetting the naval pilots on the space shuttles, it is fair to say that the gardener's barefooted boy from Scotland and his influence have gone a long way.

CHAPTER 1

TOWARDS THE END OF SCHOOLDAYS

Mr. John Paul, Snr	Mr. Craik's Gardener
Mrs. John Paul	The Gardener's Wife
Mr. William Paul	Tailor in Fredericksburg, Virginia
Mr. Craig	Estate Owner, Arbigland, Scotland
Mr. Craik's illegitimate son	George Washington's Personal Physician and Lifelong Friend
Sir Francis Drake	Famous English Sailor
Sir Walter Raleigh	Famous English Sailor
King George II	King of Britain and Colonies (1727–1760)
Duke of Cumberland	Son of King George II
Bonnie Prince Charlie	Claimant to the British Throne

In midsummer of 1761, at Arbigland, near the shores of the Solway Firth in the south west of Scotland, there was a barefooted boy, the son of a local gardener, and his name was John Paul. Being thirteen years of age, he was due to leave school very shortly, and what the future held for him only history would tell. For he had the alternatives of either working on the land, which his parents wished him to do and he did not, or answering the call of the sea, which came naturally to him but was against his parental wishes.

This area where he lived was flanked on one side by the Galloway hills and on the other side by Cumbria in the north west of England. The scenery in this area was of a placid beauty, compared with the rugged Highlands of Scotland, and the environment was rich in agriculture on land, with an overabundance of fish, both onshore in the local rivers, particularly the Nith, and offshore in the Firth itself. Because of the Gulf Stream, it experienced a moderate climate most of the year, compared with other parts of the country. But when there were changes in weather conditions, they could be very erratic. Such changes, being very unpredictable, made the Solway Firth very difficult for shiphandling and required sailors frequenting these waters to be of the highest skill, because of the currents and tides.

At that particular time the boy's father, gardener John Paul, toiled away in the garden on the estate where he worked for the local squire, a Mr. Craik by name, who lived with his wife and family in nearby Arbigland House, or "the big hoose" as it was known in the community. This was the terminology used by all members of the lower echelons to describe the residences of their masters in the rural areas of Scotland. Gardener Paul and his wife Jean lived in a small, thatched, white cottage nearby, which gave him easy access to his work. The remainder of his family lived there with him, with the exception of his older son William, who had emigrated to Fredericksburg, Virginia, in the American colonies, where he worked as a tailor. So, apart from his two daughters, there was only one other son living at home, also called John. Gardener Paul was a product of that old Scottish school of thoroughness, where everything had to be meticulously carried out. And because of this, he guarded the products and enterprises of his garden in much the same way as we today would guard the gold in Fort Knox. He was a well-built man, with a reddish beard, which had intermingling gray hairs, and a weather-beaten face. His sharp, piercing brown eyes penetrated you the moment he spoke to you. He was not only strong in physique but in character, and would not suffer fools gladly. Apart from the well-being of his family, his immediate concerns were his employer, who was very strong-headed on certain architectural designs which were the norm of the day, and his son John who, even at the early age of thirteen was in an abyss between the land and the sea as to what the future would hold for him.

Young John Paul was a small boy for his age, with sandy hair and hazel eyes and a soft-spoken manner, the latter being deceptive, for when the occasion did arise he could explode into a ferocious temper. His occupations were either working barefooted in the garden assisting his father or playing sailors with his fellow peers, using imaginary warships down on the shore, not far from the cottage in which he lived. As he was just about to leave school, this conflict between life on land and that of seafaring became uppermost in his mind. And, quite naturally, it caused a lot of concern for his parents, he being the only son left at home to carry on the gardening tradition and act as breadwinner for them in their old age. Mr. Craik, the landowner, was of a similar disposition, for he recognised the same thoroughness in young John as he did in his father. And because of this, he was over-anxious that he should follow his father's footsteps and take up a career on the land.

With no sign of young John appearing on the horizon, gardener Paul continued his laborious and intricate task of pruning rose trees, whilst at the same time he did everything in his power to swish away the midges, which, although not carriers of malaria, were equally as, if not more annoying than mosquitoes. In the meantime, young John was happy spending his time down on the seashore with fellow playmates of his own age group, fighting imaginary naval battles with makeshift model ships. Although the conflict raged in his mind between being a barefooted gardener's son working on some obscure estate and life at sea, the way he conducted those naval sorties, from the commanding heights overlooking the bay, he was, unconsciously at the tender age of thirteen, already a leader in the making. Being a curious child, he noticed a two-masted brigantine that had already dropped anchor in the bay, which caught the imagination of his maritime instincts. Nothing would do for him but to borrow a rowing boat, which was tied up alongside the quay, and row over to it. It being a calm day, when the sea was like a millpond, he managed the boat with little effort and, approaching the ship, he recognised it as being the one called *Friendship*, which plied the Atlantic between Whitehaven and the American colonies, calling at the West Indies en route. Coming alongside he noticed no sign of life aboard, so he decided to have a look around for himself. His inspection was very thorough, from the poop deck to the forecastle, but when he started climbing the ratlings on the standing rigging of the foremast to get an aerial view of the situation, the game was up. For, unknown to him, the Bosun, a Mr. George Thorpe, had just ascended from one of the holds where he had been checking the sails that were required to get the ship under way and inspecting the consignment of goods which were shortly due for shipment to the West Indies and Virginia, ensuring that the latter were securely lashed down so as to prevent movement once the voyage had commenced. Thorpe was an old salt, over six feet tall, with a dark, brownish beard, showing tinges of grey here and there. Being of rugged appearance, and built as solid as a quayside bollard, he was far from impressed at his first encounter with young John, who by this time had climbed right to the look-out on the foremast.

"What are you doing up there, you young scoundrel?" bellowed Thorpe, in his broad Yorkshire accent you could cut with a knife.

"I am just having a look around your beautiful ship, Sir," replied young John, with an air of confidence, as if he were the ship's master and not just a young schoolboy who had no right to be there in the first instance.

"What's your name and where do you come from?" demanded the Bosun angrily.

"My name is John Paul, Sir, and I come from Arbigland where my father is a gardener on the estate of the local squire, a gentleman called Mr. Craik."

"Oh, I see," said the Bosun, "I have heard about you before from the other children that hang about the port."

"That's probably true, Sir," replied young John. "But, honestly, I did not intend to do any harm to your fine ship, Sir."

"Well, why did you board it without permission?" asked the Bosun, in a rather stern manner.

"For no other reason than to satisfy my curiosity to see how it was laid out," was young John's reply.

"But you are a gardener's son, with nothing whatsoever to do with shipping," retorted Bosun Thorpe. "Is that not the case?"

"Well, to a certain extent that might be true, Sir," replied young John. "But navigational studies are one of my favourite subjects at school. Classroom theory is one thing, but to be able to board a real seagoing ship beats all the books that were ever printed on the subject, for one is learning by doing, which is much better than pure theoretical knowledge."

The Bosun was quite taken aback by the intelligent and sensible conversation of young John and only wished that some of the crew aboard his ship had the same keenness and enthusiasm about things relating to the sea as this young schoolboy had. All the questions young John put to him were very relevant to the safe handling of a ship, which impressed him so much that he spotted the schoolboy's hidden nautical talents, which were somewhat amazing, coming from a person of such tender years. Mr. Thorpe's attitude to young John began to mellow and, seeing the schoolboy was hungry and in need of a good meal, he took him into the galley before he rowed back to the shore. After a meal of salt beef, potatoes and turnips, young John's voracious appetite was once again satisfied. And by the time it was washed down with a glass of lime, which was sweetened with sugar to reduce the tang, they were both conversing like a pair of old salts that had sailed the seven seas. This might have been the case of Bosun Thorpe, but young John had never been further away than the immediate area around the Solway Firth.

"What school are you attending, my young lad?" enquired the Bosun, who now had a much calmer disposition towards John than he had when they first encountered one another.

"The village school in Kirkbean, Sir," was John's reply.

"It's a small world," replied the Bosun. "For the first time I heard of that school was from a first mate in Kingston, Jamaica, who had nothing but praise for the schoolmaster, a Mr. Lindsay, I believe."

"Yes, Sir," said John. "He is a first class teacher—particularly in the fields of mathematics, trigonometry and English studies."

"When are you due to leave school then?" enquired Bosun Thorpe, who appeared to develop a greater interest in the boy as the conversation continued.

"Funny you asked that question, Sir," replied John. "But tomorrow is my last day at school, and we will all have to be clean and smartly dressed for the great prize-giving ceremony, with everyone looking their best in front of the remainder of the Kirkbean community."

"I sincerely hope that you don't go barefooted and in those rags you are wearing today," said the Bosun, in a rather fatherly manner.

"Oh, no, Sir," said John, "I shall be prim and proper for the great occasion, for I shall present myself in such a manner that I won't let my poor family down." John continued: "You see, my oldest brother William, who emigrated to the American colonies a few years back, bequeathed me his good clothing that became too small for him and also a good solid pair of boots."

"Well," said the Bosun, "I wish you luck at the prize-giving ceremony, young lad, and make sure, when you return ashore, that the gig is well secured to the wooden jetty, and no more will be said about our unofficial, yet most enjoyable, encounter."

Having gleefully quenched his thirst at the fountain of maritime knowledge, young John rowed his way happily back to the quayside, cherishing many of the stories he had heard from an experienced Bosun of what life was like at sea. This was from a man who was many years his senior, who had encountered many aspects of seafaring life, both rough and fair, in many of the oceans and seas throughout the world. After the brief encounter aboard ship, young John stealthily made his way back to the garden in Arbigland, expecting to receive the wrath of his father, who had been toiling away all day in the heat of the glorious summer weather, which was warmer than usual in that part of Scotland owing to the hot sun and cloudless sky. In an endeavour to placate his father, young John, knowing that he would be thirsty, made him up a drink of cool, fresh spring water, mixed with a couple of handfuls of oatmeal, which was a most refreshing drink to quench one's thirst after a strenuous day's work, for it was now approaching late in the afternoon. And as the day proceeded the detestable midges became more abundant and continued to do so, until late in the cool of the evening. This, coupled with young John's long absence from his father's horticultural tasks, gave him the impression that he would not find his dad in the best of spirits. However, there was nothing more to do for young John but to take the bull by the horns and nervously enter the garden through the main privet arches his father nurtured over the years. It was a rather large sprawling garden, but once he located his father, who was struggling with large granite blocks that had been hewn in a nearby quarry, to make yet another rock garden, young John braced himself for the worst. As he slowly meandered up the gravel footpath, the sharp pieces of small rock were hurting the soles of his feet, but in his mind that sort of physical pain was nothing compared with the mental pain he would have to endure from the sharp tongue of his father whose character was such that he would not take lightly to his prolonged absence away from the garden. Approaching his father in an intrepid manner, young John said, "Good afternoon, father"—to which came the stern reply, "Good afternoon, wayfarer, where have you been all this time, considering all the work I have to do in order to keep this place prim and proper?"

"Well, father, I spent most of the afternoon on a two-masted brigantine, which had arrived and dropped anchor in the harbour", was young John's low-voiced, guilty reply as he looked at his father in a rather morose manner, nervously intertwining his fingers in front of his stomach.

"How many times have I told you in the past to keep away from these ships and some of their cut-throat crews, who are a bad influence on a boy of your age?"

"I appreciate your advice, father, but the visit aboard this ship was far from that," was John's reply, given with an air of confidence, for he sensed his father was not as angry with him for absconding as he had previously envisaged.

"What do you mean by that, young John?" asked his father, whose attitude changed from one of mild anger to that of genuine inquisitiveness.

"Well, father, the only person aboard was the Bosun, who was preparing the ship's sails and cargo for its outward voyage to the West Indies and the American Colonies."

"Do tell me, son, the name of the ship," his father said. "I might know some of its crew."

"It is a brigantine called *Friendship* that is homeported in a place called Whitehaven, which is on the English side of the water from here."

"Indeed? I have had previous dealings with that ship's crew, giving them fresh fruit from the garden whilst they were alongside the quay discharging their cargo from the New World. I think its Master's name is Captain Blake, and the Bosun is a Mr. Thorpe."

"I did not see the captain, father, nor get the Bosun's name, for I just called him Sir, being respectful of his position." Young John hadn't realised his father was aware of both the ship and some of its crew.

"Well I must take back what I said about some crew members being cut-throats, for that is not the case when we are talking about Mr. Thorpe. For although he talks with a broad and rough Yorkshire accent, beneath that he is a very sincere and genuine individual, for I know of him and his relations quite well, through our landlord Mr. Craik, who also has estates in the Whitehaven area."

"Well, father, he spoke to me in a most enlightening manner, and I could see from the way in which he presented himself to my questions that he is the humane type of Bosun, which, I am led to believe, is a rarity in the merchant navy these days. He gave me the impression, on first hearing and talking to him, that his bark was worse than his bite. And he is the type that, instead of using his rattan, manages to win the confidence of the lower deck by means of his persuasive tongue and example. I also gleaned from my discussion with him that he is fully competent on all matters as to the smooth functioning of a ship, in either a fair wind, the doldrums or severe gales."

"How on earth do you manage to pick them, John?" asked his father.

"What do you mean, father?"

"Well, do you realise that Mr. Thorpe, although he may appear to be rather uncouth on the surface, is married into one of the most famous naval families that used to be in this area?"

"No, I did not, father, but I suspected that, underneath the coarse mannerisms, there was something genuine and sincere about him, which one does not find in the majority of the run-of-the-mill tars whom one meets down on the dockside."

"Oh yes, my son," replied his father; "there is a lot of truth in what you say, for Mr. Thorpe's wife's family were very influential in the merchant marine industry at one time, both as ship-builders and makers of quality sails. And I believe the same family were the main ships' chandlers for the south west of Scotland, supplying most of the ships that plied the Atlantic in both directions, with the necessary requirements to keep a happy ship afloat, from the poop deck to the pig and whistle."

"What are his in-laws' names, father?" enquired John

"Oh, they are the one-time McLure family, whose business enterprises were not only in this part of the country, where they were big indeed, but also in Whitehaven, which is one of the most important naval ports in England. This is where Mr. Thorpe comes in, for he married one of the daughters, and, although I never met him personally, I know him through Mr. Craik the squire and Captain Blake of the brigantine *Friendship*, with whom I had a long discussion once, after delivering fruit and vegetables to his ship."

"Why is it then that Mr. Thorpe is only a Bosun now?"

"Well…," replied his father, "that's a rather long story, my son, for it started with Mr. Thorpe's wife's grandfather, the first McLure, who ventured into the shipping industry, both here and in Whitehaven. He was one of those mean, dour Scots, who worked hard all his days, building up his enterprise. As he neither drank nor smoked, he led a very frugal life, making every penny a prisoner, unless he was investing it to expand his business. He was also a staunch elder in the Auld Kirk in Kirkcudbright and ruled not only his employees with a rod of iron but also his own son Mr. Thorpe's father-in-law. When he died, he left everything to this only son; and this is where the rot set in, for he literally drank the lot, leaving not only his firm bankrupt but also his own family destitute. Before his business was wound up, Mr. Thorpe was one of his managers in Whitehaven, but, on the advent of bankruptcy, he had no alternative but to go to sea as a deckhand, as employment was very difficult to find locally. Mind you, John, although I don't know him, from what I am told he has done exceptionally well at sea, and rose to the rank of Bosun in a comparatively short time. And from what Mr. Craik tells me, should good fortune come his way again and the economy expands, he may well end up owning a ship of his own."

Young John, in the meantime, seemed to come to life with his father's last bit of information, having sat passively listening to him giving a lucid account of the ups and downs of business life and a first-hand insight as to how the real world operated.

"Thank you very much, father, for your long and thorough account of Mr. Thorpe's background", was young John's calm reply at the end of his father's discourse. Being a very mature child for his age, with an enquiring mind more befitting an adult than a schoolboy, young John intimated to his father that he had learned more of him and Mr. Thorpe that day about the ways of the world than he had in all his years at school.

John Paul Snr. was much happier now that he learned the company his young son had been keeping that afternoon, but still warned him to beware of some of the blackguards that hung around the quayside. Being part of the folklore of the mercantile marine, some of them were desperate characters, having served their time in His Majesty's prisons, and they would stop at nothing to obtain money in order to purchase a few drinks in The Crow's Nest, which was a notorious dockside public house. By drinking there, there was always the possibility of getting away to sea, as it was frequented by bona-fide seafarers who could put them in touch with a shipowner who was trying to muster a crew for a pending voyage. Furthermore, The Crow's Nest was frequented by the local daughters-of-joy, whose primary purpose was to keep the lonely seafarer happy, regardless of the venereal consequences to themselves or their clients.

In return for his father's sound advice, young John informed him that he was aware of such goings-on at the dockside but that his interest in visiting the ships that were coming and going had nothing whatsoever to do with loose women, who followed merchant seamen, particularly when they paid off ships from a foreign tour, but to further his own interest in the functional operating of sailing ships, on which his heart, much against his father's wishes, was already set. Being aware that he was about to leave school, like most boys of his age, he had three options. They were—working on the land, going to sea, or taking the high road to London. Parental influence was paramount in the young boy's life, and his father's love was reciprocated by young John, although naturally, like most boys, he was at odds with him on certain points. But this overriding concern and respect for his father was demonstrated when he knew he would be thirsty, and what drink he would like to quench his thirst.

Once his father had drunk up the oatmeal refreshment his thirst was quenched. And wiping the sweat, which had gathered in large beads on his weather-beaten brow, he thanked his son for being so considerate. Then he and young John once again set about working in the garden. And this was indeed no ordinary garden but a mixture of everything, which included all types of fruit and vegetables, various types of trees, hedges, archways, fish ponds and rock gardens. Interspersed around the grounds were summer houses, which gave one shade from the sun at the height of summer, and protection from the rain, which sometimes fell relentlessly in the Galloway region.

"I don't really know where to start, John," said his father, as he surveyed the various parts of the ground that required attention.

"Maybe you can do some weeding for me in that plot of gladiolas next to the round house, for the ground there is relatively soft and should not hurt your bare feet. I will continue building the rock-garden, as Mr. Craik is rather anxious to get it completed before some of his friends arrive from London on holiday."

Conscientiously, young John began to carry out his father's instructions; which to him was a happy task. For although he had the weeds to contend with, there was compensation in the sweet aroma that came from the honeysuckle, which crawled in abundance up various parts of the garden walls. Although he applied himself arduously to the allotted tasks given to him by John Paul Snr., there were two distractions which occupied his mind. The immediate one was the intermittent buzzing of bees, as they made their way around the garden, working like beavers to collect pollen from the vast assortment of flowers they had at their disposal. His mental distraction was his experiences on the brigantine *Friendship* down in the harbour and his most enlightening encounter with Mr. Thorpe, the Bosun. The yarns he heard from him about foreign lands that were far away were all stored in his fertile and retentive young mind. However, on this subject, John played his cards close to his chest and kept his innermost experiences and joys to himself, as he did not wish to offend his parents by letting them know that his true desires were not really life on the land, which they wished, but life on the high seas, come rain, hail or sunshine.

Having completed the weeding to his father's satisfaction, he then started leaf sweeping, in order to make the place look more respectable. In the process, however, he fell into a bunch of nettles which were growing out of a compost heap. His language on that occasion was rather blue, but with the help of some docken leaves he rubbed his legs vigorously, which had a soothing effect that eventually banished the sting. When his father returned, he noticed his son was not his usual chirpy self, and quite naturally enquired as to what had happened to him.

"Well, father, on completing the weeding you asked me to do, I then continued leaf sweeping, in order to make the place more tidy, and lo and behold, I fell among the nettles which grow out of the compost heap, next to one of the round houses."

"Is it very painful, my son?" enquired his father anxiously.

"No, not now, father, for I have rubbed the stings all over with docken leaves and let mother nature take her course. The result, apart from the rash, is that the sting has vanished"

"These blasted compost heaps and round houses," retorted gardener Paul. "They are the bane of my life, and all because of a strong-headed Mr. Craik, who is obsessed with symmetry."

"Please explain what you mean, father?"

"Well, son, symmetry means that one thing must be balanced by something similar, which, in Mr. Craik's opinion, leads to architectural beauty. For example, one tree must be balanced by one similar, one round house by another, and so on."

"Oh, I see, father. Is this the fashion of the age or one of the squire's own pet obsessions?"

"No, it is not one of his pet obsessions but a form of architectural planning in the age in which we live. The only difference from other people is, he is mustard keen on it. However, as he pays the piper—he calls the tune, and there is very little I can do about it, except grin and bear it."

"Have you ever discussed it with him?" enquired young John.

"Discussed it!" replied his father. "In your absence, some time ago, he and I had a very heated discussion on the matter, which nearly cost me my job. But having a tied cottage and a family to keep, I had no alternative but to submit to his pedantic desires."

"But what has all this to do with me falling into nettles and stinging myself?"

"Well, son, the round house that has the nettle-strewn compost heap beside it is a place I had my own ideas of what to do with, but he scrapped my plans and insisted on this structure, so as to balance the other round house on the right hand side of the Big House. And, take it from me, that's the sole purpose it serves and nothing else."

"So, would you call it an architectural eyesore instead of beauty?" enquired John, still scratching his leg where it had been stung by nettles.

"Indeed I would call it the former, for you have struck the nail on the head; for, if I had my way, it would not be there; neither would the compost heap. And with no compost heap, there would have been no nettles to sting you."

"What would you have put there in its place, father?"

"Well, I wanted to build a nice summer garden house, overlooking the pond, which is filled with tropical fish and watercress. This would have given Mr. Craik and his friends shade on a hot summer's day. But my words and reasoning were to no avail, for, the next thing, the stonemasons were at work, carrying out his instructions, very much against my will."

The conversation was abruptly stopped, when gardener Paul noticed a young hoodlum in the grounds, helping himself to as much fruit as he could carry. The lout in question was no other than Douglas Maxwell, the village bully, who had all the other children of Kirkbean absolutely terrified of him—he being of the idea that he was above the law, particularly in the village school. Both gardener Paul and his son gave chase, and with a flying tackle from John Snr. they eventually apprehended him. After gardener Paul gave him the side of his hand across the face, he immediately locked him up in one of the round houses and his son John in the other. Although this was against his will in the case of his son, he had good reasons for doing so. But considering he had done nothing wrong, young John was not only bemused but furious with his father's actions, for being treated in the same way as the village bully.

"Let me out, let me out!" cried John. "I have done nothing wrong, father. Why should I be locked up like Douglas Maxwell, when I did not steal anything?"

"Keep quiet, will you," his father replied, "and you will see the reasons for what I did very shortly."

His son was more mystified with his father's very vague answer and asked himself if he had done anything wrong to offend his father. There was nothing he could think of, except that his father might be of the opinion that he was working in collusion with the village bully. If this was the case, he said to himself, there was nothing further from the truth, so he had to be content with being locked up like a caged animal, for no obvious reason.

At this stage Mr. Craik entered the garden, on his twice daily inspection, to ensure that everything was being carried out as per his instructions, which he gave to the gardener Paul on his morning visit. He was a tall, handsome-looking man, whose pink-coloured cheeks may have given one the impression he was inclined to drink deep and over-imbibe in claret. With a greyish, white wig that flowed down to the back of his neck, he was dressed in resplendent costume of a white shirt, silk cravat and a scarlet jacket. His white breeches and black riding boots left no-one in doubt that he was very much indeed the lord of the manner.

As he walked slowly up the path leading to the round houses, he carried out his inspection with the thoroughness of a military commander inspecting his troops. On seeing his gardener approaching him in an agitated manner, he sensed something was wrong, because gardener Paul was invariably calm and self-assured, for he was very competent in everything he did for Mr. Craik.

"A very good afternoon to you, Mr. Paul," said Mr. Craik in the benign manner of a country squire.

Doffing his cap, gardener Paul replied, "And a very good afternoon to you, Sir."

"How are things looking in the garden today? Is there anything wrong at all?" enquired Mr. Craik.

"Well, things were going very well, Sir, until I caught a young lout stealing fruit."

"Pray do tell me more," said Mr. Craik, in a rather commanding manner.

"His name, Sir, is Douglas Maxwell, a bully in the local community, among the children of his own age group; so I placed him in the left-hand side balancing round house, knowing full well that you were due to carry out your daily inspection at any time."

"Oh, I see," said the squire, who, being mustard keen on symmetry, glanced up at the right-hand side balancing round house and noticed young John's terrified face.

"And your boy was at it too, I see."

"Oh no, Sir," was gardener Paul's sharp reply. "I just put him up there for symmetry."

"Pray, Mr. Paul, have your son released immediately and I will deal with the vagabond in my own good time."

When John was released, he at least satisfied the squire's idiosyncratic obsession by the balancing role he had played in his rather traumatic experience. And he could now appreciate his father's motives for putting him there, which were not so much punitive as merely a sarcastic way of ridiculing the squire, whose face by this time had become red with anger at what had happened.

As Mr. Craik and gardener Paul were discussing what to do about the scoundrel Douglas Maxwell, young John continued tidying up the garden; but, because of his recent experience, he was much more indolent in his approach to things. For such a humiliating act to be perpetrated against him was the straw that broke the camel's back, and privately in his own mind he was even more oriented towards going to sea than working on the land as an assistant gardener to his father.

In the meantime, Mr. Craik demanded of his gardener, "Before we release this scoundrel from the secure balancing round house, pray do tell me more about him, Mr. Paul."

"Well, Sir, he is known as the local bully among children of my son's age group and below, and he is prone to intimidate those who are weaker than him, even if they are slightly older than he is."

"Do you know of any particular reason for this conduct on his part?" asked Mr. Craik, who had again gathered his composure and returned to his natural colour, once the adrenalin had subsided.

"Well, Sir, you just need to look at his head and sunken eyes to see that he is of very low intelligence, and because of this he has a very large chip on his shoulder. At the same time, however, he is very sly and possesses an unusual cunning, which he probably inherits from his forefathers."

"Do you think there could have been any incestuous relationships in the past that produced an individual like this, Mr. Paul?" asked the squire.

"No, I do not know of anything of that nature happening at all, Sir," was gardener Paul's reply. "I do know, however, that he is of very low stock, for if I remember correctly, they have been a domineering and feuding family in this community for many generations. For example, they had a long-standing feud with the Armstrongs of Langholm, which led to cattle-rustling and sheep-stealing that landed some of them in jail for those offences."

"Very interesting," said Mr. Craik. "Is there anything else you can tell me, before I deal with this vagabond?"

"That, briefly, Sir, is most of what I know about them, least to say that wherever they go they are hell bent on creating trouble. They are also sleek and plausible enough to give the appearance of innocent victims of circumstances, being deliberately persecuted by all people set in authority over them."

"Most enlightening, Mr. Paul." Mr. Craik continued: "I now recollect somewhere in the back of my mind that some of them are connected with the mercantile marine."

"You are so correct, Sir, and I am sorry for omitting that fact, for there is one of his cousins I know of, a ship's carpenter called Mungo Maxwell, who I gather is also of the same temperament. For local sailors tell me that although he joined the mercantile marine comparatively recently, he is perpetually acting as a latter-day ship's lawyer and does everything in his power to create dissension aboard ship when they are on the high seas."

"So that's all you know about him and his relations, Mr. Paul?"

"Yes, Sir, but my son John probably knows more about the young scoundrel in question than either of us does, as he attends the same school as him; so why not ask him, if you are interested in finding out more about Maxwell?"

"A very sensible suggestion, Mr. Paul. Call young John over, as I want to get to the bottom of this villain and find out what makes him act like this."

"John, come over here at once—Mr. Craik would like to talk to you!" shouted gardener Paul in a very authoritative manner.

John immediately laid down his tools and came over as his father had requested, and although he looked like a lobster where he had been stung by nettles, temperamentally he had once again returned to his quiet-spoken and dignified self.

"Sorry for that rather embarrassing situation, young John," said Mr. Craik. "But putting you in the other round house was purely your father's idea of getting his own back on me, in a humorous manner, which has its roots in a long, heated argument he and I had some time ago, on the subject of symmetry."

"That's quite all right, Sir," replied young John, who by this time, being fully composed, was beginning to appreciate the humorous side of the incident.

"More important, my boy, what do you know about this thief and vagabond, Maxwell, who was caught stealing my fruit?"

"Well, Sir, to be quite honest with you, he is a rogue, a cheat, liar and bully."

"What is he like at school? He is much the same there, I assume?"

"At school, Sir..." John became emotional but managed to control his anger in front of the squire. "He has all the rest of the school so terrified that they will do practically anything he asks of them."

"For example?" asked Mr. Craik.

"Well, Sir, when Mr. Lindsay, the dominie, gives us exercises to do, all he does is copy the answers from the cleverer members of class."

"Does Mr. Lindsay know about this?"

"No, Sir, but how he has not found out is a mystery to me, as he is not only an excellent teacher but a very shrewd character."

"Not as shrewd as you think, young John," replied Mr. Craik.

"Well, Sir, you could have a point, but as this is our final week at school, examination results usually separate the wheat from the chaff, as they were set last month, under strict exam conditions, when because of invigilators it was impossible to copy."

"So you personally have nothing to worry about, John," said Mr. Craik.

"Not really, from an examination point of view, Sir, as it does not pay to be a copycat at school, for you are found out in the long run and become the subject of ridicule on prize-giving day among your classmates, relatives and friends."

"Very good, John," said the squire. "You are free to continue your work and I will have a further talk with you and your father once I have dealt with this bullying vagabond and chased him off the estate."

"One thing I must mention, Mr. Craik," said young John, "is that this Douglas Maxwell is such a confounded liar and slippery eel, he might try to swing the onus on to me, saying that I told him it would be all right to come into the garden and help himself to fruit."

"Don't worry, John, I have dealt with scoundrels like this in the past and I can normally read them like a book." He turned to the gardener and demanded in a somewhat paternalistic manner: "Mr. Paul, release that villain from the round house—bring him to me immediately."

"Aye, aye, Sir, I shall do that with pleasure," was the gardener's reply.

On his release from the balancing round house, Douglas Maxwell, far from showing any sign of guilt or remorse, was quite cock-a-hoop with what he had done and casually sauntered up to Mr. Craik. The squire stared him straight in the eyes like shafts of steel, which had a tremendous effect on Maxwell who realised, without a word being uttered, that he had maybe bitten off more than he could chew this time. Bullying in school was one thing; but on coming face to face with Mr. Craik his attitude changed completely, for he was aware of the presence of a gentleman who exerted great influence in the community, both as a landed aristocrat and as an individual who had strong political contacts in the area.

Mr. Craik, with his riding crop in his right hand, struck the palm of his left hand with it, cast his steel-like eyes over in such an aloof manner that, if looks could kill, there would be very little hope for the culprit who was caught stealing from his estate.

Surveying him over from top to toe, in complete silence for a few seconds, he angrily blurted out, "So you are one of the Maxwell tribe of vagabonds, who for some generations have been infamous in this area. You think yourselves not only to be better than the decent citizens of the community but above the law of the land itself."

"That's an utter load of rubbish," retorted Maxwell.

With the adrenalin rising again, Mr. Craik changed from anger to fury, which could be seen by the increasing redness of his face. Prodding the accused in the chest with his bull crop, he went on, in a loud commanding voice: "Don't speak to me in that manner, you insignificant, good-for-nothing lout!"

"Sorry, Sir, it is just a matter of habit," replied Maxwell.

"Yes," said the squire, "a habit nurtured by generations of treachery and ill-breeding."

Maxwell was aghast, for never had he been spoken to like that before by anyone, particularly with reference to his family background.

He stood spellbound in a complete void, as Mr. Craik continued, "I probably know more about your clan's background than you do yourself. For example, if my history serves me right, your forefathers bedevilled the poor Armstrongs from Langholm so much, they could not stand the feuding that existed over sheep-stealing and cattle-rustling, so that they had eventually to emigrate to the Ohio Valley in the American Colonies and start afresh, so that they could live in peace and harmony."

"Oh, I did not know that, Sir," was Maxwell's meek and timid reply.

"Well, you are learning every day, my boy," retorted Mr. Craik who went on lecturing the youth who, by this time, realised he had met his match, for he started to tremble in fear of what might happen next. "And here you are, the local bully, I am told, trying to carry on the same tradition in present day Galloway."

"No, I am not, Sir," replied a quivering Maxwell.

"Oh yes, you are. And let's have one thing perfectly clear here and now—such attitudes either on your own part or those of your relatives will not impress me. Do you understand?"

"Yes, Sir, yes, Sir," said Maxwell, who by this time was not only quivering but shaking like a leaf. He could not look the squire straight in the face and became more fidgety, looking askance at young John who could not help but hear the tongue-lashing he had received from Mr. Craik. The mere presence of young John at the scene really humiliated him as much as the squire's dressing down, for he ruled the roost in the village school and had never been spoken to this way before, not even by Mr. Lindsay, his school teacher, or any other members of his class.

Turning to his gardener, who stood silent throughout the whole of his discourse, Mr. Craik said, "Have you anything to say, Mr. Paul?"

"No, Sir, I'll leave all that to you, you being the landlord."

Turning then to the culprit, he said in no uncertain manner, "Should I ever have occasion to deal with you, on a case of this or a similar nature again, I shall have you charged with breaking and entering into my premises and theft of the produce of my garden."

"I understand, Sir," replied Maxwell. "It won't happen again."

"Don't interrupt, you rude rascal." And he went on: "You will then be placed in the tollbooth and eventually appear before the local justices, who will deal with you with the powers given them by Act of Parliament. So be off, you toerag and thief, and don't ever let me see you again!"

Realising he was lucky enough to get off with a verbal warning this time, Maxwell scampered out of the garden like a dog with his tail between his legs. But before he did, he managed to gather his composure and let his bullying instincts rear their ugly head once again for, on his way out he met young John, and his parting words were, "I will make you suffer for this at school tomorrow, you jumped-up gardener's lackey, whose parents cannot even afford you a decent pair of boots."

As his father and Mr. Craik were not too far away, young John thought that discretion was the better part of valour, and made no reply.

As Mr. Craik and gardener Paul finished discussing the incident, the squire called young John over to join their company.

"So your father tells me, it's your last day at school tomorrow, John?"

"Yes, Sir, and I won't be sorry to leave it."

"What do you mean by that? I always thought you liked school, my young boy."

"Oh yes, Sir, I like school and most of my classmates very much, but am squeamish at the thought of spending my last day there, in the presence of so many dignitaries—and in the company of that bully Maxwell."

Mr. Craik noticed a sudden change in John's attitude, for, far from being the chirpy lad with whom he was used to conversing, he found him to be irritable and edgy, as if something was annoying him.

"What's the matter, John?" said the squire. "You don't appear to be your usual self."

"Well, Sir, that bully threatened to get me at school tomorrow, and before he left the ground he passed some caustic remarks about the lowliness of my family. And as I simply adore them I shall get even with him by mustering all the strength and courage at my disposal. For bullying is one thing, but casting ill-founded remarks about my parents is quite another, which I will not stand from anybody, including the village bully."

"Oh, pray do ignore that," said the squire, "for in the uncharted years that lie ahead you should do well for yourself in the world, as you are a hard working and intelligent young boy."

"Thank you very much for the compliment, Sir."

Mr. Craik continued, "As for Maxwell, he will be nothing more than the village idiot, who will meet his real match physically very shortly—when he enters a real man's world."

"What do you mean by that, Sir?" enquired young John.

"Well, he will meet some real old salts, who have really roughed it in various parts of the world, when he is old enough to drink in the Crow's Nest at the dockside. And believe me, there are some rough-necks there who will cut him down to size."

As the evening sun was setting and the cool winds of the Solway Firth were causing the leaves on the trees in the garden to rustle slightly, it was time for all three to return to their respective living quarters: Mr. Craik to Arbigland House, his permanent country residence, and both Johns, Snr. and Jnr., to their gardener's cottage. It was when they were slowly meandering out of the garden that Mr. Craik said rather unexpectedly, "I think, Mr. Paul, my estate is big enough to employ another full-time member of staff; what are your views on the matter?" On hearing these words, young Paul immediately smelt a rat and glanced at his father to see what his reaction would be to Mr. Craik's question.

"Well, Sir," replied gardener Paul, "I must admit I am not as fit as I used to be, particularly when it comes to handling heavy materials. But what did you really have in mind, Sir?"

Young John's eager eyes immediately switched to Mr. Craik, as he anxiously awaited his reply.

"Well, I was thinking of young John here, who is due to leave school tomorrow and has no sign of any immediate employment in mind."

"That's very true, Sir," replied gardener Paul, who obviously expressed delight at the squire's suggestion.

Mr. Craik went on: "Do you think he would be a suitable apprentice for you, so that he could learn the intricacies of horticulture and the smooth running of the garden, without perpetual supervision?"

"As the boy has assisted me here since he was a toddler, Mr. Craik, I have no doubt whatsoever that he would be an ideal candidate for the job."

"Well, John," said the squire, "would you like to work with your father as an assistant gardener on my estate?"

Before replying, young John gave it some serious thought, but it was obvious to both Mr. Craik and his father that he was not over-zealous to become a trainee gardener. In a half-hearted manner he intimated to both of them that he would be quite capable of embarking on such a venture but, in all honesty, his heart would not be fully in it, for his heart lay only in one place and that was in the call of the sea.

"The sea is one thing," the landlord continued, "but did you ever think of your parents' retirement?"

"Indeed I have, Sir, but the mere pittance I will earn on the land is nothing to what I could earn at sea, particularly if I ever got into a situation where prize money is involved."

With this his father participated in the discussion and warned his son that he was aiming too high up for a boy of his age and that he had been reading too many chapbooks and listening to old salts tell their yarns down by the quayside.

"Remember, John," his father continued, "there are golden feathers in the birds that are far away."

"Oh yes, father," replied his son, "but life from the cradle to the grave is just a gamble." Young John continued: "You know quite well, father, the people from this part of Scotland who accumulated a modest fortune whilst serving in the mercantile marine and invested it sensibly in small farms around here, at a very early age when they were still young men. These same people, as you know, are today living in luxury, secure from poverty for the remainder of their lives, both for themselves and their families."

"That may be true, John," his father wisely told him, "but you take it from me, you can count the numbers of such-like people on one hand. For I could take you to countless others, in the various public bars down the Solway Coast, such as the Crow's Nest, Pig and Whistle and The Ancient Mariner, and you will find them spinning yarns of their experiences in various parts of the world. But what have they done with their hard-earned cash?"

"I don't know, father," said John, as he listened patiently.

"Well, to put it in a nutshell, my young lad," said gardener Paul, "they spent it on loose women and drink, in all corners of the earth, which they visited when travelling overseas."

Whilst gardener Paul was advising his son, the landlord stood by as a very interested onlooker, and then entered into the conversation: "Your father is talking a lot of common sense, John, and if I were you I would listen to his sound advice."

"Thank you, Sir," replied John.

Mr. Craik continued, "You see, working with me you will have a secure job, guaranteed wages and, should you get married one day, there will always be free accommodation for you and your family."

"Thank you very much for your advice and kind offer, Sir. I will give everything you said my most serious consideration."

The landlord wished both Johns, Snr. and Jnr., goodnight, and all three departed to their respective abodes.

The evening was now becoming much cooler and the golden sunset in the west appeared to put the sky ablaze, whilst the Solway Firth itself was reminiscent of a millpond. Slowly, gardener Paul and his young son made their way along the rugged path which would eventually lead to their humble cottage. The whole sea to their rear by this time appeared to be on fire, as the sun gradually descended beneath the inflamed horizon. A very impressive sight it was indeed, with both the towering trees of the estate and the sailing ships with their tall masts that plied to and fro, creating a most picturesque setting. If only an artist of genius could have captured such a majestic view of nature in all its glory, what a view it would have made for posterity!

Trudging wearily along the path, with the scented aroma around them from the various trees, flowers and bushes, it was obvious that they looked fatigued, particularly gardener Paul, who had had a strenuous and laborious day since first light. To the onlooker it was becoming obvious that the years of hard work on the Arbigland estate were beginning to take their toll on him, for as the journey continued, he appeared to walk unsurely, with a slight stoop on his shoulders. Being a man who was tall and possessed of a robust and rugged stature, his deportment was more obvious to the eye than would have been the case had he been a much smaller person with an insignificant physique. Young John, although obviously tired as well, was the picture of health and carried himself with a buoyancy which was only to be found in the brashness of his youth, with every moment enjoyed as a new experience in life.

As they continued silently to walk along, conversing only with the solitude of nature, John's father broke into conversation. "It has indeed been a hard day's slog in that garden, young John," he observed.

"Yes, father, particularly for you, as you have been hard at it since daybreak."

"True, John," was his father's reply. "The years eventually catch up on all of us. But youth is a marvellous gift, and whereas you have all these years ahead of you, I am afraid to say that mine are beginning to wane."

His son at this stage adopted a much more serious approach, which showed maturity well beyond his years, and said to his father, "Never mind, father, you and mother have been good to all of us, and we will not forget you in the evening of your lives."

"True, laddie, but you are really the only one I have, for your two sisters will eventually get married and go their separate ways. As for your older brother, he is now far across the sea in the American Colonies and from that distance there is very little he can do to help us."

Young John was once again entrenched in deep thought as he contemplated his father's words and looked rather sadly at him. As they walked, he said, "I am sure that my big brother William will let neither you nor mother down, particularly if he makes it as a tailor in that vast and up-and-coming part of the Empire called America."

"True, John," was his father's reply, "for he writes regularly from Virginia, and in every letter he sends home money for us and indicates warmth and concern as well."

"Oh, I know that, father, for mother has shown me and my sisters the letters he sends to us."

Gardener Paul continued, "You must remember, however, that he has his own life to lead, and as he is getting married shortly he will have enough commitments of his own to bring up a family, which will require all the money that he possesses."

"Yes, father, but if he really strikes it rich in the tailoring business, it could be quite a different story."

"Very true, my son."

"Who knows, he might invite us all out to live with him, get me fixed up in employment, and that would solve all your retirement problems," said his son.

At this, gardener Paul became rather impatient with young John and said, "Look, laddie, are you out of your mind?"

"What do you mean, father?"

"Can you imagine us emigrating at our age; I mean, your mother and myself?"

"Why not?" said the son optimistically. "You can always try something once."

"That may be the case for you and your sisters, but I am afraid that your mother and I are too set in our ways to contemplate such a venture. After all, our roots are now firmly embedded in Arbigland."

"But if I leave here, who will look after yourself and my mother, father?"

"But you have no need to leave here, in that you have the opportunity of full-time employment on the estate when you leave school tomorrow. And you could eventually take over as head gardener from me, which is just a few years from now."

Young John was apprehensive at his father's suggestion, for he appeared to be the type of boy who had the wanderlust in his blood, and gardening would be too static an occupation for him. For it would keep him pinned down to one location, something that appeared visibly, even at this early age, to be very much contrary to his nature. Proof of this was obvious by his guarded and half-hearted reply to his father's suggestion. However, he went on to give his father a pledge by saying, "Look, father, whatever the future holds for me, I can assure both you and my mother that you will both have a happy and carefree retirement; for I will never have it on my conscience to see both of you at the mercy of the parish, living the lives of semi-vagrants, regardless of which part of the world I might be in."

"That's most considerate of you, John, and it gives me and your mother great comfort to realise that you will not abandon us; but please consider Mr. Craik's fine offer to you."

As they were nearing the cottage, young John noticed a figure coming along the path in the opposite direction, and as it came nearer he recognised it to be none other than Donald Grant, Mr. Craik's head cowhand.

"Look, father, here comes your friend, Mr. Grant."

"Well, it is indeed," replied his father, "and he is one of the most trustworthy men in the neighbourhood—a stalwart to work alongside, particularly at harvest time."

Donald Grant, who had a short, black-bearded face with a rather crooked nose, was a man of stocky composure. And, although a mere humble agricultural servant, he was one of nature's gentlemen, being very learned and talented in his own particular field. As he approached, he said loudly, "Good evening, Mr. Paul and young John, so nice to see you both."

"And a very good evening to you, Mr. Grant," was the spontaneous reply from both of them.

"Did you both have a busy day?" asked Grant. And before the words were hardly out of his mouth young John replied, "Indeed we did have, particularly my father, who, as you know, always has busy days, for it is not in his nature to be idle so long as there is work to do around the estate."

"Young lad," replied Grant, "I was aware of that a long time ago, for I worked alongside your father in the heyday of his youth, and that was years before you were born."

As the gloaming was beginning to descend on the area, Grant looked at the blazing horizon across the Solway Firth and the haze which covered the fields of wheat and barley, saying, "It's going to be another fine day tomorrow, and, looking at things as they are at the moment, we should have a bumper harvest this year, which should keep our landlord, Mr. Craik, very happy indeed."

Gardener Paul replied, "I think you are a very sound judge of mother nature, for if the abundant fruit crops I have in the garden are anything to go by, and they are very good indicators indeed, then the barns should be well stocked this winter."

With this, Lassie, the family sheepdog collie, seemed to appear from nowhere; and, if animal intelligence was anything to go by, the warmth and sincerity in the Paul family was indicated by the fuss Lassie made of both gardener Paul and young John, jumping up on them and licking them all over, as all friendly dogs do. At the same time, she kept continuously wagging her tail, as much as to say, "It's a pleasure to meet you again." As young John played with Lassie,

Grant deliberately threw a small piece of wood as far as he could, and Lassie immediately ran after it.

This was obviously done temporarily to separate John from the company of the two older men, for Grant had something special to tell gardener Paul, which was not meant for his son's ears. For Grant said to young John, "Away and take Lassie for a good run; the exercise will do her the world of good." With that, both of them were happily running and playing together, quite some distance away from the older men, until they were eventually out of sight. Once young John was well away from hearing distance of both of them, Grant in a hushed and rather secretive manner said to gardener Paul, "Have you heard about Mr. Craik's son?"

"No, what do you mean, Donald?"

"I mean the one that was born illegitimate to one of his housemaids over twenty years ago; can you remember?"

"Oh, yes," replied gardener Paul; "it was all very hush-hush at the time."

"That's right," said Grant, looking over his shoulder to ensure nobody else was in hearing distance.

"To be honest, I never really met him but heard rumours of his existence," said gardener Paul, as if they were discussing some important state secret.

"Aye," said Grant, "it was all very secretive indeed; but the boy went on to study medicine at Edinburgh or Glasgow University."

"Oh yes," replied gardener Paul, "I can vaguely remember Mr. Craik going away on long trips, particularly during the summer months, to visit him on the quiet."

"Ah! You have got it now, I see," said Grant.

"Well, what's happened that you are telling me this story in such a secretive manner? Is he taking over the estate?" enquired gardener Paul in a rather anxious way.

"Oh no," said Grant, "quite the opposite, for, since graduating in medicine at University, he has evidently ended up in a real grand job."

"Where is that, may I ask?" retorted gardener Paul, in an eager and inquisitive manner.

"In the American Colonies, as a personal physician to a man called George Washington," said Grant.

"I have not heard of him," was the gardener's reply.

"Neither have I," said Grant, "but according to Mr. Lindsay, the schoolteacher in Kirkbean, this man Washington is one of the rising stars in the American part of the British Empire."

"I am delighted to hear that," replied gardener Paul, "for there was many a good person born on the wrong side of the blanket who made their way in the world, and good luck to him!"

Just as they were concluding their discussion on the subject, young John came gleefully running back with Lassie at his side, still in possession of the piece of wood which Grant threw in the first instance to break the company up.

"Well, Mr. Grant," said gardener Paul, "thank you for that bit of very interesting information. I will tell nobody except my wife; she can keep a secret. However, if this man George Washington does eventually become famous, the information will eventually filter back across the Atlantic, through the usual grapevine."

"Good night to both of you," said Grant. "And young John, look after Lassie—she's a bonnie dog."

With that they parted company, with young John very bemused as to what they had been talking about, as he just caught the tail end of their conversation. He wondered silently in his own mind whether it was about himself and his future employment. He dared not ask his father what he had been discussing with Grant, for he knew very well what confidentiality meant and the consequences of quizzing him; for, should he have dared, he either would have been given a verbal roasting or, worse still, a good old Scottish clout behind the ears.

At last they approached their humble yet happy abode, the gardener's cottage, which was part of the Arbigland estate and owned by Mr. Craik, for the sole purpose of accommodation for his gardener and family. It was a small whitewashed house, with a thatched roof, which had a large hole in the centre to let out the smoke from the peat and log fire. The fire served both the cooking purposes of the family and as a means of keeping the building warm, particularly in the wintertime, when the cold and merciless winds blew in from the Irish Sea and up the Solway Firth.

As she was just outside the cottage, having collected eggs from the henhouse nearby, Mrs. Paul was obviously happy to see them arrive back home in the company of Lassie, who began yet again to make a fuss of all three of them. Mrs. Paul was a slightly built woman, who was wearing a traditional black frock and a white-collared blouse. She had slightly greying hair, which was covered by a spotlessly white muslin cap. By observing her, one could see that in her youth she had been one of nature's beauties, and she still contained a sereneness and contentment about her, so that when one looked into her maternal blue eyes, one could see both firmness and compassion exuding from her, which were the hallmarks of both a happy and good mother.

"Glad to see you both back; what was keeping you?" queried Mrs. Paul anxiously. "I thought you'd got lost or something had happened to you."

"Well, I got involved in a rather interesting conversation with Donald Grant, the head cowhand, which I will tell you about later," replied gardener Paul.

"And you, young John," she said, "you were probably holding court as well, sorting the affairs of state out; were you not, my bonnie laddie?"

"Oh no, mother," replied young John. "Whilst father and Mr. Grant were having a discussion I took Lassie for a long run, until we practically got to the sea shore."

"Were you watching these ships of sail again?"

"Yes, mother," said John excitedly; "they were like something out of this world, as they plied up and down the Solway, their silhouettes and lantern lights looking so majestic in the twilight of the evening."

"Honestly, boy," replied his mother, "you, Columbus, Raleigh and Drake would have made great company, with your obsession for the sea."

Young John made no reply as he casually stroked Lassie's head and looked at his mother forlornly, realising that he and she were not on the same wavelength when it came to the subject of the sea.

She continued, "What's on your mind, may I ask? You were born the son of the soil, were you not?"

"Yes, that's true, mother," he replied; "but I was also born in this little cottage, which is only a stone's throw away from the sea. And honestly, mother, I just love the sea; although you may think it is an obsession I have, it's not the case, for I just take to the sea like a duck takes to water."

"Behave yourself, laddie; you are only a boy, with the natural imagination of all young boys. The only difference is that most other young boys around here, because of their relatives in America, want to be farmers, whereas you want to be an admiral; and you are only leaving school tomorrow."

Having stood patiently, listening to his wife and son discussing the merits and demerits of the sea, gardener Paul interrupted the discussion and said to his wife, "I've had trouble with him today already, but this time he did not just run away from the garden down to the quayside but actually borrowed a small boat and rowed out to a brigantine, which had dropped anchor in the harbour."

"Oh, this is most interesting indeed," said Mrs. Paul, as she cast her disapproving eyes at her son.

His father went on: "He was only caught climbing the rigging and the upper part of the foremast by the Bosun, who happened to be aboard on his own at the time. And evidently, instead of the Bosun censuring and reporting him to the authorities, they ended up the best of companions, like a pair of old salts, discussing everything from splicing the main brace to the most dangerous parts of all the Seven Seas in which to sail."

"Well I never—," his mother angrily exclaimed. "So you were a naughty boy again, I see?"

With that, young John's father interrupted his wife and told her that he had already been scolded for his misdemeanour. And he further informed her that one should never give a child a second tongue-lashing, as it was not only bad for the child but, worse still, a sign of poor parenthood.

After these few exchanges of words they entered the cottage, which was low-ceilinged, with spotless flagstones on the floor. It was also whitewashed inside and was scrupulously clean. This was a reflection of Mrs. Paul's domestication and good motherhood Although frugally furnished, it was cosy and had all the indications of sound architectural design against the elements of the wild gales in the winter. Once gardener Paul had removed his heavy boots, Mrs. Paul, who had been stoking the fire, said, "As both the girls are out with their boyfriends tonight, we will have to have dinner on our own. So if the two of you get washed I will prepare dinner, which is practically ready anyway."

Gardener Paul and his son went down to the burn, which was not far from the cottage, and had a good wash-down, which removed the grime and sweat that had accrued from their hard day's work. For young John it had to be a special scrub-down for tomorrow was his last day at school, and practically the whole village would be assembled there. Fortunately, there were no classes in the morning and prize-giving was not until the late afternoon, so he had plenty of time to prepare himself for the great event. Not knowing how he had done in his examinations, he was reasonably confident of his past record of work. However, the question of whether he would receive a prize or not would have to remain a nagging doubt in his mind, until the great moment arrived.

Walking back to the cottage, his father said, "That's much better, John, after that good scrub down. You know what they say, 'Cleanliness is next to godliness.'"

"Oh yes, father," was John's reply, but he was much more interested in the sea than either the Deity or hygiene; for he excitedly exclaimed, "Look out over the Firth, father. Is that not a beautiful three-master, with fore, main and mizzen mast, sailing so gracefully out into the Irish Sea and to who knows where?"

With this his father became rather irritable and said, "My son, will you ever forget the sea and ships, for once in your life? I have had a very hard day's work, and as it is nearly dark I could not tell the difference between a sloop or a schooner at this late hour in the evening."

"Sorry to have offended you, father, but I can see by the way they are rigged on the various masts," was his apologetic reply.

When they entered the cottage, John's mother had the spartan but wholesome meal fully cooked and ready to serve. They took their seats, with her husband sitting at the head of the table and her son sitting opposite him. Both looked fully refreshed after their clean-up in the burn outside. Mrs. Paul began to serve the meal, which consisted of mutton, boiled potatoes in their jackets and mashed turnips. After this, father said grace and she sat down to join them herself. As the meal proceeded there was initially complete silence, and all that could be heard in the background was the loud tick of a large-sized mechanical clock. Lassie was lying on the hearth, with her sad eyes firmly placed on young John, eagerly awaiting any scraps he might give her. Breaking the silence, his mother said, "Apart from your incident at sea today, what else happened, young John?"

"Well, mother, apart from helping father out and getting stung with nettles in the process, I ended up a prisoner of his in one of Mr. Craik's balancing round houses."

"Whatever on earth was the cause for that?" she asked.

"It was because of that bully and thief Douglas Maxwell, who was caught stealing fruit."

"But what has that to do with you ending up in one of the balancing round houses?"

Young John went on, "Father will explain better than I can his reasons for putting me there. All I know is that it has something to do with a peculiar word called symmetry, and I only learnt what it meant from father today and, believe me, I learned it the hard way as well."

Gardener Paul, who was quietly enjoying his meal, then explained the old battle he and Mr. Craik had over symmetry, in that one thing must be balanced by something similar at all times. When he placed Maxwell in one of the balancing round houses, knowing how Mr. Craik was mustard keen on the subject, he placed his son in the other one, in order to serve a dual purpose. One was to get his own back on the squire because of his age-old battle with him on the matter. The other was to keep him happy, for he knew very well that immediately he pointed the culprit out to him he would automatically gaze up at the other round house, because, knowing his nature, he could practically read his mind.

"Well, was he happy then?" asked his wife.

Mr. Paul replied, "Although far from happy about the incident of fruit stealing by that scamp Maxwell, whom he tongue-lashed in no uncertain manner, he was most pleased with our young son, for at the end of the incident he offered John the opportunity of working full time with me, when he leaves school tomorrow."

"Well!" exclaimed Mrs. Paul with delight. "Would that not just be wonderful?"

By the sullen look on young John's face, it was apparent that he was far from impressed by Mr. Craik's fine offer and his mother's delight. For, as she continued to show her great pleasure at the news of his offer of employment, young John glanced at a model of a schooner which was placed on the sideboard and which he had received from an old salt a few years back.

"Won't it be delightful to have you working alongside your father, my dear laddie?" said his mother, with a beaming smile on her face.

"Well, I don't know—" replied young John, with a certain lack of enthusiasm.

"What do you mean, you don't know?"

"You see, mother, much as I like working with father, I quite honestly don't think my heart is really in it, for I want to go to sea and travel the world."

But his mother replied, "This is the greatest opportunity you have, young John, and what else could you do if you missed this chance?"

"Well, mother, I can always take the high road to London, if I cannot go to sea."

Having completed their meal, young John collected all the scraps of meat and gave them to Lassie, who was sitting patiently in front of the fire. And if dumb animals could speak, she would probably have supported her true friend, young John, in his discourse with his mother. In the meantime, Mrs. Paul did not only rise to get them a jug of buttermilk to wash down the meal but her hackles rose also. For being of Highland stock herself, her son's mention of London was like a red rag to a bull to her. The reason for this was that the memories of the 1745 Jacobite Rebellion were still fresh in her mind. And not only did the London government ban the militia in Scotland but, to add insult to injury, the wearing of the tartan was prohibited also.

Coming through from the pantry with the buttermilk, Mrs. Paul joined them round the log fire, for it was much cooler now due to a strong westerly wind blowing up the Solway Firth. Father was content after his hard day's work to sit back in his rocking chair, whilst young John sat on a bench, with Lassie sleeping contentedly at his feet, having devoured the leftovers from dinner. When they were all settled comfortably down, Mrs. Paul opened the conversation by saying in a rather stern manner, "So you want to go to London also?"

"Well, dear mother, it was only an idea I had in my head, if I cannot get a billet on a ship from this area."

Raising her voice, she said, "I suppose your next ambition is to become an admiral in that murderous King George the Second's Navy, is it?"

"No, mother," retorted young John. "Wherever you get this idea of admiral from I just do not know, for I would be quite content in being an ordinary deckhand, serving my superior officers to the best of my abilities."

In a firm manner she went on, "If you go to London, my young lad, it will be over my dead body."

Young John was becoming more depressed as his father began to take an active part in the heated discussion between his wife and son.

"Look here, young John," he said, pointing his finger at him to rebuke him; "you would not want to offend your mother, would you?"

"Father, that's the last thing in the world I would ever dream of doing, for I love my mother dearly."

With this his mother became more subdued and regained her composure, saying to him, "If you only realised what King George the Second's offspring, the Duke of Cumberland (known as the Butcher Cumberland in Scotland), did to your Highland relatives after the Battle of Culloden in 1746, the year before you were born; instead of going to London to seek work you would be going there to burn it to the ground!"

"What happened then, mother?" asked John curiously.

"Well, son, when Bonnie Prince Charlie made his final stand there, they literally massacred them by the thousands, showing no mercy whatsoever."

"How dreadful, mother," he said. "Perhaps, when I grow up, I might have the chance to fight the King's soldiers."

"I don't think so, my son, for, after the defeat of the clans at Culloden, one of the first things they did was to break up the clan system, so the chances of another rebellion rising are very remote indeed."

Unconsciously to him then, the very seeds of rebellion were being planted in his young mind; for, as his mother spoke to him, you could see the fire in his belly expressed through the venom in his eyes. Listening attentively to his mother's conversation on the ills of the 1745 Jacobite Rebellion, he acknowledged the enlightenment he received from her and said, "Thank you for the sound advice on London; but, honestly, I never realised that such atrocities were perpetrated by that government against the Jacobite people, for we were given a very rough outline on the subject at school."

"The reason for that, son, is because of deliberate government policy. But, should you ever go up to the Highlands, you will get a true picture of what happened—for there are people still very much alive who can vividly remember the barbarous acts carried out by the King's redcoats. For it did not finish with the Battle of Culloden itself for, when it was all over, the same redcoats hunted Bonnie Prince Charlie throughout the length and breadth of the Highlands of Scotland, pillaging and burning as they went along."

Gardener Paul, who had been slumbering in his chair during most of the discourse, suddenly came to life again and said, "This is one day in my life I shall never forget for a long time. Little did I realise when I went out to work this morning that it would be so momentous a day, ending up listening to a historical talk on the pros and cons of the 1745 Jacobite Rebellion!"

"Well, father," said Mrs. Paul, "I am only telling the boy for his own good, so that he knows what they are really like in London."

"That's true," said her husband; "but only time will tell if your talk has had any influence on young John's mind."

As it was getting late into the night and it was prize-giving day the next afternoon, Mrs. Paul had to get young John's clothes ready so that he could look as presentable as possible among the remainder of the Kirkbean community. For they would be there in their droves, to see who would pick up the prizes and who would not.

"Time to go to bed, father," said his wife; and, after receiving this kindly piece of advice, gardener Paul rose from his rocking chair, wished them goodnight and retired to bed. After his father left the room, his mother embraced young John with a huge hug and kiss, saying, "We are so proud of you, son, but please take our advice, for after tomorrow you will have to fend for yourself."

"Regardless of what sort of work I take up, mother, or wherever I go in the world, or what I eventually become, I shall never forget the sound advice you gave me tonight. And, for one thing, London is out for me from now on."

"And remember, my dear laddie," said his mother, "be proud to wear your big brother's clothes, although they are second-hand, for I will have them nicely prepared for you in time for tomorrow."

"Will you tell William, when you write to him in America, that I wore his clothes on my last day at school?"

"I most certainly will, and this will delight him no end, as he likes these simple reminders of home." She smiled. "And talking of William, I am expecting the usual long letter from him when the next mail packet arrives from America, which should be any day now."

On the mention of the word "America" John's eyes lit up, for it was a place he had heard so much about though he had never been there. And with those last thoughts on his mind, he wished his mother good night and made his way to bed, looking forward very much to his last day at school. After she wished him good night, his mother stayed up slightly later, tidying about the house, and getting his clothes ready for the following day. But before she went to bed herself, she entered into young John's bedroom to extinguish the tallow lights by his bedside. There she found him dead to the world, the picture of childhood serenity, with a book on celestial navigation lying beside him; and, still clasped in his hands, was an open chapbook called *The Boyhood of Raleigh*, which he had been reading before he dozed off to sleep.

CHAPTER 2

LAST DAY AT SCHOOL

Mr. Robert Adam	Prominent Scottish Architect
Lord Cassilis	Chief of the Kennedy Clan. Present Chief, David Kennedy, The Marquis of Ailsa, served in the Scots Guards
Mr, Lindsay	Headmaster, Kirkbean, Scotland
Rev. Mr. Hogg	Church of Scotland Clergyman
Lord Clive	British Conqueror of India
General Wolfe	British Conqueror of Canada
St. Thomas Aquinas	Roman Catholic Saint, Philosopher, Theologian, Member of the Dominican Order
Dun Scotus	Scots Philosopher, Theologian, and Member of the Franciscan Order

Young John's last day at school was ushered in by the crowing of cocks in the neighbourhood. As was customary in a rural area at the first sign of daybreak or even slightly before, one rooster started the whole process under way, which eventually reverberated throughout the whole community. This looked like nature's way of telling the highest form of creation, the human species, that it was time to arise from their beds and face the uncertainties, joys and tribulations of the day that lay ahead. When daybreak finally arrived, there was a near cloudless sky above, and from the east of the gardener's cottage it could be observed that a merciless sun was due to appear above the horizon shortly, that would make it a scorcher of a day. Once the cock-crowing began to recede, the dawn chorus of birds, awoken from their slumbers, gradually took over. When they all got into orchestration their harmony and sweetness was, compared to the intermittent crowing of roosters, like a heavenly choir in action.

By the time young John has awoken from his good night's sleep, the sun was well above the Galloway hills, and the shafts of light that penetrated through the small windows of his room were reminiscent of the standing rigging of a ship. The first to greet him on this all-important day was his friend Lassie. She came into his room through the door, which was ajar, immediately jumped up on his bed and started licking his face all over. With this most welcoming reveille, John had no option but to arise, put on an old pair of trousers and go down to the burn for a wash; his last as a schoolboy. By the time he had returned with Lassie by his side, his sisters had departed to their place of work in another manor nearby, which was owned by a friend of Mr. Craik's. The only people left in the cottage were his father and mother, the former taking a day off work to attend prize-giving.

On meeting his mother, young John said, "A very good morning to you, mother."

"And a very good morning to you, John. Did you sleep well or did the excitement of the big day interfere with your sleep?"

"Oh no, mother, it did not keep me awake at all; I slept like a log."

"I thought so," she said, "for when I went into your room to put the light out, you were so tired that the book on Raleigh was still clasped in your hands."

"That's right, mother, it was such an excellent book; I ended up having a marvellous dream about what I had been reading."

"What was the dream all about, may I ask?"

"Well, mother, I was Sir Walter Raleigh's first officer in the Battle of Cadiz, and we really sorted the Spaniards out."

"Oh, we are back to the sea again," she replied, resigning herself to the outpourings of his subconscious mind.

"But that was not the end, mother; for, although my memory is a bit hazy now, if I remember rightly when I left the navy I ended up as an old man in a place called Annapolis."

"In the name of heaven, where is that?" she asked.

"It's the capital of Maryland, in the American Colonies."

"You are a terrible boy," she went on. "The next thing, you will be abandoning any notions of the sea or gardening and taking up politics."

"Oh no, mother, you have got to be famous to make it in politics."

"Come along then, son, get yourself ready; I will prepare breakfast for father and yourself."

John then went to his room, dressed himself in his brother's clothes and returned to his first meal of the day.

Joining his father, who was dressed in his Sunday-best and already seated at the table, young John said, "Good morning, nice to see you looking so smart, father."

Looking at him in admiration, his father replied, "And may I say the same thing about yourself. You look so different in all that nice clothing."

"Thank you, father, but, like birth and death, one's last day at school is very similar in that it only happens once, so one must rise to the occasion."

"True, son; very well said, for these three things come only once in a lifetime."

His mother then entered the room with a large plate of porridge and cream for each of them. On seeing young John, she exclaimed, "Oh, don't you look such a changed smart fellow, in your big brother's clothing!"

"Yes, mother, as we mentioned last night, I am very proud to wear his clothing."

Beaming all over, she replied, "Oh yes, son, I will be so pleased to tell him how well you looked, the next time I write to him in America."

To young John, the mention again of that magic word 'America' made him look out of the corner of his eye at the schooner that was on the sideboard.

Even Lassie realised this was no ordinary day, for, instead of lying contentedly on the hearth, which was her usual posture, she was standing on all four legs with her ears cocked up. Her head was at a side angle, looking bemused at what was going on.

"Eat your porridge, laddie; it will put hairs on your chest and make a man of you," said his father who had already emptied his plate.

Supping his porridge, young John replied, "But I will be a man when I finish school today."

"Aye, son, you may be a man by law but not by nature, for you have a few years to grow yet and a lot more porridge to eat."

Patiently listening to both of them, his mother said, "John, did you tell your father about the funny dream you had last night?"

"Oh no, mother, I forgot to mention it; I can only vaguely remember it now; can you tell him please?"

After Mrs Paul told her husband about his subconscious escapades with Raleigh, he laughingly replied, "It's not going to be another of those days, for I thought I heard enough about the sea yesterday to last me a lifetime."

His mother said, "Oh, it is just a passing boyhood phase playing on his mind, which he will soon get over."

"Let's hope he will," said his father, who, looking at the clock, rernarked, "We better make haste on our way up to Kirkbean school, for time is getting on and we do not want to rush things."

The three of them, all looking their best, made their way by foot to the village school, which was some distance away. As it was approaching midday, with only a few sparse white clouds to be seen in the blue-domed sky, the temperature was gradually rising. As they slowly trudged their way along the road they carried on a very low-keyed conversation among themselves. Their only companions to be seen were a varied assortment of butterflies, fluttering in the air in no organised grouping. Their unseen accomplices were grasshoppers on the roadside verge that chirped merrily at spasmodic intervals. All of a sudden things began to come to life for them, for when they turned left into the village they found it bustling with human activity. Children, parents and their friends were beginning to converge on Kirkbean from all directions. Those from the outlying districts were easily distinguished from those travelling by foot. They were very noticeable in that they used ponies and traps to convey them to the prize-giving. And the ponies looked splendid in their well-polished and glistening livery. With throngs of people beginning to gather more and more, it became obvious this was a very special day indeed.

Walking in the opposite direction to them, from the centre of the village, was a man gardener Paul singled out from most of the rest of the crowd, whom he knew anyway, as they attended the same village kirk on Sunday.

He said to his wife, "See this gentleman who is approaching us now? I am sure I have met him before."

"Away you go, father! You are probably getting him mixed up with someone you know well, and he just happens to look like him."

"I may be wrong, but I am sure I am right," said gardener Paul in an emphatic manner; young John nodded slightly in agreement with him.

As the gentleman came nearer, they both glanced one another in the eye, and gardener Paul said, "A very good day to you, sir!"

The gentleman replied, "And the same to you and your family, sir; I think we might have met before."

"That's what I am thinking myself, sir."

"I've got it now," he replied. "It was on the ship *Friendship*, was it not?"

"Oh yes," replied the gardener, "you are Captain Blake with whom I had a long discussion one day, when I was delivering fruit and vegetables to your ship. Correct, sir?"

"Indeed you are. May I ask your second name again, sir?"

"Paul, sir," came the reply.

"Ah yes, I remember the time well; we had a most interesting discussion. Delighted to meet you again, Mr. Paul, for, the last time we met, I was just back from the West Indies and naturally I was brown as a berry."

"Yes," said a much more relaxed gardener Paul, having satisfied his curiosity, "that's probably why I had difficulty in recognismg you, because you seemed to have lost that marvellous tan you had then."

"Believe me," said Captain Blake, who was of medium build with receding fairish hair and sharp facial features, and who spoke with an educated southern English accent, "I have had a few good tans since then and lost them. This is one of the occupational hazards of the merchant navy, for we might spend a year in the tropics and return home in the middle of the winter, amidst ice and snow."

"Aye, and it does not take long to lose a tan in our winter climate," said the gardener.

"You re so correct," replied the captain. "Since coming back from the American Colonies and the West Indies last November, the ship has been given a good overhauling, from careening and painting the hull to replacing the bowsprit."

"And she is ready for sea again?" asked gardener Paul.

"Oh yes," replied the captain. "She is now, like Caesar's wife, beyond reproach, and ready to sail across the Atlantic from Whitehaven."

"Very good," said the gardener. "May I introduce to you my wife and young son, John?"

"It will be a pleasure," replied the captain.

When the introduction was made, they carried on a mundane conversation, but young John was a mixture of delight and apprehension. He was delighted to meet an ocean-going captain like Blake but apprehensive in case he got to know about his escapades on his ship the previous day. He realised that Bosun Thorpe had been true to his word and never reported the incident to the ship's master. For, if he had, John assumed that Captain Blake would have mentioned it. And there was no indication of this in the discussion with himself or with his parents. As their conversation continued, his apprehension began to diminish, his only worry being that his mother might let it slip out accidentally—his trip to the *Friendship*. His father he could trust, for he knew the shrewd individual he was. Although Captain Blake was just visiting Kirkbean for the day, as he was taking the ship back to Whitehaven in the evening, he was well aware that this was a special day in young John's life and turned his attention to him.

"You will be very pleased with yourself today, Master Paul, this being your last day at school?"

"Oh yes, sir," he replied. "I have looked forward to this day for a long time and now the great moment has arrived."

"Are you expecting to lift any prizes?"

"Well, I don't know, sir. We will just have to wait and see."

"Whatever does develop," said Captain Blake, "you realise you get a very good education there, particularly in the field of mercantile studies?"

"Yes, sir." John had become much more relaxed now, and went on: "That is due to our headmaster, Mr. Lindsay."

"Believe me," said the captain. "I have heard of that famous name, not only on the poop deck but in various places I have visited overseas; and his education has produced some first class mariners."

"Aye, that's right, sir, but I think compared with some of the other schools around the Solway Firth they are what you would call average."

"Yes, I understand what you mean, Master Paul, but, who knows, maybe one day they will produce a really famous sailor," said the captain.

Excitedly, young John asked him, "Do you think my school will ever produce a sailor as famous as Raleigh?"

Smiling, Captain Blake answered, "Now, Master Paul, that's really asking a bit too much, but you never know, as each period in history produces great men, who, though insignificant in their early years, eventually become famous and are known and admired by millions of people throughout the world."

Whilst the interchange of conversation between the captain and their son continued, both parents, being aware of John's real interests, were on tenterhooks in case he should ask the obvious question about his chance of going to sea But he did not, and his parents managed to steer the conversation in other directions.

As the Paul family were about to bid Captain Blake farewell, Mr. Craik the squire appeared, coming up a side lane from Arbigland House, mounted on his thoroughbred. After being casually introduced to Captain Blake, the squire wished young John good luck at the prize-giving, and the family proceeded on their way. Mr. Craik then dismounted his horse and, after shaking hands, struck up company with Captain Blake. As the ship of which he was master was home-ported in Whitehaven, Mr. Craik was most interested to have a discussion with him, for he had quite a bit of property in that part of England and knew the shipowner, although he had never met Captain Blake before.

"How are things in the maritime world, particularly across the Firth in Whitehaven?"

"Very, very busy indeed, sir," replied the captain. "For, as you probably realise, Whitehaven is a very active port. And, like many others around here, it will probably get even busier."

"Is the economy going to expand again?" enquired Mr. Craik.

"Indeed it is, sir, and this is due to Britain's achievements in the war with France and the expansion of Empire."

"Oh, I suppose, with Clive taking India, Wolfe Canada, and the defeat of the French Navy at Quiberon Bay, all this will lead to the expansion of Empire," said Mr. Craik in a manner that conveyed his interest and understanding of the world situation.

"Not only the Empire expanding, sir, but both the Merchant and Royal Navies as well; one to carry the increased trade, the other to protect it," replied the captain, with an air of confidence that showed he and the squire were on the same wavelength in understanding the world situation.

"So you reckon you will be kept busy then?" said the squire.

"Busy, sir, is not the word for it; for, with the expanding American Colonies on our plate already, we will have to build many more ships of all types to cater for this recent addition to Empire."

"I understand what you mean," replied the squire; who went on to say, "Forgetting the additions to Empire as the result of the present war, the effects of trade with the American Colonies are very noticeable."

"Can you actually notice them in the countryside?" enquired the captain.

"Not to the same degree as in the expanding seaport towns, but in terms of architectural grandeur, yes."

"Most interesting," said the captain. "Can you give me any concrete examples of what you mean, in this area?"

"Indeed yes, I can," said the squire proudly. "Not far from here, plans are being made eventually to build what should be one of the most picturesque castles in the realm, when it is finally completed."

"Who is this for, may I ask, sir?"

"It is for another landed aristocrat from the Galloway region, Lord Cassilis, who is chief of the Kennedy clan. His family also has a lot of property in New York. The reason I know so much about this venture is that he is using the same architect who designed Arbigland House in 1755, the famous Robert Adam. Although it will take quite some time to complete, I believe they are going to call it Culzean Castle, when all the construction work is finished."

"That's very interesting indeed," said the captain. "I did not know the Kennedys came from this area.

"Oh yes, they are a very old Scottish family indeed, dating back to the 11th century. And when this building is complete it will be known as the ancestral home to all future members of that famous clan.

"Well, Mr. Craik, I can now see how the wealth from Empire can be noticeable in the countryside, by looking at the new palatial buildings that are being erected throughout the land."

"Well, that's one expression of Empire trade, you may say," replied the squire.

"Talking about Empire, sir, and what it entails in trade and shipping, I think it is about time I thanked you for your most enlightening company and departed."

"Have you a heavy programme then?" enquired the squire.

"Very heavy indeed, sir, for I have to take my ship from here to Whitehaven, as we are sailing across the Atlantic from there very shortly."

"How long will you be away for, captain?"

"Around a year this time, sir, depending on the discharging and loading of cargo, not forgetting the weather, particularly the trade winds."

"Well, if you will be away all that time, please do join me and my good lady for supper, as she would be delighted to meet someone like yourself who has travelled frequently to the various parts of the Empire, across the Atlantic."

Considering how long it would take him and his crew to cross the Solway Firth to Whitehaven, Captain Blake stood with his arms crossed over his chest glaring up into vacant space. He momentarily hesitated, then said, "Well, sir, as it is you, it will be my pleasure to join you for a meal, and I'll sail with the high tide late this evening."

"Excellent!" said the squire. "But before we go back to Arbigland House, I have an obligation to go to the village school and watch the prize-giving ceremony, which is a great event here; so you must come and join me."

"I would be delighted, sir," said the captain, "for, apart from my own shooldays, I have never been to a prize-giving since. And it will delight me no end to witness a Scottish one, particularly in Kirkbean School, as they have a tradition of producing some excellent sailors."

"Good!" replied the squire. "I dare not miss it this year of all years for, as you are aware, this is my gardener's son's last day at school."

"Oh, is this master Paul you are talking about?"

"Indeed it is, captain," replied the squire, "and a bright hard-working boy he is as well. The only thing is that he is a child with conflicts between working in my garden with his father or going to sea. But between his parents and myself we hope to tip the scales in favour of his working on the land."

"Yes, he did appear to be reserved and slightly apprehensive when I first met him with his parents. However, after a while, he came out of his shell and we had a very intelligent conversation indeed."

"Yes, once he gets going he can certainly converse and ask probing questions," replied the squire. "However, it is time for us to make our way up to the school, only hoping that he picks some prize up today."

The Paul family had arrived in the school grounds, to be greeted by many of their friends from the surrounding neighbourhood. And as father and mother made their way into the school assembly hall, young John met his best friend Dominic Archer, who was leaving school that day also. Dominic was a medium-built boy, with a fresh complexion, dark, curly, shoulder-length hair with sideboards, and possessed of a vivacious personality. His father was a retired Royal Navy captain, whose last ship was H.M.S. *Triumph*. He was now secretary of the local training association.

On meeting his friend, young John said, "Good afternoon to you Dominic. You look well turned out today."

Dominic replied, "And I can say the same for yourself, for had I not known you all these years back I would have mistaken you for the squire's son, you look so well presented."

"Thank you," replied John, "but I am afraid that I feel rather odd in this outfit, particularly as, you know, it belongs to my older brother William."

"Oh, don't worry about that, John, I am sure that your brother would be very proud of you if he could see you now."

"Dominic, you should have been with me yesterday. What a time you would have had!"

"What do you mean, John?" enquired Dominic curiously.

"Well, I was out on a brigantine in the harbour, and oh boy! What an interesting experience it was!"

"Marvellous, please do tell me more."

"First, I thought it was just lying at anchor with nobody aboard, but, to my surprise and shock at the beginning, the Bosun was down the holds and when he ascended the companion and caught me up the standing rigging I thought I was for the high jump."

"Did nothing happen to you then, John?"

"No, the Bosun was naturally a bit wild at first, but after a while we got on like a house on fire. For I ended up spending around two hours with him, which included a real tar's slap-up meal."

"He must have been a good type not to report you to the authorities, for they are very strict on that, in case people are trying to stow away to this great up and coming part of the Empire called America."

"Yes, he was a man of trust, for he told me that nothing more would be said about it. And, mind you, he was true to his word, for I was in a rather awkward position today when I accidentally bumped into the captain of the same ship, not knowing whether he had been informed of the incident or not."

"How on earth did you manage to do that—I mean meeting the captain of a real sea-going ship?"

"It was on my way here that I met him in the company of my parents, for my father knew him previously. Believe me, I was in a sweat when we were first introduced, for I did not know whether the Bosun had told him about his experience with me yesterday; that's assuming he met him, of course."

"And what next, John?" asked Dominic, his eyes lighting up as the story unfolded.

"Well, once I got over the first barrier of realising he was not aware of my escapade, the other thing I was really worried about was that my parents might mention it to him in passing conversation; but it never entered into the discussion."

"Oh good," said Dominic. "And where is the captain now?"

"We left him in the company of the squire, Mr. Craik, whom we happened to meet also. He was on his way from the Big Hoose, going to Kirkbean village at the time."

"He is in excellent company then," said Dominic, "which is befitting a man of his experience and position. Did you ask him the inevitable question, John?"

"Great minds think alike, Dominic," replied John. "No, I did not, for, had I mentioned going to sea in the company of my parents, they would have seen red, particularly my mother."

"That's a pity," said Dominic, "it was your golden opportunity, which would have fulfilled all your schoolboy ambitions."

"Yes, I know, Dominic," he replied, "but should the opportunity ever arise again, I will definitely ask him about going to sea; but it will have to be well away from the ears of my parents at the time."

As the parents, relatives and friends were beginning to fill the assembly hall, the children had to remain outside until the bell was rung. This was to be the signal for them to enter at the rear of the hall, the front part of it being reserved for their elders. When John intimated to Dominic that rather unsavoury incident he had with Douglas Maxwell the previous day, his friend's face just squirmed at the mention of his name. But when one of John's other friends told him that Maxwell was telling untrue stories about him regarding the incident in the garden, he changed from a quiet, happy and reserved boy to one fuming with rage. His mates gathered round him to try to placate him, for fear of the consequences if the school bully should attack him. The fury of his temper could now be seen by the whiteness of the pupils in his eyes. Trying to reason with him at this stage was of little avail.

As his face became redder and redder, young John angrily demanded, "Where is that swine and bully Maxwell?"

When one of his friends informed him that he was with some of his mates outside the stable at the back of the school, John said, "They are not real mates as we are; they only act as his mates because he completely dominates their lives. Let's go and get him, for I have a bone to pick with him."

His best friend Dominic did his utmost to persuade him not to go, but his advice fell on deaf ears.

When John and his comrades made their way to the stables, they crept quietly and listened to Maxwell holding court with his underlings. He was boasting in a callous manner that on the previous day young John had invited him into Mr. Craik's garden to help himself to some fruit thinking this had the squire's approval. He went on to inform his henchmen that when the landlord found this out he locked up young John, after giving him a sound thrashing with his bull crop.

On hearing this, John became more livid, and what should have been a happy day for himself and his mates became instead rather tense, in view of what was being said about him. So, making their way to where the bully was, young John immediately confronted him by saying, "That's a load of lies you are telling, Maxwell."

"They are not," came the bully's abrupt reply, "and if they were, what could you do about it, you gardener's barefooted lackey?"

"You will soon see, you bully, for I have a very special bone to pick with you. This is for what you said about my family yesterday and the lies you have been telling your henchmen just now."

"Pick a bone with me!" Maxwell replied. "You could not pick a chicken bone, let alone fight me, even in your brother's boots which you are wearing. And he probably stole them from some drunken sailor down at the docks."

"Right, Maxwell, enough is enough, let's have a square go, with clean fists and nothing else."

"Are you serious, you bloody insignificant, good-for-nothing weed?" said Maxwell, who was very indignant that his authority should be challenged on his last day at school.

With that said, they both took their jackets off; the remainder of the boys present formed a circle around them, for they were going to witness a piece of social history in the annals of Kirkbean school. Maxwell lunged violently at young John, who ducked, got the bully off guard, and with his right hand fist struck him as hard as he could in the pit of the rib cage, temporarily winding him. As he was reeling from the effects of this, the majority present were shouting in unison, "Get stuck in John, show the coward what you're really made of"—whilst Maxwell's so-called friends remained very subdued.

As Maxweell was slowly gaining his wind back, young John smashed him with a right beauty on his left eye, did the same on his right eye, and said to the bloodthirsty onlookers, "I have not yet begun to fight." On Maxwell's part, now, there were no holds barred; so with his two hands he grabbed John's shirt at the front, just around his neck, with the intention of butting him in the face and knocking him out. After taking a firm grip, he drew his head back, so as to make the maximum impact on John's face with the temple of his head. The plan, however, badly misfired. As he came forward with the full force of his head, all John did was to lower his as far as he could. The result of this was that Maxwell's face hit the crown of John's head with one mighty smack, which was so hard that it broke his nose and completely dazed him, so that he was staggering about, almost unconscious. By this time there was blood and cheers everywhere. Maxwell's face was more reminiscent of a butcher's apron than of somebody who was going to attend a prize-giving ceremony. The cheers came from the rest of the school children, who all, including Maxwell's underlings, unleashed their animal tendencies in this lust for blood. Now that the bully had had an overdose of his own medicine by being well and truly thrashed, his henchmen deserted him, for they were not really his true friends but weaker ones, whom in the past he had perpetually dominated with threats of violence.

As Maxwell lay groaning on the ground the rest of the group congratulated young John on what he had done. His closest friend, Dominic, came up and shook him by the hand and said, "Well done, John! You have done us an excellent service. It's a pity that you did not do it a few years ago, for we would have had a much happier school. Just wait until the rest of the boys hear about it, and I bet they will all be overjoyed." John by this time had composed himself, and said to Dominic, "I am sorry that my last day at school had to end this way, but that lout Maxwell drove me to it and I could stand it no longer."

"Don't worry, John; take it from me that everybody will be behind you and not a word will be said until everything calms down."

"Oh, thank you, Dominic. As long as the headmaster does not get to know until I leave school, which is only a few hours away, I will be happy."

Dominic continued, "Just think that this great deed of yours today, in cutting that bully down to size, will be spoken about in the village, in quayside bars, who knows, maybe on the high seas in years to come!"

"Oh, I think you're slightly exaggerating now, Dominic," John said with a wry smile, "for in that statement of yours you included every place but the moon!"

"Well, you never know, John; when we are purely pages in history, you might be known of on the moon as well," said Dominic humorously.

Dominic and his friends then took John down to a nearby stream where the horses usually watered themselves, and cleaned the blood from his face, hands and jumper. Luckily, they had just completed this important task when the bell rang, summoning them all to make their way into the prize-giving ceremony.

When they arrived at the assembly hall, their elders were all seated, but it was so full that some of the children, including John and Dominic, had to stand up in the side aisles of the hall. The hall was a solidly built, stone building, with a raftered roof, and the walls inside were whitewashed. Because of the hot sunny day most of the windows were opened to let in fresh air. This greatly reduced the temperature, so that the children, parents and guests did not have to endure an oven-like atmosphere. At the front of the hall there was a table bedecked with bunting, on which lay the prizes that were to be given out that day; and around the bottom of the table was a large assortment of flowers, donated from the Arbigland House gardens. This put the icing on the cake of what was a most convivial setting. By the happy smile on his face, one could see that gardener Paul was proud of the fruits of his labours, for everyone sitting near him congratulated him on his first-class floral display. The only thing that was dreaded by the parents and pupils, on this flower-bedecked table, was that instrument of humiliation to some, motivation to others—the dunce's cap. This was given to the boy with the poorest examination marks in the school.

As they settled down, awaiting the arrival of dignitaries to make their speeches and present the prizes, those standing up had a good opportunity to have a look around the hall. John and Dominic recognised their parents and gave them a smile. Then John whispered excitedly in Dominic's ear, "Guess who is sitting down there, talking to Mr. Craik?"

Down where?" said Dominic in a hushed voice.

"The front row, far right," whispered John.

Peering across the heads of all present, Dominic said in a low voice, "I have no idea. I have never seen that gentleman before. Who is he?"

Whispering, John said, "That's Captain Blake, I told you about."

"This is marvellous: a real ocean-going captain in our midst!" replied Dominic, as if King George himself were present.

"The squire must have invited him along, as he has no connection with this school at all," said John in a hushed tone of voice.

"I hope he is not here with a press-gang waiting outside until it gets dark," whispered Dominic humorously in John's ear, so that no-one could hear him.

"No, I don't think so," said John in a practically inaudible voice, "for, with our class, he would not need a press-gang, as we would all be volunteers."

"I would give my right arm to be introduced to him," whispered Dominic.

"One up on you, Dominic!" said John, "I have already met him." As there was by this time complete silence in the hall, Dominic and John were conspicuous by their whispering and the secretive manner in which they conducted their discussion; so much so that quite a few stern-looking eyes began to stare at them.

At last the dignitaries, led by Mr. Lindsay the headmaster, entered the hall and, apart from the noise from the movement of their feet, you could have heard a pin drop. Mr. Lindsay was tall, a youngish-looking man for his age, slim-built, with a well groomed black beard. Wearing his academic robes and mortar board, it could be seen from his mere presence behind the prize-giving table that he was a man of intellect and that knowledge exuded from him.

Calling the hall to order with his wooden gavel, he stood up and said, "Good afternoon, ladies, gentlemen and pupils. It is my pleasure to see you all here today." He then went on to make a brief report on the academic year which they were all witnessing coming to a close. To those boys who were leaving school that day he spoke briefly of the opportunities that lay before them, both at home and in the expanding Empire. And, as many of the Scottish coastal towns were in one way or another connected with the mercantile marine, he went on to explain the opportunities that awaited those who were interested in a life at sea. When he mentioned this point, Dominic nudged young John, and John in return winked back and gave a nod of the head, as much as to say that things were looking good for them in the uncharted years that lay ahead. Mr. Lindsay then went on to thank them all for turning up in such large numbers, and then intimated that the thing they were all anxiously waiting for, the actual prizegiving ceremony, was about to commence. For the presentation of the prizes he called upon the local minister, the Reverend James Hogg, to present them, as he called out the names.

The prizes were to be presented in backward order, the third one first and so on, for each subject at a time.

When Mr. Lindsay sat down and the local minister stood up, the silence in the hall was once again broken by the enthusiastic clapping and cheering of all present, for both the headmaster and the minister were well respected members of the community. They were the sort of people that the less enlightened populace practically revered, for they were the linchpins of most communities in Scotland at that time—the ecclesiastical and educational representatives of society. When the cheering and clapping had subsided, the headmaster started to call out the prize-winners' names in reverse order, and they went up to collect a book from the minister, in recognition of their achievements at school. Young John became more dismayed and depressed looking, as he was not among the first three for all the subjects mentioned so far. You could see in his face, as the prizes were given out to some of his best friends, that his spirits were ebbing lower and lower as time went on. When it came to the last prizes of the day, he looked so glum as if to be beyond caring. When it came to the last ones, Mr Lindsay said, "Although last on our long list, the following awards in Navigational Studies are equally, if not most important, to many of the boys leaving school today."

Young John whispered in Dominic's ear, "This is our last chance, what do you think?"

"Well, after our showing to date, very slim indeed."

Mr. Lindsay then called out, "Third prize in Navigational Studies is Master Dominic Archer."

His name was called out amidst the cheers of his friends. Young John clapped him on the back as he made his way up to the minister to collect his prize. On his return, his best friend John was the first to congratulate him on his achievement.

When the second prize-winner was called out, it could be observed that, although John had been pleased by his friend Dominic's getting third prize, he was once again very sad and practically on the point of tears, because of his poor performance that afternoon.

Then Mr. Lindsay said, to his delight, "The last award of the day, which is the first prize in Navigational Studies, goes to none other than Master John Paul."

As John was so popular at school and in the village community, the whole assembled crowd went into raptures on hearing this. And as he collected his coveted prize from the Reverend James Hogg, the minister said to him, "Congratulations, Master John! Maybe, with what Mr. Lindsay said in his speech about the increase in the mercantile marine, waiting all afternoon for this prize might be a good omen for you."

"I hope it is, Mr. Hogg, and thank you so much," said John, now much more confident and cheerful than he had been since the start of the ceremony. Turning on his heels, he proudly made his way back up the hall, and as he did so he acknowledged a smile and a nod both from the squire and Captain Blake, who were in the front row. When he met his friend, the first thing Dominic did was to congratulate him with a sincere handshake with the words, "John, your schoolboy ambitions have been fulfilled."

"Thank you, Dominic," he replied. "This prize means more to me than all the others put together."

Mr. Lindsay's attitude changed from one of joy to one of sadness as he said, "As prize-giving is now over, I have an award to make which I sadly regret doing. But in the tradition and interests of the high standards of our Scottish education, I have no other choice but to ask Master Douglas Maxwell to come forward, so that the minister may place this dunce's cap on his head."

When these words were uttered, there was complete silence in the hall; there were merely looks, nudges and nods; and when Dominic Archer heard this news, he winked at young John and, with a smile on his face, without a word being spoken, he gave him the thumbs up. When Douglas Maxwell made no appearance, his name was called out again, and this time there was a voice from the centre of the hall which said, "Excuse me, Mr. Lindsay, but my name as you know is Allan McLennan and I am the village blacksmith. You will excuse me for just arriving, but permit me to tell you my reason for being late."

"Certainly, Mr. McLennan," said Mr. Lindsay, "do carry on, by all means."

"Well, Sir, if I can explain the reason for my delay. On my way in here, I saw Master Douglas Maxwell and he was in a very bad way."

"Was he ill?" enquired the headmaster.

"Worse than that, Sir," replied McLennan. "He had two beautiful black eyes and his face was streaming with blood."

With this statement before the whole forum, young John was once again on tenterhooks.

Mr. Lindsay then asked, "Is he all right, and what in heaven's name happened to him?"

"Well, Sir, when I was helping him up, I tried to find out what happened, but when this gold watch, with your name inscribed on it, fell out of his pocket, he ran away home, crying like a baby and muttering, 'Please don't tell Mr. Lindsay I stole his watch.'"

With that said, there were gasps to be heard all over the hall. Young John became much more relaxed when he realised the cat had not been let out of the bag.

"Thank you very much, Mr. McLennan," said the headmaster, who continued, "I think you have done us all an excellent service, for although I had my suspicions as to who stole my watch out of my study I had no concrete evidence until today. Kindly leave the matter with me, and I shall get in touch with the legal authorities."

After the prize-giving was over and each and all bade one another farewell, they all went their different ways through a much cooler countryside than they had experienced earlier in the day, for the temperature had dropped by this time and, although the sun was still shining, the shadows of the tall trees in the neighbourhood were becoming longer and longer as the day progressed. Shortly after leaving the hall, young John and his friend Dominic were personally congratulated by Mr. and Mrs. Paul, the squire and the captain, on their achievements that afternoon.

Walking behind the Paul family and Dominic Archer were captain Blake and the squire. As they ambled slowly out of the school grounds Captain Blake turned to the squire and said, "My sincere thanks for a most pleasant and enjoyable afternoon. It was only a pity that it was marred by that incident about Maxwell at the end of prizegiving."

"I am glad you enjoyed it," said the squire to the captain. "I would not worry too much about what happened to that Maxwell character, for, believe me, he got all he deserved; he is nothing but a lout, a bully, a thief and a vagabond."

"Oh, I did not know that," replied Captain Blake.

"Oh yes indeed," said the squire; "for there is an old biblical say-ing, 'You shall reap as you sow,' and believe me that's what happened to him."

"Excuse my ignorance," said the Captain, "but can you tell me what this dunce's cap means and the history behind it, as they have one at the school I went to?"

"Well, to put it crudely," said the squire, "it is for the stupidest boy in the school. Historically it goes back a very long time."

"Very interesting," said the captain. "How far does its history go back?"

"Well, captain, if you can listen to me," said the squire, "we had a Franciscan monk from this part of Scotland, very famous in philoso-phy in fact, from a place called Duns, whose name was Duns Scotus. He attended the University of Oxford away back in the twelfth cen-tury, as a member of his religious order. At the same university there was another religious house called Blackfriars, run by the Domini-can Order. As they followed the writings of St. Thomas Aquinas, they were known as members of the Thomite school of philosophy and thought themselves to be much superior to the poor humble Fran-ciscans, whom they considered intellectually inferior. Hence, the dunce's cap got its name from this man from Duns."

"Well, that's really most interesting," said the captain. "I am delighted you told me, as I like to know the reason for something I see that interests me yet I cannot understand."

As the Paul family and Dominic had met some of their friends on their way home, the distance between them, the squire and the cap-tain began to narrow. And, coming in the opposite direction in great haste, was a face that young John immediately recognised.

"Hey, Dominic," John said excitedly, "look who's coming up the road."

"Who is it then?" said Dominic, with Mr. and Mrs. Paul looking bemused, for they had never seen the gentleman in question in their lives before.

"It's Mr. Thorpe, Captain Blake's Bosun," said young John, "let's go and show him our prizes."

"All right," said Dominic, "but I hope it is not the press-gang I mentioned earlier in the day."

"No, don't be so stupid," replied John. "He is probably looking for Captain Blake, who is just behind us."

Running eagerly up to him young John said, "Good afternoon, Mr. Thorpe—so pleased to see you again."

"And a very good afternoon, Master Paul," replied the Bosun. "So nice to meet you again. Man, you look a much smarter boy today!"

"Did you see the prizes Dominic and I got at school?" said John, proudly showing him their books.

"Is that not marvellous?" replied the Bosun, as he scanned through the books; and finding they were navigational studies, he was even more delighted.

"Yes," said John, "I got a first and my friend Dominic got a third."

"Excellent indeed!" said the Bosun. "And whilst we are on about navigational studies, have you seen Captain Blake?"

"Yes, he is just up the road there with the squire, talking to my father and mother. I hope you are not going to tell him about my visit to your ship yesterday," said John apprehensively.

"Remember what I told you on leaving the ship, master John?"

"Yes, Mr. Thorpe."

"Well, don't worry," said the Bosun, "but come along with me, both of you, because what I am seeing the captain about could be of interest to you."

As they made their way to meet the ship's master, John and Dominic had no idea what he wanted to see Captain Blake about which could concern them. As they approached, all four of them were in good humour, laughing heartily at some joke that had been cracked by the squire.

Meeting the ship's master, the Bosun said, "Good afternoon, Sir. No doubt you will be surprised to see me here."

"Indeed I am, Mr. Thorpe," replied the captain. "I hope there is nothing seriously wrong."

"No, not really, Sir, except that a sloop came over from White-haven with an urgent message from the shipowner."

"Not a change of plans then?" enquired a concerned skipper.

"Oh no, Sir; a ship came in from the West Indies yesterday and two of the crew went down with fever and were buried at sea, in the middle of the Atlantic."

"So what! That's not unusual in the merchant navy, is it?"

"I appreciate that, Sir," said Bosun Thorpe, "but the two cabin-boys on our ship, now that they are old enough, have to be trans-ferred to that ship as deckhands, which leaves us two boys short. That's what I came to see you about, Sir."

"Oh, I see now, Mr. Thorpe," replied a concerned looking captain. "Well, we will need to put our thinking caps on, won't we?"

With this news, young John looked at Dominic, gave him a small wink and a half smile, then cast his eyes on his parents to see what mood they were in. They were of course thrilled with their son that day and cherished him for being first in the class on a subject he ate, drank and slept.

Captain Blake then said humorously, "You know, Mr. Thorpe, that on the high seas, under severe gale storm conditions, I have to make snap decisions. Well, I have made one this very moment!"

"What is that, Sir?" said the Bosun, as he looked down on John and Dominic, who were listening attentively to every word that was uttered.

"We have two cabin-boys right here in our midst—should they wish to take the job."

"Great minds think alike, Sir; I was thinking the same thing myself," said the Bosun, who was now in the company of a beaming pair of potential mariners.

Captain Blake then turned to the boys and said, "Masters Paul and Archer, would you like to join my crew as cabin-boys?"

He need not have asked them, for they were already jumping with delight and replied, "Oh yes, Sir, you have made our day!"

"Of course, it will be up to your parents whether they wish you to go or not," said the captain.

Turning to his parents, John pleaded with them to let him go, and, since they realized he was going to be in good company with Captain Blake, they gave their assent. The squire himself had a great influence on their decision, and his blessing on the offer by the capitain helped to put the final seal on it.

"Very well, Master Paul," said the captain. "You catch the sloop *Gloria* from the quayside, which will be leaving in two days' time, at nine o'clock in the morning, for Whitehaven. And on arrival there, report to the *Friendship* and we will take it from there. And finally, the Bosun will give you a list of all your requirements to take with you."

"Yes, Sir, I shall be there on time, with my chest packed and ready to obey your commands."

The captain then turned to Dominic and said, "Master Archer, the same thing applies to you, subject to your parents' approval. Do you understand?"

"Yes, Sir, I do. It's just a matter of courtesy to tell my parents, for I know they will give their approval."

So young John's last day at school was crowned with something he had always yearned for—a job at sea, on an ocean-going ship.

CHAPTER 3

FROM CABIN BOY TO
SHIP'S MASTER

Leonardo da Vinci	Italian Genius on many Subjects
Mr. Patrick Henry	American revolutionary
Mr. Guy Fawkes	English Conspirator (1570–1606)
Flora MacDonald	Fearless and Faithful Friend of Bonnie Prince Charlie
Mr. Sam McAdam	Scottish Shipowner
Captain John Newton	Slave Trader; Abolitionist; Author of 'Amazing Grace.'

It was a sad and forlorn young John Paul who, with his chest packed, waited at the quayside for his voyage on the sloop *Gloria* which would take him to Whitehaven to join the brigantine *Friendship* as cabin boy. Not only was he leaving home for the first time, he was going alone, as his best friend, Dominic Archer, failed to get his parents' permission to join the mercantile marine as a mere cabin-boy. Dominic's father, being an ex-Royal Navy Captain, considered such a menial occupation to be well below Dominic's station, and he had more ambitious ideas as to what his son should do: he should enter the Royal Navy as a midshipman and eventually follow in his own footsteps.

However, at the quayside, to bid young John farewell, were his parents and the squire, Mr. Craik, who had made a special effort to be present, as he held young John and his father in great esteem.

"This is a very important day in your life, young John," said the squire.

"It certainly is, Sir; one could say the fulfilment of a boyhood dream. For since my earliest childhood days, when I witnessed the various ships of sail plying up and down the Solway Firth, I can now honestly say, in the presence of my dear parents, that the call of the sea had a greater hold over me than working as a labourer in your garden."

"Good, young John," said the squire; "for I would sooner see you doing something that you really enjoyed than carrying out a task which your heart was not really set on."

"Thank you for these sentiments, Sir, and please do not think that I am in any way insulting your dignity in not becoming an apprentice gardener to my father on your estate."

"Not in the least, young man," replied the squire. "On the contrary, you have the great Scottish attributes of single-mindedness and independence, which are great virtues to possess. But remember, should you ever wish to leave the sea, there will always be a job awaiting you on my estate, working alongside your father."

"Thank you very much, Mr. Craik," replied young John. "For should my wish to make the sea my career be nothing more than a boyhood fantasy, I will most certainly eat humble pie and return to life on the land."

Meanwhile his parents, in the company of his favourite Border collie, Lassie, stood by with a look of sadness in their eyes. His father was very composed, being the type of person he was; but his mother was much more emotional, as the tears began to stream slowly down her cheeks: it would be the last time she would see her beloved son for, to her, he was venturing into the unknown.

"Now, young John," said his father seriously, "remember what I told you about the various bars of ill repute up and down the Solway coastline?"

"Yes, father, I remember those lectures from a very early age, really too young to understand what it was all about at the time."

"Well, my lad, you will find most seaport bars the world over containing that sort of woman, whose sole purpose is to entertain the desires of the wayward seaman, who is far from home and has some spare cash to spend."

"But, father, I can assure you these are the last thoughts in my mind at this moment; however, if and when temptation presents itself, I will remember what you told me."

"It is not the act of sex itself, which, to be honest, most young virile males like yourself yearn for, but the serious consequences it can have on your health."

"What do you mean by that, father?" asked young John eagerly.

"Well, my son, you can catch certain diseases that are in many ways incurable, some being so serious that you can either die at an early age or suffer serious ill health for the remainder of your life, which will rule out the possibility of marriage and the happiness of bringing up a respectable, God-fearing family."

Whilst this heart-to-heart talk between father and son was taking place, Mrs. Paul and the squire were conversing quietly out of hearing distance, in order to eliminate any embarrassment between mother and son, for, because of the puritan ethic of the time, sex was very seldom spoken about. From the manner in which the squire was speaking to his mother it could be observed that he was reassuring her that young John would be in safe hands once he was under the command of Captain Blake and the experienced Bosun Thorpe.

When the skipper of the sloop *Gloria*, which was a single-masted sailing vessel, rigged fore and aft, instructed him to go aboard his ship, the time came for final farewells. Young John first of all doffed his cap and, shaking the squire's hand firmly, he thanked him for all the advice he had given him and intimated that, should his endeavours as a seaman prove fruitless, he would return to his native land and serve his apprenticeship as a gardener. Likewise, he wished his father farewell and thanked him for the advice he had given him since early childhood. He also asked his father to convey his sincere thanks to Mr. Lindsay, his educator at the village school in Kirkbean, for all that he had done for him during his days as a schoolboy. The most emotional aspect of his departure was his final farewell to his mother, who by this time was unashamedly crying, to such an extent that her husband and the squire had to placate her and wipe the tears from her eyes. Occasions like these were not uncommon in this area, for the call of the sea had been answered in the past by many boys of young John's age group, so the people on the quayside and the crew aboard the *Gloria* quite well understood the situation, for many of themselves had been in the same position in the past.

Once she regained her composure, Mrs. Paul strongly embraced her young son, saying, "God bless you, my dear laddie, and look after yourself wherever you go."

"Please, mother, do not fret for me, as I am quite capable of looking after myself."

"True, son, you are talking a lot of common sense, but do take care of yourself and, for my sake, keep out of trouble and never cultivate low company that would bring disgrace on your family and your beloved Scotland."

"Mother, that advice you gave me the other evening, in the presence of my dear father, will always remain in my mind, particularly the way we were treated by the English."

"But don't hold any animosity against individual Englishmen, for they are only doing what their King and superiors order them to do."

"Yes, mother, I shall never forget a sermon we once got from the Reverend Mr. Hogg, where he quoted from the Good Book, 'Do unto others as you would unto yourself'."

"Well, remember that, my dear son, and that philosophy throughout your life; regardless of what you aspire to, you should not go far wrong."

"No, mother, you are so correct in what you are saying, for, if we all used this quotation from the Holy Bible, the world would be a much happier place; for, before we can free the world from the chains of serfdom and evil, we must first of all change ourselves."

At this stage the squire, Mr. Craik, interrupted and said, "By the way, young John, I have spoken to Captain Blake and, at the first opportunity available he will give you permission to visit your brother William, whenever you are in the Fredericksburg area of Virginia."

"That's really kind of you, Sir," replied young John, "for I shall be delighted to meet him and give him all the news from home."

His mother's final words of farewell to him were to make sure he called on William, for, once in his company, he would have a good person to guide him, for Willie was a very sensible and levelheaded boy, who was prospering quite well in the American Colonies. And before boarding the sloop *Gloria* his final goodbye was to his old true and faithful canine friend, Lassie. Her animal intelligence seemed to be at its peak, for there was none of the usual excitement about her; she seemed to be aware of what was happening around her and, far from being joyous, it was a very sad occasion indeed for her. Finally, patting her on the back and shaking her paw, young John made his way along the gangway and boarded the ship, which was to take himself and some other passengers to Whitehaven and finally on to the New World.

It was under a heavy cloud-laden sky, and with a slight westerly wind, which made the starboard side the weather side, that the sloop finally departed from the small quay and made its way across the Solway Firth to Whitehaven. As the *Gloria* was kedging out of port, the only indication in young John's composure of any emotion beginning to show itself, were the tears welling in his eyes, as he waved a final farewell to those wishing him bon voyage ashore

"Well, that's him away at last, father," said Mrs. Paul sadly, as she wiped the final tears from her bloodshot eyes.

To comfort her and give her further assurance, gardener Paul said, "Don't worry too much about him, mother, for he is a very sensible and mature boy for his age."

"Well, I hope you are right," replied his wife, "for I like to see the boy do well as a seafarer; for we all knew that his heart was in nothing else but this, since he started to talk and became observant of the world around him."

"Very true, mother," replied gardener Paul, "and I know in my own mind that he would never have been truly happy working alongside me, for his heart would not have been in it, good and conscientious as he is."

"How do you think he will fare at sea then, father?" enquired his wife.

"Well, I think that if he listens to the sound advice of Bosun Thorpe, he may well end up a Bosun himself in future years."

The squire, who had been very subdued during this discourse, went on to say, "Well, being a fairly good judge of character, I am prepared to say that young John, given the right opportunities, will go a lot further, for, when he fully develops into manhood, he should become quite a character and an expert on all aspects of seamanship."

"So you think he might make the rank of Bosun one day, Mr. Craik?" enquired his mother anxiously.

"Yes, I do, and if my intuition is correct, he will probably go a lot further."

"That would be nice," replied his mother, "for I would like to think that his education was not wasted."

"Well, I can assure you and your husband that his teacher Mr. Lindsay told me that, of all the boys he has taught over the years, young John Paul should take to the sea as a duck takes to water."

Gardener Paul then interrupted and said, "I am inclined to agree with you, Mr. Craik, but we will just have to wait and see, for we all know that luck plays a big part in enhancing one's opportunities."

"True, Mr. Paul," said the squire, "but to get promotion in the mercantile marine, there is something that must complement this luck and that is leadership, determination and professional competence, in the handling not only of a ship but the crew which one commands."

"However," said gardener Paul, "let us just take things step by step and see how he will progress as a cabin-boy, and the future should sort itself out one way or another."

By this time the sloop was well out of sight of the harbour, so they all decided to make their way home, with an aura surrounding them as if they had just been to a funeral. There was no mirth or joy in their discussion but only an air of sadness at young John's departure.

After an uneventful but pleasant voyage across the Solway Firth, the sloop *Gloria* eventually arrived in the Cumbria town of Whitehaven. To young John, this was another world completely, for Whitehaven was a bustling naval port, both for the Royal and Merchant Navies of Great Britain. And he had never witnessed such an assortment of men-of-war, schooners, brigantines and all other various types of ship, down to the common or garden gig, in his life before. But having read a lot about them and watched them ply the Solway Firth as a boy, he was not completely unfamiliar with what was going on in this beehive of mercantilism.

Amidst the array of ships that were there, he eventually located the brigantine *Friendship*, and, alighting the gangway, he finally sought out the Bosun and duly reported for duty.

As he trudged up the gangway, precariously balancing his chest of belongings on his right shoulder, the Bosun, Mr. Thorpe, looked down on him from the poop deck, like a buzzard surveying his prey.

"So you have made it at last, Master Paul," said the Bosun, as he eagerly watched him come aboard. Being an old salt with years of experience behind him, Bosun Thorpe could usually tell whether a new recruit to his ship would make it or not by observing the individual's attitude and deportment.

"Yes, Sir," replied young John. "Glad to be aboard the *Friendship* at last."

Surveying him with his beady eyes, the Bosun said, "Now look here, Master Paul, there are one or two do's and don'ts I must advise you on, which help in the overall smooth running of a ship of this nature.

"First, you don't call me 'Sir', but just plain 'Bosun'. Do you understand that?"

"Yes, indeed I do," said young John in a confident manner.

"The only people you call 'Sir' are the Captain, his Chief Officer, Third Mate, and of course we cannot forget the Purser."

"Fully understood, Bosun," was John's reply as he eagerly awaited Mr. Thorpe's further instructions.

"Before I further introduce you into the daily routine of this ship and what everything stands for, what happened to your school friend Master Archer, who was supposed to be joining our crew today?"

"Well, Bosun, he himsejf had every intention of coming, as he was most anxious to join the crew, but his parents would not assent to his wishes, as they have other things in mind for him."

"Like what?" enquired Bosun Thorpe.

"Evidently his father would like him to go to sea, but not as a cabin-boy in the mercantile marine."

"Did his parents consider such a job to be too menial a task?" enquired the Bosun.

"To put it in a nutshell, yes, Bosun," replied young John, "for his father would like him to join the Royal Navy as a midshipman, with the hope that he would eventually obtain a permanent commission in His Majesty's Navy."

"Of course, I believe his father is a retired naval captain himself," said the Bosun.

"Yes," replied John excitedly; "before he left the Royal Navy he was captain of that very famous ship called H.M.S. *Triumph*."

"Oh, that explains it then," said the Bosun; "for, to be accepted in the Royal Navy as a midshipman one must have influential friends in high places, and Master Archer certainly has that."

"Yes, Bosun, that's where he is lucky, in that he has a lot of contacts with the right people. Mind you, to be fair on him, he never considered himself a cut above the rest at school. Quite the opposite in point of fact, for not only was he my best friend, he was also very popular with the remainder of our classmates, many of whom came from poor and humble homes."

"Well, maybe it will be better for the boy in the long run, if he joins the Royal Navy," said the Bosun; "for some of the old hands aboard this ship would have given him a rough time as a boy sailor, once they learned his father was a retired sea captain in His Majesty's Navy."

"But surely they would not hold that against him, Bosun?"

"Oh yes, they would, Master Paul, for as you will find out sooner or later, there are some roughnecks among the crew who would have made his life unbearable, to such an extent that they would have sickened him on the first voyage, if he made it, to such a degree that he would have thrown in the towel after his first trip, or maybe have jumped ship in America, where we eventually hope to arrive."

"I am certainly learning fast, Bosun Thorpe," replied young John. "But what did you mean when you said, 'If he made it'?"

"Well, when we are in severe-force gales in the middle of the Atlantic and the ship is pitching like a cork in turbulent water, the term 'man overboard' can mean murder in disguise, particularly when it is pitch-black at night and, because of the severity of the gale-force winds, we have to reduce sails. On occasions like these, many unsavoury things have happened in the past, and will no doubt repeat themselves in the future."

"So is it an advantage to me to be of poor humble stock then?"

"Very much so, Master Paul; because you come from the same social background as the rest of the crew this is a tremendous advantage to you. For, once you get familiar with them, they will do everything in their power to show you the ropes."

"From this I gather they are not all cut-throats and blackguards, then?" he enquired.

"Far from it!" was the Bosun's reply. "Because of some rather ugly incidents aboard in the past, the ship's owner insists we have to be very selective in picking a crew, so that we have complete harmony throughout the ship's company."

"That's very reassuring to know, Bosun," replied young John, who by this time was becoming very much more at ease in his new surroundings.

"We do, however, have our incidents," said Bosun Thorpe; "for all you need is one or two potential troublemakers to slip through our selection process and they can create havoc among the rest of the crew."

"And what do you do in situations like that?" enquired young John.

"Well, breaches of discipline are dealt with by the Captain and administered by Mr. Mills, my deputy, who is known as the Bosun's Mate."

"So that I can familiarise myself with discipline aboard ship, can you give some examples, Bosun Thorpe?"

"Well, in extreme cases such as murder or mutiny, the felon in question is hanged to death from one of the lower yard-arms and then thrown overboard without any pomp or ceremony. And if we are in tropical climates, they become known as shark-meat. But the normal punishment that's most administered and—remember this does not happen every day—is that the accused is lashed on the bare back with the cat-o'-nine-tails."

"Does this apply to boy seamen like myself?" enquired young John anxiously.

"No," replied Bosun Thorpe, "for any breaches of discipline by boy seamen are dealt with by making him, in naval jargon, 'kiss the gunner's daughter'; for you will notice that because the war is still going on, this ship is armed."

"Oh, that's the reason for merchant ships being armed, because of the war?"

"Yes," replied the Bosun; "and should any boy have to be disciplined, he bends over one of the guns; then he is lashed across the backside, although he is still wearing his trousers. In cases like these, Mr. Mills will use this rattan, which is different from the cat-o'-nine-tails."

Young John nervously viewed the instrument which the Bosun was holding in his right hand, and said, "I hope I am never on the receiving end of that!"

The Bosun went on to say, "Master Paul, take it from me that when discipline on this ship is administered, it is the exception rather than the rule, for, by and large, we have a very happy crew indeed. And I am only telling you all this so that you will learn the traditions and customs of the sea at an early age, as they are so different from life ashore."

"I understand," acquiesced young John.

"Before Captain Blake arrives, I shall explain the layout of the ship to you, as it is very strict company policy that all new crew members are familiarised with the ship's layout and how it functions. When we are under way and operating in the midst of a storm or severe gale, you will appreciate the value of such instruction, for you will know what to do in the case of an emergency. The sea can be a merciless place at times, and without an enlightened crew who know exactly what to do at the right time, they could have an early watery grave, because of stupidity and inexperience."

"I am only too eager to learn from you, Bosun," replied young John, as he listened attentively to what Mr. Thorpe had to say.

"Now, Master Paul, ignore anything you might know or might think you know, so that, like all other new arrivals, you start from scratch and get into my way of thinking," said Bosun Thorpe, as he stood upright on the poop deck, facing the front of the ship. The Bosun went on to explain that the front of the ship was called the bow, and the rear was called the stern. "And any part of the vessel on the right hand of the fore and main masts is known as the starboard side. Likewise, any part of the ship on the left hand side of these masts is known as the larboard side. Being a two-masted ship, the fore mast is the one nearest the bow and, as you can see, it has square sails. And the one immediately in front of us is known as the main mast, and it has fore-and-aft sails.

"Do you understand me so far, Master Paul?" enquired the Bosun.

"I most certainly do," was young John's confident reply.

"So far, so good," said Bosun Thorpe, realising that young John was studiously absorbing every word he was saying.

"Now," the Bosun continued, "a ship never sails in a straight line but zig-zags, as it cannot sail straight into the wind. Therefore, once we get under way, we will be tacking and wearing ship, in accordance with the way the wind is blowing."

Absorbing every word of advice, as a sponge takes in water, young John interrupted and said, "Can you explain in detail what you mean by tacking and wearing ship, Bosun?"

"A very good question, my lad," was the Bosun's reply; "for this is a thing we will remember throughout the whole voyage. And if you remain a seafarer, which I hope you will do, you will encounter it for the rest of your career."

The Bosun continued, "I shall start by describing what tacking means. The order is given first of all to stand by to tack. And when this manoeuvre is carried out, it means bringing the wind from one bow to the other, with the head of the ship going through the eye of the wind. If, for example, the wind is blowing on the starboard side of the ship, this side is known as the weather side, as it is the side the wind catches the sails. In times like this, the larboard side will be known as the leeward, pronounced 'looard', side of the ship, or the sheltered side. So if we begin to tack when the starboard side is the weather side, once the operation is completed the larboard side becomes the weather side and the starboard side becomes the leeward or sheltered side."

By this time it could be observed that young John was beginning to understand more fully the basic rudiments of sail-handling, even although the sails were not already set, as the brigantine was still stationery in port.

Mr. Thorpe then asked him, "Are you understanding what I am telling you so far?"

"Yes, Bosun," was young John's confident reply; "for I had a vague idea about the subject anyway."

"Now forget about your vague ideas or those you have picked up as a schoolboy, for these simple briefings that I am giving you now are prerequisites for making you a good sailor one day," said the Bosun in a fatherly manner.

Young John nodded.

"Blast it!" exclaimed the Bosun, hitting the palm of his left hand with his fist. "There is another important thing I forgot to mention, and that is the bowsprit. This is the spar running out from the ship's stem on the bow, to which the forestays are fastened."

The Bosun went on, "Now Master Paul, we will now turn to the subject of explaining what is meant by wearing ship, which is otherwise known as gybing. When the order is given to wear ship, the manoeuvre is carried out by bringing the wind from one side to the other, with the stern of the ship going through the wind. Do you understand that simple, yet important piece of information, Master Paul?" asked the Bosun.

"Indeed, I do," was John's candid reply.

The Bosun went on, "Well, my lad, from what I can observe of you so far, you should take to life at sea like a fish takes to water, as you are very quick on the uptake."

"Thank you for the compliment, Bosun," replied the latest recruit to the ship.

The Bosun continued and said, "Now relax, Master Paul, and we will sit on this companion, which leads from the poop deck down onto the main deck below us."

So they both squatted, the mature and experienced Bosun and the young trainee, who showed no sign of homesickness whatsoever but was oozing with enthusiasm to obtain more knowledge from his mentor—knowledge that would hold him in good stead in the unknown years that lay ahead of him.

Casually the Bosun continued: "You know, Master Paul, that what I have told you here and now is one thing, but it will only be put to the test on the high seas, under extreme and precarious circumstances, when we run into foul weather."

"Did any of your young boy seamen in the past ever panic?" young John asked the Bosun.

"Panic!" replied Mr. Thorpe. "I have had trainees come aboard my ship who would have been far better off assisting the town crier, for they had as much chance of making good seamen as I have of going to the moon."

On that note, young John asked the Bosun, "With the advancement of this great subject called science, if the theory of flight is ever put into practice, do you think that man's knowledge will so advance that he will land on the moon?"

"Master Paul, I know you have been reading that famous man called Leonardo da Vinci," said Bosun Thorpe, with a broad smile on his face and a twinkle in his eye.

"No, I have not read him myself, but my friend Dominic Archer's father had a book on some of his writings and he had some remarkable stories to tell about that great man."

"Well, lad," replied the Bosun, "mankind is slowly progressing day by day in knowledge of the world around us, and who knows where it will end up? What I am prepared to say, however, is that, should mankind ever ascend to these great heights, with the advancement of science, I bet you my last farthing that it will be a sailor who will be there first." The Bosun smiled broadly.

Just as young John was laughing away to himself at the Bosun's remarks, a seagull's dropping landed on top of his hat.

"Blast it!" said young John, "this new hat I bought to go to sea is soiled already and we have not left port yet."

"You should not worry about that, Master Paul," said the Bosun, "for that's a good omen for you, a sign of luck; and you might remember these words of mine one day."

"Can you tell me more traditions of the sea that will be able to help me?" young John enquired of the Bosun, after cleaning the seagull's droppings from his hat.

"Well, Master Paul," replied the Bosun, "time does not permit me to go into detail here, as the folklore of the sea has a very long history and tradition, going back to the first time primitive man took to water."

"So it is a subject in itself?" enquired young John.

"Indeed it is," said the Bosun, "and you will only pick it up as your career progresses. All I will say at this stage is that sailors are a very superstitious breed of men—quite different from the types you will meet ashore, as they have a culture of their own."

"I know you are a busy man, Bosun, but, to satisfy my curiosity, can you just give me two examples that you consider important?"

"Yes, I will give you two important incidents which influence sailors on the high seas. First, if you find albatrosses following a ship at sea, it is supposed to be a sign of danger. Whereas, if you get dolphins following the ship, this is understood to be a sign of peace."

"Thank you very much for that enlightenment, Bosun. I suppose I will pick up the remainder of the traditions and folklore as time goes on?" said young John in an enquiring manner, still on the companion with his legs crossed, with both hands between them below his knees.

"Yes, you will pick a lot up from the crew, once you get to know them. However, there are one or two other important points I wish to tell you, before Captain Blake arrives—and he will fully brief you as regards your duties."

Young John stood up from his relaxed position and listened attentively, with both arms folded, as the Bosun poured forth his knowledge of seamanship.

"Well, you already know what standing rigging is; for that's what I caught you climbing up the other day. They are also known as shrouds and are permanent fixtures to the masts; and the ropes you were climbing up are known as ratlings."

"Thank you, Bosun," he replied; "that is one piece of information I will always remember, as it was my first introduction to a real sailing ship, at very close quarters."

Now the Bosun went on to explain that the running rigging consisted of such things as halliards, which were ropes that were used to hoist the sails. Sheets were ropes which were clewed to the sails to control them. And a down-haul was any rope rigged to pull a sail down when it was hoisted. And he finally explained the importance of backstays, which were very important when tacking and wearing the ship or hoisting the sails.

"Are you beginning to understand what it is all about, Master Paul?" enquired the Bosun.

"Yes, Bosun, I am picking these important points up slowly, but I have a lot to learn yet."

"You most certainly have," said the Bosun, "but I think what I have told you today is sufficient to start with, for if I went on any further it would only confuse you and defeat the whole object of this very important briefing. However, I shall get my assistant, Mr. Mills to brief you further as the voyage proceeds, so that you will eventually be familiar with all aspects of how a sailing ship operates. And once you have mastered the basic principles of this ship, you should be able to apply them to any ship you sail in. For most ships are sailed on the same lines, except for a few differences depending on what type of ship it is, of course."

"Well, thank you very much Bosun, for explaining something very complex in a very simple manner, which I hope I will be able to put into practice once we get under sail; for I am fortunate, in the sense that when I do a thing once or twice practically I never seem to forget it."

"Oh, here comes Captain Blake," said the Bosun. "Away down to the gangway and present yourself for duty, when he comes aboard."

"Aye, aye, Bosun," was young John's reply as he made his way down the companion to the main deck, in order to meet the ship's Master.

As Captain Blake boarded his ship, to the eerie shrill of the Bosun's whistle, all hands turned to, as they knew the routine of the sea as a cat knows her kittens. For, once he was aboard, it was a sign that they were shortly to prepare the ship to get under way. All the preparatory work had already been done, and all that was required now were his final orders, and shortly they would be on the high seas once again under full sail, plying an Atlantic Ocean which, on some occasions, would be as calm as a mill pond, and on others very turbulent; all this depending very much on the elements of nature.

As the Captain stepped onto the main deck from the gangway he had an air of command about his deportment that made all crew members realise he was very much the ship's master and from now on they were all very much at his mercy. Young John just stood in a state of amazement, for it was a very different Captain Blake he was seeing now compared with the one he saw a few days ago. Resplendent in his captain's uniform of breeches, tailed jacket, silk muffler and tricorn hat, young John admired the air of authority he displayed from the moment he set foot on his ship.

"Good afternoon, Mr. Thorpe," Captain Blake said to the Bosun.

"Good afternoon to you, Sir," replied the Bosun, awaiting further instructions.

"Prepare sails to weigh anchor in about an hour's time, Bosun," said the Captain, studiously looking westwards towards the overcast horizon, as if anticipating what sort of weather they would expect.

"Aye, aye, Sir," replied the Bosun, who immediately bellowed his orders to the crew, many of whom, through experience, were already in their positions by their respective masts, depending on which watch they were on once she got under sail.

"By the way, Sir, Master Paul has arrived, but his mate could not make it."

"Yes, I understand, Bosun, for I met Master Archer's father, who told me he was entering him as a midshipman in the Royal Navy."

"Oh, good! You know about him, Sir," said the Bosun.

"Yes, I wish the lad well, and he should have an adventurous career ahead of him, for, after the Quiberon Bay affair, the French will be just biding their time until they have another crack at us."

The Captain then turned to young John and said, "Good to see you, Master Paul. Come with me to my cabin and I'll explain your duties aboard ship so that you will know what to do once the voyage commences."

"Very good, Sir," was young John's immediate reply, and they both made their way to the Captain's cabin, which was situated at the stern of the ship, aft of the poop deck, immediately below the main deck.

"So I see your friend could not make it, Master Paul."

"No, Sir, his father wishes him to join the Royal Navy."

"Well, I am afraid, Master Paul, this will mean more work for you, for we really are a cabin-boy short now."

"Aye, aye, Sir," was the boy's confident reply. "Once you give me my instructions I will be able to cope, although it may mean an added effort on my part."

"That's what I like," replied Captain Blake; "a person who is prepared to take on added responsibility without shirking it."

"No, Sir, I shall carry out your instructions to the letter, for I am most grateful for having the pleasure of serving under you and learning all the ins and outs of seafaring the hard way."

"Very good, then, Master Paul," replied the Captain, "we seem to be starting off on the right approach. Well, you are primarily employed as a cabin-boy, which will mean you are on permanent days. You see, the ship's company is split up into two watches, fore and main. Each watch does twelve hours on duty and twelve hours off. Mind you, if there is an emergency, such as severe weather, when we have to reduce sails or when we are tacking or wearing ship, it can be a case of all hands on deck, and that includes you. Do you understand what I have said so far?"

"Yes, Sir," was young John's assured reply.

"Now, your duties as cabin-boy primarily mean that you keep my cabin and those of the other officers clean at all times. Daily, ensure that our cots are kept tidy, and remove all litter from our cabins, leaving it in the dustbins provided."

Young John was listening attentively, taking everything in that Captain Blake was telling him, as if he was hearing his old schoolmaster, Mr. Lindsay, giving him lessons on some subject that really enthralled him.

Captain Blake continued, "Furthermore, you will ensure that our uniforms and footwear are kept clean at all times. And when we arrive in port, should I or any of the other officers decide to go ashore in off-duty uniform, you will also ensure that such clothing is kept clean and presentable to wear. Any questions, Master Paul?" asked the Captain.

"Yes, Sir," was his forthright reply. "The Bosun told me that, as soon as we get under way, I will be taught the basic rudiments of ship and sail-handling."

"A very good point you mentioned there, for, after all, it is my responsibility to turn you into a first-class seaman one day."

"Well, Sir," was John's reply, "I am only too keen to learn the trade as soon as possible."

"Very well then, I shall inform the watch officers that, when the occasion arises, you will be given the opportunity to act as look-out and messenger and read the log and, when we arrive in really shallow waters, to act as leadsman."

"Excellent, Sir!" replied young John. "All these things appear to be very exciting."

The Captain went on, "All these duties are very important indeed and have to be carried out in a diligent and trustworthy manner, particularly the last one I told you about, when we are in shallow waters and you are acting as leadsman. For if you fail to give the duty officer proper readings, namely the distance between the lead when it touches the sea-bed and the markings on the rope at sea-surface level, it can spell real trouble, for the ship can run aground and create a lot of problems for all concerned."

By this time young John was beginning to realise that there was more to ship-handling than he had previously realised, and this made him all the more keen to learn those basic tasks which were so important to the safe functioning and smooth running of a ship under sail.

Realising that he was going to enjoy his ventures at sea, young John brazenly asked the Captain about his opportunities to act as helmsman and learn sail-handling. The Captain indicated to him that his opportunity to act as helmsman and help steer the ship would only be given to him, in the first instance, when they were sailing a smooth course in relatively calm conditions. From there he would progress gradually, so that he could eventually handle the helm under much severer conditions. Likewise with sail-handling, for the Captain informed him that he would instruct his Bosun to ensure that he would gradually be given the opportunity to handle all types of sail, from the bowsprit to the main mast; but he would have to learn gradually so that he would eventually have a firm grounding in the overall purpose of sails, how to operate them and when and where not to use them.

Captain Blake continued, "I think you have enough to go on with. Make your way now to the forecastle, which is forward near the bows, and once you have settled in your accommodation, make your way to the galley and have something to eat."

"Thank you very much, Sir, for these orders and pieces of advice, for I can assure you that I will conscientiously carry them out, as I want to learn fast."

"Good," said Captain Blake. "I think you should do very well for yourself, as you have all the essential qualities that will make a good sailor of you one day."

Once again he thanked the Captain who, after briefing him, made his way to the poop deck to consult with his First Officer and the Bosun, so that the ship could get under way at any moment.

"Master Paul," bellowed the Bosun, "as we are about to sail, go down into the anchor cable locker, which is below the forecastle, and help the other two deckhands down there store the cable neatly, as we slowly take it in."

"Aye, aye, Bosun!" was his prompt reply, as he hurriedly made his way to have his first experience at sea. It was a dank, dark and cold part of the ship to which he made his way down the ladder. On arrival there, the first thing to cross his path was a big, ugly rat, which seemed to appear from nowhere and immediately darted through a hole to the seclusion of one of the holds down below.

Reporting to the two deckhands, who were already in their positions to take in the anchor cable once it lost the strain, he said quite boldly, "Master Paul, reporting to help you."

"Who the bloody hell are you?" growled one of the weather-beaten-faced old salts.

"Master Paul, the new cabin-boy," was his assured reply. "The Bosun sent me down here to give you a hand."

As the deckhand spat the tobacco he was chewing out of his mouth he retorted in a brusque manner, "Look, it's a man we want down here, not a damned schoolboy!"

"I'll do my best," was young John's anxious reply.

"A young boy like you should be getting the Captain's lime juice prepared instead of trying to do a man's job before you are ready for it; this is typical of Bosun Thorpe," said the old hand, whose name happened to be Victor Fear. And Fear by name and fear by nature he certainly was, for young John was rather fearful after their first encounter.

"Take no notice of him, boy Paul," said the second deckhand. "Victor is slightly gone in the head. I think it was that last dose of venereal disease he caught in Tobago that has affected his brain and his whole attitude to life."

Young John Paul said silently to himself, "What have I let myself in for?"—remembering his father's stern advice that morning.

"First day at sea, then, boy?" enquired Victor.

"Yes, indeed," replied young John.

"Well, boy," Victor went on, "you should have your head tested."

"Why's that?" enquired young John, in rather a low tone.

"Well, Master Paul, I have been in this game for over the last forty years, both in the Royal and Merchant Navies. I have seen the lot and, having done the lot, I have come to the conclusion that one has to be slightly touched to have anything to do with the sea in the first instance."

"Well," said young Master Paul, "I suppose it affects different people in different ways, does it not?"

"Well, Master Paul, you probably have a point there, but I fail to see it. However, you will find out for yourself as time goes on. Wait until we get you initiated in Jamaica."

"I don't understand what you mean," was young John's anxious reply.

"Once you are in the motherly arms of those mulatto ladies you will soon find out. They will not only make your dreams come true, but you will think you are in paradise at the time."

Not wanting to appear ignorant of the social life of seafarers whilst ashore, and conscious of his parent's warning, young John replied, "Oh, we will take things as they come."

In the meantime, with the clanking of the capstan pawls on the main deck above them, there were indications that the ship was beginning to get under way, as it was obvious that the anchor was away, with the slack cable coming through the hawsepipe. And the quicker it came through, the more exasperating was the task of stacking it neatly. It did not take young John long to have his hands, arms and legs a complete mass of filth from the slime there was on the anchor cables, and as the process went on it became more and more rapid, until sweat began to break out on young John's brow. At certain points he felt like throwing the towel in, because of sheer physical exhaustion—but determination made him persevere with this gruelling and very unpleasant task, for he did not want to let himself down in the presence of two old salts.

When the arduous task of taking in the anchor chain was completed, Victor said to his mate, "You know, this is the keenest boy seaman I have come across in my whole career. Some of the ones we have experienced in the past would have been better off at home, attached to their mother's apron strings, for they had as little chance of making good seamen as I would have of becoming one of their lordships at the Admiralty."

"Yes, I quite agree with you, Victor," was his friend's reply. "This young boy worked like a beaver, and I think he will get on well with the rest of the ship's company, as he is keen to learn and apply himself."

Young John was greatly elated by this compliment from two old hands, who had sailed the Seven Seas in all types of ships and weather conditions; for, although he was filthy all over the front of his clothing, his first task at sea had been completed to his delight and jubilation.

By the time young John had ascended the ladders up to the main deck, he noticed that the remainder of the crew were not there, for the first thing he observed with his eagle eyes, on popping his head through the main deck hatch, was that the *Friendship* was proceeding westerly under full sail. And all he could see, immediately looking above him, were the last two sailors coming down the ratlings of the foremast standing rigging, having just shaken the last reef of the square topsail. The ship was on the starboard tack and, as it gained speed on its way into the great Atlantic, all indications were that things were going to get rough. As the wind sang in the taut weather rigging, young John was so delighted with his first introduction into the real art of seafaring that he took no notice of the blustering north-easterly wind which was billowing around his ears. And as he made his way along the main deck, contentedly walking in unison with the roll of the ship, the Bosun, who by this time had his pea jacket buttoned up to his neck, had to shout in young John's ears so that he could be heard above the intensity of the wind.

"Master Paul, well done!" shouted the Bosun in his ears. "You're off to a good start, for I have had very complimentary remarks about you from the two men with whom you were working."

"Thank you very much, Bosun," shouted young John, having had his first ego trip in the mercantile marine.

The Bosun went on, "Stowing in the anchor cable requires a lot of muscle and sheer grit, and that's why I put you down there. For, believe me, if you win the approval and confidence of an old hand like Victor Fear, it is a feather in your cap, for, take it from me, if anyone has been around, he has."

"Yes, Bosun," shouted young John eagerly in his ear; "he was telling me some of his experiences, when we were working down below, and I can see that I have a lot to learn."

"Don't worry, Master Paul," said the Bosun, who was holding the fife rail on the leeward side of the main mast, in order to stabilise himself because of a sudden pitch in the ship. "You re better picking things up gradually and getting them right than trying to learn everything at once, so that you're so confused you make a right mess of things."

"Thanks for the sound advice, Bosun," was John's reply.

"You see, Master Paul," the Bosun continued, once we are on the high seas, we are purely at the mercy of mother nature, and if we don't know how to play her at her own game she very soon gets the better of us, and a watery grave can await the whole ship's company; or, if we are lucky, we might just be able to survive the havoc of a shipwreck and all the misery it entails. So, knowing what to do, and doing it at the right time, is of paramount importance, both in ship and sail handling."

As the ship began a more acute roll, young John replied, "Yes, Bosun, I fully understand what you mean already, and this is only my first introduction to real life at sea."

"However, Master Paul," continued the Bosun, "as you are on permanent days, you can stand to and go to your hammock, but, before that, I recommend you clean all that slime off yourself, so that you are spick and span for Captain's duties in the morning."

"Aye, aye, Bosun, a good clean-down will do me good, and I will be careful not to waste any water, for I know that it is as precious as claret aboard ship."

"Now, before you go, I shall get the messenger on morning watch to give you a call around 0500 hours and the first duty you have to do is to get the Captain a hot beverage from the galley. And after you have served him, you will do likewise for his Chief Officer on the poop deck, whom he will be relieving at 0600 hours. Do you understand these instructions then?"

"Aye, aye, Bosun, instructions fully understood."

"So away you go then and have a good night's rest."

As young John made his way along to his sleeping quarters in the forecastle, he was already acquiring the art of balancing himself with the roll of the ship, as the roaring wind lashed one massive grey wave after another relentlessly at the brigantine. As the starboard bow received the first wave, she began a leisurely climb, which heaved the bowsprit up towards the sky. But young John could already observe that his first night at sea was going to be far from calm, as she continued to pitch, heave and roll, with the bowsprit being visible to his eyes one moment and invisible the next.

Having had a good wash-down, he eventually managed to get the art of swinging into his hammock and, once he mastered this skill in the privacy of his own sleeping quarters, the only indication of tears and homesickness came when his mind went back to home. He was thinking of his dear family, particularly his father and mother, not forgetting his favourite pet, Lassie. He remembered vividly his parents since his early childhood; as long as he could remember, in fact; and he came to the point of tears when he contemplated his happy and carefree childhood days in the Solway Firth. His memories took him back to his days at school and his beloved Dominie (old Scots word for teacher) Mr. Lindsay; the many days he spent working barefooted with his father in Mr. Craik's garden; and finally his parents' parting advice. As to the future, he asked himself what it would hold for him. Certainly his first introduction to the seafaring life, being put into the anchor cable locker, was a severe test of both his physical capabilities and ingenuity. Remembering the compliments he had received, he was quite happy and looked with confidence to the future. Mentally he said to himself, "Once I get onto the first rung of the ladder, if things continue as they are, I should become an accomplished seaman. But will I ever become a Bosun or even someone more famous?" He had enough commonsense to realise it was futile to go into the realms of fantasy about life at sea, of which he had dreamt from his earliest days; he must just take things step by step and, for good or ill, history would be the judge.

As he was getting comfortable in his new surroundings, his hammock remaining stable as the ship listed gently from starboard to larboard, suddenly he felt something crawling on top of his blanket. "A damned rat!" he yelled, as he sat up in terror, for he abhorred such vermin which naturally gave him the creeps. As he lay, with his heart pounding for fear it would come back again, he could not forget the ugly and monstrous creature he had seen earlier on that day. Eventually, however, with no sign of its return, he calmed down and prepared himself for a good night's sleep. From behind his head he could faintly recognise a gentle purr, which grew louder and louder as it came nearer to him. Although it was dark by now, he soon realised it was a cat crawling down the ropes which were used to sling his hammock. Surely this must have been the poor creature that gave him a fright earlier on and not the gruesome rat he had envisaged—for he realised that cats and rats were not the best of playfriends. When the cat eventually landed on his hammock, it snugly made its way to the space in the hammock next to his head and contentedly purred him to sleep—for he was much more relaxed now, having learned who his four-legged friend was. When he awoke next morning, before the messenger had arrived to give him his duty call, daylight had broken. And there still beside him, lay this large black tomcat, still purring away, obviously with no concern whatsoever about the world around it. As he was eventually to learn, this tomcat was none other than Sooty, the ship's cat, and its purpose on board as a member of crew was to keep the rats at bay. From that time on, Sooty and John became the best of friends, and remained so for the rest of his tour of duty on the *Friendship*; for Sooty made a marvellous companion and substitute in the place of his dear Scottish border collie, Lassie, whom he thought of often.

Young John made many enjoyable voyages between the West Coast of Scotland, the West Indies and America. And within a couple of years he became so proficient a seaman that he won the admiration of all those he served under and alongside, particularly Captain Blake and Bosun Thorpe, not forgetting old salts like Victor Fear, who knew all the ropes and would soon give a phoney the bums rush and tell him to get lost.

His great delight came, however, on the first trip the ship made to Fredericksburg, Virginia, when the opportunity arose to visit his brother William there. Captain Blake had such trust in him that he not only allowed him to visit his brother but to conduct business with the local traders in order to dispose of surplus cargo, which the *Friendship* could not convey back across the Atlantic to the Old World due to lack of sufficient space.

His meeting with his older brother was, naturally, a very emotional experience for them both.

William exclaimed excitedly: "John! I can hardly believe it's you; you are a young man now; and to think, the last time I saw you, you were just starting to go to school in Kirkbean!"

After throwing his arms around his big brother and tightly hugging him, John said, "You know, Willie, this is not real; I can hardly believe this, after all these years."

"Never mind, John," replied his brother. "As you are staying with me a short while, when you conduct some business in this bustling town of ours we will make up for all those lost years, for the day I departed from that beloved country of ours I thought it was the last I would see of you."

"Yes, Willie, it is amazing what fate is, because it was sheer luck I joined the merchant navy as a cabin-boy and did not remain on the land, helping father look after his favourite garden."

John went on to explain to his brother, who was much taller than he was but had the same features, including a refined air about him, how, by accident, he had met this Bosun Thorpe one day and Captain Blake the next; and thanks to those meetings, he had ended up fulfilling a childhood ambition by going on the high seas and serving before the mast immediately he left school.

"Well, that's marvellous, John," replied his brother William. "And how do you like being a seafarer?"

"Well, William, I can honestly say that I have enjoyed every minute of it. Mind you, it does have its ups and downs, like every other occupation in life; one has to take the rough with the smooth."

"Do you think you will make it your career?"

Here John hesitated, then said, "William, being my oldest brother, I must let you into a secret."

"What is that?" enquired his brother anxiously, thinking he might have contracted one of those repugnant diseases caused by seafarers' visiting houses of ill repute.

"Well, William, I fell in love with America on first seeing this vast, beautiful and inspiring country. And I hope to end up here, come hell or high water."

"Yes, John," replied William; "it is a marvellous country; it's so vast that it will take a long time to develop its full potential."

"Do you think you could get me a job here, William?"

"How old are you now John, fourteen or fifteen?"

"Just coming up for fourteen next July, William."

"Oh, I don't think it would be too difficult to get a fit young man like you fixed up, as I have a lot of good contacts through my tailoring business."

"That would be excellent, William, for I could tell mum and dad on my next voyage home what my intentions are, and eventually pack in the seafaring life, before emigrating as a permanent resident."

"What sort of employment were you thinking about, John?" enquired his brother.

"Well, William, as you know, apart from life on the ocean wave, the only sort of work I really am familiar with is working on the land."

Placing his left hand on his forehead, William closed his eyes, reclined back in his chair and started to think.

"Yes, John, leave that one to me," said William, after considering whom he might know who could get his young brother fixed up on the land as a farm labourer or something of that nature.

"That would be really good of you, William, if you could do your best for me; for, once I get settled in and save some money, I could eventually purchase a piece of land of my own, build a house, and marry a local girl and settle down."

"Talking about land, John," enquired his brother, "how are the old folks and our sisters at home?"

"Well, William, as you know, our sisters are engaged to be married shortly and father and mother are both keeping well."

"As you know," his brother replied, "I correspond with them regularly and mother's letters are so long and detailed that they take such a long time to read, but I must admit that she has kept me fully informed about what is going on in the old country."

"Oh, she certainly goes into detail when she starts," replied John. "But she is a marvellous person, for all that. For she gave us all a good grounding in life, though she has an obsession about the 1745 Jacobite Rebellion, and once she starts off on that subject, it is difficult to get her to stop."

"Oh, I know only too well, John, for I have had pages upon pages about it from her, about that evil London government."

"Aye, she certainly takes her politics seriously. Mind you she has fairly enlightened me on many points, so much so that they will remain with me until my dying days."

"Yes, John, there is a small group of Scots in Edenton, North Carolina, she would get on well with, for they are hell bent on continuing the 1745 Rebellion over here."

"Are feelings that strong then, William?" asked young John curiously.

"Curiously, it's the émigré Scots whose relatives were involved in the 1745 Jacobite Rebellion who are the worst. Have you ever heard of Patrick Henry, whose parents come from the North of Scotland?"

"No, I must say I have not," replied John. "What sort of character is he?"

"Well, you have heard of Guy Fawkes, haven't you?"

"Indeed I have."

"Well, Patrick Henry is another one, if you listen to his ravings, who would blow the Houses of Parliament up and justify it in conscience."

"Do you ever think there will be a revolution here, William?"

"No, I don't think so, John, for, although you get malcontents like Patrick Henry knocking about, they are very much in the minority as the overwhelming majority of the population are very loyal to the Crown in London."

"So you think it is just wishful thinking on the part of this man, Patrick Henry, and his like?" asked John, as he mentally recalled his mother's long discourse on the ills of the London government under King George II, the night before he left school a few years back.

"Yes, that's all it is, I think, John," said William, in a calm and objective manner. "Mind you, as this country grows economically stronger, which it is doing every day, should the London government seriously mishandle its administration to any great degree, people like our dear Patrick Henry would be only too keen to fan the flames of discontent amidst the entire population. But, as I said already, I think the whole thing is highly unlikely."

"Getting back to your seeking employment here, John," said William, in a true brotherly manner, "are you quite certain that you want to leave the sea?"

"Yes, William," was his serious reply; "for since stepping on shore of this great land mass, it was what you would call 'love at first sight' for me."

"But are you sure it's not just a youthful infatuation you have, seeing a strange place for the first time, which you happen to like?"

"No, William," was his assured reply; "there is something about this majestic virgin land that appeals directly to the sentiments of the heart. For after all, if I remain in the merchant navy, or any other navy for that matter, I might just reach the dizzy heights of Bosun, and that will be my sole contribution to the world of seafaring. But, should I eventually acquire a nice piece of land here—and I believe it is quite plentiful—I could improve myself and my offspring and maybe end up being somebody very important in the community; somebody who would be remembered locally in years to come."

"Well, if you are adamant on that way of life, as against the sea, as a long-term objective, I will start making enquiries immediately among my business contacts, and, as you are sailing for home today, I will forward all the information to you shortly, on the next sail packet departing for Scotland."

Over the next three years similar meetings were made, and young John's determination to settle in America was forefront in his mind. Before making his way back to the *Friendship*, on what he thought was just another routine visit, the ship being due to sail to Whitehaven via Jamaica, the trade winds being in its favour, young John, having sold all his merchandise on behalf of Captain Blake, bade farewell to the large number of business contacts he had made. They were all greatly impressed by the shrewd and diligent manner in which he carried out his transactions, and observed how he was a stickler for detail, even down to the last penny, when selling his commodities. Like previous farewells to his brother William, this one had no tinge of sadness about it, for he was adamant about returning as a fully-fledged settler to this up-and-coming part of the Empire. Eventually, in grasping both his hands strongly, his brother William said, "John, I am so proud of you because of the impact you have made on the local business men you have met in so short a time."

"Yes, William," replied John, "and as I have said previously, I am very proud of your being my oldest brother and making a name for yourself in this thriving community. The family back home will indeed be pleased to hear my firsthand report on how you are progressing."

"That will be very good of you, John. Please convey my love to all of them, particularly father and mother, when you return to our native Scotland."

"I most certainly will do that, William; and is there anything in particular you want me to tell them?"

"Nothing really, which I have not told you, John; only to say that, next time you return, I should be married."

"It's only a pity that I never met your bride-to-be, William."

"Aye, that was unfortunate, John, but she is away up country staying with her mother, who is not just keeping too well at the moment."

"Not to worry, William," replied John. "There will be plenty of opportunities of meeting her when I return here for good."

"Well, you can trust me to get everything organised, and, when you eventually arrive here, we shall have a comfortable room awaiting you in my house, and it will be like home from home, just as it was in Kirkbean."

"Do you seriously think I will make an impact on America, William?"

"Well, John," replied William in a paternal manner, "I think 'impact' is too strong a word; but you can make a nice niche for yourself, and who knows what the future will hold for you?"

"As previously, William, I will eagerly await your letter back home, and once I receive instructions from you to come over here I will pack my job in and work my passage across, in one of the ships."

"Good luck then, John," replied William, "and have a safe voyage back across the Atlantic."

With these parting words, young John meandered slowly from his brother's residence in the centre of Fredericksburg and made his way down to the docks in order to board the *Friendship*, which would eventually take him back to his home port in Whitehaven.

On arrival at the quayside, he found the *Friendship* fully laden and looking very resplendent, awaiting her departure over the wide ocean to the Old World. In his absence, the crew had been far from idle. As well as discharging the cargo they had carried across from Whitehaven and reloading her for the return journey, they had also carried out one or two minor repairs to the rigging, and added sails, which would ensure a faster journey home, calling at Kingston, Jamaica, for a change.

Immediately he was spotted by the remainder of the ship's company there were claps and cheers all round, for they could tell by the smile on his face and the confident manner in which he walked up the gangway that his mission ashore had been successful. Acknowledging the compliments paid to him by the remainder of the ship's company, he proudly made his way to the ship's Master, to report on his business feats ashore.

"Good afternoon, Captain Blake," he said in a crisp and business-like manner; "I have completed your tasks ashore, Sir."

"Delighted to see you, Master Paul," was the Master's reply. "I don't think I need ask about the errand I sent you on, for I can sense by your disposition and deportment that you did not fail me."

"No, Sir," was John's enthusiastic reply; "I had an excellent time ashore, for, as well as meeting my good brother William, I sold all our merchandise as usual to local businessmen, against great competition from other ships' agents."

"Excellent, Master Paul," replied the jubilant Captain. "Please do tell me more."

"Well, Sir, in view of the contacts I made, I should not worry about surpluses at any future date in this port, for I have found an outlet for all our commodities. I could quite easily have sold twice as much again."

"That's really good," replied Captain Blake, who went on to say, "I can see that you are not only becoming an excellent seaman, slowly but surely, but also an astute businessman as well."

"Thank you for the compliments, Sir," said John, beaming all over his face.

Having collected the money young John had made from his ventures ashore, Captain Blake checked it against the bill of lading and found everything thereon as accurate as the bearings on the ship's compass. He then went on to say, "Now, Master Paul, now that you have distinguished yourself so well on behalf of the company in Fredericksburg, I am afraid it's back to the old routine. You know your duties well enough by this time, so there is no need for me to elaborate any further, except to say that we are due to sail shortly for home, and once we kedge off we shall sail the first leg of our journey on the larboard tack before we change to the starboard one. Judging from the haze on the horizon and the relatively small white horses that are forming on the crest of the waves, it should be a reasonably smooth passage to Jamaica. After that, we are entirely at the mercy of mother nature, but we will take things as they come; so report to Mr. Thorpe."

"Aye, aye, Sir," was John's sharp reply. Remembering the compliments that had just been paid to him by Captain Blake, he was oozing with pride and a greater determination to keep his well-earned reputation whilst afloat as well.

Once the *Friendship* got under way en route to the West Indies, the voyage was so leisurely that they had to rig additional sails to give the ship more thrust. During this operation young John assisted

'Sails', which was the name of the man responsible for the rigging, care and maintenance of all the ship's sails. And as sails were the sole means of powering a ship, he was a very important member of the ship's company.

The name of the gentleman in question was Mr. Boyd, who hailed from the Whitehaven area and had many years experience in the world of shipping, having served on all types of vessel. He was tall and broadly built and had sharp facial features. He was a doer rather than a talker, and young John picked up much sound advice on sail handling from him, and came to respect him immensely for what he had learned from him. He had young John so well taught after a while that he could leave the apprentice under his charge to antici-pate the ship's requirements in accordance with the prevailing condi-tions of weather that existed at any particular time. This foresight on young John's part impressed Captain Blake and the remainder of his crew immensely, for the young cabin-boy was learning the tricks of the sea very fast. He developed the art of sailing—an important one on the high seas, particularly in turbulent weather conditions of knowing when it was necessary to reduce sails during a storm and, when the storm ebbed, the exact moment to exercise sail power so as not to lose any speed.

It was whilst young John was on lookout duty up on the main mast that he eventually sighted land, which surely must have been the signal that they were about to complete the first leg of their voy-age. And, having an aerial view of the distant islands which were Jamaica, he excitedly shouted, "Land ahoy, Sir!" to Captain Blake, who was on duty on the poop deck below. Captain Blake immedi-ately raised his glass and, scanning the horizon he knew so well, immediately picked out the port of Kingston, where they were due to dock in a few hours' time. Once having confirmed this on the ship's charts, the Captain shouted up to young John: "Very well done, Mas-ter Paul; it's Kingston, Jamaica, right enough!" Signs of approaching land became obvious from the increased activity aboard the *Friend-*

ship, for, being a very competent crew, all hands knew exactly what to do when the ship was due to enter port, so that everything would run smoothly and there would be no last-minute hitches.

Appearing from the bowels of the ship was young John's old friend Victor Fear, to whom he had grown very attached as they got to know one another better. Although they were the opposites in temperament, in that young John was reserved and diligent in his duties, working like a beaver in all the mundane day-to-day tasks aboard ship he was allotted, Victor was the opposite—a gregarious, outgoing devil-may-care sort of character, who, because of his nature and experience, was the type that took risks but at the same time laughed at life. Whether on board or ashore, he was the life and soul of the party and, as such, was very popular with the remainder of the crew.

Spotting John up in the mainmast lookout, Victor started to climb the ratlings so that he could hold an audible conversation with him.

"So we are nearing Kingston at last then, young John," he said in his melodious Welsh voice.

"Indeed we are, Victor, and it looks most picturesque from up here," John shouted back.

"Give Bella Houston, Mary Hill and Flora MacDonald a wave from me then, young lad, for I bet they are at the quayside waiting for us," said Victor humorously.

John did not know what to say, for he realised that Victor was talking about the ladies of the night or daughters of joy who were known to him on these sun-drenched and plague-ridden islands, where not only tropical but venereal diseases were rampant. And as he descended the ratlings, he had a contemplative expression on his youthful sun-tanned face, which prompted Victor to ask, "What are you thinking about, John? Your mind appears to be miles away from here."

To which John replied, "You are so correct, for I remember my mother telling me in a long talk, or should I say lecture, on the 1745 Jacobite Rebellion, of a certain Flora MacDonald who helped Bonnie Prince Charlie to escape after Culloden. Is this the same one, I wonder?"

At this, Victor doubled over, laughing, and said, "If this is the same one, she has changed her colour very quickly, for she is as black as the Earl of Hell's waistcoat."

"So it must be a different one then, Victor?" asked John in a curious manner.

"Yes, she and the other two I just mentioned were slaves from the West Coast of Africa, and they were probably given their names by the plantation owner who purchased them—probably a Scot into the bargain."

"How cruel!" protested John.

Victor burst out in his excitable Welsh accent and said, "How do you mean, 'cruel'? Are we not living in a cruel, bloody world, boy?"

"Yes, in certain ways you are right, Victor, but these people are still human beings—God's creatures, the same as you and I are, entitled to respect for their human dignity," said John philosophically.

"Human dignity, my backside!" retorted Victor, who went on, "You will learn, before you are much older in this man's navy, that some of these slaves are treated better than we are by their masters."

"What do you mean?" John enquired curiously.

"Well, look here, young John," said Victor, who by this time had adopted a very fatherly attitude towards him. "This has been your first ship, and we are all very lucky to have such a humane skipper as Captain Blake, who, as you notice, has a very happy crew. But I can tell you that you will meet others in this game who will make your life a living hell and treat you a lot worse than these slaves are being treated by their masters, so don't give me this claptrap about human dignity, for we are living in a world where it is the survival of the fittest, and the sooner you get to know that the better, young lad."

Young John, having listened attentively to Victor's verbal discourse, went on to say, "Yes, you might have a good point, Victor, for Captain Blake is a very fair ship's Master indeed; and, for a man who has the power of life or death at sea I must say that, from what I have observed, although he is strict, he has compassion as well."

"Look, lad," retorted Victor; "you have got to be strict handling these sailing ships, for, if we don't follow a strict law of nature in handling these sails, we could all end up in a watery grave; so there can only be one boss in making decisions, with no room for discussing what should be done."

"So is that what we mean by saying 'working hard afloat and playing hard ashore'?"

"You've got it, John; you are learning the rules fast," said Victor with a smile. "And when we get ashore shortly, as in the past, we will play very hard indeed. Mind you, I must warn you, John, avoid these three whores like the plague."

"Why is that?" enquired John.

"Well, lad," replied Victor, talking with years of seafaring experience behind him, "these three I have just mentioned are notorious on these islands and have spread more disease among merchant seamen visiting here than all the malaria-carrying mosquitoes in the West Indies."

"Thanks for the advice, Victor," said John, who by this time had reverted to his schoolboy memories, as if he had been once again listening to his old school teacher, Mr. Lindsay.

"Mind you, John," Victor went on to say; "Flora MacDonald has a daughter, who is a real cracker, for, being a half-caste, she is not only very elegant but has a beautiful coffee colour, with the most succulent lips I have ever seen. She is known locally as Naughty Susanah, and I must introduce you to her."

John's mind was in conflict between what his father told him before leaving home and the desires of the flesh. But he realised that, in keeping with the customs of the navy, he must take the plunge some time or he would be treated as odd among the remainder of the crew, as if there were something biologically wrong with him. He would not be rash, however, for he realised the terrible consequences of catching the dreaded disease, so would follow the advice of his trusted and experienced friend Victor, who would find out through the local grapevine who was clean and who was to be avoided at all costs.

After the *Friendship* had docked, most of the crew, apart from the officers, made their way to the notorious quayside tavern known as Betty's Bar. This establishment was one of the focal points for the local prostitutes who catered for the demands of visiting seamen whenever they called in at Kingston, and was consequently part of naval folklore.

On entering the tavern, which was low-ceilinged and humid but buzzing with conversation, it became obvious to John that Victor was well known in this place, from the manner in which he was received by all and sundry.—And after secretively conversing for a short while with one of the locals, he was fully aware of who to avoid and who not to avoid. Returning to the remainder of his friends who were there, which enchanted John, he kept them all up to date as to what the situation was, and they were all pleased for the advice he had to offer. When they had consumed a fair quantity of local hooch, which had a kick like a mule, reason and inhibitions went overboard and the passions of the flesh began to take over, which was accompanied by singing and hilarity. And intermingling with far-from-home seamen were the ladies, who were only too willing to offer their sexual services to the highest bidder, or maybe cheaper to an old customer who had been a regular client over the years when his ship visited port.

Victor surveyed the ladies in the tavern until he spotted Naughty Susanah, and in his loud voice, which boomed as if he were up in the yards in severe gales, he beckoned her over to join the company. As she approached gracefully, with her long dark hair, which was shoulder length and covered the upper part of her breasts, she immediately caught the attention of young John, who looked at her in awe, having confirmed with his own eyes what Victor had previously told him about her—a picture of natural beauty.

"Long time no see," blurted Victor. "How have you been keeping since I last saw you, Susanah?"

"Very well indeed, Victor, but my mama says I should have nothing to do with you, for you are a very bad man."

"What do you mean by that, my dear?" said Victor, who by this time was quite inebriated.

"My mam says you gave her a baby last time you slept with her, and I have another young brother to look after now."

"How old is your brother now, Susanah?"

"Just under a year, and he is so pretty," was the curt reply.

"Not guilty then," replied Victor; "for it is over three years since I was with your mother, and unless you believe in delayed action and miracles it cannot possibly be me; she must be getting me mixed up with somebody else who looks like me."

"Oh, it does not really matter, Victor, as it is one of the risks of this trade, and we must accept the consequences if pregnancy occurs; another mouth to feed."

Victor went on, "No, Susanah, my conscience is clear, because of the time factor involved. However, let me introduce you to the youngest member of the crew, young John from Scotland."

Warmly holding John's hand, she said, "So pleased to meet somebody so virile looking, who is all the way from Scotland. Would you like to come to bed with me, and I will give you a good time as you are a friend of Victor's?"

John was hesitant at first at taking up the offer, because of his childhood environment and the lectures he had had on the subject from his father, but when Victor noticed his indecision, he said, "Look, boy, you are no longer attached to your mother's apron and you have got to take the plunge sooner or later, or you will definitely be the odd man out amongst the crew; and just think of the ribbing you will have to take on the voyage home if the rest of them hear you declined such an offer—in Betty's Bar, of all places!"

John was still slightly hesitant but much less so than he had been before, and when Victor leaned over and whispered in his ear, "She's clean; I checked with Ebenezer behind the bar. You have nothing to worry about, lad, so away and get the dirty water off your chest, and you will be a real man, fully initiated into the customs and traditions of all seafarers. After all, you have been with us over three years now and you have not lost your virginity yet."

This was enough to dispel any previous hesitations in young John's mind, for he just could not lose face with the remainder of the ship's company; so, throwing caution to the wind, he said confidently to Susanah, "Let's go then."

Making his way to a small room at the rear of the bar, young John was to emerge about three hours later, physically exhausted but fully sexually satisfied and a much more outgoing individual, because of his first experiences in a Jamaican brothel. Amidst his comrades, he could now hold his head up high and look them straight in the face for he would now be considered a fully fledged mariner, from the worldly point of view, among his peer group aboard the *Friendship*.

As the brigantine sailed leisurely across the Atlantic, en route to its home port, there was nothing unusual about the voyage, except that John was no longer treated as a boy; for, because of his experiences in the West Indies, he was now accepted as a fully fledged member of the crew. However, had he not taken the plunge in Jamaica, he would probably have been ostracised and ridiculed by the remainder of the ship's company, which would have made life aboard, if not unbearable, indeed very difficult, for he would have been considered the odd man out.

Two days prior to entering Whitehaven, one of the crew spotted a pair of albatrosses circling overhead and, pointing upwards to the sky, he immediately shouted to Mr. Thorpe who was on the poop deck with Captain Blake: "Mr. Thorpe, can you see what is following us?" Looking upwards, the Bosun replied, "Indeed I can, and I don't like it! The last time I saw birds like that following our ship, which was a few years back, we went aground off Savannah." Captain Blake likewise looked up and confirmed Mr. Thorpe's sentiments by saying, "I don't like that sort of omen, for, although I have only experienced it twice in my career, on both occasions it brought tragedy. First, we were shipwrecked off Portugal, on a ship called the *Don Juan*, when we were making our way to Gibraltar and encountered rough weather that drove us against the rocks."

"Was it serious, Sir?" enquired the Bosun anxiously.

"Serious!" said Captain Blake. "All hands went down, including the old man, apart from four of us who managed to swim with the current and remain perched on a large rock until the storm subsided."

"And what happened on the second occasion you were followed by albatrosses, may I ask, Sir?"

"Well, Mr. Thorpe, that was when most of the crew went down with black vomit, when we were coming home from the Windward Islands."

"That would have been quite a nerve-racking experience then, Sir."

"Indeed it was, Mr. Thorpe, for, apart from being unwell ourselves, the remainder of us that remained alive had the awesome task of burying some of our best comrades at sea and, after that, we had to sail-handle the ship back to port three-quarters under strength. How we did it, God only knows."

Being a very superstitious lot, as most sailors were, on seeing their escorts flying overhead and sometimes nestling in the crow's nest, the whole crew became very depressed and despondent; for those who had experienced such a situation before knew what it was all about, and those who were encountering this situation for the first time were aware of what it meant from the folklore of the sea.

As conditions were relatively calm, the crewmembers were mystified as to what the bad omen could represent. Amongst them there were as many views as there were stars in the moonlit sky. Could it be a pending collision? Had another war been declared whilst they were sailing home, and were enemy ships now at hand? Or would they all be struck down by the plague? Surely not the latter, as they were only one day from home and they all looked fit and healthy. When, however, the *Friendship* eventually docked, the ill omen came true, fulfilled by something not one of them had even thought about: the firm had gone bankrupt and they were all paid off.

Once the ship was unloaded of its merchandise, Captain Blake and one of the firm's representatives mustered the whole crew on the forecastle and explained the situation to them all. Fortunately there was sufficient money left to pay them their wages in full, and when that was done, before they all went their different ways, Captain Blake thanked them for being such a loyal and trustworthy crew and said that when he eventually took over another ship, if any of them were looking for employment aboard, he would go out of his way to secure them a billet.

As they all dispersed, Captain Blake, in the company of Bosun Thorpe, called young John into his presence to bid him a special farewell, saying, "Well, Master Paul, you were an eager young boy the first day I met you and over these last few years you have gone ahead by leaps and bounds and, I may say, you have matured immensely since our first voyage out of Whitehaven."

"Thank you very much, Sir," was John's proud reply; "and may I take this opportunity to thank you and the Bosun for all the sound knowledge you have imparted to me, which will no doubt hold me in good stead for future seagoing experiences. For I will always be able to fall back on the basic anchorage I received from both of you should an awkward situation arise under any climatic conditions."

At this the Bosun interrupted and said, "Yes, Master Paul, I knew the first time you officially boarded the brigantine that you would make it, and you have proved me right. And may I say that, if you keep the right company and avoid low types of sailors, the future should indeed be bright for you, as you are an intelligent, level-headed and ambitious youth."

"Well, Mr. Thorpe, should I ever reach the dizzy heights of Bosun or go further in the world of seafaring, I will always consider any achievements that come my way as due to the sound advice you gave me on my first few days at sea."

With that said, they all shook hands, both the Skipper and the Bosun wishing young John luck as he went on his way.

The great boom that was supposed to follow the conclusion of the Seven Years War, which ended in 1763, was a non-starter in many ways, for expansion was slow in the economy with the result that many shipping companies went to the wall and consequently employment in the mercantile marine was very tight; so tight, in fact, that one could no longer choose what type of ship one wanted to serve on, but had to take anything that was going or starve. And it was circumstances like these that John experienced in 1764, when he found himself, much against his will, as Third Mate on a slaver from Whitehaven, which plied between the West Coast of Africa and Kingston, Jamaica. On first meeting the skipper of this blackbirder, his memory went back to what his old crew mate on the *Friendship*, Victor Fear, had told him about some seagoing captains. And his new skipper fitted to a 'T' Victor's description of what the worst type of Master could be. For John's new boss, Captain Wright, was a far cry from his old skipper, Captain Blake. Whereas the latter was a gentleman with a humane disposition, his new one was the exact opposite. In point of fact, he was more animal than human. His physique was ape-like, with a thick neck and stooping back. He was of medium height, stockily built, and smothered all over in hair. His sunken eyes were reminiscent of a baboon from the jungles of Africa. 'Conscience' was a word that appeared to be completely alien to him when it came to dealing with his crew. As for the poor slaves he carried from their homeland to Jamaica, they might as well not have existed, for the degrading manner in which he kept them in the holds below was an insult to the very term 'human dignity', a term as strange to the garrulous skipper as sunshine was to his poor and wretched human cargo below deck.

Remembering the sound advice he had received as a boy from his mother about how to treat his fellow human beings, John was far from happy with his lot, but, because of the recession in the mercantile marine, he had to grin and bear it until something better appeared on the horizon. During his short stay aboard this slaver, he kept himself very much to himself, carrying out the skipper's instructions, never querying them or offering any navigational advice on the more sophisticated points of seamanship which he had learned from his experiences aboard the brigantine *Friendship*. When he compared the crew aboard the slaver with those of Captain Blake's ship, it made him very sad indeed, for here he was, because of the economic whims of the time, a gentleman of finesse amidst a band of cut-throats, many of whom would not have found a billet on an ordinary sailing ship. There were no Victor Fears aboard to liven the rest of the crew up with jokes, ploys and humorous talk, for they were really the dregs of the mercantile marine, carrying out the most despicable task of all—transporting human beings from their natural habitat to the sugar plantations and cotton fields, where they would be sold like cattle, having no say in the matter whatsoever.

John did several trips on this slaver, but he used it merely as a short-term expedient, hoping that something better would turn up which would be compatible with his humanity and concept of human dignity. Although under extreme pressure to try and enlighten Captain Wright, he knew very well that such a course of action would have been fruitless, so he carried out his duties as Third Mate in his usual diligent and meticulous manner. And although the skipper was far too ignorant a man to appreciate or even concede his talents, it was noticeable to the remainder of the crew that he was a cut well above the run-of-the-mill officers that were encountered on a slaver.

It was the cargo of human beings, shackled down in the holds, that pricked John's conscience. For not only was there the stench of the slaves wallowing in their own vomit and excrement, but their cries for help fell on deaf ears; for Captain Wright treated them as if he were carrying a cargo of animals or ordinary materials. Indeed, ordinary materials were cared for much better, for a new philosophy was fermenting. This new Anglo-Saxon thinking was the God Almighty right to property, where human beings became very much secondary to this commodity.

His last trip on this ship ended in Kingston, Jamaica, when he was offered a post as Chief Mate on another slaver, called *Two Friends*, which carried around ninety to one hundred slaves from Africa, taking merchandise on the return trip. John, on joining this ship, thought that nobody could have been as bad as his previous skipper, Captain Wright, but how wrong he was! If his old master was treacherous to his crew and the slaves, his new one, Captain McCarron, was the devil incarnate himself. Bluntly, he could have been described as nothing more than a massive sixteen stone, sadistic brute, who used to delight in satisfying his perverted instincts by personally lashing not only erring crew members, whenever it took his fancy, but also the poor helpless slaves, who were manacled down in the darkened holds and were in more need of medical attention than the merciless whippings that were administered to satisfy the lustful desires of a depraved skipper. All this and similar actions were playing on John's mind, to such an extent that he could not reconcile such barbaric actions with his conscience. And although he was seething within, he could not take any positive action against the skipper, whilst being a member of his crew, for that could have been construed as mutiny, and the penalty for such an act on the high seas was death by hanging from the lower foremast yard-arm. For if John disliked his introduction into the slave trade on his first ship from

Whitehaven, he doubly disliked it on this one, his second and last ship, which was no more than a floating hell, for both crew and slaves, under a skipper who had not one ounce of human decency in his whole make-up. And because of these brief encounters with the slave trade, John by this time had decided to quit what he called "this degrading insult to humanity" at the first opportunity when they arrived at Kingston, Jamaica, from Africa. It was this last passage that filled his heart with remorse and disgust, for, because of the actions of the skipper, many slaves died at sea, and it was John's duty as Chief Mate to organise their burial, something that left a lasting impression on his mind.

Having abandoned the slave trade in disgust, John found himself without a ship and with few friends in the always bustling port of Kingston. It was a sweltering hot mid-July in 1768, and, booking temporarily into a local tavern, he went about the town and docks looking for employment in anything but the horrid slave trade. He managed to control his emotions about what he had encountered on the two ships he had served on, for, had he reported the matter to the authorities, word would probably have got back through the grapevine, rightly or wrongly, that this Scottish upstart was nothing more than a trouble-maker, and his chances of securing employment would have been very slim indeed. As plantation owners exerted a great deal of influence in the local world of shipping, he thought that, in the circumstances, discretion was the better part of valour, and silence on the subject until he could find somebody to confide in was the order of the day.

Having exhausted all possible avenues that might have given him employment, he was afraid he would end up destitute in Jamaica. Then one day as he was by chance walking down to the quayside, he met an old acquaintance from Kirkcudbright, a Mr. Sam McAdam by name.

Approaching with outstretched arms to greet him, he said, "Good afternoon, Mr. McAdam; it's a nice surprise to see you in this part of the world."

Mr. McAdam, who had not seen John since he was a schoolboy, stopped in his tracks, momentarily gazed at him and said, "Am I see-ing right? Are you not John Paul, the gardener's son?"

"Indeed I am, Mr. McAdam, and it's many years now since we met."

Grasping him heartily with both hands, McAdam said, "Goodness me, I can hardly believe my eyes, for the last time I saw you, you were just a barefooted schoolboy hanging about the docks back home and listening to us old salts spinning our yarns about life on the high seas and our visits to foreign ports."

"Yes, that's some time ago now, Mr. McAdam, but I could recogn-ise you straight away, the moment I set eyes on you."

"How old are you now Master Paul, or should I say Mister?"

"Just turned twenty-one years of age, at the beginning of the month," was John's manly reply.

Mr. McAdam, who was a stout, jovial character and fifty years old, with a dark beard and similar hair, which had slight touches of grey here and there, went on to say, "Is it not amazing how time passes! I can distinctly remember the day you were born, for I had just returned from a trip to West Africa and I met your father in one of the dockside bars and we both, in the company of others, celebrated your birth."

"You may remember that day, Mr. McAdam, but for obvious rea-sons I certainly can't; but it is very nice to meet someone so far from home who drank to my health on the day I was born," said John humorously.

Mr. McAdam went on, "Yes, I distinctly remember that when we drank your health your father said that he hoped you would make a good gardener one day, and I said in fun, just being back from a foreign voyage, that I hoped you would make a good sailor; and my words have come true."

"Oh, yes," replied John, "many a true word is spoken in jest, for I made the grade as a sailor; but whether I am a good one or not I will leave to my superiors, shipmates and history to be the judge."

"Well so far you have certainly made it in seamanship, but I still find it difficult to believe it is you, as you have matured so these last few years."

"Well, Mr. McAdam, I was very fortunate on the first ship I sailed as cabin-boy, for I had an excellent Skipper in Captain Blake and a first-class Bosun in Mr. Thorpe, not forgetting the ordinary, every-day crew members, some of whom were very experienced and highly skilled indeed."

"Aye, and you are fogetting three other very important people in your life."

"Who are they?" enquired John curiously.

Mr. McAdam's quick reply was, "Your father, mother and Mr. Lindsay, your old teacher."

"I have not forgotten them, Mr. McAdam, for they gave me the basics of sound knowledge and good old Scots commonsense that will be with me until the day I die."

Mr. McAdam went on, "Yes, I have seen the protégés of Mr. Lindsay on many a poop deck, and he has certainly produced some good ones over the years, particularly when it comes to navigating a ship in all types of conditions."

"Yes, I was able to put his theories to the test shortly after sailing from Whitehaven on the *Friendship*. How sorry I am that they went bankrupt, for I was enjoying every minute of my time with that company."

Mr. McAdam said, "Aye, but they have started up again, with three beautiful new ships, and I think they are in partnership with that Captain and Bosun you just mentioned."

On hearing this, John's eyes lit up and he said excitedly, "You don't mean to tell me they have started up again, have they?"

"Oh, yes, they have," was McAdam's reply, "and with much bigger ships; but I think the brains behind it all is this man called Captain Blake, for they are getting plenty of work in both directions."

John then went on to say, "If only I could see Captain Blake now, my problems would be solved, for he would put me to work straight away, if only I could meet him."

"You mean to say that you are unemployed at the moment, and so far from home? Whatever has happened to you to end up like this?" asked Mr. McAdam, in a manner that meant he was concerned about John.

"Well, Mr. McAdam," John went on, "after the firm that owned the *Friendship* went bankrupt, because of the economic recession at the time, the only thing available was the slave trade, so it was either that or starving."

Shaking his head forlornly, Mr. McAdam said, "You don't mean to tell me you ended up on a blackbirder, did you?"

"Yes, unfortunately, Mr. McAdam, I did, as I had no other alternative, but never, repeat never, again, as it is impossible to describe some of the things that went on in these two slavers I sailed."

"Oh yes, Mr. Paul, I know how you feel, because the crews of these slavers are the dregs of humanity, most of whom are pressed into it, for no sailor with a shred of human conscience would venture on such an undertaking."

"Well, Mr. McAdam," John continued seriously, "I can think of no commerce so iniquitous, so cruel, so oppressive and so destructive as the African slave trade; hence the reason I am here, looking for work."

"You are now talking from experience, whereas I am purely going on hearsay, as I have never ventured on to a slaver, for it's just enough to sail windward of them to get the foul stench in one's nostrils from miles away."

"Yes, we really have a lot to answer for," said John, who went on; "Should I ever be in a position to exert my influence in the world of politics, I shall go all out for its abolition, for the very concept of slavery is an insult to the dignity of mankind. For we were all created in the image and likeness of God, regardless of the colour of our skin."

"Well, Mr. Paul, if I can enlighten you, there are moves afoot for its abolition already, and a powerful figure in the movement is a former Captain Newton, who spent nine years in the slave trade and is now a man of the cloth."

It could be seen now that John could openly confide in Mr. McAdam without any inhibitions on this subject, so he said, "Should I ever have the pleasure of meeting this man Newton, he and his abolitionists will find a true ally in me."

McAdam went on and said, "Well, Mr. Paul, all that is in the past and it says a lot for your principles and courage that you packed in the abhorrent trade, especially when you are so far from home. I am only sorry I cannot offer you a billet, but, should you wish, you can have a free passage home and maybe you can meet Captain Blake on the other side of the Atlantic."

John's eyes lit up and his face exuded delight as he went on to say, "Mr. McAdam, this is really kind of you, and if there is anything I can do aboard to help you, don't hesitate to let me know."

"No, there should be very little to do, as we expect a relatively quiet passage home; but I am sorry you will have to sling a hammock for yourself, as there are no spare cots."

"Sling a hammock!" replied John, "I would sleep in the crow's nest or even in the bilges to get away from those abysmal experiences I had on the blackbirders I just mentioned to you."

"There is only one thing I might mention, and that is at the end of the voyage the ship is going in for a good overhaul, and maybe you will be able to give us a hand careening the hull once we have got everything organised."

"That's the least I can do, Mr. McAdam," was John's grateful reply.

When the brigantine *John* eventually sailed, it was under a practically cloudless blue sky, and the wind was so light that they had to put up studding sails to get the ship under way. And this continued for the first few days of the voyage, with nothing beyond them but a blue hazy horizon, and a scorching sun overhead during the day, with a relatively cool breeze after nightfall. This, however, was not to last long, for one morning they awoke to find a heavy-laden mid-Atlantic sky, and their maritime instincts told them that things were going to get much rougher than they had previously experienced.

And rougher it did get, with the white horses from the crest of the waves pounding the starboard side of the bow so mercilessly that they had to batten the hatches and operate the bilge pumps down below. In the midst of this, the wind and rain lashed in gale-force conditions, so that they had greatly to reduce sail in order to control the ship. During all this activity John was delighted that he could put his sail-handling experience to good use and be of assistance to the crew.

When the storm receded and everything was back to plain normal sailing, the Captain said, "Mr. Paul, your assistance was greatly appreciated by the crew during that bad patch we encountered."

"Glad I've been of help to you so far, Mr. McAdam."

"You certainly know how to handle these sails."

"Well, as this ship is similar in many ways to the one I sailed as a cabin-boy, I have had plenty of experience over these last few years."

When John had just uttered the last sentence, the Skipper, instead of continuing the conversation, suddenly said, "You know, Mr. Paul, I am not feeling well at all."

John's reply was, "Well, Mr. McAdam, if you don't mind my saying so, you look far from well. Are you feeling feverish or beginning to break sweat?"

"I am both, actually, Mr. Paul;" and, as he said this, beads of sweat started to form on his brow and eventually all over the remainder of his body.

"I would recommend that you go down to your cabin straight away, and I'll inform the Mate," said John, who, knowing what the symptoms were, was becoming very concerned for the Skipper.

When John informed the Mate what had happened, he immediately threw his hands up in the air and said, "Oh, no, not the dreaded fever!"

John's reply was, as he sadly shook his head, "I am afraid so, but I did not want to tell him as much. But from the experiences I have seen over the past few years, I am sorry to say that everything points in that direction."

The Mate, in great consternation, said, "Mr. Paul, can you take over the poop deck, and I will go down below to see the Skipper. But not a word to the rest of the crew, for, as you see, they are a close-knit hard-working happy bunch and I don't want to lower their morale in any way."

"Not a word will be said, Sir, and it will be my pleasure to help you out. And don't worry, because I am quite confident of handling this ship."

Shortly afterwards, the Mate came running up the companion on to the poop deck, looking very sad and in something of a panic, and excitedly said, "Mr. Paul, things look very bad; the Skipper is not only sweating heavily all over, but he is gasping for breath. He is so bad, in fact, that he could not take the medicine I offered him. As a matter of fact I think he has lost consciousness."

John coolly answered him by saying, "Sir, I think things are for the worse, but remember, this is the time for us, and especially for you if you don't mind my saying so, Sir, to keep a clear head."

"Are you sure you can manage up here?" enquired the anxious Mate.

"Manage, Sir! That will be no problem at all, for, when I get my next bearing it will be time to change from the starboard to the larboard tack and I will execute that with no difficulty at all. Just you go down below," said John, with all the confidence of an experienced skipper.

John duly changed tack; took the ship through the eye of the wind; released the starboard running backstays and secured the larboard ones simultaneously. The ship was on its new course, and everything went so smoothly that he did not make any mistakes or have to reprove any member of the crew.

Some time later the Mate emerged from down below, looking ashen-faced and appearing to stare into space with a void expression on his face. Approaching John, the Mate said, "I am afraid it's bad news, Mr. Paul; the old man's gone."

"I expected the worst, Sir, for that blasted fever is one of the curses of seafaring, and it can come on all of a sudden."

"Yes, indeed," said the Mate; "it's a good job we don't know what is in store for us."

"Very true, Sir, but we must look to the future, and I'll give you all the assistance you want."

"Well, Mr. Paul, from now on you will act as Mate, and I am now the legal Captain."

"Very good, Sir; I am at your disposal from this very moment on."

When the word of the Skipper's death spread among the crew, there was great sadness indeed, for to most of them Mr. McAdam was more of a father figure, for whom they had the greatest respect. This was confirmed by the welling of tears in their eyes on the day he was given a Christian burial at sea, in the highest traditions of the mercantile marine.

Things were just about getting back to normal, and the new Skipper was beginning to find his feet, when, lo and behold, he went down with the same fever as Mr. McAdam. When his death was announced, there was near panic among the crew, for two reasons: first, would this horrific fever spread among the whole crew or most of it, so as to make the ship unmanageable? And secondly, what would they do, with both their original Skipper and Mate dead? To attempt to answer these questions, John immediately took control of the situation and, to allay their fears, he assembled all the crew on the quarterdeck. So far as health was concerned, he ordered them all to take preventive medicine. So far as ship and sail handling were concerned, he addressed them in a cool confident manner, explaining what his background and experience was. Once they had all heard of his previous experience, since winning the prize in navigational studies at Kirkbean school until his position at the present moment, they all returned to their respective duties, knowing that the ship was in both confident and competent hands. And competent hands they were indeed, for young John skilfully handled both the navigational and sail aspects with such ease that they all successfully and safely arrived at their home port of Kirkcudbright. On the ship's arrival, the owners were naturally saddened to learn of the death of both Master and Mate, but were delighted with John, once he had given a full report of what had happened and presented them with the ship's log. They were so impressed by the cool manner in which he had taken control of the situation, which was confirmed by all crew members, that they offered him the job of Captain on the ship's next voyage out. This was indeed a great honour to bestow on someone who was just twenty-one years of age; unprecedented, in point of fact.

So, once again, the sun shone on Captain John Paul, now a fully-fledged Skipper in his own right.

CHAPTER 4

MUNGO MAXWELL AFFAIR, JAIL AND FREEMASONRY

Mr. Mungo Maxwell	Ship's Carpenter

Before Captain John Paul took over command of the *John*, it had to be made one hundred per cent seaworthy again before it proceeded on its next voyage across the Atlantic. So, whilst the owners were in the process of having the ship overhauled, they granted their young Skipper leave of absence to go and visit his relatives and friends in Kirkbean; for since he had last visited them his father had died, in 1767, whilst he was away from home and employed in the barbarous slave trade. So it was a rather saddened John who made his way back by stagecoach to the village he had left as a small boy to embark on a life on the high seas.

On arriving at the gardener's cottage, he could sense the absence of his father and his dear old canine friend Lassie, who had died of old age some few years back. There was no longer the buoyancy about the place he had experienced as a young schoolboy, and as he made his way to the cottage door his head was bowed in grief as he nostalgically took a trip down memory lane, thinking of the happy and carefree days he had spent there in the formative years of his life. Knocking gently on the door, he called, "Mother, mother are you home?" And rushing out to meet him she unashamedly burst into tears, threw her arms around him and exclaimed, "John! My darling son—am I not pleased to see you!" And hugging her tightly he said, "Dear mother, I am delighted to see you after being away for so long."

"Yes, my dear son, this place is a shadow of what it used to be, since your dear father passed away last year."

"Yes, mother, there is nobody more grief-stricken than I am, and I only got to hear about it when I returned to Kirkcudbright yesterday. For the ship I sailed back on had a rather tragic ending, for the Skipper and Mate died of the fever. I had a long talk with the Skipper, a Sam McAdam, who knew father well, so he must not have known about his death."

"No, he would probably have been away from home on a foreign trip at the time. I know, because quite a few sailors have visited me since then to convey their condolences, as they had been away abroad. They assured me that had they been at home at the time of his death they certainly would have been at his funeral."

"I am sure they would, mother, for they all thought very highly of him," was John's low-voiced reply.

Having gathered her composure, she said, "Oh yes, that was very noticeable by the large turnout at Kirkbean cemetery, for I never knew he had so many friends, from so near and far."

John described to his mother the horrific and detestable experiences he had had in the slave trade and why he quit it; and how he had ended up working his passage home from Kingston, Jamaica, to end up taking the ship safely into Kirkcudbright. He told her about the death of the Skipper and his Mate on the voyage home, and explained how he had been promoted to Skipper and that, as Captain John Paul, he would shortly take the same ship out to the West Indies, as Master in his own right. Temporarily regaining some of her old self, as John knew her in his youth, although the years were beginning to tell now, she excitedly exclaimed, "John, you mean to say that you are a *captain* of a ship at *your* age?"

"Yes, mother," was his proud reply, and going on he said, "Having kept a cool head in mid-Atlantic and taking control of the situation at the time by means of celestial navigation, I won the confidence of the crew, who were on the verge of panic, and sailed the ship safely into its home port to the delight of its owners."

"Well, that's incredible," his mother replied, and continued, "You very rarely get skippers of these ocean-going ships who are under thirty, let alone someone who has just turned twenty-one!"

"You know there are exceptions to the rule in everything, mother, and maybe there is somebody above looking after me."

"Somebody above!" she exclaimed. "Well, your dear father, who no doubt is in heaven now, would be proud of you if he were alive. And his dying words, before he lost consciousness, were about his dear son John, and they appear to be coming true."

"What were they, mother?" John asked anxiously.

"Well, my dear son—now your sisters, who were at his bedside when he was in the throes of death, will vouch for what I say, when you see them—his last utterances were to remember him kindly to you, for he had had a premonition on the last day before his death; he saw you one day becoming famous in what would eventually turn out to be one of the most powerful navies in the world."

"But, mother, I am only master of a small trading brigantine, with very little influence whatsoever in the merchant navy, let alone one of the up and coming navies of the world."

"You know, my dear son, your father had the second sight, although he never mentioned it to you as a boy," said his mother, who went on to say, "I can give you many instances of things that he told me and, sure as God is my maker and judge, they all eventually came true."

"Well, mother, only history will tell if he was right in what he said on his deathbed," was John's humble reply.

His mother, after explaining everything about his father's illness, eventual death and funeral, with the finer details of the whole sad and mournful affair, took up the subject of gardening.

"You know that Mr. Craik might approach you about taking father's job as head gardener?"

"No, I did not know that," was John's reply.

"Yes, he has a couple of young lads there from the village, keeping it in shape, under his constant supervision at present, until he gets somebody full time, and from what I have heard he has you in mind."

"But mother, I have just been given the golden opportunity of a lifetime—the captaincy of my own ship—at the early age of twenty-one years!"

"Yes, my son, and as far as I am concerned, you remain with the sea, for I would be the last one on earth to thwart your father's deathbed prophecy, for we all loved him far too much for that."

"Anyway, mother, I can help you a lot more by being at sea, for my wages will be three or four times more than I would earn from being a gardener."

"Yes. I'll be quite happy here on my own, for your sisters and your brother Willie are also very good to me."

On her mentioning his brother Willie's name, John made enquiries as to whether or not any mail had arrived in his long absence from home. The original letter his brother promised from the American colonies, relating to employment there, never arrived, and John assumed it had gone astray. After his enquiry his mother said to him, "Yes, John, there is a letter awaiting you through in the room, which has been there for some time now."

"Oh good, mother, I must read it and find out what Willie has to say."

On opening it, he found that it was no ordinary letter but reams and reams of paper, which took him some time to read through to get the gist of what it contained. He found Willie's first concern was the death of his dear father and the importance of their mother's being looked after in her old age. He intimated that he had previously sent correspondence regarding John's emigrating to America but had assumed that because he had received no reply John was no longer interested. But after making one or two enquiries he had found that for a variety of reasons none of his letters could have reached home; for example, in the case of one letter the packet ship which was carrying it from the American side of the Atlantic went down with all hands after a midnight collision in heavy fog at sea. So, in this letter, he was renewing his offer of good employment, but also advised John to remain at sea so that he could visit his mother as long as she was alive, for because of his father's death circumstances had changed drastically and their mother's welfare was now of paramount importance to all the family. In the final analysis he did, however, leave the decision entirely in John's own hands.

Having digested all the contents of this long letter, John once again found himself in something of a quandary and, turning to his mother, he said, "Mother, why is it that all my life so far has been dogged with conflict, and there has been nothing straightforward for me?"

"Can you explain what you mean?" she enquired maternally, as she was beginning to prepare him something to eat.

"Well, as you know mother, as a boy I had conflict between the land and the sea, and when I was briefly in the slave trade I had great conflict of conscience for getting involved in that ghastly business. Where is it all going to end up?"

His mother said, "You know, John, that some people are born with a straightforward, mundane life ahead of them, where things work out very simply for them; whereas others have conflict throughout their lives from the cradle to the grave; and I think, my dear son, that you fit into the latter category. However, you are lucky in the sense that you have the resilience to overcome such conflicts and still come out on top."

He went on, "Well, I hope you are right, mother, for resilience is what I need. For one moment I was practically destitute in the West Indies, after leaving the slave trade, with no job and nowhere to go; and the next thing I find myself a ship, am offered a job as a gardener, and now I find, reading Willie's letter, that he has excellent employment prospects in America."

On mentioning Willie's offer of employment in America, his mother looked at him rather concernedly and said, "What has Willie been saying and what has he got to offer?"

Turning to her, John said, "There is the letter, mother. Read it for yourself and tell me what you think."

As John ate the meal she had prepared for him, she studiously went through Willie's letter, very carefully, and said, "Willie is like myself; he leaves the decision solely in your hands as regards what course of action you should take."

"Well, what would you advise, mother?" he said anxiously, in order to settle the conflict that was raging in his mind.

"Without a doubt, my son, in memory of your dear father, remain at sea, for I think you have a lot going for you. You have done exceptionally well at such an early age and remember, you have your whole life before you."

"Decision made, mother! Gardening is definitely out, as is America at the moment; so the call of the sea wins once again," said John, who now relaxed like a mature man in his dear old father's rocking chair.

"Well, I am glad I was once again in that happy position to enable you to come to a decision on what to do, and I'll inform Willie in the next letter I will be sending him, which shall be very shortly."

"That's good of you, mother, for Willie will understand once you explain things to him. As time does not permit me to write him in detail at the moment, please tell him that I will call and see him in Virginia at the first available opportunity, when our ship sails there."

Having spent a few days at home with his mother and meeting his sisters and friends, Captain John Paul made his way back to Kirkcudbright to inspect his new command, the brigantine *John*. And a thorough inspection it was, for he was meticulous in everything he did. So he and his First Officer, a Mr. Robin Wignall, carried out their inspection of the vessel from stem to stern, ensuring it was once again one hundred per cent sea-worthy, having had the hull careened of all barnacles and foreign agents that would slow its speed once it got under sail. His First Officer, Mr. Wignall, was a lot older than John and he had just recently joined the ship as well, replacing the Mate who had died of the fever on its previous voyage back from the West Indies. Mr. Wignall was a tall, quiet-spoken and reserved gentleman, from the great naval areas of southern England. Having grey hair and a reddish complexion, he had a benign and pleasant face, and he and his new Skipper hit it off on first meeting one another, for Captain John Paul soon realised that under the reserved veneer there was a rock-like character who could be relied upon at all times and who was nobody's fool.

After inspecting sails, running and standing rigging, and everything that was above the upper deck, which included a repainted bowsprit, they went down below. Likewise, down below there was just as thorough an inspection of the bilges, pumps, men's sleeping accommodation, the galley where they ate, and the holds where the cargo was stored. And finally, as Captain John Paul was very keen on hygiene, he had all outlets sealed below deck and had the whole ship fumigated to get rid of vermin. This was done by lighting a combination of sulphur and combustibles in the bilges, the resulting vapour slowly but surely making its way upwards into every other part of the ship, even penetrating into the most obscure nooks and crannies of the vessel. Once all this was done to the young Skipper's satisfaction, he gave the crew permission to load the general merchandise for their outward voyage to the West Indies.

The voyage to Tobago was in many ways like most that did not encounter bad weather. It was quiet and pleasant, with everyone getting on with his allotted duties, whether he was a messenger, helmsman, or handling the sails and the rigging. Being a small ship with a very compact crew, it gave Captain John Paul the opportunity to familiarise himself with most of the men, and he got to know Mr. Wignall a lot better, finding him a first class Mate although he was older and of a very different cultural background from his own. As the *John* plied gracefully through the wide Atlantic, Captain John Paul, proudly and quite rightly, strode the poop and quarterdeck on many occasions, deep in thought. Would not his old school teacher, who taught him the basic rudiments of navigational studies, and his dear father, who had gone to his rest, be proud of him now, being probably one of the youngest skippers on the high seas, with life and death control over his crew! He was also indebted to Captain Blake and Bosun Thorpe for the excellent training he had received from them. And as time slowly ticked away, with nothing but the solitude of the vast ocean all around him, his passing thoughts, apart from those on the slave trade, were always memorable and mostly happy ones, although they were sometimes tinged with sadness. Where was his old friend and advisor, in his most impressionable years, Victor Fear? Was his old school mate Dominic Archer now a lieutenant in His Majesty's Royal Navy? Such thoughts the young Skipper cherished as he made his way down memory lane.

His second and last trip on the *John*, from Kirkcudbright to Tobago and back, was a far cry from the peaceful and joyous experiences he had had on his first trip. And it was to reveal the Skipper's character—that he could be as quiet as a lamb one moment and roaring like a lion the next. This trait in his character betrayed itself after the brigantine had been out of port a few weeks, when he casually asked his Bosun, a Mr. George Fitzpatrick, who hailed from Liverpool, how things were getting on aboard ship. The Bosun's reply took him aback when he said, "Everything is going on all right, Sir, except the ship's carpenter who is a bit of a troublemaker down below with the rest of the crew."

"Thanks for telling me, Mr. Fitzpatrick," was the Skipper's concerned reply.

"Yes, Sir, he fancies himself as a bit of a ship's lawyer. He is certainly the only odd man out among the rest of the crew, for he really can upset them sometimes, especially when they all get stuck in and work as a team and he tries to lower morale."

"He's not encouraging mutiny, is he, Mr. Fitzpatrick?"

"Oh no, Sir, not exactly mutiny, but really creating dissension among the ship's company."

"And what's his work like then, Bosun?" enquired the Skipper, who was becoming annoyed that he had a bad apple in the midst of his crew.

"Well, I can't really say, Sir; we have not really put him to the test, as he just signed articles with us for the first time before we left Kirkcudbright."

Turning to his First Officer, Captain Paul said quite strongly, "Mr. Wignall, did you witness the signature of our new ship's carpenter when he joined our ship?"

"I did indeed, Sir."

"And what is his name, may I ask?"

"A Mungo Maxwell, Sir. Why, is there anything wrong?"

Hearing the name Maxwell was enough to turn the pupils of his eyes white, for his mind went back to the incident in the garden and his fight on his last day at school with Douglas Maxwell, the village bully. And he recollected, as a boy, hearing what Mr. Craik the squire had said about one of his cousins being a ship's carpenter and a bit of a lower-deck lawyer.

In the presence of his First Officer and the Bosun he went on to say, "You know, gentlemen, I think we do have a trouble-maker aboard with this man Maxwell."

"Well, Sir, he was sent down from the firm's office to me and I must say that I never knew anything of that nature about him, for it was the first time I had set eyes on him," was the First Officer's candid reply.

"Will we have to keep a special eye on him then, Sir?" enquired Bosun Fitzpatrick.

Addressing both of them, he said, "Gentlemen, had I known who it was in the first instance—although it is no fault of yours, Mr. Wignall—he would not have been allowed within miles of this ship for, take it from me, I know the family only too well and they can only be described as a bad lot."

"Oh, you know of the family then, Sir?" enquired Mr. Wignall, as he tapped the taff rail of the poop deck with his fingertips, as if he were playing a tune on some musical instrument.

"Yes, Mr. Wignall, one of them was the bane of my life at school and he made life miserable for us all, as he was the village bully."

"Oh, one of that sort of family I see, Sir," said Mr. Wignall, who was now grasping the taff rail firmly with both hands, as the *John* was beginning to roll more than had been experienced since the start of the voyage.

Turning to the Bosun, Captain Paul said, "As you said, Mr. Fitzpatrick, keep a close eye on him, ensuring there is plenty of work to do so as to occupy his time, for you know what they say, 'the devil makes work for idle hands.'"

"Aye, aye, Sir," replied the Bosun smartly, "and if he in any way steps out of line I will bring the matter to your attention immediately."

A few days elapsed, when sure enough the Bosun was back to Captain John Paul, complaining to him about Maxwell; and, rather flustered, he said "Sir, I have had trouble with that ship's carpenter,

Maxwell again, both with the hash-up of a job I gave him to do, plus his insolence and insubordinate manner, when I told him in no uncertain way that it was not up to standard."

Immediately the Bosun's information was understood by the Skipper, he changed from a passive individual to one of anger, for although his voice was normally soft-spoken, he could roar like a bull when the occasion arose. "Right then, Mr. Fitzpatrick, we will nail this character here and now, before he gets too big for his boots, otherwise he might create such dissension among the crew, by lowering their morale and confusing them, that we could have mutiny on our hands."

"Very good, Sir; do you want to see him now?"

"No," replied the angered Skipper, "not until you have given me all the facts about the case."

"Well, Sir, I asked him to divide a rather large cabin down below into two, by building a bulkhead, so that I could have two separate stores instead of one. This was to separate the spare sails from the rigging and blocks and tackles."

"And did he carry out your instructions, then?" enquired the Skipper.

"Well, after moaning that he did not consider it necessary, he finally did it after a fashion; but what an amateurish job he made of it!"

"Carry on, Bosun," said the Skipper, jotting all these details down.

"Well, Sir, when I told him it was far from up to standard, he said that if I could do any better I should do it myself."

"Thanks, Mr. Fitzpatrick. Now, there are two things I will not tolerate aboard my ship—insubordination to a superior; and slipshod workmanship, whether it's in the rigging, galley or the carpenter's department." Turning round, the Skipper said to the messenger, "Get me Mr. Wignall from his cabin immediately."

"Aye, aye, Sir."

Shortly afterwards, the First Officer presented himself on the poop deck and said, "You wanted to see me, Sir?"

His authoritatively-spoken reply was, "Yes, Mr. Wignall, I have a rather serious disciplinary problem to deal with in my cabin; it is that confounded ship's carpenter Maxwell. So you take over from me here until I come back."

"Aye, aye, Sir, I will do that with pleasure."

"Bosun, fetch Maxwell down to my cabin straight away, will you?"

"Aye, aye, Sir. I'll go down below and get him immediately."

When the Bosun escorted Maxwell into the Captain's cabin and presented him in front of the Skipper, the Captain immediately noticed the resemblance between him and his cousin, Douglas Maxwell. He even had the same cock-ahoop attitude. But the Captain did not let these factors influence the case before him, for he was as meticulous in administering justice as he was in reading the noon latitudes.

Looking at the carpenter, who was standing to attention at the front of his table, straight in the eyes, he said, "Look here, Maxwell, there are very serious charges being laid against you here: first, insubordination to the Bosun; and secondly, slipshod workmanship, which I have just been told of before I came into my cabin. What have you got to say for yourself?"

"Well, Sir, I am the only qualified carpenter aboard this ship and nobody who is not a qualified carpenter should tell me what to do."

Jumping to his feet, the Captain pounded his table with his fist and angrily exclaimed, "Look, Maxwell, you are nothing but an insubordinate lout and it is something I will in no circumstances tolerate aboard my ship, for you, like any other member of the crew, will carry out an order given to you by any of your superiors, without any argument. And as you have been blatantly insubordinate to the Bosun and insolent to me, you will receive six lashes of the cat-o'-nine-tails immediately, and don't let me ever see you on Captain's report again."

"Take him away out of my sight, Bosun, and prepare him for his punishment on the forecastle side of the main mast. I will be out shortly to supervise it myself; and, incidentally, summon all the crew that are not on the deck to watch, so that it can act as a deterrent to any potential trouble-makers."

When the Skipper appeared shortly afterwards to carry out his duties by ensuring that his instructions were carried out to the letter, the whole scenario was set for the quick administration of punishment, which would be carried out by the Bosun's Mate and witnessed by the ship's Surgeon, the remainder of the ship's company being merely observers. By this time, Maxwell's shirt had been removed and both his hands secured tightly to part of the main mast by rope, so that he could not move from that position until the punishment had been carried out on his bare back. Summoning the Bosun's Mate to carry out the flogging, the Captain said, "Mr. Holgate, administer six lashes of the cat-o'-nine-tails to the accused for his misdemeanour in being insolent, insubordinate and incompetent in his workmanship."

"Aye, aye, Sir," said the assistant Bosun, who was short and stockily built and as solid as a rock. After the first and second lash, Maxwell's screams could be heard by the remainder of the ship's company, who stood by passively, with their heads lowered, as if observing a burial at sea. They did not like to witness anybody being lashed, as it could be their turn next time, should they be unfortunate enough to step out of line. The only time the remainder of the crew showed no sympathy for anyone being flogged was if that person were found guilty of stealing from one of their own comrades. But thefts of this nature were usually dealt with by the culprit's being hanged from the lower yard-arm of the foremast, and, once he was certified dead, his body was immediately thrown overboard. Mind you, that was formal justice, if it ever got that far; for seamen had a very strict ethical code when it came to stealing from a comrade, and lower deck justice was usually administered by the crew themselves, in that the culprit just 'accidentally' fell overboard after nightfall, after falling heavily and being stunned. This was to ensure that he would sink and drown immediately he landed in the water, limiting his chances of swimming away from justice. And when he was reported missing, all lips were sealed as to what had happened to him. Such were the strict unwritten customs and traditions of 18th century sailing ships.

After the third lash, the ship's Surgeon inspected the accused's back, and then gave the go-ahead for the Bosun's Mate to administer the remaining three, to make it a total of six. When the fourth one was being administered, Maxwell was squealing like a pig and begging for mercy. When the last and final lash was administered, he appeared to be lifeless, as if he had passed out, with beads of sweat running down his face and back. When the whole gruelling task had been carried out by Mr. Holgate, the Surgeon carried out his final inspection of Maxwell's bare back and reported to Captain John Paul that the punishment had been justly carried out and that the culprit was still alive, with a sound heart-beat. On receiving this advice from the ship's Surgeon, the Skipper then ordered Maxwell to be released from his bondage and addressed the ship's company thus: "We have today witnessed for the first time aboard this ship the use of the cat-o'-nine-tails, and may this be an exception rather than the rule, for ensuring the smooth functioning of the brigantine. May it also serve as a warning that insolence, insubordination and slipshod workmanship will not be tolerated aboard my vessel. You may all now return to your respective duties, and those who are not on duty can stand down."

After being given this final talk by the Skipper, the ship's company that were present dismissed themselves and made their way from the forecastle to their respective destinations, some muttering quietly under their breath and others remaining completely silent, with their own thoughts on the matter. The Captain now made his way to the poop deck, and, after consulting the ship's log and making an entry in it, said to the First Mate, "Thank you, Mr. Wignall. I'll take over the rest of the watch; you may return to your cabin."

"Thank you very much, Sir," said Mr. Wignall, who then made his way down the companion to the quarterdeck and thereafter into his own cabin and into his cot, where he had a quick nap before his dinner, for, after he had had his meal he would be taking over the next watch from the Skipper himself.

As the voyage across the Atlantic to the West Indies was nearing completion, things again got back to normal, and everybody on the brigantine appeared to be working away happily and very much looking forward to their arrival in Tobago. The crew, naturally, observed discipline, and, as far as the Skipper was concerned, the unfortunate incident of the Maxwell affair was something of the past. But little did he realise, as the brigantine gracefully sailed on through the greenish-blue ocean, with a merciless sun beating overhead, that his problems were really only starting. The first indication of this was when he met the Bosun on the quarterdeck one day and said, "Good morning, Mr. Fitzpatrick: how is the morale among the men now that we are nearing our destination?"

"With one exception, Sir, everybody appears to be very happy indeed as they go about their tasks preparing the ship for entry into Tobago harbour."

"And what is the one exception, may I ask then, Bosun?" said the Skipper rather anxiously, thinking that all the problems of the past had blown over.

"Well, Sir, it is the ship's carpenter, Maxwell, again," relied the Bosun.

At this, Captain Paul threw his hands up in the air and sighed, "Oh no, not Maxwell creating more trouble, is it?"

"Oh no, Sir, he is not creating any trouble at all, but he appears to be brooding over something deep down within him, for he keeps himself very much to himself, saying very little to anyone; but, mind you, doing everything he is told to do."

"So he is no longer the lower deck's ship's lawyer, is he, Mr. Fitzpatrick?"

"Oh no, Sir; on the contrary; for if one could charge him with anything it would be for dumb insolence, for he is that quiet these days."

The Captain then continued, "Good, better for him to be completely silent and getting on with his work than creating dissension among the crew."

"Yes, Sir," replied the Bosun, "but from my own experience in the past, when anyone was disciplined they grinned and bore it at the time, but after a few days everything was back to the old routine as if nothing had happened. But I am afraid to say that there appears to be something deeper here with this character Maxwell."

"Well, we will see what will happen when he gets a run ashore in Tobago, lets his hair down in some local taverns and meets the ladies of pleasure. After a session with them he will probably put everything behind him and return to normal, a much more humble man. For I know his pride will be hurt, once news of this business reaches back home," said the Skipper as he checked the charts for their exact bearings, in order to avoid a dangerous sandbank at the entrance of Tobago harbour.

It was when the *John* had safely entered Tobago harbour and was tied securely at the quayside that, unknown to him, Captain Paul's troubles were really starting; for the first thing Mungo Maxwell did was to go to the Court of the Admiralty and report the matter there. On meeting one of the members of the Court, a Mr. Forbes, an émigré Scot whose father hailed from Aberdeenshire, he said, "Excuse me, Sir, my name is Mungo Maxwell and I am a ship's carpenter on the brigantine *John* which has just arrived today from Kirkcudbright. I wish to lodge a formal complaint against my Skipper, a Captain John Paul."

"Yes, Maxwell," said Mr. Forbes, who was a stout, dapper man with greyish brown hair and around fifty years of age. "What's your complaint then?"

He then patiently listened to Maxwell's verbal complaint, noting down the salient points mentioned. Declaring that he was cruelly lashed under the Skipper's supervision, Maxwell also claimed victimisation, because he was a cousin of a particular Douglas Maxwell with whom the Skipper had crossed swords many years ago when they were at school. Turning to him, Mr. Forbes said in a stern manner, "You realise, Mr. Maxwell, that you are lodging a very serious complaint indeed which, if proven, could make the Skipper of your ship answerable to criminal charges?"

"Yes, Sir, I do, but I am sure it all comes about because of my relationship to the individual he has had a long-standing grudge against."

"Did he mention this matter to you at the formal hearing of evidence aboard ship?"

"No, Sir."

"Well, how do you know that he was aware of the fact that you were both related?"

"Well, Sir," Maxwell continued, "we are a close-knit family at home, and my cousin told me all about him, and I assumed he realised he was my relative."

"Now then, Mr. Maxwell," retorted Forbes, "assuming is a lot different from concrete facts, is it not?"

"Well yes, Sir, but he could have no other reason for picking me out from the remainder of the crew."

"Well, Mr. Maxwell, you go into that room across there," said Mr. Forbes, pointing to the door marked 'Admiralty Medical Authority', "and I will have you examined by our port doctor in the first instance. Do you understand?"

"Yes, Sir," was the carpenter's reply.

Mr. Forbes then instructed one of his assistants to go without delay to the brigantine *John* and ask for Captain John Paul and his Bosun to come and see him immediately regarding a very serious allegation being made against him by one of his crew, who considered he had been unfairly flogged on the high seas.

About half an hour elapsed, by which time Maxwell had been thoroughly examined by the medical officer, who was in the process of preparing his report for Mr. Forbes when the Skipper and the Bosun entered the office.

On meeting Mr. Forbes, the Skipper doffed his tricorn hat and said, "Good afternoon, Sir. I am Captain John Paul of the brigantine *John* which arrived in port today from Kirkcudbright in Scotland, and this is my Bosun, Mr. Fitzpatrick."

"Good afternoon, Mr. Fitzpatrick," said Mr. Forbes, who bowed his head towards him as he sat behind a very large mahogany desk—which indicated that he was a very important person in the world of the mercantile marine.

"Good afternoon to you, Sir," replied Bosun Fitzpatrick, who realised that he was in the presence of an educated individual, well versed in maritime law, and a rather different kettle of fish from the everyday seaman he encountered aboard ship.

Turning to the Skipper, Mr. Forbes said, "Now, Captain Paul, I have before me some serious accusations made against you by one of your crew, a ship's carpenter called Mr. Maxwell. He is one of your ship's company, is he not?"

"Yes, Sir, indeed he is," was the Captain's sharp reply.

"Now, Mr. Fitzpatrick, will you kindly wait outside my office, and I will call your evidence once the Captain has given his."

"Aye, aye, Sir!" and, turning on his heels, the Bosun made his way outside and took a seat in the shade on the verandah.

"Now, Captain Paul, ignoring for the moment the alleged brutal punishment, which Maxwell accuses you of inflicting on him, was this punishment the result of charges you personally initiated?"

"No, Sir."

"Well, how did you get to know about Maxwell's insolence, insubordination and slipshod workmanship?"

"It was merely brought to my attention by the Bosun, for, up until then, I was not aware of anything unusual happening."

"Did you mention the fact to Mr. Maxwell that you had had occasion to fall out violently with one of his cousins many years ago, namely a Douglas Maxwell, who was in your class at school?"

"No, Sir; although I was aware of the relationship between the two I did not let that affect my decision in any way," said Captain Paul, with an air of impartiality about him.

"Let me continue about his workmanship, for you claimed that it was sub-standard; is that right, Captain?"

"Indeed it is, Sir, and if you so wish you are very welcome to inspect the bulkhead in question and come to a decision about what you think of it; for, may I say respectfully, Sir, even you will observe the atrocious craftmanship involved."

Mr. Forbes then went studiously through his notes and said to the Skipper, "Thank you, Captain Paul. Once I have heard the Bosun's evidence I shall accompany both of you down to the brigantine and carry out my own inspection. Will you be kind enough to retire now and send the Bosun in, please?"

"Certainly, Sir," said Captain Paul, as he made his way smartly out of the room.

When the Bosun came in, he was thoroughly grilled by Mr. Forbes. After he was satisfied, from Mr. Fitzpatrick's evidence, that he had initiated the disciplinary action and that the charges were preferred by him and not personally by Captain Paul, he thanked him for his evidence and asked him to retire outside until he was ready to accompany them down to the ship in order that he could carry out a personal inspection of Maxwell's work. In the meantime, Mr. Forbes told Maxwell to wait in the room adjoining his office until he came back from the ship.

Accompanying Captain Paul and his Bosun, Mr. Forbes made his way down to the dockside and boarded the *John* to see the bulkhead that Maxwell had made. Once it was pointed out to him, with the assistance of a tallow lamp—for it was fairly dark below the main deck—Mr. Forbes shook his head and said, "I see what you mean. Even I, who studied law at Oxford, can see that the craftsmanship is of such poor quality that my young son, who is still at school, could do better." After rigorously inspecting the bulkhead and testing it for strength, the three of them returned to Mr. Forbes's office.

Once seated at his desk and drinking a large tankard of lime juice to quench his thirst, Mr. Forbes wiped the perspiration from his brow, then added some more comments to his report. Having completed this part of his investigation, he called for the medical officer's report on Maxwell. On receiving it, he went over and over it again with his eagle eyes, to ensure that he missed nothing important.

Having collated all the evidence he had at his disposal, Mr. Forbes sat back silently in his chair for a few moments, with his eyes closed, and then said to the Skipper, "Captain Paul, you are completely exonerated as regards the whole thing, fairly and justly, in accordance with the highest traditions of maritime law. So you are free to go. Thank you both very much, gentlemen."

With that, they all shook hands. Before they left the building Mr. Forbes said to Captain Paul, "I shall be seeing Maxwell shortly, but in the meantime look for another ship's carpenter, for, when incidents like this do arise—which, thank goodness, are very rare indeed—we usually find the accused another ship back home so that there are no recriminations either way on the ship where the complaint was made."

"Very good, Sir," replied the Captain. "I know where I can lay my hands on a good carpenter within a stone's throw from here." And with that they made their way out of the building in search of their replacement.

Mr. Forbes now found it necessary to inform Maxwell of his findings; so, once his assistant had asked him into his room, he said, "Mr. Maxwell, I have thoroughly investigated your complaint, and, on all the evidence I have before me, your claim of being victimised and cruelly treated is completely unfounded, for there is not a shred of evidence to support your allegations. Do you fully understand what I am saying?"

Hesitantly and dismayed, Maxwell, realising there was no appeal against this court, said, "Yes, Sir, yes, Sir, but my life will be a living hell aboard that ship now, for I will be a marked man."

"Oh no, you won't, Mr. Maxwell, for you are not going back aboard that ship, for we will find you another one; as a matter of fact, my assistant is making enquiries now and, if my reckoning is correct, you will be sailing tonight and, as your old ship will be in port for a few weeks, you will be home long before them."

"Thank you very much, Sir," said a somewhat more cheerful Maxwell, who was pleased to learn of the possibility of a new ship.

"Away you go, then, and see my assistant who will fix you up with your new ship; and be more careful in future, for you are starting off with a clean record. It's up to you."

"Aye, aye, Sir," said Maxwell, as he made his way to find his new ship.

Having spent a few weeks in Tobago selling his merchandise that he had brought from the Old World, Captain Paul, having secured another ship's carpenter, sailed for Kirkcudbright fully laden with rum. With cargo like that, the ship's discipline had to be very strict indeed, for if the crew had access to this potent liquor it could spell trouble aboard. So the officers and the Bosun had to keep strict supervision at all times. Thus, after an uneventful passage, with none of the experiences he had encountered on the outward one, it was a contented Captain John Paul who took his ship safely into Kirkcudbright, thinking to himself that it was good to have had the sordid Maxwell affair behind him. However, unknown to the Skipper, his real troubles were just about to begin once again, and they were troubles of a greater magnitude than he ever had experienced in his previous seafaring career.

Unknown to Captain Paul, Mungo Maxwell, who had shipped home on another vessel much earlier than he, had died and been buried at sea en route for home. And as Captain Paul was entering harbour in the ship's home port he was unaware of the unwelcoming party awaiting his arrival at the quayside; for although subsequent enquiries proved that Maxwell had died of the fever, word had got back to his father that the death was primarily due to the flogging he had received under the orders and supervision of Captain John Paul.

Some time after the ship berthed he made his way down the gangway and there, waiting to arrest him on a charge of murder, was the local dispenser of justice. Sheriff McTaggart was a grumpy, granite-faced, dour and humourless, puritanical Scot, whose broad philosophy in life was that if anything was enjoyable it must be bad and an instrument of the devil. So, approaching the Skipper with Maxwell's father at his side, he said, "Captain John Paul, in the King's name I arrest you on the charge of murder of one of your former crew members, a Mungo Maxwell, whose father is here laying the charge before you in that you had him beaten so cruelly that he died as the result of your actions. Anything to say for yourself?"

"Not guilty, my lord." His crew looked on in dismay, some of them quietly mumbling to themselves, having never seen anything like this in their lives before.

"Escort the prisoner away to the tolbooth without delay," said the Sheriff, in a gruff and rasping voice.

When he was led away and placed in the cells, which were in the dungeon part of the jail with the court house up above at street level, the Skipper silently contemplated his situation, saying to himself, "This is the end of the road. Why in God's name am I here of all places, when I was only carrying out my duties on the high seas, as all competent skippers would do!" Forlornly he sat in his cold, dark and poorly-ventilated cell, which reminded him momentarily of his first few days at sea in the anchor cable locker, and of his times on the slavers. The only factors absent here were the intense heat and the unbelievable stench. But it gave him a faint insight into what the poor slaves must have suffered: this, in many ways, was paradise compared to what those human souls had to endure.

As he lay in his cell awake at night, accompanied by the noise of squeaking rats (another reminder of his boyhood days at sea), he gradually gained his composure and convinced himself that if he handled his defence properly he had no need to be where he was at all. To this end, he requested to see a lawyer. After the whole situation had been explained to him, the lawyer consulted the Bosun who was a crucial witness in the whole affair at this stage. Once this defending lawyer had presented all the facts before the Sheriff, supported by the evidence of Mr. Fitzpatrick, Captain Paul was granted bail and released from prison, but it was essential that he stand trial at a later date.

In the meantime the story, as all stories do, spread like wildfire throughout the whole community, and naturally it became grossly exaggerated, for when one person or a group of persons told some other there was always something added to the tale, distorting the original story completely. But Captain Paul's friends in the community (and he had many) stood by him and believed his version of what had happened, because it was supported by the same story that came through the crew's grapevine. Their belief was also supported by the fact that they all knew the notorious history of the Maxwells and some of the things they had done in the past and what they were likely to get up to in the future. So these friends were inclined to take old Maxwell's version of the story with a pinch of salt.

Captain Paul terminated his contract with the owners of the brigantine *John*. With this cloud hanging over his head the owners could not retain him for they had to find another skipper very fast, to take the ship on its next voyage to the West Indies. They did, however, promise him that when the case was over, and if he were found not guilty, they would be only too pleased to take him back, as his record with them was second to none for what he had achieved in so short a time. Having interviewed members of the crew privately, they were of the strong opinion that there was no case against him once all the true facts were known. And they informed him that if there were any assistance he required in preparing his case, they would be only too pleased to help him.

It was now crucial for Captain Paul that he obtain firm evidence in black and white from two independent sources so that he could clear his name once and for all from this ignominious and baseless charge filed against him. He had to think quickly because one source of his evidence, difficult though it would be to obtain, was not as difficult as the most crucial evidence of all—the medical officer's statement in the West Indies. So nothing would do now, if he were to save his skin, but that he should get a free passage out there and see Mr. Forbes in person. This he duly did; but before he departed, he informed the legal authorities of his movements and intentions so that they were aware of what was happening. Had he left without informing them, they may have construed his act as that of a fugitive escaping from justice, by making his way to the American Colonies where he could get lost by assuming a new name.

When he arrived in Tobago and explained the situation to Mr. Forbes, the latter furnished him with a certificate, signed by himself and the port medical officer. This certificate was going to be the very document that would get Captain Paul off the hook, for it contained the important information that there had been a flagrant breach of discipline by Maxwell and that the punishment he had received was executed in accordance with the laws of the mercantile marine. The medical report tipped the scales finally in his favour when it stated that the punishment was not excessively administered and had had no adverse effect on Maxwell's health. With all this very important information in his safe keeping, John thanked the authorities in

Tobago for all their help and made his way back across the Atlantic on the first available fast ship making its way to the Solway area. On his arrival home he lost no time in contacting Maxwell's last employer, who furnished him with a certificate signed by the ship's captain and surgeon, intimating that the man had died of the fever and that no further causes had led to his death. Furnished with these two certificates, it was a very happy John who presented them to the local justices, who, after reading them very carefully, decided to drop the charges that had been preferred against him. They told him he was free to go, as there was no longer a complaint to answer. This was the case in the formal sense; but local folklore and gossip had it in certain quarters that he was the man who had had a sailor flogged to death, a stigma that remained with him for the remainder of his life.

Once the news that the charge of murder had been dropped against him was heard locally, word spread quickly throughout the community, and his popularity could be observed by the manner in which his friends came up to him and congratulated him in public. One of his friends, who was of some standing in the community, a Bob Edgar, said, "John, justice has been done, for I realised all along that the whole thing was a complete fabrication after I spoke to some of my friends in the lodge."

"What lodge are you talking about, Bob, may I ask?"

"The local Masonic lodge, of course. What other lodge do you think I would be talking about?"

"Oh, I see," said John, who went on to say, "I quite understand what you mean now, as I have many good friends apart from yourself who are proud members of that organisation. You will excuse me but it really slipped my mind at first, Bob, as with this awful charge hanging over my head I have been slightly confused of late. However, I am coming back to normal now."

Bob went on to say, "Who would not be kind of mixed up, with such a terrible accusation being made against one; the more ridiculous thing being that it was completely false!"

"Not to worry, Bob," John went on, "it's all water under the bridge now and I shall be looking forward to the day when I am on the high seas again."

"Well, I hope it's not long from now," said his friend Bob. "And I hope everything will be plain sailing from now on for you."

"Well, I sincerely hope it will be," said a contemplative John, "for things so far, since my schooldays, have been very traumatic indeed."

"It's funny you said that," Bob went on, "for I was just discussing with a mutual friend of ours who happened to comment that since your schooldays life has been one of conflict for you."

Resigning himself to fate, John said, "Yes, some people have life running for them very smoothly, whereas with others there is stress and conflict from the cradle to the grave. And the way things are going for me, I appear to be in the last category—unless my fate changes, which I hope it will."

Bob, who was now sitting on the dry stone dyke with his legs dangling about a foot above the ground, said philosophically, out of the blue, "John, my friend, did you never think of joining the Freemasons?"

His reply was, "Quite honestly, Bob, I never gave it a lot of serious thought, for I have never been in port long enough to give it much consideration. Mind you, as you know, I have a lot of very good friends in the organisation."

"Well, my friend," Edgar went on, "now that you have some time to spend amongst us before you go to sea again, why not come to the Masonic lodge on Tuesday evening? I'll propose you at tonight's meeting and should you not be black-balled, which I doubt will happen, I will sponsor you at the initiation ceremony on Tuesday."

John, leaning against the stone dyke, now became very pensive and deep in thought, thinking it over. And looking upwards with his chin resting in the palm of his hand, John nodded and said, "Yes, Bob, I think I will take up your suggestion, for who knows, it might break the spell of bad luck which has plagued my life so far."

Bob went on, "Well, I can assure you, John, that once you become a member, you will be joining a world-wide fraternity, which will do you more good than harm. For I know that when I was at sea myself it gave me many contacts on the continent of Europe, particularly in France, and it is very influential in the American Colonies. Take it from me, friend, it's a very fine brotherhood."

"How about the mystical rules and such-like things?" asked John. "Such practices have always intrigued me."

"Don't worry about that," said Bob Edgar, with an air of confidence. "You will find out soon enough about all these things. Just you present yourself at the door of the lodge on Tuesday night and leave the rest to me."

"A million thanks then, Bob; I shall be there," said John, as they parted on their separate ways.

When John turned up at the appointed time on the Tuesday evening, looking his best in his Sunday attire, there was an aura of apprehension about him, as he was in the process of going to join a very important brotherhood that was surrounded by mysteries outsiders could not understand because of their secrecy. As promised, he was met outside the lodge by his friends, Bob Edgar and Robert Findlay, the latter being delighted that he was going to join the brotherhood. So they took John to a side room and prepared him for the ceremony, which to him at this stage was very much like venturing into the unknown. First, they loosened the front of his shirt from above the waist and blindfolded him, at the same time offering words of encouragement and telling him to relax, for it was essential that he would have to go through the ritual.

Being blindfolded, he was taken into another room, the main part of the lodge and, being in complete darkness, all he could hear were the strange voices and the strange words that were spoken as part of the initiation ceremony. When the blindfold was removed, he was aware of the glittering point of steel against his flesh. And in the midst of all this a certain fear crept over him as everything seemed so strange, and he began to tremble and break sweat. Then, however, came a voice whispering encouragement and telling him to have no fear—the voice of his friend Bob Edgar. With his friend's reassuring words, he ceased to tremble and his fears vanished. When the initiation ceremony was complete he was elected into the Masonic Order; his brothers congratulated him and they all celebrated with alcoholic refreshments, and good discussion followed. His sponsor, Bob Edgar, came up to him and put his arm round his shoulders, saying, "John, my fellow brother of this illustrious circle, look to the future with head held high. We all in here started the same way and maybe one day you will help the brotherhood just as we helped you tonight."

"I am most grateful to you, Bob, for what you have done for me this day. Henceforth I shall always uphold the high principles of this fine organisation, of which I am now happy to be a member."

"Well, John, I sincerely hope that from now on the conflict which has dogged you all your life is, as we would say, water under the bridge, and that you can look to a tranquil and harmonious future."

"Let's hope so as well," said John.

But the gods thought otherwise.

CHAPTER 5

ALLEGED MURDER OFF TOBAGO, CHANGE OF NAME, AND ESCAPE TO AMERICA

Mr. Joseph Hewes	Chairman, Marine Committee
King Robert the Bruce	King of Scots (1306–1239)

Through the maritime grapevine, John Paul was not only establishing himself as a first-class captain but also as an excellent business-man in the buying and selling of merchandise. He now possessed the ideal qualifications that made him an asset to many potential shipping companies, who were only too eager to employ an individual with the outstanding talents he possessed. To this end, the release from the justices in his home town of Kirkcudbright found him a free man in charge of a large square-rigger called *Betsy*, which plied between Britain and the New World, always making a point of calling in at Tobago in the West Indies.

It was on his second outward voyage towards the end of 1773 that an incident took place which not only changed his name but also world naval history. For, as the *Betsy* lay anchored in the Bay of Tobago on that historic December day, the Captain, who was on the poop deck, observed quite a number of the crew assembled on the forecastle in the throes of serious discussion. Being somewhat concerned about the manner in which the assembled crewmembers were conducting their conversation, he turned to his First Officer, a Mr. Boylan, and asked what the crew were discussing. His reply was, "I don't honestly know, Sir. At this stage all I can say is that that chap McGregor, with whom we had trouble once before, appears to be acting as the chairman or ringleader of the group."

"Well, Mr. Boylan," said Captain Paul, "I want you to find out immediately what they are discussing. It looks rather unhealthy from here, whatever is on their minds. Let's get to the root of it straight away."

"Aye, aye, Sir; I will make enquiries on your behalf right now and inform you without delay."

Discreetly, Boylan made his way down the companion from the poop deck and, crossing the quarterdeck, he descended among the crewmembers on the forecastle like a cat among the pigeons. Immediately his arrival was known there was a complete hush among the crew. From his experience at sea he could sense at once there was discontent around; what it was, however, he still had to find out. So, bracing himself to his duties, he anxiously enquired what their problem was. At the start they all remained long-faced and sullen, but McGregor, who appeared to act as their spokesman, blurted out, "It's about our wages, Sir."

Looking slightly taken aback, Mr. Boylan said, "What's the problem with wages then?"

"Well," said McGregor, who by this time had become the leader of the discontented crew, "we want our wages for the journey paid here and now, so that we can spend it ashore."

Boyland replied, "Well, there is nothing I can do about it, except to see Captain Paul on the matter."

To which McGregor replied, with the obvious support of his ghoulish-looking mates, "The sooner you see him the better, as we are serious in what we say; it is action we want, not words."

"There is no need to take that attitude now," replied Mr. Boylan who wished to calm down the situation and placate those present.

Making his way, deep in thought, back on to the poop deck where Captain Paul was eagerly awaiting his return and reply, Boylan said to the Captain, "I think we have the making of trouble on our hands, Sir."

"What do you mean by that, Mr. Boylan?" asked Captain Paul.

"It's about their wages, Sir," said Mr. Boylan, knowing that there was very little he could do about it, apart from report and maybe offer advice to his Master. Pacing slowly up and down the poop deck, with his hands behind his back, Captain Paul went on, "Mr. Boylan, they were aware of the fact that they would not be paid their wages until we returned to our home port, for I need all the money in my possession to purchase cargo for our return journey, and that's the end of it."

Timidly, Boylan, who was also pacing the poop deck with the Skipper, said, "If you don't mind my saying so, Sir, I think the situation is more serious than you realise, for I felt the atmosphere of revolt whilst I was in their midst a few moments ago."

"Mr. Boylan," the Captain went on, "are you implying that we have the making of a mutiny on our hands?"

"Well, Sir, if the situation is not taken in hand and the matter sorted out, I would say that it could lead to something none of us really wants, for their spokesman McGregor appears adamant that they want some positive action, and he has the passive support of the remainder of his cronies, as you can see this very moment if you look down on the forecastle."

The Captain, who had an overall view of the forecastle from the poop deck, said, "Yes, I can see what you mean, Mr. Boylan, for they are not all conferring there for the good of their health, are they?"

"I should not think so, Sir," replied his concerned First Officer.

"So it's McGregor who appears to be leading them on," said the Captain, with his chin in his hand, as he contemplatively stroked his cheek.

"Yes, Sir," said Boylan, "but he appears to have the backing of them all, for although they were fairly mute when I was among them, letting McGregor do the talking, you can see from here, by the manner in which they are openly responding to his haranguing and gesticulating, that they are all far from happy."

Captain Paul continued, "I hope that McGregor realizes the seriousness of the trouble he is fermenting, for, if he is inciting mutiny, you know the penalty for that, Mr. Boylan?"

"Indeed I do, Sir, only too well: death by hanging from the mainmast lower yard-arm."

"Well, come with me, Mr. Boylan, and I will go down amongst them and try to get the matter sorted out."

"Aye, aye Sir," said Boylan, as they both made their way down to talk to the discontented crew.

As they were approaching the forecastle, the discussion among the crew was becoming more heated, and the Captain then realised, on hearing McGregor's voice above the rest, that they were quite serious in what they had said to Mr. Boylan when he first met them, and that now he had a delicate problem on his hands which would require all the negotiating skills he had at his disposal. So, being in full ceremonial dress, which included his tricorn hat, but not his sword which he had left in the Master's cabin below the poop deck, Captain Paul squarely faced up to the problem and openly confronted the crew by saying, "Right then, you lot, what's this problem of wages I hear about from my First Officer, Mr. Boylan?"

They all fell silent at first, suspiciously looking one another up and down and casting their eyes on McGregor, who had been openly holding court prior to the Captain's arrival. The silence was short-lived, however, for their spokesman was not backward in coming forward and explaining their discontent. And after listening patiently to them at first, the Captain then said, "Let's get one thing straight from the start: there will be no wages until we return home and I have sold the cargo which I am about to procure. Do you all under-stand that?"

There was practically inaudible mumbling among them all, and then McGregor said, "Well, that's not good enough, Sir, for we want our wages to spend ashore."

"Well, as I told you already, you can't have them, so just get on with your work, and you will be well recompensed when we return to England," said Captain Paul in a firm manner, hoping that they would heed this authoritative approach to the matter.

"Return to England, my foot!" blurted out McGregor, who, on uttering these words, got an encore from his comrades and went on to say that all other shipping companies he and most of the crew had served with previously had faithfully paid their wages on the first leg of the voyage, once they had sold their merchandise. Getting rather impatient with them by this time, Captain John Paul was beginning to show signs of his fierce temper rising to the surface; but, after his Mungo Maxwell experience, he managed to control his feeling of contempt for McGregor. He did, however, go on to say, "Look, McGregor, shipping companies have different policies, which even vary from one ship to another, as happens with the firm that owns this ship. And, in our instance, no payment will be made to any crew member until we arrive back home—and that includes officers as well, myself included."

McGregor was becoming more argumentative and brash in his approach to the subject, for he went on to say, "Look, Sir, it might be all right for officers and people like yourself, but it certainly is not good enough for us, regardless of what the company's ruling might be."

The Captain angrily went on, "McGregor, you appear to be the ringleader of this group and, if I were you, I would cool things down among the rest of them, otherwise you will end up in serious trouble; probably something you never thought about. Do you understand what I mean?"

"Indeed I do, Sir," retorted McGregor, "but all we are asking for is our recognised rights and nothing more."

In the company of Mr. Boylan, the Captain said to the assembled crew, "I am sick and fed up with this discontent about wages, and I warn you all to return to your duties or accept the consequences of violating maritime law."

As he and his Chief turned their backs on them and made their way to the quarterdeck, the Captain said, "Well, Mr. Boylan, let's hope that the matter is cleared up once and for all; but it's that damned man McGregor who is leading them on; I am sure of it, but it is a bit premature to pin anything on him."

"Yes, Sir," said Mr. Boylan, nodding in agreement. "We will keep a close eye on that chartacter on the voyage home, for I think he could be a dangerous individual indeed; he exerts a tremendous influence on the remainder of the crew."

"Yes, indeed, Mr. Boylan, you are right. I think I will ditch him on our arrival in England, for you know what they say, one bad apple can ruin the rest of the barrel."

As they were ascending the companion from the quarterdeck to the poop deck, Mr. Boylan turned round and excitedly reported to the Captain what he observed: "Look, Sir, they are lowering one of the gigs and going ashore." At this the Captain, shaking his head, loudly exclaimed, "The bastards! This amounts to nothing less than mutiny, which cannot be tolerated. We will have to deal with it and deal with it fast, Mr. Boylan. Go and fetch me the Bosun and his Mate immediately."

"Aye, aye, Sir," replied Mr. Boylan, who now realised they had some real trouble on their hands, and God only knew where it would end.

By this time Captain Paul was livid. He hurriedly made his way to collect his ceremonial sword, the hallmark of his authority aboard ship. Having done so, he at once confronted the mutinous crew, hoping to discourage them from their felonious deed, at the same time avoiding another Mungo Maxwell incident. Pointing the drawn sword at them, he said furiously, "Right then, you lot! Get back aboard ship immediately and nothing more will be said about it. Failing that, this is mutiny, and you are the ringleader, McGregor."

"Mutiny, you swine!" yelled McGregor, who was now getting the active support of his comrades in the form of verbal remonstrations against the Skipper. "If I get out of this boat, it won't be mutiny I will be guilty of but pure bloody murder!" When the Skipper shouted, "McGregor, consider yourself under arrest for mutiny," the accused immediately jumped out of the gig and, picking up a bludgeon, said, "You bastard! I will swing for you!"

McGregor, being a tall sixteen-stone brute of a man, with red hair and beard, and having arms as thick as the main brace, approached the Skipper, who by this time realised that everything was for real. The Captain, on retreating from the oncoming mutineer, not being able to see behind him, caught his heel on the coaming of a hatch, and thus now had the choice of either defending himself or falling down into the hold and being killed, as it was some considerable distance to the bottom. So, as McGregor, in a furious rage and shouting "You swine! You asked for this!" was in the process of delivering a lethal blow, Captain Paul had no alternative but to lunge forward with his sword and stab the mutineer—for it was either the one or the other of them that would arise as victor. As it turned out, the Captain's thrust was fatal in that it went straight into McGregor's heart, and the mutineer immediately keeled over dead, to the great dismay of all those present.

Looking at McGregor dead in front of him, in his own pool of blood, the Captain, who was by this time trembling, said to his First Officer, "Oh God, I've killed him, Mr. Boylan! But, believe me, it was not intentional for I had no alternative."

"I appreciate that, Sir," said his Chief Officer, who went on to say, "You are quite right in what you say, Sir; you had no alternative but to do it, for it had got to the stage where it was either you or him."

"But will the authorities ashore believe my story that it was self-defence and not murder on my part, Mr. Boylan?"

"Yes, Sir, I see no reason why not, for, tragic though the circumstances are surrounding the case, in the final analysis you had no choice but to defend yourself."

"Very good, then, Mr. Boylan; you take over, for I am going to report the matter to the Justices ashore."

"Aye, aye, Sir," said Mr. Boylan loyally, realising that the Skipper needed his utmost support at that very unfortunate moment. And, as the Skipper was making his way to the quayside, Mr. Boylan wished him good luck and reminded him to quote him as witness when the Justices ashore asked for corroboration of his story.

As Captain Paul slowly trudged his way from the quayside to the local Justices' office it could be seen that he was burdened with many thoughts, not pleasant ones at that. For, of all the traumatic experiences in his past, there were none as serious as the one which now confronted him. The Mungo Maxwell affair, which had caused a furore at the time, was chicken-feed compared with this incident; but in his own mind, although he deeply regretted the incident, he justified his actions to his conscience and therefore did not consider himself in any way a murderer. However, the nagging worry at the back of his mind was how the Justices would look at it from a purely legal point of view, for that was all that mattered if his name was to be cleared of the charge of murder.

Entering the local Justices' office, he said to a stout gentleman, who was well on in years, practically bald, and wearing a monocle, "Excuse me, Sir, but I would like to speak to one of the local Justices."

The reply from behind the desk was, "You are talking to one now, the only one here in point of fact. What can I do for you, may I ask?"

"Well, Sir, my name is Captain John Paul from the square-rigger *Betsy*, which is anchored out in the bay, and I have just come to report the death of one of my crew, whom I killed in a shipboard brawl." On hearing this, the Justice Officer, a Mr. Granville Sharp, sat back in his chair aghast; and, after calling for his clerk to witness the reporting of the incident, he said, "Gad, Sir, you don't look like a murderer to me!"

"No, Sir," replied the Captain, "it was purely a matter of self defence, and anything I say here can be substantiated by my First Officer, a Mr. Boylan, who is aboard ship at the moment."

"All right, Captain Paul," said Mr. Sharp, and continued, "Any deaths which occur within my jurisdiction that are not due to natural causes have to be investigated to determine whether they were the result of foul play, accident, or suicide. So you understand my position in law, do you, Captain Paul?"

"Indeed I do, Sir," replied the Captain.

"Very well then, Captain Paul, will you explain in detail, very slowly from beginning to end, what happened, and my clerk will take down every word that you say."

Slowly, Captain Paul gave the Justice a comprehensive report of what happened, from the very beginning of the episode to its culmination in the ringleader's death. After Mr. Sharp had read it through twice, he turned to Captain Paul and said, "Well, Captain, on the evidence I have before me here, providing it is corroborated by your Chief Officer, Mr. Boylan, you have very little to worry about, from what I can see."

Somewhat surprised that he was not placed in custody, Captain Paul said to the Justice, "Does that mean that I am free to go?"

"Yes," replied the officer; "but I must warn you that you will have to appear before an Admiralty Court on the charge of murder. Not to worry, however, as it's purely a technicality, for all the evidence points to the fact that you really acted in self defence, and you will therefore be acquitted."

Being reasonably satisfied with these encouraging words, the Captain said, "What will I do now, Sir?" Checking the documents to ensure that he had all the shipowner's relevant details, the Justice said, "You can return to your ship and, as the court only sits twice a year, we will send you adequate warning so that you can make the necessary arrangements to come back here in plenty of time before sitting commences."

The Captain pondered this and then said to the Justice, "Should I seek legal representation now or wait until I come back over for the case?"

"No, there is no reason for you to take legal advice at this stage: as yours appears to be a very clear-cut case of self-defence it will suffice if you consult a lawyer just before the trial is due to commence."

"What about witnesses, Sir?" he asked Mr. Sharp.

"Yes, that is a good point, Captain Paul; if I were you, I would ask them to be in attendance when the case is being heard, particularly your First Officer, Mr. Boylan, for his evidence will be crucial to your obtaining an acquittal."

Wiping the sweat from his brow, Captain Paul went on to say, "As I would like to get this case cleared up as soon as possible, particularly as the ship is here for some time and my main witness, Mr. Boylan, could corroborate what happened here and now, would it be possible to be tried in a civil court, Sir?"

"That is a possibility, Captain Paul, but normally cases like yours are tried in an Admiralty Court and, funnily enough, although they are not an everyday occurrence, they are normally about ship-board brawls that inevitably result in death or serious maiming."

"Very good, Mr. Sharp, I think I will strike while the iron is hot and opt for a civil trial, if it can be organised within the next few weeks," said the Captain, who was determined to get his name cleared before embarking for British waters.

"Well, if you so wish, Captain Paul; once I have interviewed Mr. Boylan I shall make the necessary arrangements to have you tried in a civil court," said the sympathetic Justice.

"Well, thank you very much for your sound advice, Sir," said the Captain, as he made his way out of the Justice's office into the dazzling sunshine, a much calmer man than he had been when he entered it.

When he left the Office of the Admiralty Court, Captain Paul took a seat in a shaded verandah nearby and began to work out his defence in his own mind. He had regained his composure and could look at things in a much clearer light, having received such encouraging words of comfort from Mr. Sharp, the local Admiralty Justice. Whilst he was quietly relaxing, deep in thought, a very good local friend, John Summers, happened to pass by and noticed him sitting forlornly in the shade. Coming up to him, John Summers said, "Look, John, I know that you are in trouble and you have to act quickly, so listen carefully to every word I say; for your future, indeed your very life, may depend on what words of advice I have to offer you."

The Captain said, "John, so sorry to meet you in such circumstances, but how did you hear about the incident?"

"How did I hear!" retorted Summers. "It has spread like wildfire throughout the port and, if I were you, I would get out of here fast."

Being rather taken aback, the Captain said, "What do you mean by 'getting out of here fast'?"

"Well, you see, this man you killed is not only a local man, as you know, but the McGregor clan practically run this place—and if they get their hands on you I am afraid it will be 'goodbye, John Paul!'"

"But John," the Captain went on, "I have just made arrangements to clear my name; will you listen while I give you all the circumstances surrounding the story?"

"Now, John," exclaimed his friend, "time is getting very short. Listen to everything I say to you, and you can tell me about the whole sordid affair later." The Captain, very sensibly taking his advice, said, "John, I know you are a reliable friend of mine, and it will give me great pleasure to listen to every word you have to say."

"Well, to put it bluntly, you will have to get off the island as soon as possible and ignore the civil court, for it would be suicide to appear before them."

"Why is that?" the Captain asked indignantly, "I am clear in my own conscience that I did not murder him but acted just as any other person would have done in my situation. Is not the first law of nature self-preservation?"

"Now look, John," said Summers; "I happen to know this area a lot better than you, and, take it from me, it's not worth the risk of going before a civil court, even although, as you say, the killing of McGregor was a last resort on your part." The Captain paused, then said, "Yes, John, you are probably right. So what have I to do then?"

"The first thing you must do is to come with me immediately round the back of the township and discard that uniform, forgetting you ever were a sailor, and I will fix you up with some clothing to see you on your way," said Summers, who already had a get-out route planned in his mind.

So, after they had stealthily made their way to Summers's house, the first thing the Captain did before he had a meal was to have a good washdown and a complete change of clothing. And, whilst they were tucking into a sumptuous meal, the first solid food the Captain had taken since the incident aboard the *Betsy*, Summers said to him, "John, my friend, from what you have told me of the incident you are completely innocent, for I would, like any other normal man, have done the same thing myself. So put everything behind you and start afresh." Just as John Summers was finishing his discourse with the Captain, his young brother Allan came rushing in, but, not knowing the Captain, he suddenly stopped in his tracks. It could be observed, however, that he had something to tell his brother.

"What's all the excitement about then, young Allan?" asked his older brother.

"It's about a murder on a ship called the *Betsy*, which is anchored in the harbour, and the dead man's relatives are at the quay-side going mad looking for the Captain of the ship."

Although Captain Paul remained perfectly calm throughout Allan's discourse, it could be seen from the consternation in his eyes that he was far from calm within. Turning to Allan and at the same time winking at the Captain, John said, "Thanks very much for the information, but it's really nothing to do with us, is it?"

"Not really, John," was Allan's reply to his older brother, "but I thought I would let you know, as there is quite a furore going on about it."

"By the way, Allan, may I introduce you to my friend, whom you have not met before, a Mr. Jones by name, who just happens to be passing through to the other end of the island."

"Pleased to meet you, Mr. Jones," said Allan politely.

"Pleased to meet you, Master Allan," said the Skipper, who had now assumed a new name in response to the quick thinking of Allan's older brother. Playing the whole thing very coolly, John said to his younger brother, "Allan, I want you to go over to Neil McLaughlin's farm straight away and get me a set of stirrups he promised me the other day. And as you won't be back until near midnight—that is, if you don't stay the night there—borrow this lantern to help you in the dark."

"That should be no problem at all, for I like going to Mr. McLaughlin's; he is a great guy."

When Allan had left on his errand, his brother John turned to the Captain and said, "John, I had to think quickly there in front of my younger brother, for if it ever got back to the McGregor family that I was giving you refuge, it would be the end of me also in this community of ours."

"Yes, I am very grateful for the way you handled things, by God, am I not glad now that I took your advice!" said a much relaxed Captain.

"Well, that's what friends are for, John, and I know in my own conscience that I am not harbouring a murderer," said Summers.

"Well, that's very noble and kind of you thinking that way about me," said the Captain.

"Now, John, as you realise, the heat is on, and so it is imperative that you leave here as soon as nightfall arrives," said Summers, as he watched the sun begin to descend slowly into the western horizon.

"Right then, John, what do I do from here?"

"Well, under cover of darkness, now that I have given you a new name, make your way to the other side of the island on horseback, and catch the first available ship to the American colonies," said the only friend he could really trust at this late hour in the day.

The Captain then said, "I told you of my brother Willie's death. There is nobody else in America that I really know."

"Don't worry about that, John," continued his friend; "for, once you get there, that country is so big you can quite easily lose yourself. As nobody will recognise you by your previous name, you can settle down there in complete freedom, with a clear conscience behind you, and just become another insignificant cog in that vast part of the Empire."

"Oh yes, John," said the Captain. "Once I can make it there, I should be able to work something out for myself; but it's only a pity I did not have someone I could contact."

"Hold it, John," said Summers, "I have just been thinking. There is a friend of mine from back home in Scotland living in Philadelphia, called Bob Hannah, and I think he has something to do with the maritime world there."

"That would be really good of you if you could give me his address. A contact of that nature is just the thing I want, for honestly, the sea is the only thing I know, as it has been my life since leaving school thirteen years ago." Rummaging through his old correspondence, Summers said, "We are in luck. Here is his address; write it down and remember to call on him if you ever make that part of the country."

"John, I don't know how much I can thank you for all you have done for me. You've certainly got me out of a tight corner this time and I will always be grateful to you for it."

"Well, John, you never know your luck. I know Bob Hannah and the type of character he is, and the network of his friends he will have in Philadelphia, and think you may make your name on the high seas once again," said an assuring and confident John Summers.

"The high seas!" said the Captain with a sigh; "that's the last thing I want to think of at the moment. A job on the land would suit me fine. However, I shall just take things step by step and look forward to the future with courage and confidence."

"Yes, you should be all right once you leave the island. As far as I am concerned, you were never here," said Summers.

"But how about your young brother, Allan; won't he ask questions? And if he finds out, won't he spread the word around?" asked an uneasy-looking Captain, not wishing his friend to get into trouble because of his unfortunate misdeeds.

"No, that's why I deliberately made the excuse to send him away, for I have regular people passing through here who are complete strangers to him, so he would have found nothing unusual in your presence."

"How about my naval uniform, then? Will that not give the show away and lead him to ask awkward questions?" asked the Captain curiously.

Taking the Captain by the hand, Summers led him out of the house and into the rear garden; and, showing him the ash-covered remnants of what had been a fire, he said, "That's all that is left of your uniform, John. For the first thing I did when I gave you a set of new clothing was to destroy what you had been wearing, before Allan could see it."

"Well, John, I must give you full marks for everything, even to the destroying of my uniform, and I am most grateful to you," said the Captain.

"Well, John," Summers went on, "if you knew this place as well as I do, and the influence of the McGregor family in particular, that's the very first thing you would have done yourself. Take it from me!"

As it was getting late now and darkness was falling, the time was ripe for the Captain to take leave of his host and make his way stealthily by horseback across to the other side of the island, where he would be treated as just another traveller passing through to another part of the expanding empire. So, thanking John Summers for all his help in getting him off the island, a much more confident and a calmer Captain left his host than had met him earlier. For he was very confident now that as soon as he set foot on the land of his dreams things would eventually work out all right and that his conflict-ridden days of sailing the high seas would be a thing of the past—something he would want to forget. To this end, he still wished to settle down, eventually to own a small farm, take a young bride, and become a contented husband and father.

On arrival in America, however, he still had a twinge of conscience regarding the incident off Tobago, and even planned to return and face trial. He also used the name of John Paul for some time, but finally reverted to the one given to him by his friend Summers. And, because of political developments, he never returned to the West Indies.

As the current political climate between Britain and her unruly daughter was deteriorating rapidly, John, now a fully mature man of twenty-eight years, after finalising his deceased brother's estate, found himself making his way to Philadelphia in 1775. Because of the political rift developing between America and the mother country, intuition drove him to this area, as it was the seat of maritime power existing at the time. So it was of paramount importance for John to call in and see the Bob Hannah his friend Summers had told him about, and convey to him his friend's compliments. In doing this, he thought it might provide him with the opportunity of obtaining a berth in some ship that was going on the high seas, for his maritime instincts were now becoming stronger than his desires to settle on the land. And having put all his previous troubles well behind him, he thought that a second chance at the seafaring life could not possibly be as disastrous to him as his initial one had been.

On locating Bob Hannah, who was a tall fair-haired man of Nordic complexion and a member of the local militia in Philadelphia, he was rather cautious of how he would approach him, not wishing to disclose his tragic past. So, being determined to keep his family name intact, he went up to Hannah on first seeing him and said, "Good day to you, Mr. Hannah; my name is John Paul Jones; pleased to meet you."

Shaking his hand warmly on recognising his accent, Hannah said, "And a very good day to you. Is it Mr. Jones I call you or Mr. Paul Jones?"

"Paul Jones, if it please you, Mr. Hannah."

"Well, Mr. Paul Jones, what can I do for you in this bustling town of ours?" asked Hannah, who on looking him over, realised that he had in his company an individual who was not only of refined character but a person who had a certain seriousness and an air of leadership about him.

John Paul Jones, who was now seated comfortably on the verandah of Hannah's house overlooking the docks, said to him, as he casually surveyed all those ships of sail before him, "Some time back I met a friend of yours in Tobago, who is also a good friend of mine, a Mr. John Summers by name, and he sends his warm greetings to you."

Sitting back in his chair with a big smile on his face and roaring with laughter, Hannah said, "Oh no, this can't be real! You mean to tell me you met John Summers and that he is a friend of yours?"

"Indeed he is," was John Paul Jones's reply, "and a very genuine friend he is indeed."

"Well, I never!" exclaimed Hannah. "If you are a friend of his, you are a friend of mine. So relax and consider yourself in good company."

"That's very kind of you, Mr. Hannah," said a very relaxed John Paul Jones, realising he was now in the company of someone who had more influence in the community than he had and that, if he played his cards properly, employment of some sort or another should be forthcoming.

Hannah, delighted that he was in the company of a friend of Summers, went on to say, "Yes, John Summers and I studied in the same class in Scotland, and what an enlightening time we had! Did he happen to mention one of our teachers, a Mr. Smith by name?"

"No, I am afraid he did not, Bob," replied John, who was now on first-name terms with his dynamic host.

"It's a pity he did not, for this man Smith was some character himself, and John Summers could have told you some very interesting stories about the happy times we spent together."

"No. What he did mention, however, Bob, was that if I saw you, you might be able to get me fixed up in employment," said John, as he once again surveyed the large array of ships on the Delaware River.

"That will be only too easy, John; would you like to be in the militia with me?"

"Do you think there is any future in it, then Bob?" enquired John anxiously.

"Any future in it! That's an understatement, for with the recent incidents at Lexington and Concord, we will not only have all-out revolution on our hands but I guarantee a declaration of independence within a year or so," said Hannah, obviously looking forward to a long-drawn-out struggle with the British.

"Well, you know, Bob, my philosophy is very much for the concept of liberty and I would be only too pleased to take up the sword in its honour; but I am not so sure about independence, are you?"

"Well, John, now the first shots have been fired, it is difficult to see us going back. Because of the attitude of the King George III government in London, the only way I can see true liberty in this vast country of ours is by going for independence, as they are complementary," said his new-found friend, whose eyes betrayed his eagerness to take up arms.

John, who listened attentively to the words being uttered by Hannah, realised that things were never going to be the same again on either side of the Atlantic, and went on to say, "Sad to say this, Bob, but if your ultimate views bear fruit, there will be a lot of blood spilt in the process."

"There sure will be, John, my friend, but that's the price we will have to pay for our liberty and freedom," said Hannah philosophically.

John's mind went back to the long lectures his mother used to give him, as a young boy, on George II and what he did to suppress the Jacobites and how he eventually crushed the Scots' hard-earned liberty, the liberty which had its roots in the Battle of Bannockburn in 1314 when Robert the Bruce was triumphant in the cause of his country's freedom. And he thought to himself that here we had the same George II's son, trying to deny his subjects in the American colonies that same degree of self expression which his father had denied to his own kith and kin. His mind wandered back to his childhood days, when he told his mother that when he grew up he might have the chance to fight the English, and she never thought that the opportunity would arise again. History, however, had proved her wrong, for here was his ideal opportunity to fulfil his prophetic childhood statement, not in the land of his birth but thousands of miles across the Atlantic.

Hannah, noticing that his newfound guest was deep in thought, turned to him and said, "I notice that you have been thinking deeply over what I have said."

"Indeed I have, Bob," said John; and went on to say, "If this war does continue, no doubt they will require some sort of navy to try and upset Britain's maritime might."

"Yes, John, but I am afraid that is where we are particularly weak, in taking on the might of the British Navy. However, moves are afoot in the Continental Congress to organise a navy and a marine corps."

"This is most interesting indeed, Bob, and how does one go about volunteering for such a navy?" asked John enthusiastically.

"That should be no problem at all, John," replied his new friend. "I have a very good companion, Joseph Hewes, who has just been appointed Chairman of the Marine Committee in Congress, so I must introduce you to him. Thereafter it's entirely up to you."

"It would be excellent, Bob, if you could arrange for me to meet this gentleman, Mr. Hewes. But how do we go about it?" asked an eager John, now visualising himself once again back on the high seas and serving a cause he believed in strongly, which was this great concept of liberty, a word which was on everybody's lips throughout the thirteen colonies.

"That will be easily done," replied Bob. "We will make our way along to the Masonic Lodge tonight where I will not only introduce you to Mr. Hewes but also the community."

"Good!" said John. "It will be a pleasure to meet these people who have some say in the community, particularly Mr. Hewes."

In the warm conviviality of the Masonic Lodge, John was delighted with the atmosphere, which to him was home from home. From the manner in which his friend Bob Hannah was sociably conversing with many of the other members, John realised that he had made a worthwhile contact in the community, for anyone who was anybody appeared to be on very good speaking terms with his friend Bob. Having purchased some light refreshments at the bar, his friend said to him, "Oh, here is Mr. Hewes coming now—I will need to introduce you."

"Lovely!" replied a grateful John. "This is the very opportunity I have been waiting for."

As he approached them, Mr. Hewes, who was tall with rugged features, seemed to tower over John, who was relatively small compared with this very important contact of his friend Bob.

"Good evening, Mr. Hewes," said Hannah with a smile all over his face, which indicated that they were bosom friends. "And a very good evening to you, Bob!" replied Mr. Hewes. "So nice to see you again. May I join your company?"

"Most certainly," replied Bob in an affable manner. "Do sit down and tell me what has been happening."

"What has been happening!" replied Mr. Hewes, as he slowly sipped his ale. "I think it would be more appropriate if you asked what has not been happening, as I am up to my eyes in work with one thing and another."

"Oh, it's like that, I see," said Bob sympathetically.

"Yes, indeed it is, Bob," replied Hewes, who then continued, "Since I have become Chairman of the Marine Committee I have been working flat out to get this navy of ours under way, which is a tremendous task; but we will make it eventually one way or another."

On hearing the word 'navy' mentioned, John took an eager interest in their conversation, thinking anxiously to himself that his ideal opportunity had arrived.

Turning to John, Bob Hannah said, "Mr. Hewes, please let me introduce a good friend of mine from Scotland, Mr. John Paul Jones."

Giving him an outstretched hand of welcome, Mr. Hewes said, "Delighted to meet you, Mr. Paul Jones. Have you just arrived here?"

"Yes, I have just recently arrived, and I must say that I am very much impressed to date with what I have seen."

"Good!" replied Mr. Hewes. "Welcome to Philadelphia, and I hope you will like it here, for you could not be in better company than with the people you will meet in this Lodge."

"That's really good to know, Mr. Hewes, for I know that, since meeting Bob here, I have been introduced to some marvellous people in this fine community of yours."

"Are you just over from the old country, then?" asked Mr. Hewes of his newfound acquaintance, as Bob Hannah silently listened to the conversation developing. Here John had to choose his words very carefully, so as not to divulge his harrowing past and change of name.

"No, Mr. Hewes, I came to the American colonies via Tobago, where I met a mutual friend of both Bob's and mine, who told me that should I ever be in this area I must call on him. Well, here I am in his company now."

Only too eager to interrupt, Bob Hannah said, "John here tells me he has quite a lot of sailing experience behind him, since his school days."

With this added information, Hewes became even more interested in his new social contact, and went on to ask, "What did you do in the navy then, Mr. Paul Jones?"

"Well, Sir, I ended up as a deep-sea captain before I quit the life, hoping to settle in America," was John's proud reply, realising that things were beginning to look favourable for him.

"A deep-sea captain!" exclaimed Mr. Hewes. "Well, indeed, a man of your experience is the very type I am at this moment looking for."

"I gathered that from Bob here," replied John, in a low voice, being a soft-spoken individual until his temper was roused.

"You see, Mr. Paul Jones, this Marine Committee of which I am Chairman is responsible for the running of our new Continental

Navy, which is only in its infancy. At the moment we are just slowly beginning to find our feet—or should I say water?"

John, who was becoming more engrossed in everything he heard from Mr. Hewes, went on to say, "And how are things developing, Mr. Hewes?"

"Well, they are coming along very nicely, Mr. Paul Jones," said a proud Mr. Hewes, "for we have a few ships already fitted out with guns, with more on the stocks to be launched within the next year or so."

"But you don't intend to take on the might of the British Royal Navy, do you?" enquired John, in a very sombre manner.

"No, that would be impossible at the moment, Mr. Paul Jones, but what we can do is harass merchant shipping to such an extent that it greatly affects their supplies and thus weakens the ground forces on land," said Hewes, talking as a man who possessed a great flair for organisation and the deployment of the scarce resources at his disposal.

"And how about all these privateers I see floating around?" enquired John.

"Oh yes, they are a tremendous help to us in one way, but a drawback in another," said the new naval supremo.

"In what way are they a drawback to you, may I ask, Mr. Hewes?" enquired John.

"Well, when it comes to taking prizes, the spoils are shared out among the crew, which is not the case in the Continental Navy; hence it is difficult to recruit good and reliable sailors, for their loyalty is given to cash rather than to their country."

"And do you intend to do anything to have this situation rectified?" asked John, before considering joining Hewes's newly formed navy.

"Indeed we do, Mr. Paul Jones; it is a matter to which I am giving priority, for as things stand at present they are far from conducive to the creation of a strong, disciplined and harmonious navy."

"I think it would be very wise to get this sorted out as soon as possible, for it will give you the opportunity to plan your navy without this terrible millstone round your neck," said John, talking in an authoritative manner by virtue of his past experiences in the merchant navy.

By this time Bob Hannah was becoming very much an observer, but he was delighted that John and Joseph Hewes were getting on so well in their long drawn-out discussion of the pros and cons of the infant navy. And once Mr. Joseph Hewes had probed John's background, learning of his rise from cabin-boy to ship's master (John omitting the Mungo Maxwell affair and the murder at Tobago), the man in charge of the newly-founded navy was so impressed by John's record of seamanship that he saw a golden opportunity for a man of his talents to serve the rebellious daughter of mother England on the high seas. So, striking while the iron was hot, Mr. Hewes put the question, "Would you like a commission in our navy, Mr. Paul Jones?"

"Indeed, Mr. Hewes, I would be delighted, for, from what I gather from my friend Bob here and yourself, it would give me great pleasure to serve your glorious cause."

"Excellent!" replied an equally delighted Hewes, who realised he had an individual of not only tremendous talent but also of integrity, who would make first-class officer material.

"Can you come round to my office in the morning for the swearing-in process, and I will have you allocated to a ship immediately?"

"It will be my honour and humble duty to report to you, first thing in the morning, Sir," said a beaming and happy John, who was once again taking a step into to the unknown. And, bidding Mr. Hewes a final farewell, both John and Bob Hannah left the Masonic Lodge and retired for the night.

The following morning it was a jubilant John Paul Jones who presented himself before Mr. Hewes and his Maritime Committee to take up his new appointment in the cause of the liberty he most greatly cherished. And having duly taken the oath of allegiance to the new Continental Congress, he now became a First Lieutenant in the infant American Navy, the time of year being late 1775. And, being assigned to a ship of twenty guns called the USS *Alfred*, it was to him that the honour fell of raising the Grand Union Flag for the first time ever to its jackstaff on the Delaware River.

So the former cabin-boy got off to a glorious start in his adopted country of America. And, considering his precarious past, it would have been somewhat premature to anticipate what the future would hold for him.

CHAPTER 6

U.S.S. RANGER

Dr. Benjamin Franklin	American Representative in Paris
The Earl of Selkirk	Scottish Aristocrat and Landowner
The Countess of Selkirk	Wife of the Earl of Selkirk

By the year 1777 the rift between Britain and her American colonies was becoming much greater, with the latter having declared independence on 4th July of the previous year. Naturally, in an environment of this nature, hostilities between the two countries were gathering momentum, both on land and at sea. At sea the infant American Navy was still haphazardly organised, but it was expanding at a greater speed than hitherto, with new ships being launched or acquired as the war proceeded. In these circumstances, John Paul Jones had excelled himself in all the tasks allotted to him by the Maritime Committee, to the extent that he was now a Captain in his own right. Being a determined Scot, however, and hewn in the traditions of the British mercantile marine, he was a stickler for organisation and sound discipline, which he considered to be of paramount importance for the efficient running of a fighting navy. And although he proved his capabilities as Lieutenant in charge of gunnery on the USS *Alfred* and as Captain of the USS *Providence* in Caribbean waters, he made many enemies among his superiors and peers as well as his subordinates within the Service. Like many other great leaders, he was the type of man that was either loved or hated. He did, however, have the trust and confidence of the Marine Committee in Philadelphia. Had he not had this, his career in the Navy would have been very short-lived indeed, for another disadvantage he had was that he was an outsider serving in the midst of colonial-born Americans. Being a Scot into the bargain did not endear him to the homebred sailors, for the Scots, because of their independence, zeal and enterprise were looked on as a race to be watched, due to their resourcefulness. There was, however, within the colony of America tremendous rivalry between the elements from the different States that made up the new Continental Navy, which did little to encourage streamlined efficiency. As with most new organisations or societies, nepotism was rife, and Captain John Paul Jones had no family or friends to support his cause. In the professional sense, however, he did have friends in the Marine Committee, who recognised his skills and potential as a great leader and who, with this in view, acted accordingly.

Because of his excellent record to date as a professional seaman and because of his vast experiences in the Atlantic trade, the Marine Committee decided to isolate him from the local naval infighting that was going on and send him into European waters where he would be his own boss, in sole command of the crew; and also, apart from taking prizes, he would be able to create the maximum possible havoc that would serve the cause of independence. Now that privateers were given the formal backing of Congress, they could assist the Navy in the harassment of British ships, inflicting the maximum damage on them whenever possible.

On hearing of this new venture the Marine Committee had in mind, Captain John Paul Jones was delighted to be embarking on such a mission, as it was a challenge which would vindicate him as a natural leader of men, who could fight independently on the high seas, without any superiors breathing down his neck. What Congress had in mind for our young and aspiring Captain was a three-masted, twenty-gun sloop of war, just recently built and called USS *Ranger*, with a ship's complement of over two hundred men; and, although coincidental, it was appropriate that Captain John Paul Jones's appointment to the USS *Ranger* was on the same day as the birthday of the 'Stars and Stripes.'

With the USS *Ranger* fully fitted out in full fighting condition, Captain John Paul Jones left the New World to visit the old one, arriving in France, then proceeding on his specific mission after consulting with the American Commissioner in Paris as to what would be his most effective destroying tactics.

On meeting the American Commissioner in France, Dr. Benjamin Franklin, and his Assistant, Captain Paul Jones, presented himself by saying, "Good day to you, Sir, pleased to meet you. I am Captain John Paul Jones of the USS *Ranger*, and I believe you have further instructions for me."

"Good day to you, Captain Paul Jones. It is indeed my pleasure to meet you, after sailing across the Atlantic from my beloved homeland," said the sprightly American representative in France, who, although advancing in years, had a mind as sharp as a razor.

"How are things in Paris?" enquired the Captain.

"Pretty good, Captain," replied Dr. Franklin, "but they could be better."

"What do you mean by that, may I ask, Sir?" enquired Captain Paul Jones.

"Well, diplomatic activity is very fluid, and if I can only swing the French behind me in our war effort with Britain I shall be a happy man, for we all might then begin to see light at the end of the tunnel in this war of independence."

"Yes, I very much appreciate what you say, Sir, for without French naval backing we have a difficult task on our hands."

"How are things faring in our infant Navy back home then, Captain?" enquired the anxious Dr. Franklin.

"Well, Sir, as you said, it is very difficult indeed to take on the might of the British Royal Navy and expect to defeat them with the limited number of ships we have at our disposal, so it's imperative that we get the backing of the French Navy if we want to see this war fought to a successful conclusion."

"Yes, Captain, that's the problem. But give us time, and I think things will come our way very shortly, for I am working very hard to that end," said the hopeful diplomat.

"Well, with our resources, Sir, all that privateers are any good for is purely commerce destruction; whereas our young Navy, because of its size, should not only be used in harassing the British Fleet but also in attacking their defenceless places which, in turn, they would have to defend with ships they would otherwise use to attack us."

"Oh, I see you are on the same wavelength then as the Marine Committee in Philadelphia, Captain," said Dr. Franklin.

"Yes, Sir, if we could organise effective hit-and-run-type raids where they are most effective, I think it would be good utilisation of our scarce resources, plus the fact that it would greatly weaken the power of the British Royal Navy on the high seas, as they would have to protect their home bases."

Paying great attention to what the naval strategist was saying, Dr. Franklin went on to ask him, "Have you any specific place in mind, Captain Paul Jones?"

"Indeed I have, Sir, and it is on the west coast of England."

"And what is the name of the place, may I ask?" enquired a most interested Commissioner, wishing to learn more about the Captain's schemes for attacking mainland Britain.

"It's a place called Whitehaven, Sir," replied the Captain.

Unfolding a map of the British Isles, the Commissioner said, "Please point it out to me then, Captain."

Pointing to the map the Captain said, "There it is, Sir, lying slightly above the Isle of Man on the right-hand side."

"Oh, I see now," said Dr. Franklin, "but why, in heaven's name, did you pick Whitehaven of all places? It is the first time I have even heard of it. Why not Plymouth, which is nearer?"

"Plymouth, Sir!" retorted Captain Paul Jones. "I sincerely hope you are not serious, for entering Plymouth sound, even under cover of darkness, would be suicidal; once we were spotted we would not have a snowball's chance in hell of surviving."

"Oh, I see, Captain; so it's not worth risking a raid on Plymouth at this stage, is it?"

"No, Sir. Not that your intentions are not sound and fully coincide with mine, but the risk would be too great and survival chances minimal. With such scarce resources at our disposal it will be much safer to opt for Whitehaven."

"But going back to what I said, why Whitehaven in particular? Have you any special reason for choosing that place?" asked a probing Dr. Franklin.

"Well, my reasons for selecting this particular place are, first that I know the port like the back of my hand as it was my home port when I first joined the British merchant fleet. Secondly, it is a large naval base, and if I could put it alight before escaping it would not only be of great propaganda value back home and on the continent of Europe but it would also be a great psychological blow, not only to the British Royal Navy, which would have failed to protect its coastline, but also to King George's politicians in London."

"Excellent then, Captain Paul Jones. I see you are not only expert in ship handling but you are also a good strategist as well," said Dr. Franklin, as he relaxed further back in his chair, contemplating the wisdom of the Captain's suggestions.

The Captain, now beginning to show his true natural talents of leadership, went on to inform Dr. Franklin of his ideas by saying, "You see, Sir, if a raid like this is successful it could be a blueprint for others throughout the remainder of the war, for the only chance of our challenging the Royal Navy is on a one-to-one basis—where they do not frighten me at all!"

"You know, Captain," said Dr. Franklin philosophically, "should you be successful with this bold plan of yours, you might be setting a precedent for future commanders yet unborn."

"Well, Sir, this is how traditions are made, and, should I be successful in my endeavours throughout this war, I have many more ideas under my hat which I will offer to the Marine Committee and which would lay the basis for a formidable navy one day. However, that's looking to the future; our immediate concern is our attack on Whitehaven."

"Very true, Captain, but before we go on to discuss that please permit me to tell you, hoping it does not inflate your ego, that you are the most enlightened member of our new Navy I have met so far, and I think you have a lot to offer it."

"Thank you very much for that kind compliment, Sir, but we have a long way to go to get this Navy of ours put on a truly professional footing."

Dr. Franklin went on to say to the Captain, "Do tell me your other reasons for going into this area, for you only explained the first one."

"Ah, glad you mentioned that, Sir. Sooner or later—for I think this is a very bold scheme indeed which will enrage the London Government should I get your permission to embark on it," said Captain Paul Jones, greatly impressing the American Representative to France the more he poured forth his ingenious ideas.

"Yes, do tell me your views, Captain, for I will be delighted to hear them, as your first one has my one-hundred-percent backing."

"Well, Sir," the Captain continued, "American sailors being held in British jails is a very sore point with me, and I see no reason why we could not take some form of action which would make their jailors sit up and do something about it instead of letting them rot away in prison for the duration of the war."

"Again, Captain, my concern for these sailors is as great as yours, but the British don't recognise them as prisoners of war but as pirates, in the same way as they recognise you; so anything you can suggest to alleviate the situation in which these poor men are unfortunately placed I shall listen to most attentively," said Dr. Franklin, who now fully realised that he was discussing more serious government policy with Captain Paul Jones in their short meeting than he had done with all previous Captains he had met in the past.

Captain Paul Jones began explaining his strategy to the Commissioner by saying, "One reason I chose Whitehaven to raid is that further north in my own country of Scotland there lives the Earl of Selkirk; and, should I be able to kidnap him, we can hold him in America until such time as our sailors are exchanged for British troops in our jails."

Dr. Franklin, who was somewhat taken aback by this proposition, said, "But why on earth capture this poor Earl in particular?"

"Well, the reason for taking him, Sir, is that he is a peer of the realm, and consequently his capture should have some influence with the North administration in London," said the Captain with an air of confidence, as if the plan presented little difficulty to execute.

"You realise that by taking this aristocrat you would be holding him as a hostage until such time as a prisoner exchange scheme could be put into operation?" said a rather unsure and concerned Dr. Franklin.

"Indeed I do, Sir," replied the Captain, who went on say, "but we are in the middle of a war, and something drastic must be done to alleviate the plight of these prisoners."

"Oh, I understand that perfectly well, Captain Paul Jones, but you realise you are setting another international precedent by taking a hostage who is not directly involved in the hostilities?"

"I perfectly understand that," replied the Captain, who appeared to be becoming rather impatient, since he and his men would have to carry out these raids, not merely discuss them in an office.

"Well, Captain, as you appear very keen to kill two birds with the one stone, I'll have to consult my instructions from Congress before the raid is finally authorised," said Dr. Franklin, picking up the document he had received from Philadelphia on the role which the USS *Ranger* had to play in European waters. Captain Paul Jones sat in a rather edgy manner, as the Commissioner studiously perused the *Ranger's* operations orders from beginning to end. Having read the document thoroughly, Dr. Franklin said, "Captain, you are in luck, for this document is very flexible indeed in that it empowers you to do anything you think fit, either on land or at sea, that would benefit the war efforts of America."

"Excellent, Sir!" said a delighted Captain. "So I have your permission to embark on this perilous mission forthwith, have I?"

"Indeed you have," replied a relieved Dr. Franklin, who was glad that he had been able to satisfy the Captain's aspirations, "and may I wish you and your crew every success in this exacting mission which you hope to accomplish."

Before leaving the Commissioner's office the Captain thanked him for authorising the venture, and went on to say, "After the mission is successfully completed, I hope to return to France with a few more prizes in my possession."

It was a cold, miserable March 1778, with a heavily laden sky that overshadowed the USS *Ranger* as it made its way stealthily out of Quiberon Bay, hoping ultimately to arrive at Whitehaven to execute the first part of its mission. In the roadstead there was a squadron of French men-of-war, and it gave Captain Paul Jones great pleasure and honour to salute them, the first time ever a gun salute had been given by a ship showing the Stars and Stripes; and when the French Admiral reciprocated the compliment, it was a proud Captain that stood on the poop deck of the USS *Ranger* having the American flag recognised for the first time by a foreign power. This was yet another indication that the French were slowly but surely beginning to move into the American War of Independence and support the rebellious colonists in their struggle against the might of the British Royal Navy.

The further northward the USS *Ranger* sailed through the Irish Sea the more inclement the weather became, so much so that by April heavy sleet and snow were making the passage thoroughly wretched; and, as the crew could not understand Captain Paul Jones's strategies, they became very restless and unhappy with their lot. Apart from the gruelling weather, one of the reasons for this state of affairs was that many of them could not understand or grasp the political implications of embarking on a mission of this nature. To most of them it was a fruitless endeavour to attack Whitehaven and then go on to capture an earl; it meant nothing to them. The opportunity of taking prizes appealed to the crew as being much more lucrative, for the more ships they took the greater financial remuneration there would be at the end of the day when they returned home to their beloved America. But, although there were rumblings in the lower deck among the crew that could have led to a mutinous situation, Captain Paul Jones managed to quell them before they got out of hand by his sheer grit and determination to accomplish his mission successfully.

Whilst the ship was on course between the northern part of Ireland and Scotland, just before altering course for Whitehaven, one of his boy seamen up in the foremast lookout shouted down excitedly to Captain Paul Jones: "Ship ahoy, Sir, on the larboard bow!"

"Keep your glass trained on her and report back to me immediately once you get further information about her," shouted the Captain.

"Aye, aye, Sir!" replied the cold and shivering boy seaman from aloft. The reply came back shortly from the lookout that it was a twenty-one gun sloop of war. The boy seaman continued, "It must be British, Sir, but it is heading away from us in a westerly direction."

"All right, boy seaman, I have already got it in my glass, so you just keep scanning the horizon, and as soon as you have spotted anything report back to me or my Executive Officer without delay."

"Aye, aye, Sir!" came the sharp reply.

Looking through his glass, the Captain could get a much better view of this armed sloop as every minute passed. As he was getting a better view of the vessel, he noticed that it carried twenty guns; but, at the distance the *Ranger* was from it, it was difficult to determine what size they were. What he did notice, however, was a small fishing boat travelling towards him from this sloop of war. To satisfy his curiosity, he ordered his helmsman to take the ship in the direction of this small vessel, at the same time ordering his Executive Officer, Lieutenant Leadbetter, to change tack from the starboard to the larboard side.

Coming alongside the fishing boat, which proved to be crewed by harmless fishermen, he hailed them loudly, asking, "What's the name of the sloop of war you fellows have just passed?"

In a strong Irish brogue one of the fishermen replied, "To be sure it's the HMS *Drake* of the British Navy, just making its way to Ireland."

In order that they would be unable to inform HMS *Drake* of the USS *Ranger's* whereabouts, Captain Paul Jones immediately arrested the Irishmen, but released them from custody unharmed and well reimbursed once his mission in that area was successfully completed. It was a jubilant and excited Captain Paul Jones who said to his Executive Officer, "Lietenant Leadbetter, did you hear that about HMS *Drake*?"

"Indeed I did, Sir, and what a jolly prize it would make!" replied his uncaring right-hand man, who had a very difficult task and was now sorry for earlier fermenting dissent among the men behind the Skipper's back.

"A jolly prize!" the Captain went on. "Not only that, but what propaganda value it would be to us if we captured a ship named after such a famous British sailor!"

"I think we should clap on all extra sails, including the studding sails, and make straight for it, Lieutenant Leadbetter," said a zealous Captain, not wishing to let such an important prize as this slip from under his nose.

"My sympathies are fully with you, Sir, but, if you don't mind my saying so, I would strongly advise you to leave it, because the crew want to get this Whitehaven raid over and return home," said his Executive Officer.

"Well, if that's the way you think they feel we will change course and head for Whitehaven, ensuring that we arrive there under cover of darkness," said a reluctant Captain, who realised that, in view of lack of homogeneity among his crew, trouble must at all costs be avoided at this late stage of the exercise.

Approximately two miles from Whitehaven, in a cove that was out of sight of this important base, Captain Paul Jones briefed his landing party of around fifty men, which he himself was going to lead, on the quarterdeck of the USS *Ranger*. With them all assembled before him in a semi-circle and listening attentively, he said, "Tonight we hope to make history, first by showing to the world that the famous Royal Navy is incapable of defending its own coasts one hundred per cent, and secondly—as I know this area like the back of my hand and the shipping it contains—by doing more harm in a very short period of time than the whole of the United States Navy has done since the war started."

"Let us hope we're successful, Sir," said Lieutenant Leadbetter.

"Lieutenant Leadbetter, this is our golden opportunity to put our infant Navy on the map; all that it requires is sound planning, guts, courage and a nerve of steel. We must all keep cool, calm and collected, otherwise our efforts will be in vain."

The Chief Quartermaster then interrupted and said, "The boats are ready for lowering and all the oars have been muffled, Sir."

"Very good, Quartermaster, slowly lower them. I'll take the first boat and Lieutenant Coyle will be in charge of the second one, for he has been fully instructed on what to do; so, you members of the second boat, take your orders from Lieutenant Coyle and remember, they have to be carried out without any debate or argument; and, should you have to talk, make sure it is only in a whisper," instructed the Captain, now showing himself a man of true leadership; "I hope you understand what I have just said?"

"Lieutenant Leadbetter," Captain Paul Jones continued, "you assume complete command of the *Ranger* until I return, and have the minimum of crew on duty so that the rest can get to sleep, for as soon as we return we shall have to get under way hastily, before daybreak, for sure enough the Royal Navy will be on our tails."

"Aye, aye, Sir," replied his Lieutenant. "I will ensure that your orders are carried out to the letter."

Rowing hard against the tide was more difficult and took longer than anticipated. Neither of the boats' crew could complain of feeling cold by the time they reached the entrance to Whitehaven harbour, for it had been a long time since they had broken sweat. When they eventually arrived at their destination, the Captain and Lieutenant Coyle left guards on their respective boats, for a quick get-away when their mission was accomplished. As both the north and south side of the harbour was guarded by a battery, the first thing they had to do, practically simultaneously, was to capture the guards and put the guns out of action. After scaling the wall of the south battery, Captain Paul Jones had the good fortune to find the guards asleep, so it was very easy for him and his men to capture them. And once they had accomplished this, it was relatively easy to put the guns out of action.

In the midst of the operation, the Captain was imagining that everything was going according to plan, when suddenly half the town was swarming on to the quayside.

"What the hell is happening?" the Captain enquired of one of his young Midshipmen.

"I am afraid I don't know, Sir," was the nervous and timid reply.

"Well, I think I bloody well do," replied the angry Captain Paul Jones. "We have a swine of a traitor in our midst, and if I could lay my hands on him I'd shoot him on sight, without a court martial."

"Yes, Sir," said the petrified Midshipman, who had never seen action as bold as this in his life before, "I think there are one or two here who only joined us in Portsmouth, New Hampshire, just to get a free trip home, Sir."

"Well, my young man, you have learned at an early age that if in your future career in the United States Navy you ever go on a mission of this nature, make sure you have a picked crew which you can thoroughly trust," said the Captain, who was beginning to mellow after getting over the original shock.

"Thank you for your sound advice, Sir," said the young Midshipman, who was learning fast in this young man's navy.

However, the exercise was not completely thwarted, for Captain Paul Jones managed to set some ships alight before departing. As they rowed back to the *Ranger* just before daybreak they were followed by cannons let off from some of the guns they had failed to put out of action, but fortunately for Captain Paul Jones and his merry men they went wide and missed them.

Because of the inclement weather and the presence of the townsfolk, who were all up in arms by this time, the damage done to the shipping was minimal compared with what Captain Paul Jones had originally envisaged and what he would have inflicted but for the traitors, who were conspicuous by their absence when the hit-and-run boats returned to the *Ranger*. The effect of the raid on morale was, however, a different matter, for that anyone should defy the might of the Royal Navy and attack one of Britain's major land bases was simply unbelievable, something that the London Government, and particularly Their Lordships at the Admiralty, just could not swallow. There was so much consternation throughout the British Isles that demands were made from all quarters for naval protection against any future raids of such nature. To this extent the USS *Ranger's* mission had proved successful, for the Royal Navy had to re-allocate their resources, which otherwise could have been deployed in the American War of Independence, to protect the shore bases around mainland Britain. If it had not been heard of prior to this escapade, the name John Paul Jones now became feared and hated throughout the land. Orders went out to the Royal Navy to capture this American 'pirate' at all costs, before he could inflict further serious damage, both in destroying ships and damaging morale, particularly among people living in coastal towns who were vulnerable to such maverick attacks which could be carried out like 'a thief in the night' under cover of darkness.

The *Ranger* had sailed from its place of hiding to meet the raiders coming back from Whitehaven, and once they had rendezvoused and the boats' crews were all safely aboard, it then shaped its course for the south west of Scotland, to carry out the capture and kidnapping of the Earl of Selkirk as a hostage.

Captain Paul Jones, after a good night's rest, was now ready to embark on the second part of the mission. As he knew every corner of this part of the Solway Firth from his boyhood acquaintance with it, he was confident that he could pull off this coup with little effort, for the Earl of Selkirk lived in a very secluded spot called St. Mary's Isle and his capture would be a much less dangerous part of the mission than the raid on Whitehaven had been. But the Captain still encountered problems with the awkward crew of the *Ranger*, the majority of them acting very much under duress in everything they did. So he promised them that, once this final part of the mission was completed, he would capture as many prizes as possible on their return journey to France, in order to relieve their moodiness and low spirits; for he thought the money obtained from the sale of the prizes would act as a spur to raise their morale.

In view of his experience with the two traitors who had betrayed the Whitehaven raid, Captain Paul Jones personally selected and vetted the men who were going to carry out the kidnapping. So he chose Lieutenant Richard Woods of the United States Marine Corps as his deputy, and ten other reliable men of the utmost loyalty and integrity to be members of the landing party. Turning to his young New Hampshire officer, he said, "Lieutenant Woods, I am putting you second in charge of the party; you will row ashore with me and capture our aristocratic hostage."

"Aye, aye, Sir," replied the youthful-looking and fair-haired Lieutenant.

"We will row in, first light tomorrow morning, when everything should be dead quiet, and kidnap the Earl."

"Will there be much life about the area, Sir?" enquired the anxious young officer.

The Captain's mind wandered back to his carefree boyhood and said, "I can vividly remember from my childhood days that the Selkirk mansion is in a very secluded area indeed, so we should have very little difficulty in entering the area. And, if I remember rightly, the only other signs of life that will be near the 'Big Hoose' will be two or three estate-workers' cottages, which are well out of sight and some distance to the rear of it."

Ensuring that no stone was left unturned, the young Lieutenant, being a thorough sort of individual, then enquired of Captain Paul Jones: "Will there be no estate workers about to raise the alarm then, Sir?"

"No, there should be none about when we arrive, for they will be on various parts of the estate carrying out their daily duties. They very seldom come about the Big Hoose anyway, if my memory serves me correctly," said the Captain, talking with an air of authority on another matter he knew very well, the daily routine operations of an estate in the Solway Firth area in the land of his birth.

Scanning the map in the chartroom, Lieutenant Woods said, "Right, Sir, this is our destination here, so if we just row round that peninsula which is jutting out there, we should come in sight of this famous Big Hoose you are talking about?"

"That's correct," replied the Captain; and pointing to the peninsula on the larboard bow of the *Ranger*, he said, "Once we get round that, the beach should be directly in front of us, with the Big Hoose standing out on its own, next to the shore."

"Will it be essential to muffle the oars, Sir?"

"As a precautionary measure, yes, plus the fact that it's good training for you and your raiding party to get to know the importance of stealth in this and in any future operation you may have to carry out, for the element of surprise is one of the most important factors in such raids," said Captain Paul Jones.

"Right then, men, get the boat ready for lowering, and we will be on our way," ordered an eager young marine officer, who was only too keen to get his name in the annals of United States naval history.

"Another thing I must insist on," said the Captain, "and that is that in no circumstances must we use violence of any sort in capturing the Earl."

"Aye, aye, Sir, I'll instruct our landing party on that matter also," said the young officer.

"We will be on our way," said the Captain, looking at his watch.

It was a grey, dull morning, but with a much calmer sea than they had encountered on the raid on Whitehaven as they slowly made their way some distance from the *Ranger*, rounding the peninsula and eventually coming in full view of the Selkirk 'Big Hoose.' As the rest of the crew had their backs to the shoreline, it was an excited Lieutenant Woods who first spotted the ivy-covered, rambling piece of architecture and exclaimed to Captain John Paul Jones, "I have sighted our destination at last, Sir, and everything is as you fore-told—perfectly quiet."

"Right then, men, ease the boat gently and we will turn it round manually, for a quick getaway once we have captured the Earl of Selkirk," said Captain John Paul Jones.

"How is the tide running, Sir?" enquired one member of the crew.

"Good point, my man," said Lieutenant Woods. "It's going out, so we will not be left stranded by an incoming tide taking the boat out in our absence."

"Hey, Sir, see what I see on my starboard side?" said a young, nervous crewmember.

"No, what is it?" enquired the marine officer.

"It's a couple of workmen, I think," was the reply.

On sighting the boat coming near the shore, the two workmen immediately scampered into the hinterland beyond the Selkirk mansion. Surveying the place where the men had been working, one of the crew remarked to Lieutenant Woods, "I see they have taken to their heels in a bit of a hurry, Sir."

"Oh yes, I see them now at a distance, and they are fairly moving. They must obviously think we are a press-gang, trying to muster up a crew, but how wrong they are, for we are after a much bigger fish than either of them!" said a jubilant Lieutenant.

As they eased the boat gently on the beach and positioned it for a quick getaway, the Captain said to his crew, "All right, men, follow me, and we will approach the house from the side, making ourselves less conspicuous by going through the undergrowth."

As they all crept along in single file with the Captain leading them, to their surprise they encountered a rather old estate worker. So as not to give the show away, Captain John Paul Jones gave him to understand that they were members of a press gang, looking for some of the younger members of the community to serve in His Majesty's ships of war. And after a short conversation with the white-haired old gentleman, they soon established that the Earl of Selkirk was not at home, as he was away down in England on holiday. On hearing this the Captain was far from pleased and very despondent indeed, and turning to Lieutenant Woods he said, "Blast it, can we get nothing right in this operation at all after all this trouble?"

"It does not seem to be our day, Sir," replied an equally fed up and forlorn Lieutenant Woods.

With spirits very low, the Captain said, "There is nothing else for it but to return to the *Ranger*, so let's make our way back now. It would be futile to capture the Countess in place of the Earl, as it would be bad propaganda—it will go right against the British grain and do nothing whatsoever to help release our prisoners."

As the crew by this time were beginning to murmur words of discontent among themselves at the abject failure of the mission, the young Lieutenant of the Marines said, "But, Sir, surely we can scuttle something of propaganda value out of this mission, even if we don't capture the Earl himself. After all, look at the pillaging and burning the British have done in America."

After pondering the Lieutenant's words, in order to raise the morale of the men the Captain said, "You made a good point there, Lieutenant Woods, which could have some propaganda value after all, especially when it filters back to the central government in London and throughout the country, through the media of the press. So what I suggest is that you obtain the Selkirk silver, informing the Countess that your main purpose of the visit was to take the Earl himself as hostage, for the release and exchange of American prisoners in British jails."

"Very good, Sir," said the eager young Lieutenant and his more optimistic crew. "At least it will show we were here and the main purpose of our mission."

"Very well then, Lieutenant Woods, you and your men make your way along to the mansion and I'll wait at the boat for your return with the silver plate."

"Aye, aye, Sir," replied the eager officer, as he and his men made their way to the Selkirk house.

Observing the peace, solitude and tranquility surrounding the house, the only sign of life the landing party noticed was smoke rising from the chimney, an indication that someone was at home. Security was such that the main front door was half opened when Lieutenant Woods chapped the knocker. To their surprise the first thing to greet them was an affable golden retriever which, instead of barking at them to frighten them away and raise the alarm, came up to them wagging its tail as much as to say, "Nice to see some strange faces around here for a change!" Shortly afterwards, the Countess of Selkirk, who was a tall, graceful and very attractive and aristocratic lady of the first order, appeared before them, and in a very cool manner said, condescendingly, "Pray, gentlemen, do tell me what you want at this early hour in the morning?"

The quick, firm but polite reply came from the leader of the party, who said, "My name is Lieutenant Woods of the United States Marines, and we are here from the United States Navy sloop USS *Ranger*. Although we came here originally to take your husband hostage, having learned that he is not at home, we demand your silver plate instead."

Being taken aback at this bolt out of the blue, the Countess said, "In heaven's name, what is all this about—what on earth are you up to?"

"We came originally to capture the Earl, Madam, and take him back to America as hostage, until such time as all sailors in British jails are exchanged with their counterparts in America", said a very cool and competent Lieutenant Woods.

The Countess, being of blue blood, showed very cool composure and, half laughingly, said, "Pray do tell me, who on earth ever put you up to this—trying to take my dear husband, of all people?"

"It's our Captain, Madam," said the officer in charge of the party. "He left here many years ago and emigrated to America."

"Pray do tell me his name then, will you?" asked the inquisitive Countess, who by this time was surrounded by her nanny and young children.

"Captain John Paul Jones, Ma'am," was Lieutenant Woods' reply.

"I am afraid I never heard of that name about this area, for as you may not know, Jones is a Welsh name, and a name like that in this area would stick out like a sore thumb," said a much more relaxed Countess.

"Well, he certainly comes from this area, Ma'am, for he is very familiar with all the creeks and peninsulas around here, as if they were his own five fingers," said the young officer.

"No, I am afraid I am none the wiser," said the Countess, who went on to say, "The nearest we ever had to that name around here was a John Paul, who went to sea as a cabin boy many years ago, whose father was the gardener on the nearby estate. But it was the British merchant navy he joined, for he first of all sailed from White-haven which is further down the coast."

Even with this information supplied by the Countess, the Lieuten-ant never thought of the possibility of his Captain adding Jones to him name, and was still none the wiser of his stormy past.

After a prolonged conversation, the Countess showed no objec-tion to their taking her silver plate, providing she obtained a receipt for it. She did, however, think that it was a very poor substitute for an aristocratic Earl! After they had collected everything and placed it in a bag, they bade the Countess farewell and made their way back to Captain John Paul Jones, who was waiting to take them back to the USS *Ranger*. Although he had missed capturing his main quarry, the Captain was pleased to have the silver plate, which was purely an instrument of propaganda value eventually to be returned to the Earl of Selkirk.

If the mission was to prove anything, it was that it struck fear into all coastal resorts and ports. At the same time it made the London Government sit up, and particularly the Admiralty, who had thought their coastline was impregnable with their 'wall of wood.' As Captain John Paul Jones had proved, both here and in Whitehaven, this was no longer the case. It was a severe blow to the pride of the Royal Navy!

Back aboard the USS *Ranger*, Captain John Paul Jones, being a determined character, was adamant in his desire to scuttle something greater out of this mission; so he said to his Executive Officer, "Lieutenant Leadbetter, get out the charts and log book and see where we last located HMS *Drake* a few days ago."

"Aye, aye, Sir; I will get that information immediately." On being informed of the last location of the British sloop, the Captain said to his Executive Officer, "Right then, Lieutenant Leadbetter, we will weigh anchor and set sail for that location without delay, for I am determined to pin down this golden propaganda opportunity, capture it, and take it back to France, with as many other prizes as we may collect en route."

"Very good, Sir," replied Lieutenant Leadbetter, who went on to say, "But will the crew stand it, Sir; they appear to be very fed up."

"To hell with the crew!" retorted the angry Captain. "They can like it or lump it. Who is running this ship, them or me?"

"You are, Sir, but I thought I should tell you that they are far from happy, which could lead to trouble, as many of them are homesick, being away from America for the first time," said the cautious Executive, knowing well the moods of his Skipper.

The Captain, realising the gravity of the situation—for his Executive Officer was the type of man to give an opinion which was well worth heeding—said, "Once we get all sails filled and are on our way, I want to address the whole ship's company from the poop deck. That includes those who are stood down as well, for I am determined to knock some form of discipline into this unruly lot and make them worthy of the name of fighting sailors. Will you organise that straight away, Lieutenant Leadbetter?"

"I shall do that as soon as all the sails have taken the wind and she is sailing on a course which will not require changing tack in the middle of your address to the crew, Sir," said a grateful Executive Officer, who was pleased to see the Skipper taking a firm hand in an awkward and potentially dangerous situation.

Once they were all assembled around the mainmast, Captain Paul Jones addressed them in a forthright manner, which left them in no doubt of who was in charge and the severe consequences if they ignored his orders: "Right, you lot, I have not gathered you all here this afternoon for the good of your health but to make quite clear what your shortcomings are and what is required of you, not only for the good of this ship but also that of our infant Navy. First of all, in any fighting unit at sea, undivided loyalty to the Skipper is demanded from all those under his command. Many of you are acting here as if you were on a pleasure cruise on Lake Champlain instead of fighting for your country and, if need be, dying for it, as I am prepared to do. So let it be clearly understood that all orders given in my name by any of your superiors must be carried out immediately in a cheerful manner, regardless of what the order might be. And let me inform you here and now that any grumblers or troublemakers will be most severely dealt with, which means, in the case of the most serious breach of discipline, death by hanging. For unless we become a highly efficient fighting unit, how, may I ask, may we lay down the traditions for the future United States Navy in the centuries that lie ahead of our young nation? With that said our next operation order is to capture HMS *Drake*; after that, on our way back to France, we will capture as many prizes as the number of officers on this ship permits. When we eventually arrive back in France, the spoils of our captures will be divided amongst us all in accordance with Navy Regulations, so we should all be a lot better off financially at the end of the day. Now, with that said, all return to your respective duties forthwith."

"That was an excellent speech, Sir," said Lieutenant Leadbetter, the Executive Officer.

"Well it was what I considered necessary to inject some sense of discipline and loyalty into them. And when I arrive in port, I shall be forwarding a long letter on the subject back to the Marine Committee in Philadelphia," said the Captain, who now appeared to be much more satisfied that they all understood what was expected of men serving on a fighting ship.

The Captain did not have very far to go to find HMS *Drake*. Unknown to him, the *Drake* was looking for the *Ranger*, for instructions had gone out from the Admiralty to the Royal Navy, "Capture this man Paul Jones, at all costs"; and they had placed additional ships in the Irish Sea and English Channel to carry out this specific task. This was the very thing Captain Paul Jones wanted: re-deployment of resources on the part of the Royal Navy! The Captain must have had the second sight or some intuition about a situation of this nature arising for, whilst he was in these very dangerous waters, he was like a Christian in the lion's den.

To reduce the risk of discovery, he deliberately kept his crew below deck, with the minimum number on the upper deck, and whenever possible kept his ship stern-on to approaching ships, so that they could not see his gunports; and, in order to pass as an innocent merchantman, it was essential that he did not fly the Stars and Stripes, for it would have given the whole game away.

When the *Ranger* eventually tracked down the *Drake*, Captain Sutherland of the *Drake* enquired on his loud-hailer: "What ship is that and where are you from?" To which Captain John Paul Jones made immediate reply, "The USS *Ranger* from a former British colony."

Then, running up the Stars and Stripes, he let him have a broadside of grapeshot right along his decks. The element of surprise again proved an advantage to the Captain, who instructed his Executive Officer, "Lieutenant Leadbetter, in no circumstances must we go alongside and grapple, for I think that their crew far outnumbers ours."

"Aye, aye, Sir!" replied the Executive Officer, just as a cannon-shot from the *Drake* whizzed past the Captain's ear only inches away, then landed in the sea.

"That was a near one, Sir," said Lieutenant Leadbetter.

"Well, that's life," replied Captain Paul Jones humorously. "Here today and gone tomorrow! Now I want you to instruct the gunnery officers to concentrate their cannon-shots on masts, yards and sails, but leave the hull intact, for I want to take this treasured prize back to France."

"Aye, aye, Sir" said the Executive Officer, who immediately sent the messenger boy down to the gun deck below with these specific orders.

By the time the fight had been going on for over an hour, Captain Paul Jones was relishing every moment of it—and so were his crew, for they were more active now than ever they had been since leaving the coast of America. This was real war, with human life at stake every moment. In the end HMS *Drake* paid dearly for the encounter, for Captain Sutherland and one of his young officers, Lieutenant Malcolm Miller, lay dead with many other members of their crew on a blood-soaked deck, and the other senior officers aboard had no alternative but to surrender. By this time the *Drake* was so badly damaged aloft, with the upper parts of the fore and main masts shot away and most of the rigging in tatters, that it became completely unmanageable.

When the boarding party went aboard the *Drake*, the first thing they had to do was to take over one hundred and fifty prisoners and bury over two dozen seamen. As Captain Paul Jones was a stickler for naval custom and tradition, the HMS *Drake*'s Captain and young Lieutenant Malcolm Miller were buried at sea with full military honours. At first the USS *Ranger* had to tow the *Drake* because of its appalling condition, but Chips and Sails and their men worked like beavers day and night to get it fully operational, and to the proud satisfaction of all it was safely crewed into Brest on the starboard side of the *Ranger*, accompanied by four other prizes which Captain Paul Jones had taken on their return journey to France.

It was a proud crew of the USS *Ranger* that eventually berthed in Brest under the forthright and domineering captaincy of John Paul Jones. And although the Captain had mixed feelings about the whole operation, particularly in its earlier stages, his doubts about the mission were swept away when he eventually met Dr. Benjamin Franklin, the American Commissioner in Paris, who warmly shook his hand and said, "Captain Paul Jones, you have done more for the American cause in Europe in a matter of weeks than the whole of the American armed services have done since the first shots were fired at Lexington and Concord."

"Has it been well reported then, Sir?" enquired a proud Captain Paul Jones.

"'Well reported' is not the word for it, Captain, for since your daring raid on Whitehaven and the episode at the Selkirk mansion you have been the talk of Europe. And in capturing the prestigious HMS *Drake* you have struck a hard blow at the British nation's morale," said Dr. Franklin.

"Well, Sir, I never realised that my mission was as successful as that."

"Well, you can't argue with the reporting in the British press," said an equally proud Dr. Franklin, who went on, "Here are some newspapers we got over from Britain; just read the large print that makes up the headlines."

The Captain, with a beaming smile on his face, was more than satisfied when he read such headlines as: "CAPTURE THIS AMERICAN PIRATE JOHN PAUL JONES AT ALL COSTS"; "AFTER DARING WHITEHAVEN RAID—NO BASES SAFE"; and "RAID ON SELKIRK MANSION MAKES NO COASTAL HOME SAFE."

"Well, Sir," said a satisfied Captain to his political superior in France, "I am glad that I did my bit for this infant Navy of ours."

"Take it from me," replied Dr. Franklin, "over the years I have seen many captains and ships visit France, and I say quite candidly and in all sincerity that most of them are amateurs compared with you and what you have achieved in so short a time. For, thanks to your courageous action in this mission which you have just accomplished, whatever the future holds for the United States Navy in the years that lie ahead, you and the USS *Ranger* will hold a formidable and cherished place in its history."

CHAPTER 7

U.S.S. BON HOMME RICHARD

Admiral Keppel, R.N.	British C.-in-C., Battle of Ushant, 1778
Lieutenant Horatio Nelson, R.N.	Future Admiral Lord Nelson of Trafalgar Fame
Lieutenant Richard Dale, U.S.N.	Executive Officer, USS *Bon Homme Richard*
Captain Pearson, R.N.	Captain, HMS *Serapis*
Captain Landias, U.S.N	Captain, USS *Alliance*
King Louis XVI	King of France (1774–1793)
King George III	King of Britain and her Colonies (1760–1820)
Lord North	King George III's Prime Minister

By the year 1779 France had officially entered the war with America against Britain, an event of crucial importance for the rebellious self-declared independent colonies if they wished to wrest power from mother England. Supported by the Spaniards, the French Navy made a somewhat indecisive entry into the war; for after they had engaged the British Royal Navy off the Ushant they and Admiral Keppel on

HMS *Victory* returned to their respective bases, with neither side claiming victory.

After his triumph on USS *Ranger*, Captain John Paul Jones was at a loose end and only too eager to embark on another mission which might give him and those under his command greater glory and at the same time help the cause of his adopted country America. To this end he struck up conversation with his old friend Dr. Benjamin Franklin on one of his many visits to him in Paris. Entering the American Representative's palatial office, he was warmly greeted by Franklin, who said to him, "Good afternoon to you, Captain Paul Jones. You are looking rather depressed. Is there anything the matter with you?"

"Anything the matter, Sir! Well, I am like a fish on dry land, and I am afraid that I am becoming rather impatient with hanging around here," was the Captain's despondent reply.

"Well, you proved yourself very well on the USS *Ranger* and, take it from me, judging from the correspondence I am receiving from Congress in Philadelphia, you are very highly thought of indeed, particularly by the Marine Committee," said the Commissioner, trying to reassure him that he had not been forgotten. But the Captain, who was of the opinion that he was missing an opportunity of proving himself of even greater value as a thorn in Britain's flesh, said, "I fully appreciate your sentiments and the attitude of Congress, but let's look at what we achieved on the USS *Ranger* as being part of the general struggle; and, as you know, Sir, that is far from over."

"I appreciate that," replied Franklin, "but now that the French are on our side I personally can see the light, dim though it may be as yet, at the end of the tunnel," replied a proud and more confident Franklin, who by his diplomatic skill had drawn the forces of King Louis XVI to the side of America.

"Yes, Sir, I must congratulate you on the excellent work that you have done for our country, but, so far as naval operations are concerned, wars are won on the high seas and not in offices, either in

Philadelphia or Paris," said the Captain in a polite but firm manner, being aware of the influence his political master had with the French Marine.

"So, to put it in a nutshell, Captain, you are once again eager to go back to sea and carve a name for yourself. Is that not the case, may I ask?"

"Indeed it is, Sir, for I did not join the young United States Navy to be hanging about ports but to help this great cause of liberty and freedom. As regards carving a name for myself, that is a secondary consideration, for one has to be at sea in order to prove oneself. And, who knows, there might be something of a fiasco, like the joint French and Spanish Battle of the Ushant against the Royal Navy or, worse still, one could have one's head blown off by a cannon, or one might obtain a great naval victory. But whatever the result, something must be tried."

"Yes, Captain," replied Franklin, "your valour and courage are in no way in doubt, and I will see what I can do to get you on the high seas once again, as soon as the opportunity arises."

"Well, Sir," retorted the Captain, "it is ludicrous being land-bound when there is such an important war being waged, and for my part I am determined to play an active role in it, so that we will eventually arrive at a victorious conclusion."

"Well, if it is of any interest to you, Captain, I am awaiting instructions from Congress which will authorise me to purchase a new frigate, which I will have no hesitation in placing under your command," said Franklin.

"That's very kind of you, Sir. When will I come back and see you?"

Pondering, Franklin looked at his calendar and said, "If my estimates are correct there should be a mail packet in, any day now, containing correspondence from Congress and instructions as to the ship to be purchased and the role it should play. So that I can liaise with the French Minister of Marine on the matter, can you call in and see me a month from today?"

"Thank you for all your help then, Sir, and I will be looking forward to seeing you in a month's time. In the meantime I shall keep my fingers crossed hoping that something positive develops between now and then," said the Captain, who was much more optimistic now that he had won the favour of his political superior in France.

Being a highly organised and competent individual, it was exactly one month later that Captain Paul Jones presented himself to Dr. Franklin, only hoping that there was something on the cards for him at last. Although he had been inclined to be sceptical, his hopes were eventually to be fulfilled when the Commissioner said to him, "Relax, Captain Paul Jones, I have good news for you. But this is a much bigger task than you undertook on the USS *Ranger*."

The Captain, beaming like a child with a new toy, said excitedly, "What is the news, Sir?"

"Well, Captain, Congress has authorised me to purchase an excellent second-hand frigate of 40 guns, which is in first-class condition and will be under your command on this next mission, on which we shall jointly embark with the French Navy."

A much more relaxed Captain said in reply, "That's the best news I have heard for a long time, Sir. Please tell me more about it."

"To start with, Captain," said Dr. Franklin, who was meticulously reading through the correspondence he had received from both Congress and the French Minister of Marine, "it is called *Le Duc de Duras* and will have a complement of around four hundred men."

"That is indeed a challenge, Sir," said a confident Captain. "But don't worry, I will accept it, as I did for my first duties as a cabin-boy, when I sailed to sea as a boy at the age of thirteen."

"Oh, there is no worry about that," said Franklin, "for your track record to date speaks for itself; hence the high esteem in which you are held by the Marine Committee in Congress."

"Well, Sir, I don't know how I can thank you for getting me away to sea again."

"Only one way to thank me and America, Captain," said Dr. Franklin, "and that is, victory on the high seas."

"Oh, I appreciate that, Sir, for once I get to sea it will be my intention to seek victory at all costs. But I was thinking of something more personal than that," said the Captain, with a twinkle in his eye.

"Very good then, Captain; let me know what you have in mind, will you?" said a rather curious Dr. Franklin, not knowing what Paul Jones would come up with next.

"Well, Sir," said Captain Paul Jones, "isn't it right that, as well as your government duties, you write almanacks in your spare time?"

"That's quite correct, and I get great enjoyment following this harmless pursuit. Why do you ask that, may I ask?" enquired Franklin.

"Well, as your *nom de plume* for your almanacks is "Poor Richard," I would like to rename this frigate I am about to command after you and call it the *Bon Homme Richard*, which as you know is the French for Poor Richard."

"Goodness me!" exclaimed Dr. Franklin, holding his hands in the air and with every sign of delight. "That would be a great honour indeed, and it is very kind of you to think of me in that way."

"Not in the least, Sir," said Captain Paul Jones. "It's the least I can do to honour you, for you have been exceptionally good to me since I arrived in France from America, and this is my humble way of showing my very great appreciation for all you have done."

"Well, Captain, I will inform both Congress and the French Minister of Marine about the change of name, just to keep records straight," said the Commissioner, who felt himself greatly honoured to have a ship of the United States Navy named after him and, moreover, the largest ship the infant Navy had possessed since its foundation.

"Well, Sir, I will go away and start planning the sort of crew I will require, for a ship of this size requires a lot of organisation and sound discipline. It is therefore imperative that I select the right officers and men if we are to have any hope of achieving our objectives," said the Captain with an aura of contentment and authority surrounding him; for since the advent of this news he had become a changed man.

"Yes, I think you are very wise in what you are saying, Captain, for, thanks to your experiences on the USS *Ranger*, you have learned the importance of choosing the right sort of crew," said Dr. Franklin.

"You can repeat that again, Sir!" said the Captain. "To have a crew of misfits such as I had on the *Ranger* would probably mean that a battle would be lost before it commenced."

"Mind you, Captain, misfits although many of them may have been, you achieved your objectives, for as you know the British are beginning to exchange prisoners; so the idea of capturing the Earl of Selkirk was not as far-fetched as it sounded, and your actions have had a positive impact on the British Government in London."

"Well, all's well that ends well, Sir, and I hope to muster a crew from among the released prisoners once I know who they are, for some of them have probably served with me before, so I shall know what they are made of."

"Well, Captain, as the King of France has personally decreed that the French will defray all the expenses of making this frigate—which we will now call the *Bon Homme Richard*—one hundred per cent fighting fit, I want you to go straight away and look it over thoroughly from stem to stern and give me a list of what you require in the way of armaments, sails and anything else you may consider necessary for its efficient functioning in battle. I will liaise with the authorities here, so that you can get ready to go to sea as soon as possible," said Dr. Franklin, who was beginning to show strain caused by his long-drawn-out negotiations with the French Government on behalf of Congress.

"Very good, Sir, I will go and draw up a comprehensive list for you and report back as soon as I have appraised the whole situation," said a very cool and confident Captain.

"That's first class then," said Dr. Franklin. "And in the interim I will liaise with the French Ministry of Marine, for by the time you come back there should be something thrashed out formally between the two Governments as to what role you should play—which may be, I think, to lead some form of task force against the British. But I will have more definite information the next time we meet."

It was a zestful Captain Paul Jones who returned a few days later from Lorient to Paris, having looked over his new command and found out what was required to make her 'ship shape and Bristol fashion' so that she might challenge the might of the British Navy. On entering Dr. Franklin's office, he found him sitting behind his large oak-panelled desk, browsing through some important documents that had just come into his possession and were related to the role which Captain Paul Jones would play in his pending mission.

"Good afternoon, Sir. So pleased to see you again. I have just arrived by stage coach from Lorient, and have a full list of items required for the *Bon Homme Richard*."

"Excellent, Captain. Delighted to see you. Or should I say 'Commodore'!"

"What exactly do you mean by that, Sir?" enquired a rather inquisitive Paul Jones.

"Well," replied Dr. Franklin, "I have before me, this very moment, the finalised agreement with the French Minister of Marine, which is entirely in accord with the sentiments of the Marine Committee of Congress."

"Give me the good news then, Sir," said an anxious Paul Jones.

"Well, Congress thinks so very highly of you that you will lead a joint American/French task force, which will consist of six other ships, with the *Bon Homme Richard* being the flagship, you being given the rank of Commodore in charge of the squadron," said a delighted Dr. Franklin.

"Sir, I find this difficult to believe, but it will give me great delight to shoulder such responsibility. But what about the officers senior to me back home in America?"

"Never mind them, Commodore—which I will call you from now on! You have done something which all of them failed to do—that is, to prove yourself an astute and capable officer, from the first day you joined the Navy. So you are getting your just reward."

"With that said, Dr. Franklin, can you give me some further details of the task force and its purpose?" asked Commodore Paul Jones, being now more aware of the added responsibility being placed on his shoulders.

"Well, in all, if my calculations are correct, Commodore, you will have approximately one thousand men under your command, consisting mainly of French men," said Dr. Franklin.

"Does that mean we will come under French Naval Regulations, Sir?"

"Oh, no, Commodore, far from it, for they will sail under the American flag and consequently under United States Naval Regulations, with which you are well familiar by now."

"And the purpose of the mission, may I ask, Sir?" enquired the Commodore, meticulously writing down all the details the Commissioner was giving him.

"Well, Commodore, the primary purpose of the task force which you will command will be to pin down ships of the British Royal Navy off the east coast of Scotland and England."

"And the reason for this?" asked the Commodore.

"Well, it's to distract the attention of the Royal Navy so that the French can launch a joint military and naval attack on southern England."

"That sounds most interesting, Dr. Franklin," said the Commodore, who was gazing over a map of the British Isles, having already formulated in his mind the route he and his ships would take from France.

"Yes, the French have at present over twenty thousand highly trained soldiers ready to embark on such a venture," said the Commissioner.

"Well, let's hope their endeavours this time are much more fruitful than the affair of the Ushant," said the Commodore, who by this time was roughly working out the number of nautical miles to the North Sea via the north of Scotland.

"Yes, Commodore, they will have to make amends for the poor showing in that battle; but I believe that failure was as much due to the illness of the crews as it was to poor seamanship," said Dr Franklin, who was by now becoming an expert on naval affairs as well as in general diplomacy. The Commodore, appreciating the power of the British Royal Navy, went on to say, "The British fleet under the flagship of HMS *Victory* is some force to reckon with. It is my contention that if they had had any Admiral on the *Victory* other than Keppel things might have turned out differently."

"Yes, I believe Admiral Keppel was court-martialled over the affair. The trouble is that, next time round, they might put a much more capable individual in charge, for you are well aware of the fact that they have tremendous resources of manpower to pick from."

"Yes, Dr. Franklin, I am well aware of that, and their reserve of potential flag-officers appears to be limitless. One in particular I was told to look out for in future years is a young chap called Nelson, for I was talking to an old salt just recently who knows of this individual Should he ever attain flag rank and take over HMS *Victory*, he is so hot that he will carve his name in naval history."

"Yes, I also have heard of this young up-and-coming star called Nelson; but if I may say so, Commodore, you already have carved your name in history by your daring raids in the USS *Ranger* and by taking the USS *Bon Homme Richard*, plus the supporting ships that go with it. Now you have the opportunity of enhancing your name even further," said Dr. Franklin, as he slowly paced up and down his office, which was an even more important venue for visitors now that the might of France was behind the American cause.

"Well, Sir, I will make my way to Lorient. One thing I am determined to do is to select the right crews, particularly the officers, for it is my opinion that there are not many bad seamen, just bad officers. From experience, I have found that, given the right living conditions and good leadership, the average sailor will respond to orders under the most trying sailing conditions."

"There is a lot of sound common sense in what you say, Commodore, so I wish you a safe journey on your way to Lorient. My final instructions to you will be delivered by hand in a few weeks, which will give you time to get things organised to your satisfaction," said the Commissioner, warmly shaking Paul Jones's hand and wishing him luck in his next perilous venture.

Making his way to Lorient by stagecoach from Paris, the Commodore was deep in thought, planning his new command. As he quietly mulled things over in his mind he had the face of a man who was very much looking forward to the new challenge set before him. Death or the prospect of it were never words that entered his mind or vocabulary, for his make-up was such that it could be claimed he was fearless of dying; and with a first-class fighting squadron under his command, he would have to instil into his officers and his men an undaunted scorn of death, if the mission were to prove successful.

On arrival in Lorient he found it a beehive of naval and military activity, something he relished. Word got around of the future squadron he was to command and there were men released from Plymouth jail who were clamouring to get on his flagship, the USS *Bon Homme Richard,* for they had previously served with him and knew that he was a man of iron who, although quick-tempered on occasion, was an individual very much in control of a situation. And those who knew him trusted him so much in a difficult situation that they would go to the ends of the earth to serve alongside him, for they were only too well aware of his capabilities on the high seas, come hail, rain or sunshine. To the Commodore's delight, he saw the fruits of his attack on the Earl of Selkirk's estate and of the capture of HMS *Drake* pay off, for the British Government reluctantly exchanged the men for American sailors in British jails. These prisoners, on release from jail, had made their way across to France and were to form the bulk of the *Bon Homme Richard's* crew. It was, however, crucial during this operation that the Executive Officer on his Flagship should be of the temperament and high calibre that would meet his requirements. This requisite was satisfied one day when a tall youngish-looking officer came up to him and said, "Good afternoon to you, Sir, my name is Lieutenant Richard Dale. I have just been released from a British jail and I would just love to serve under you on your flagship for, although I have never met you before, I have many friends that were with you on the USS *Alfred* and the USS *Providence*, and they report highly of you."

Cautiously, the Commodore looked Lieutenant Dale up and down and, after a very thorough and prolonged questioning about his past experience, said, "Lieutenant Dale, you will be my Executive Officer on the USS *Bon Homme Richard*, for I think you have the wherewithal and ability for such an arduous post."

"It will be my honour and pleasure to serve under you, Sir," said a very levelheaded Lieutenant Dale.

"You mentioned in your conversation that had you not been taken prisoner you would probably have been Executive Officer on our recently commissioned frigate, USS *Saratoga*—is that correct?" asked the Commodore, who was happy in his choice of such a levelheaded and energetic young officer as his right-hand man.

"Yes, Sir, that is quite correct, and I am extremely sorry that I missed out on such an appointment, for I am led to believe she is a beautiful ship and a pleasure to handle."

"Yes, Lieutenant Dale, although I have never seen the ship myself; like you, my second-hand information of her is much the same. Mind you, if she lives up to her name she will certainly be a famous ship one day, for I think the Battle of Saratoga, 1777, from which she derives her name, where we decisively routed the British, was a turning point in the war. This paved the way for France's entry into the war, on our side," said the Commodore in a very serious and contemplative mood.

"Well, one never knows, Sir, but if we get out of our pending mission with flying colours, on your recommendation I might become Captain of the USS *Saratoga* one day!" said the young Lieutenant humorously, with a smile on his face.

"Well, I must warn you now, Lieutenant, that it will be no easy task, and you will play a key role in this operation," said the Commodore, as he checked the list of potential officers and crew.

Coolly, Lieutenant Dale said, "Sir, I am at your command as from now. Fire ahead with any orders you wish me to have carried out on your behalf."

"Well, Lieutenant, as you know many of those who have been released from British jails better than I do, you can tell me the good from the bad amongst them," said the Commodore.

"I am a pretty good judge of character, Sir, and what I don't know about them I'll find out through the grapevine amongst the officers and men I do know," replied Lieutenant Dale.

The Commodore continued, "Well, ignore the crewing of the six other ships in the squadron, as that is their own Captain's responsibility, and just concentrate on the personnel we require for the flagship. Remember, I want all officers to be of the highest quality, from the ship's surgeon down through gunnery officers to an efficient purser for accounting purposes—for I intend to take many prizes on this mission."

"Aye, aye, Sir! Leave that to me. However, although I don't want to be disrespectful, Sir, about my superior officers, in the interest of the overall success of our mission I am bound in conscience to tell you about one Captain before we set off on the high seas."

"Yes, that's an important point you raise, Lieutenant Dale We may as well get these problems sorted out whilst we are on dry land, instead of waiting until we are about to go into battle," said the Commodore, having learned his lesson dearly, during his previous mission, about unruly and slovenly men.

"Well, Sir, if you permit me to say so, it is Captain Landias of the USS *Alliance*. He seems to be bragging among the other officers that, being a naturalised American and also senior to you, he should be in command of the Squadron," said Lieutenant Dale, not wanting to give the impression that he was formally complaining about a senior officer in the presence of the task force commander.

"Oh, I see," said the Commodore. "Thank you very much for keeping me informed, for I expected something of this nature and I should imagine there will be greater jealousy on the other side of the Atlantic."

"Well, I don't see why there should be, Sir, for you have at least proved yourself. Having spent some time in a British jail, I have become aware that your name is by now well known throughout the whole of Britain. And believe me, Sir, an awful lot of ordinary people have great respect for you," said the Commodore's young Executive Officer.

With a smile on his face, the Commodore said, "That's very nice to hear, and I must say that it has pleased me indeed. As a matter of fact, I have nothing whatsoever against the ordinary British people, for my bone of contention is not with them but with their pig-headed Government in London. Hence the reason for my taking up the sword in the cause of liberty against oppression." The Commodore spoke in a fatherly manner, beginning by this time to show great affection for his young Lieutenant, for he appreciated the latter's coolness, common sense and maturity—assets which would be tried to their extremity in the months that lay ahead.

Hesitantly, Lieutenant Dale said, "I don't like to be harping on about it, Sir, and if you think I am wrong in what I am saying, please tell me to refrain from discussing the matter. But do you know this Captain Landias of the USS *Alliance*?"

"I have only heard about him vaguely in the past; is there anything you know about him that I should be told? You are quite free to talk; being my Executive Officer, there will be many things that you and I will confide to each other which will be of a confidential nature relating to the rest of the Squadron," said a rather inquisitive Commodore, realising that his Executive Officer would be a source of strength to him in the smooth functioning of the pending operation.

"Well, to put it bluntly, Sir, although I have not personally served under him, many of the people who know him of old reckon he is slightly insane," said Lieutenant Dale.

"Well, I don't know. You could be right in what you say, but I think jealousy plays a big role in his temperament. However, time will tell what sort of character he is," said a rather concerned Commodore.

"With that bit of information between ourselves, Sir, will I now go and get this crew of yours organised?" enquired his Executive Officer, who was rather proud to be serving as the Commodore's right-hand man on his flagship the *Bon Homme Richard*.

"Yes, Lieutenant, you go and acquire these officers, and once you have located them, bring them to me for vetting. And one final point I omitted—get a good Chief Quartermaster, who will be in charge of the wheelhouse, for tricky ship's movements will be of paramount importance when we engage the enemy."

"Aye, aye, Sir, I shall do that for you right away, for I know where to find the right man you are wanting," said Lieutenant Dale, as he smartly saluted the Commodore and swiftly got on his way in seeking the type of men who would come up to the Task Force Commander's high standards.

A few weeks later, with all the victualling complete and crews assembled, the Task Force was ready to sail on its way round the British coast, via the west coast of Ireland, then round the north of Scotland, for they were hoping to meet their first encounter with the enemy somewhere in the North Sea. It was the only sensible route they could have taken to achieve their objective, for going through the Irish Sea or the English Channel would have been very dangerous indeed as they would probably have encountered the enemy much sooner and defeated the purpose of the exercise, which was to engage the Royal Navy in the North Sea off Britain's eastern seaboard.

The crew of the *Bon Homme Richard* was international, the highest single national group being American. Surprisingly, there were a very high number of Englishmen, who had transferred their allegiance to the American flag, along with quite a large number of Irish and Portuguese sailors. All the marines on board were French, in their resplendent uniforms of red coat, white waistcoat and breeches. Their officers were dressed in a blue uniform, with white lapels. This type of turnout suited Commodore Paul Jones, as he was a stickler for smartness and presentable deportment from all men under his command. As he himself set a very high standard in his dress, befitting one holding the rank of Commodore and necessitating even the wearing of his ceremonial sword, his crews were enthralled by his good example and imitated his attitude.

The night before the Task Force sailed, the Commodore had all the remaining Captains aboard his flagship, and explained the operation order to them in detail. As for his own crew, he could see by their cheerful manner that he had men who had willingly volunteered to serve under him and not a bunch of homesick and indolent seamen such as he had had on the USS *Ranger*. The only thing that was required of them now was to put their keenness into action and show what they were made of under fire of battle. Apart from Captain Landias on the USS *Alliance*, the only other factor that gave the Commodore cause for concern was that there were converted privateers in his force. Throughout his career in the United States Navy privateers had been a sore bone of contention with him. Apart from weakening the overall strength of the official Navy by luring sailors away because of slacker discipline and greater prize money, they were only good at commerce destroying. Before the assembled officers returned to their respective ships, the Commodore, being the epitome of naval efficiency, went over the main points again, emphasising the importance of the whole operation, down to who would crew prizes when captured and into what port they would take the prizes.

In early August 1779 the USS *Bon Homme Richard*, in the company of some of her escorts, sailed from Lorient to Croix Roadstead, where she picked up the remainder of the Squadron. They then all set sail on their perilous journey into the unknown. A few days away from France, two of the privateers parted company with the rest of the Squadron. That was the sort of thing which the Commodore had envisaged from the outset, as he had no faith in them whatsoever, whether American or French. In this case they happened to be the latter. They were very fortunate, however, in picking up many prizes en route and, as preplanned, sent these to their respective ports with the crews that had been allocated to them before leaving France. Prizes taken further north, around the north-west coast of Scotland, were, however, sent into Bergen in Norway, where there was an agent appointed to receive and dispose of them.

Apart from the breaches of discipline on the part of one or two ships, such occurrences were not uncommon in that period of naval history, and apart from the taking of the prizes, it was a relatively calm passage, until they rounded the north of Scotland in the first week of September. Then, making their way slowly down the east coast of Scotland, the Commodore hatched the grandiose plot of raiding Leith, which is the port of Edinburgh, and of demanding a ransom instead of razing it to the ground. The Commodore, realising the defenceless position of Scotland after the 1745 rebellion, thought that if he levelled his guns on the old port of Leith, the ransom would be there for the picking without a shot being fired. However, his plans went wrong when the winds changed and he had no alternative but to proceed on his journey southward. Again, a few days later, he had the same idea in connection with Newcastle, as this was an important town on England's east coast supplying London with coal. His strategy was that, if he could cut off the winter coal supply to London, the nerve centre of power in Britain, he would be greatly helping the overall cause, which was, in the European theatre at least, to create as much havoc and inconvenience as possible on the east coast of England, enabling the French to have a good crack at England's southern flank. This plan, like that on Leith, for tactical reasons failed to bear fruit. So he continued south to rendezvous with his main quarry near Flamborough Head, which lies between Hull and Scarborough in a most picturesque part of Yorkshire.

It was on a relatively calm afternoon that the Commodore spotted on the horizon a fleet of forty-one ships of sail, whose encounter was just too good to be true. For here was the opportunity he yearned for—to have the chance of carving his name in the annals of history of the United States Navy as being its ablest and most dashing commander. From local seamen recently captured he learned that this was a convoy of merchantmen from the Baltic, escorted by HMS *Serapis* and HMS *Countess of Scarborough*. The former was a frigate of 50 guns, the latter a sloop of 20 guns. The Commodore, having trained his glass on both ships, realised that, if the outcome of any foray were to be successful, he would need to use all his skill and naval ingenuity, for HMS *Serapis* in particular was a much more modern ship than the *Bon Homme Richard*, with much greater striking power due to the number of large guns she possessed. Realising the disadvantage they were at before a shot was even fired did not perturb the Commodore or his crew. Yet they realised that, once they engaged with the enemy, it would be a fight to the kill. Therefore, strategy on the part of Commodore Paul Jones and his men, particularly his officers, was of paramount importance if they wished to attain victory against an enemy which, on paper at least, was greatly superior to them. The Commodore was eager to engage the convoy, knowing that it was carrying supplies for the Royal Navy; but before he could have a go at it he had either to capture or sink the escorting ships. So from now on this was the aim on which he primarily concentrated his thoughts and efforts.

Once the Commodore had fully sighted his enemy, the crews took up their assigned positions, whether they were aloft, on deck or below. At the same time, the marines marched up and down, beating their drums, which was the call for general quarters. Everything was ready for action now, with all guns being shotted, the gunners standing by waiting for the sole command, "Fire!"—which would trigger off the battle between the United States Navy and the British Royal Navy. As the hour was getting late, a full moon was beginning to rise; the sea, like a mill pond, was so calm that it required additional studding sail on the *Bon Homme Richard* to make any headway at all in the slight breeze that overcame that part of the North Sea.

When both ships came within range of one another, with HMS *Serapis* being practically parallel with the USS *Bon Homme Richard* on the former's larboard side, Captain Pearson, RN, hailed the Commodore, who was flying British colours, and enquired what ship it was. When the reply from the *Bon Homme Richard* could not be heard properly on the *Serapis*, Captain Pearson blurted out on his hailer, "If you don't answer immediately, I'll open fire!" No sooner had he said that than the Commodore lowered the British flag and, raising the Stars and Stripes, gave the order to fire his starboard guns. Firing simultaneously, the *Serapis* gained a distinct advantage due to a mishap on the *Bon Homme Richard* when the battery was put out of action by two eighteen-pounders which killed many gunners and blew up part of the upper deck. It looked a very bad omen indeed for the Commodore, who ordered his Quartermaster to get the frigate in a position so as to rake the *Serapis*. But Captain Pearson thought likewise; and, seeing the condition of the *Bon Homme Richard* after they had exchanged a few broadsides, the Commodore said to Lieutenant Dale, "Because of their gunnery supremacy, a gun-to-gun battle is out; so we shall have to grapple, and reduce the encounter to hand-to-hand fighting when we board."

"Aye, aye, Sir, I'll inform the Officer Commanding the Marines of your intentions." With that, he had a boy seaman messenger deliver the Commodore's instructions. Reducing the topsails, the Commodore ordered his Chief Quartermaster at the helm to take the *Bon Homme Richard* across the stern of the *Serapis*, on the starboard quarters, so that they could grapple and board it. But because of the awkward angle at which the *Bone Homme Richard* crossed the enemy's ship, Captain Pearson had little difficulty in warding off the potential boarders, which left the Commodore in no position but to try and work out his next move. In the meantime, the sky was alight with a mixture of fire and gunsmoke. The gun-deck of the *Bon Homme Richard* was like a river of blood, with dying men groaning from the wounds they had sustained. In the midst of all this mêlée, with yards and sails all over the place, the Commodore was adamant that his force should continue to fight to the death, and encouraged his men not to give up, even though the odds by now were stacked against him.

Captain Pearson saw the hopeless position the *Bon Homme Richard* was in, with sailors running all over the place extinguishing fires. He realized that, if he crossed the American's bow, all he had to do was rake her with the full power of the armoury at his disposal, and the fight would be over, with the Commodore having no alternative but to surrender. But the helmsman's angle was too acute, and instead of crossing the 'T', all that happened was that the *Bon Homme Richard's* bowsprit ended up in the stern of the *Serapis* getting stuck in its mizzen mast. Chaos aboard the American frigate was such that Captain Pearson thought it opportune to call out, "Are you going to surrender then?" This enquiry was like a red rag to a bull to Commodore Paul Jones who, his mind flashing back to his schooldays when he confronted the local bully, Douglas Maxwell, responded with his famous reply: "I HAVE NOT YET BEGUN TO FIGHT!"

Because of his adamant determination not to surrender, where lesser mortals would have thrown in the towel, Commodore Paul Jones, because of his indomitable spirit, planned his next move in order to outwit HMS *Serapis*. And with the few guns he still had at his disposal he ordered the Chief Quartermaster to turn the helm to larboard so as to take the *Bon Homme Richard* round to starboard and inflict on Captain Pearson what the latter had tried on him. This was to take his frigate across the bows of the *Serapis* and, in naval jargon, cap the 'T', so that he could rake the enemy's deck. However, instead of achieving this in one clean sweep, all that happened was that the bowsprit of the *Serapis* ended up in the *Bon Homme Richard's* shrouds. And in the midst of all this, *Serapis's* forward upper deck guns were booming away creating havoc with the *Bon Homme Richard's* sails and shrouds.

The Commodore now had to think quickly, for the longer the bloody debacle continued the sadder the outlook for the *Bon Homme Richard* became, with fire, blood, displaced rigging on the decks, and injured men rolling about in agony, not forgetting the dead bodies, which were from a strategic point of view at least of little use to those left to fight it out. So, turning to his Executive Officer, the Commodore said, "Lieutenant Dale, our only chance left is to grapple and hope that our maintop men can make short work of the enemy on deck with their sharpshooting and grenades. For if we fail to do this and they aim their two decks of eighteen-pound guns at our three masts simultaneously, and were these to go, I am afraid that those of us left alive will end up prisoners of dear old mother England."

"Well, Sir, that's the last thing any of us want but I must say things look pretty bleak at the moment. However, as soon as we get into the position to grapple, I'll have all other officers and men fully briefed on what to do," said his very competent Executive Officer, who was showing his true colours as a real protégé of the Commodore. Meanwhile USS *Pallas* and HMS *Countess of Scarborough* were pounding away at one another some distance from either of them. And USS *Alliance* was keeping her distance, not wanting to join the affray. In the height of battle, this prompted the Commodore to remark to Lieutenant Dale, "I think this Captain Landias is not only insane but also cowardly."

"Yes Sir, as I told you earlier, he will be more of a liability than an asset to us."

Because of the rising wind, the *Bon Homme Richard* backed her top sails, and this checking of her speed proved to be the Commodore's blessing in disguise for, with it, both ships manoeuvred until the *Bon Homme Richard* was facing due south and the *Serapis* due north. And in the process of this move the starboard anchor of the *Serapis* got caught up in the *Bon Homme_Richard's* bulwarks on the starboard quarter. Both ships were so close to one another that their guns were touching. It was a delighted Commodore, with sweat pouring down his face, which was partially blackened now with gunsmoke, who said to his Executive Officer, "Excellent, Lieutenant Dale, this is what we were waiting for; so now that we have secured the grappling irons I want you to relay my order to all crew members that I want my previously-mentioned plan put into action."

"Aye, aye, Sir," replied the Lieutenant, "I will send the messenger boys to the respective officers in question without delay."

Captain Pearson on HMS *Serapis* was quick to realise the Commodore's strategy. As the *Bon Homme Richard's* condition was so pitiful, with the bulk of her guns out of action, all the Commodore had left was the use of musketry to kill the sailors and marines on the main deck of the *Serapis*. The Captain of the *Serapis* realised that all that was required of him was to break away from the *Bon Homme Richard* and deliver the full cannon volley from both his starboard gun decks, and that would put an end to the Commodore's aspirations once and for all. When he endeavoured to cut the grappling hooks he had a surprise awaiting him, because the accuracy of *Bon Homme Richard's* sharpshooters killed or injured the party of sailors as they were trying to carry out their orders. Captain Pearson's next move was to drop anchor, in the hope that the wind and tide would assist him in breaking the deadly grip of the *Bon Homme Richard*. All this did, in point of fact, was to swing both ships round in the opposite direction, as the American frigate clung to the *Serapis* as the tentacles of an octopus cling to rocks. So the move was really counter productive. As the status quo remained, the only difference now was that the bow and stern of each frigate was in the direction opposite to that in which it had previously been. What this manoeuvre meant for Captain Pearson was that his larboard guns were no longer of any use to him; and his starboard gun-ports, which were shut during the earlier part of the battle, could not be removed, as they normally could, being so close to the *Bon Homme Richard* that they had to be blown off by cannon fire. Once the British had done this, however, they created further havoc on the American frigate, for their perpetual pounding away at the *Bon Homme Richard* put its main battery of twelve-pounders out of action also, leaving the Commodore with only three nine-pounders left on the quarter-deck.

If the Commodore started the battle at a disadvantage because of having fewer guns and, after a while, losing all his eighteen-pounders because of their dangerous and unserviceable condition, then losing his twelve-pounders in the last incident, he was now reduced to three nine-pounders with which to challenge an enemy who was still fighting fit from a gunnery aspect—all the odds of winning were stacked against him now. His only chance, and it was very difficult with the movement of both ships, was to pound the masts of the *Serapis*. So, informing his Executive Officer, he said, "Lieutenant Dale, ensure that the maintopmen concentrate on killing every one of the enemy as soon as they appear on the main deck from below. And, as our main guns are out of action, ensure that the powder boys supply them with all the grenades we have left in the ship's magazine, for they can be put to good use."

"Aye, aye, Sir," said his Executive Officer, wiping the sweat off his brow.

In the midst of this furore, with *Serapis's* guns still booming wildly away, slowly battering the internal parts of the *Bon Homme Richard* to pulp, with fire breaking out all over the place, the only beacon of hope left for the poor frigate was that the fore, main and mizzen masts were still standing, even though part of the gundecks had collapsed. And, to add insult to injury, the USS *Alliance*, which appeared from nowhere, started to rake its own flagship. On the first occasion, Captain Landias attacked the stern of the *Bon Homme Richard* and, veering wildly to starboard, delivered some lethal shots to its bows. Not only holing it below the waterline, he killed a few men into the bargain.

"What the hell is up with Captain Landias?" shouted the Commodore to his Executive Officer.

"I told you, Sir, the man's a raving lunatic. But see him move away now, Sir. I bet I know what he's up to, which is for us to sink—then he will attack the *Serapis* and snatch all the glory."

"Snatch all the glory!" shouted the Commodore. "All the glory he will snatch, if we get out of this alive, is a court martial, and I'll see to that."

"I agree with your sentiments, Sir," said Lieutenant Dale, "but he will probably argue that because of the fire and smoke around here he thought we were the enemy. For that's the jealous sneak he is, Sir."

"He will argue that line over my dead body," replied a furious Commodore.

Running up to the Commodore, gasping, a boy messenger said, "Sir, Sir, we are taking in water fast, where we were holed on the larboard bow just below the waterline. The deck officer down there sent me up to tell you!"

"Right, boy seaman, go and tell the officer in question to do his best to get the hole patched up, and get all the released prisoners to man the pumps, telling them to pump like hell if they value their lives."

"Aye, aye, Sir," said the boy messenger, who was so excited that, on turning round, he bumped into Lieutenant Dale and nearly knocked him down the companion leading from the poop deck.

In the meantime, the marksmen on the tops were doing a first-class job, for they were popping the enemy off like flies on the British frigate. But just with that an excited officer appeared and said to the Commodore, "Sir, we have taken in over five feet of water. For God's sake surrender or we will all drown." Determinedly the Commodore replied, "I will *not* surrender, for I would sooner sink first. But I will make the *Serapis* surrender." Whilst everyone around him was losing their nerve, apart from his able Executive Officer, Paul Jones said to one of the men standing near a nine-pounder: "Give me a hand to take this gun across to the starboard quarter and then double-shot it for me immediately."

"Aye, aye, Sir" And they both prepared the gun for action, for the normal gunner had just been seriously injured in the head. The Commodore then manned the gun himself. The *Serapis* guns still boomed away, but to little avail for the shots were now going straight through the *Bon Homme Richard* and into the sea, as a result of the perpetual pounding both the starboard and larboard tops had been taking. As the main yards of the *Bon Homme Richard* were now well over the deck of the *Serapis*, the Commodore said to his Executive Officer, "Right then, Lieutenant Dale, get as many men as possible along to the end of the yards overhanging the enemy, and let them have it with all the grenades at our disposal."

"Aye, aye, Sir," said the Lieutenant, who went on to ensure that the Commodore's orders were promptly carried out. This appeared to be a crucial move on the part of the Commodore, for while his marines bombarded the *Serapis* with grenades, not only leaving the top deck desolate, strewn with blood and covered with dead bodies, they also managed to get the grenades through the hatches to the main gun decks below, causing untold havoc, which could be seen by the number of fires that were alight on many parts of the ship. As all this was going on, the Commodore kept up the double-shotted nine-pounder unremittingly, until the main mast of the *Serapis* started to creak. With all these things happening at the same time to the British frigate, Captain Pearson panicked and surrendered, as he had no men to assist him, for the minute anyone appeared from the decks below he was immediately bumped off by the Commodore's marksmen.

With Captain Pearson's surrender, the Commodore sent Lieutenant Dale and a boarding party across to the captured *Serapis*. Things were looking up for the Commodore, for HMS *Countess of Scarborough* had just surrendered to USS *Pallas*. Having established United States Naval authority on board the *Serapis*, Lieutenant Dale escorted Captain Pearson aboard the *Bon Homme Richard* (or what was left of her) and introduced him to the Commodore, who accepted the formal surrender. This was carried out in the high traditions of 18th century naval procedure, with the defeated handing over his sword to the victor, a symbol of laying down arms. Accepting Pearon's sword, the Commmodore congratulated Captain Pearson on his excellent fight, and duly returned the weapon to him. And taking him into what was left of his ramshackle cabin he shared a glass of wine with his enemy. During this piece of important naval etiquette, the Commodore said to his prisoner, "Yes, Sir, I thought of bumping you off on many occasions, as you were a sitting target; but I ordered my men to leave you alone, as I wanted you as prisoner."

Even in defeat, Captain Pearson had a sense of humour, for he said, "Great minds think alike, Sir, for I ordered my men also not to interfere with you, for I similarly wanted you as my prisoner. As things turned out, however, it did not happen that way, as you are the victor."

Just as Captain Pearson finished talking, there was a terrible thud on the quarterdeck of the *Bon Homme Richard*. Looking out of his cabin, the Commodore said, "There goes your main mast, Sir. It has just landed on our ship. However, when I see all those poor souls lying dead, all around us on both frigates, we are lucky to be alive to fight another day."

As the Commodore had just completed the last part of his statement, instead of living to fight another day, both of them nearly ended up in eternity at the same time. For there was an almighty explosion, which neither of them had never experienced before, on board the *Bon Homme Richard*. The frigate's magazine had blown up—throwing both of them from one end of the Commodore's cabin to the other, with part of its deck collapsing underneath them. Luckily, Lieutenant Dale was just outside the cabin at the time and managed to get them both out before the whole cabin floor caved into the deck below, which by this time was on fire; but although the blaze was spreading, the crew managed to contain it and eventually have it extinguished.

The bloody and gruelling battle, which had gone on relentlessly for nearly four hours, took a terrible toll of lives, injuries and severe damage to both ships. Casualties were heavy for both frigates, with the *Bon Homme Richard* losing around one hundred and fifty men, whilst the *Serapis* lost something over one hundred marines and sailors. Whilst all the dead were consigned to the deep, with full naval honours, the surgeons of both ships worked unsparingly to attend to all those injured. The Senior Surgeon, Jones, who bore the same name as the Commodore had added to his original one, was a medium-built dark-haired Welshman with a sallow complexion and a very affable manner. Because of his medical skill, there were many sailors and marines from both frigates walking the highways and byways of their respective countries many years later, who had this genius of a man to thank for saving their lives.

For nearly a day and a half after the battle, the carpenters and their mates worked like beavers, with the prisoners operating the pumps continuously. Unfortunately, their courageous efforts were of no avail, for it got to the stage that water was coming in as quickly as they were pumping it out. When it reached the lower deck, the Commodore saw his flagship to be beyond saving so he ordered all remaining crew, together with the prisoners he had captured on his way to the scene of the battle, to be transferred to the *Serapis*. Sadly, when everyone was safe, he then himself made his way aboard his coveted captured frigate, at the same time transferring his flag from the beleaguered *Bon Homme Richard*. A few hours later it was a very emotional Commodore and crew who witnessed the frigate, which was to make them famous in the annals of United States naval history, go down slowly and gracefully, bow first, into the cold salty waters of the North Sea, to join the gallant heroes from both countries who had just previously preceded her to a sea-bed grave.

Having severed the grappling irons after he transferred his flag, the Commodore immediately set about getting the *Serapis* into ship-shape condition again and fully seaworthy once more. To this end, all crew members, particularly carpenters and sail-makers, worked as they had never worked before, for they were all very proud of their heroic achievement in battle and now looked up to Commodore Paul Jones not as their task force commander but as if he were the Deity himself. But the Commodore, who was as keen on a ship's administration as he was on its fighting ability, started checking the list of Royal Navy prisoners he now had in his possession. And calling over his Executive Officer he said, "Lieutenant Dale, this is beyond all realms of belief, for see your opposite number on the enemy side, Lieutenant Dominic Archer?—if it is the same one I am thinking of, and I am a hundred per cent sure I am right, then he was my best friend at school in Scotland." Checking the list over, Lieutenant Dale said, "Well, Sir, if this is true, it is incredible but not improbable. For you know I have met friends of mine from the same small town in Virginia in the oddest of places."

With a smile on his face, the Commodore then told his Executive Officer to release Lieutenant Archer and send him to his cabin straight away. When Lieutenant Archer arrived at the Commodore's cabin he touched his hat and they both looked momentarily at one another in complete dismay. And Lieutenant Archer then said in excitement as he shook his head, "Sir, am I seeing things? I would recognise you anywhere, but I still cannot believe it is you." But the Commodore, hugging him warmly, said, "I can't believe it's you either, but I know it is you, and isn't it a small world indeed? Come, sit down and let's have a small glass of wine and talk about old times. Goodness me, don't we have a lot to talk about! And only call me 'Sir' in the company of others, for when we are on our own it's still like schoolday first-name terms."

So he and his old schooldays' friend discussed in depth for over an hour what had happened to them both since they went their own different ways after leaving school. And when Dominic intimated he was leaving the Royal Navy as soon as this ghastly war was over, which in the opinion of each of them need never have been started had things been handled properly by London at the outset, the Commodore was quick to offer him a commission in the United States Navy. On Dominic's leaving the Commodore's cabin, the Commodore shook hands with his friend and his final words were, 'Dominic, you will be the best-looked-after prisoner of war who was ever captured on the high seas!"

After getting the *Serapis* fully seaworthy again, in the company of the other captured Royal Navy ship, they all cruised in a leisurely way over the North Sea and pulled in at the Texel, which was an island off the coast of Holland. After some time there, until they thought the coast was clear of British Navy ships, they made their way back to France; the Commodore having transferred his flag to the USS *Alliance*. By this time there was such a furore throughout Britain that the

Admiralty in London had sent out additional ships to attempt once again to capture the Commodore, at all costs.

The ironic thing was that they looked for him everywhere but in the right place—the north and west coasts of Scotland, the Irish channel, the west coast of Ireland; but the slippery Commodore Paul Jones managed to evade them all and eventually made his way back to France through the English Channel, the most dangerous area of all, it being so narrow. It was therefore a proud Commodore John Paul Jones who sailed into Lorient, with a jubilant crew, not realising that in the annals of United States Naval History this was to be his finest hour.

On arrival back in France, the Commodore was given a hero's welcome, beyond his own belief, for the great victory he had achieved at sea, against all the odds. For having the inferior ship of the two and losing his armaments at the commencement of the engagement, he should have lost the battle shortly after it commenced. And at one stage he was not only fighting Pearson but also the mad, jealous and spiteful Captain Landias of the USS *Alliance*. However, the Commodore came out on top in the case of Captain Landias, for when he submitted his report to the Marine Committee of Congress, the Skipper of the *Alliance* was court-martialled and dismissed from the United States Navy.

When he met his political superior and old friend in Paris, Dr. Franklin, the American Representative said to him, "How in the name of God did you achieve such a victory in these circumstances?"

"Well, Sir," replied a proud Commodore, "it was a matter of keeping one's head and encouraging the crew, when all the others round one were losing theirs."

"Well, Commodore, I have a letter here before me from the King, making you a Chevalier of France," said Dr. Franklin.

"That's very kind and considerate of the French authorities to bestow such an honour on me, Sir, which I really do cherish."

"Well, may I say that your decisive action in the North Sea against the British has been reported so much on either side of the Atlantic and has so greatly boosted the American-French Alliance that things are beginning to look up now, both on land and at sea. And if we persevere the way we are doing we should achieve victory very shortly."

As the Commodore sat listening to Franklin, as proud as a peacock, one of his secretaries came in and said, "There is a letter here for you, Sir, under the Royal Seal, from the Palace of Versailles."

"Thank you very much," said Franklin, who on breaking the seal and reading its contents, looked up at the Commodore with a beaming smile all over his face and said, "Commodore, there is a Royal Command here which says you have to be presented before the King."

"Goodness me, Sir! This is indeed an honour, which will give me great satisfaction and joy. Although I will go there personally, I will not only be representing that gallant crew of mine but also those courageous men of the *Bon Homme Richard* whose grave is the cold icy waters of the North Sea."

"Yes, Commodore, although you will deserve it, you really have to be someone to be presented at the Palace of Versailles these days; and may I, on behalf of the United States Government, congratulate you on your great achievement," said the aged Diplomat, who intimated that all this information would be officially reported to a grateful Congress in the United States.

"Once again, Sir, thank you for the compliments, for the way things are going I will soon have more honours than Catherine the Great of Russia has lovers," said the Commodore, with a twinkle in his eye and a broad smile on his face.

To which Franklin humorously replied, "You will be going some, for I don't think that if you put all the international honours available at present on your chest they would equal the number of lovers our Catherine has gone through—she goes through them as a hot knife goes through butter!"

In full naval regalia, wearing the insignia of a Chevalier of France, it was a smart and elegant Commodore Paul Jones who made his way to the Palace of Versailles outside Paris, to be presented to His Most Christian Majesty, King Louis XVI of France. On arriving there, he slowly made his way through the architectural splendour of the Palace until he arrived at the Royal Chamber. Being ushered in by one of the royal household, and having removed his tricorn hat, he duly paid homage to His Most Christian Majesty by kissing hands. Being a man of very few words, King Louis thanked him for the courageous battle he had fought off Flamborough Head and how he had turned what looked to be an obvious defeat into a resounding victory; and said that his success had played a very important role in raising the morale of France, for which the whole nation was greatly indebted to him. And, in recognition of the fruits of his valiant battle, the King presented him with a personal gift of an inscribed gold-hilted sword. And the Commodore indicated that when his memoirs were published, he would present, as a personal gift from himself, a gold-embossed leather-bound copy to His Most Christian Majesty, who said he awaited them with much pleasure. Before the Commodore took leave of King Louis, he thanked the Monarch for the most precious gift of the sword and for the honour he had bestowed on himself and those who served under him by granting him an audience. So, bidding the King farewell, he entered the dazzling sunlit royal courtyard and made his way back to Paris, to spend what he later termed the happiest and most joyous time of his life. Little wonder that he had such pleasant experiences there, for, being treated like a hero everywhere he went, he was showered with congratulations and invitations to join in the stream of high society's social life. Being an amorous individual, he did this with the same enthusiasm as when directing a battle on the high seas. But being a refined Officer at heart, he reverted to his soft-spoken and romantic mannerisms, leaving behind him the language of the quarterdeck, which was purely for sailors in a right situation and not for the sophisticated *mesdemoiselles* he enthralled by his dynamism. And with them he had many happy and memorable encounters but nothing of a permanent nature, for Commodore Paul Jones epitomised the eternal sailor from time immemorial—a girl in every port.

CHAPTER 8

FAREWELL TO EUROPE
AND A TRIUMPHANT
WELCOME IN AMERICA

Mr. Robert Morris	United States Agent of Marine
Admiral de Grasse	Commander-in-Chief, French High Seas Fleet
Lord Cornwallis	British Commander-in-Chief, Yorktown
General Washington	American Commander-in-Chief Yorktown; and First President of the United States of America (1789–1797)

Having been treated as a celebrity everywhere he went in France, the Commodore now had to return to America, which he had not seen for over three years. Apart from being known in United States naval circles, he left that country, like so many other captains before and after him, comparatively unknown. His return this time, up the Delaware River to Philadelphia, from which he had set out on his first ship of the United States Navy, the USS *Alfred*, was very different for him. For every one who had heard of a captain in the infant navy, thousands throughout the whole nation, from General Washington downwards, had heard of John Paul Jones who, without a shadow of doubt, was now the jewel in the crown of the United States Navy, with a solid track record behind him to give justification to this claim.

As he was by nature an individual with no strong roots, his attitude with the fairer sex was to root them out, cultivate them, entertain and seduce them, and then (in the age-old maritime tradition) forget them. And this was most certainly true of his experiences in France, with the exception of one, who was of more trouble to him than any enemy on the high seas had ever been. She could only be described as 'la belle'—the young daughter of a French aristocrat, her beauty being stunning to say the least. Called Mademoiselle Thérèse, of medium build, five foot two inches tall, with brown eyes and long, flowing dark hair, she was the epitome of what is seductive in a lady. She was also the determined type who would not take 'No' for an answer if her mind was set on a specific goal; for, when it came to the point of her having a particular objective in mind, she would use all her feminine charm to obtain her goal.

The Commodore during his stay in Paris was having a very strong affair with this young lady, but it was becoming rather too serious for his roving nature; so he decided to give her the slip, as he would do with any ships in awkward circumstances, by making some genuine excuse that he would be unable to see her for a few days. This gave him time to pack his belongings and make his way to the port of Lorient, where his sloop of war, the USS *Ariel*, was now fully rigged out and laden for him to take back to America. He was not clever enough, however, to elude Thérèse for, with her feminine intuition, she suspected something was amiss. Making tentative enquiries at the French Ministry of Marine in Paris, which only a woman in her social position could do, she found out the name of the ship, the port, the date, and the time it was due to sail across the Atlantic. And, lo and behold, the charming and vivacious Mademoiselle Thérèse presented herself at the gangway of the USS *Ariel*, much to the delight of the crew who were getting ready to be on their way the following day. She was stopped from boarding the sloop, however, by two swarthy members of the United States Marine Corps, who were on guard duty to ensure that no unauthorized persons boarded the ship. The marines on guard duty realised, on seeing her, that she was someone special and very different from the high class daughters of joy whom they had occasionally seen about docksides when they were being entertained by certain ship's officers. So one of the guards addressed her politely, "Yes, Madam, can I help you?"

An indication that she had received a good education was apparent when she replied in impeccable English, "Yes, marine, I think you can; is this Commodore Paul Jones's ship?"

"You mean the most famous officer in the United States Navy, Madam?" smiled the tall marine, who was clearly very proud to be associated with the Commodore and the true stories he could tell when they arrived back home about his gallant and heroic exploits.

Having confirmed it was her lover's ship, she said to the marine, "Being a long-standing and true friend of the Commodore's, can I come aboard and see him?"

"Sorry, Madam," was the marine's firm but polite reply; "all the entertaining has now ended aboard, with the last guests leaving about two hours ago; and the Commodore has given strict instructions that no civilians are to be allowed on board for we are preparing to sail tomorrow."

There ensued a somewhat heated debate between the young mademoiselle and the guards. And if they were firm, she was equally adamant that she should be allowed to see Paul Jones. To the delight of the crew, who were carrying out their seamen's tasks aboard ship, they could not help but hear what was going on, particularly those who were working near the gangway. The commotion she was causing caught the attention of one of the officers who descended the gangway to investigate the problem.

"Good evening, Madam. Officer of the Watch. I am Lieutenant Joseph Lyden. What can I do for you?"

As he was a tall, good-looking, well-mannered and educated New Englander, Thérèse was not long in calming down and directing her charm to Lieutenant Lyden. After her very long, smooth and convincing story, Lieutenant Lyden, having established that she was not just a one-night stand but meant something more to the Commodore, said, "Well, Mademoiselle Thérèse, I will deliver your message to the Commodore, so please wait until I return, for I am sorry I cannot take you aboard as it is strictly against regulations."

With appealing, come-to-bed eyes, she said, "Lieutenant, that is so kind of you; just you deliver my message, please."

Making his way to the Commodore's quarters, which were below aft, Lieutenant Lyden knocked on the door and, when he was told to enter, went in and saluted the Commodore. Standing smartly to attention he said, "Sorry to disturb you, Sir, but there is a very attractive young lady alongside and she has something important she wants to see you about."

"A young lady!" exclaimed the Commodore, who had been studiously checking charts in order to plan their impending voyage. "What's her name, Lieutenant Lyden?"

"A Mademoiselle Thérèse, Sir."

"Oh, no!" exclaimed the Commodore, burying his head in his hands and sighing, at the same time shaking his head. "How on earth did she know we were sailing from here, for I gave her a different port from this!"

"Well, if you don't mind my saying so, Sir, you know the cunning of a female when she gets something into her mind," said his Officer of the Watch.

"Yes, I do, Lieutenant Lyden; and knowing her only too well I can see that she probably used her charm and influence with the powers that be in Paris to find out the real port we're sailing from. However,

Lieutenant, go and escort her to my cabin, informing the marine guards that she has my personal permission to come aboard."

"Aye, aye, Sir, I shall do that for you right now," said a very conscientious Duty Officer.

"When she entered the Commodore's cabin, he stood up and, with open arms, said, "My darling Thérèse, how did you know I was here?"

Having been his lover for some time she was naturally on very intimate terms with him, and she went on to say, "John, my heroic sailor, that's the advantage of having friends in high places—in the Department of the Marine in Paris."

"Well, as we are due to sail tomorrow, it's very kind of you to come along and say goodbye and wish me bon voyage," said the Commodore, as he strongly embraced her and kissed her forehead. Looking forlornly at the Commodore and still in his embrace she said, to Paul Jones's absolute astonishment, "John, darling, I am pregnant and I am sailing with you to America tomorrow."

The Commodore, taken completely aback by this statement, said to her in complete astonishment, "You're what! Pregnant?"

Holding his cheeks in both hands she continued, "Yes, my sailor boy, I had a medical check-up with a prominent physician in Paris who confirmed it. And, as you know, my darling John Paul Jones, you are the only one I have been with these last few months and, as far as I am concerned, the only one I will ever be with, for you are the love of my life."

The Commodore, being a man of integrity, could not deny the affair he had been having with Thérèse. He said, "My darling Thérèse, we have to be reasonable about this, for, if your allegations are correct, and I have no reason to doubt your claim, then I'll proudly say that I am the father of your child; but, apart from that, there is very little I can do, for the idea of your sailing to America with us is, unfortunately, out."

"But, darling!" she said, as she started to sob, "Why is that?"

The Commodore, who was as cool now as he had been in the height of battle, went on to say, "Thérèse, you must be reasonable and keep a level head in this situation. This being a ship of war, it is strictly against United States Naval Regulations to carry any civilian passengers with us, unless they are on official government duty."

Gathering her composure and wiping the tears away, Thérèse then said, "Darling, I love you so much that I would sail the seven seas with you, purely as your humble mistress."

"Be reasonable now, Thérèse," said the Commodore, gently caressing her hair. "If I took you with me on the *Ariel* back to America it would be an automatic court martial on arrival, for we are sailing into Philadelphia which is the centre of governmental power, and because of our past achievements all eyes will be on us."

"But, John, my darling, what can I do without you, my adorable hero?" said Thérèse.

"Well, my darling, you live in a magnificent chateau outside Paris, with the material comfort of the world at your disposal; whereas my home is where you are now, and that will be only a temporary home until I get my next assignment from the Board of Admiralty in Philadelphia."

Beginning to sob again, Thérèse became very emotional and said, "My dearest, adorable sweetheart, I would swap my château and all the glories of high social life in Paris to share a humble log cabin with you in America."

Calming her down, the Commodore said, "Please, Thérèse, as you are a very reasonable girl, you realise that my mistress is the sea, as it has been since I was a teenage youth."

"Yes, my darling," she continued, "but you will have to settle down some time."

"Well, Thérèse, we will leave that to the future, for my immediate concern is to take this ship safely back to the United States tomorrow." Then, inflating her ego, he said, "Being an intelligent and sophisticated lady, you will understand the position."

As it was getting late, Thérèse, putting both arms round the Commodore's neck, said, "Darling, as there is no stage coach to Paris until tomorrow morning, can I stay aboard with you, and we will have our last night of love, to set the seal on the happy times we have spent together?"

Without hesitation the Commodore said, "Yes, Thérèse, for spending this last night with you will set the seal on my visit to this side of the Atlantic."

"Oh, John, my darling, my courageous sailor," said Thérèse passionately, "this will be a night I shall never forget to my dying day."

"Mind you, Thérèse, this won't be as comfortable as your lavishly furnished château. But don't worry, the two of us won't have to sleep in my cot as I have a collapsible bed that will serve the purpose well," said the Commodore, as they started to undress.

Once they had both undressed and settled comfortably in bed, they embraced passionately, as they had done on so many previous occasions. When their passions were fully aroused they made love frantically, as they had never done before. When it was over, Thérèse said, "Darling, I would go to the ends of the earth for you," as she lay beside him stroking his face and looking seductively into his eyes.

"Yes, my darling Thérèse, as you know, I had many society ladies before I met you; as many as I wished for; but I must say there is something special about you compared with the rest of them. Unfortunately the United States Navy will separate us tomorrow; but we must keep in touch, in view of the impending birth of our child," said the Commodore, who was proud of the fact that he had proved himself not only in battle in engaging the enemy but also in the act of human reproduction.

Thérèse continued, "My darling John, we will most certainly keep in touch, for if I don't get you, I know that I will remain a spinster for the rest of my life."

"That's taking it a bit far now, Thérèse," said the Commodore, who was only now realising how keen she was on him.

"Now, darling John, when the child arrives and is at the age when it can travel by sea, I'll sell all my possessions in France and emigrate to that great country of America, for we will have the opportunity of meeting again, I hope," said a very serious Thérèse.

"That is really considerate, Thérèse," said the Commodore, "for I would just love to see my offspring."

"Well, my darling, I make this solemn promise now, that should I give birth to a boy I will give him the finest education money can buy, get him acquainted with the sea at a very early age, and when he grows up he will enter the United States Navy as an officer, in the steps of his most gallant father."

"If you did that, Thérèse, it would delight me no end; so, remember, we must keep in touch so that I know what develops," said Paul Jones, who was more than happy with the sensible approach Thérèse was taking to the whole situation, realising the predicament he was in, with his loyalties to the United States Navy taking precedence over all others.

As it was now approaching midnight, there was practically complete silence aboard the USS *Ariel*, for apart from the occasional noise of the footsteps of the marines who were guarding the ship, the only other intermittent sound was that of the gently incoming tide breaking against the hull of the ship. So, extinguishing the cabin light, they both went to sleep in one another's embrace, for the last time in France at least, as Thérèse would be making her way back to Paris in the morning, leaving the hero of the United States Navy not only with the most happy and pleasant of memories, but also with the arduous task of safely taking his ship of war across the sometimes treacherous Atlantic.

On this occasion, 'treacherous' was the only word to describe the tempest-torn Atlantic off the north west coast of France.

After the first day out at sea, things became so bad off the infamous Penmarch Rocks that the Commodore had first to reduce sail greatly and then take down all sails. Finally, the howling wind proved so strong that he even had to cut down the masts, which left *Ariel* floundering about helplessly in a boiling sea. This lasted for two days and, as was later verified by the crew, had it not been for the cool-headedness and skill of the Commodore in ship handling, they would have smashed against the perilous rocks, ending up in a cold, watery grave at the bottom of the Atlantic.

When the storm had calmed down, the Commodore ordered his crew to rig a jury mast and thus managed to take his ship back safely into port, to the astonishment of all the port officials, for the chances of any ship surviving a tempest of such magnitude as that which the coastline had just experienced, were zero, or minimal to say the least. This was evident to the crewmembers of the *Ariel* as they made their way back into port, for the coastline was strewn with wrecks that had been dashed against the rocks during the course of the storm. Because of this unforeseen blow struck by nature and the havoc caused to the *Ariel*, the ship's departure was delayed for some considerable time until new masts, sails and rigging were acquired and fitted, so that the sloop of war was once again fully seaworthy to tackle the temperamental Atlantic, which could change very rapidly depending on the weather conditions that prevailed at the time.

The second attempt to make the voyage was much easier in the calmer water the *Ariel* encountered. The Commodore, because of the important load he was carrying in order to supply General Washington's troops, deliberately sought to evade the British Royal Navy. For this reason only he had to change his course drastically to avoid ending up in their claws. Because of the important consignment, Paul Jones told his men that they were making their way back home as quickly as possible, and this delighted them no end for, once back home, they would collect quite a large sum of money from the prizes they had taken previously which had not yet been distributed to them. However, although the capturing of prizes was definitely out, according to the Commodore's plans, a situation arose which he found very tempting. A British privateer of twenty guns, called the *Triumph*, came within such easy reach of him that he thought the opportunity of capturing her too good to ignore. So he decided to have his last fling against the British in mid-Atlantic. By closing gun-ports, keeping crew below deck, and lowering the American flag, the Commodore used the ruse of masquerading as an innocent British merchantman. This move on the part of the Commodore once again paid off, for thanks to the element of surprise he outgunned the pri-vateer and accepted the surrender of the British Captain. But as he was in the process of sending a boarding party on to the *Triumph*, under the command of Lieutenant Carter, USN, the Captain of the privateer, taking advantage of his position and the strong wind, clapped on sails and, to the Commodore's disgust and dismay, gave him the slip.

The remainder of the voyage was very quiet indeed. This was due to the relatively trouble-free sea-lanes the Commodore had specifi-cally chosen. Apart from the few ships that loomed on the horizon, the *Ariel* and its crew practically had the rest of the Atlantic to them-selves. So after a few days, he safely berthed the *Ariel* in Philadel-phia—in the same dock he had left as a relatively obscure Captain a few years before. The situation was very different now, for he was returning as the United States Navy's first hero of the War of Inde-pendence against the British. And the moment he set foot ashore it became perfectly obvious he was the first publicly declared hero of the young and vigorous America, after George Washington, when he was surrounded by reporters wishing to interview him, after word had spread around that the Task Force Commander of the famous USS *Bon Homme Richard* Squadron had returned home to his adopted country.

As the war was nearing its conclusion, Philadelphia was a beehive of political, naval and military activity. The emergent nation was indeed very optimistic that things were developing in its favour. Any chance now of reconciliation between Britain and her fast-maturing unruly daughter had long ago vanished, the young nation now emerging slowly but surely with a confidence that would one day dismay not only her old colonial masters but the rest of the world also.

In consequence of the large-scale movement of troops in Philadelphia, the Officers' Club was particularly busy with naval and army officers passing through. It was into this Club that Lieutenant Richard Dale, USN, went one day for a refreshment, only to meet Lieutenant Mike O'Hara, USN, with whom he had served on the *Bon Homme Richard*. On spotting him in the reading room quietly reading a book, he crept up behind him and said in a low voice, "I have not yet begun to fight." On hearing these words, Lieutenant O'Hara immediately turned round and excitedly said, "Goodness me, Richard! I was in dreamland there, still hearing the spine-chilling echo of the cannons as they went off in that battle we both fought in. And you had to come up from behind, uttering those now famous words to me."

Shaking his hand warmly, Lieutenant O'Hara said, "How pleased I am to see an old comrade-in-arms! When did you arrive back?"

"Just today, Mike, but we nearly didn't make it, for we got caught in one of the worst storms ever recorded, near the Brittany coast of France, which would have claimed the whole crew but for the skilful handling of the Skipper," said Lieutenant Dale, beaming all over his face, so pleased he was back on dry land.

"Who was the Captain of the ship, may I ask?" enquired Lieutenant O'Hara.

"Now, Mike, who do you think could handle a ship in that situation? I am surprised at you of all people asking me that question," said Lieutenant Dale humorously.

"All right, Richard, you win. Ask a stupid question and you get a stupid answer. Where is he now?"

"Well, after we came off the USS *Ariel* he had to report to the Chairman of the Board of Admiralty, which is a new name in my vocabulary," said Lieutenant Dale.

"Oh yes, it was new to me also when I came back, but it has just replaced the old Marine Committee and is more streamlined," replied Lieutenant O'Hara.

"Well, knowing him, once he gets talking to this new Board he will streamline it further," said Lieutenant Dale with a smile on his face.

"Yes, Richard, he certainly is some man, for he undoubtedly has carved his name on this young Navy of ours; he leaves all other senior officers well down the league as far as I am concerned," said the man who was so proud to have been one of John Paul Jones's gunnery officers in his greatest moment of triumph.

"Well, I bet you that by the time he is finished with the Board of Admiralty (excuse the pun!) he will be the anchor on which our future Navy is built," continued Lieutenant Dale.

"That's without a doubt, Richard," said Lieutenant O'Hara, "for his tactics and ingenuity against HMS *Serapis* were simply incredible. And I am so glad you are here with me, so that you can vouch for what I am saying, for until Commodore Paul Jones's official memoirs on the battle are published in detail, it is very difficult to describe to anyone who was not there."

"Well, Mike, I thought the situation at Flamborough Head was bad, but, quite honestly, I was much more frightened when I was caught in the middle of that tempest-tossed sea on the USS *Ariel*, for we were in pitch darkness when it commenced, with the wind and rain lashing down mercilessly. Added to this, when the storm was at its height, there were waves that must have been over twenty feet high, trying to drive us on to the rocks. And had they succeeded, none of us would be here today to tell the tale. How on earth he managed to handle that ship—and remember this lasted for two days—clear of those rocks is a mystery not only to me but to the rest of the crew."

Trying to show his experience of seamanship, Lieutenant O'Hara went on to say, "There would have been plenty of reduced sail then, Richard?"

"Yes, Mike, we started with that; ending up with no masts at all, as Paul Jones had all three cut down in the end."

"What!" exclaimed Lieutenant O'Hara, "he had the masts cut down! Well, I have had some experiences myself but have never heard of that before; but, knowing the man on the poop deck, I believe every word you tell me, Richard."

"Well, we know him only too well, particularly you, Mike, having been his Gunnery Officer, so it's not difficult for us to understand what he is capable of achieving. But to try and explain it to someone who has never served with him is rather difficult, for you end up being accused of telling tall stories," said Lieutenant Dale, as he looked around the room.

"As I said earlier, Richard, this is how glad I am that you are with me here, for you can substantiate some of the things I say," said Lieutenant O'Hara, as he closed the book which he had been reading just before Lieutenant Dale's entry. Lieutenant Dale, having a further look around the reading room, said to Lieutenant O'Hara, "I am afraid there is nobody in here I recognise, Mike. Let's go through to the bar and have a drink, for old time's sake."

"Of all people, Richard, it will be my greatest pleasure to have a drink with you," said Lieutenant O'Hara, as they both made their way into the bar, which was naturally much more boisterous than the reading room. Making their way up to the bar, which was busy with officers swapping stories of their war exploits, Lieutenant Dale asked the bar steward politely, "Two refreshments, please." As the bar steward was very familiar with most of the faces in the bar, he said to both of them, having served them their drink, "Excuse me, gentlemen, did you serve on the famous USS *Bon Homme Richard*, which everyone has heard so much about?"

Lieutenant Dale answered, "Indeed we did, Sir, and we are two of the lucky ones to return home alive."

"Well, gentlemen," said the bar steward, "all drinks are on the Officers' Club."

"Oh, thank you very much; this is a pleasant surprise indeed," said Lieutenant O'Hara, who, with his companion, was aware of a silence in the immediate vicinity of where they were standing, as the rest of the members looked on them in awe for what they had achieved for the struggling young nation, so many miles from home, on the other side of the Atlantic.

Although he did not know them, Bob Hannah, who was sitting near to where they were standing, on hearing the mention of the *Bon Homme Richard* came up to them and said, "Excuse me, Lieutenants, did I overhear you saying in conversation that both of you served in Commodore Paul Jones's Squadron in the North Sea?"

"That is correct, Sir," came the proud reply from Lieutenant Dale.

"So you will know the great man himself, do you?" asked a curious Hannah.

"Know the great man, Sir!" exclaimed Lieutenant Dale; "although I say it in all humility, I was proud to be his Executive Officer. Lieutenant O'Hara here was one of his Gunnery Officers."

"So you're Lieutenant Dale, then?" enquired Hannah.

"Indeed I am, Sir."

"Oh, I have heard and read a lot about you, Lieutenant. Very proud to meet you." Introducing himself, he said, "My name is Colonel Hannah, 15th Cavalry Regiment. It is a pleasure to meet you both. Would you like to join my table?"

"That's really kind of you," said both of them, as all sat down at Colonel Hannah's table.

"Yes, gentlemen, believe it or not but I am a very good friend of the Commodore's. I am also proud to say that I am the man who got him his original appointment in the Navy, through a very good friend of mine, who is now unfortunately dead. He was Mr. Joseph

Hewes and was the first Chairman of the Marine Committee in Congress,' said a rather verbose Colonel Hannah, ensuring everyone at the bar heard him.

"Oh, it is sad to hear about poor Mr. Hewes's death," said a concerned Lieutenant Dale.

"Yes, he just passed away not so long ago," said the Colonel.

"The Commodore will be very sorry to hear that, for I have heard him speak very highly of him on several occasions," said Lieutenant O'Hara as he slowly sipped his refreshment.

"Well, it's amazing, gentlemen; when I met your now most famous Commodore, an out-of-work merchant seaman, just over five years ago, little did I realise for one moment I was in the company of a gentleman who would make the international headlines in so short a time. I realised he was very competent, but I honestly thought he would end up as another run-of-the-mill skipper," said Colonel Hannah, as the two young officers listened most attentively.

"Well, Sir," said Lieutenant O'Hara, "he certainly has made the headlines on both sides of the Atlantic, particularly in Europe, for he has half the British Royal Navy searching for him everywhere on the high seas but in the right place!"

At this, Lieutenant Dale interrupted the conversation and said, "That was part of his overall strategy, both in the raid on Whitehaven with the *Ranger* and in his battle in the North Sea on the *Bon Homme Richard*."

Lieutenant O'Hara added, "His plan certainly paid off, for, apart from the tremendous psychological blow he has struck on mainland Britain, he has the British Royal Navy at sixes and sevens, not knowing where he will turn up next."

Colonel Hannah then asked, "How did you find him, gentlemen? Or is that a ridiculous question?"

"Well, as far as I am concerned, Sir," replied Lieutenant O'Hara, "there is only one word to describe the Commodore—brilliant!"

"Well, Sir, if I may say so, having been his Executive Officer, or right-hand man, throughout the whole battle of Flamborough Head, he is cool, competent and highly efficient in everything he does, whether it's controlling a battle from the poop deck or looking after the crew's welfare in respect of food and hygiene."

Lieutenant O'Hara, who was sitting in his chair with his legs out-stretched and his hands behind his head, went on to say, "If I can add to what Lieutenant Dale has just said—and I think he will agree with me—the Commodore does not suffer fools gladly and, quite hon-estly, he is a man you either love or hate." Nodding at Lieutenant Dale with a smile, he went on to say, "We all know that he has a fero-cious temper—quiet as a lamb one minute, and roaring like a lion the next if things are not going smoothly. Another great quality he has is that he has no fear of death whatsoever; he seems to inspire all his officers and crewmembers, because of this quality, so that they end up adopting the same attitude in the heat of a battle. And, lastly, I would say that he would never ask any man to do anything he can-not do himself. This was proved when we were reduced to three nine-pounders on the *Bon Homme Richard*—he took one over him-self and mercilessly pounded away at the main mast of HMS *Serapis*, until they capitulated."

"Well, gentlemen," said Colonel Hannah, as he ordered another round of drinks, "it has been most enlightening meeting both of you and getting first-hand information about my friend. Unfortunately I shall not be able to see him as I am on my way down to Virginia to join General Washington's staff, for I think we are going to have a right dust up with Cornwallis at Yorktown. And if the French High Sea Fleet under Admiral de Grasse can knock out the Royal Navy and cut off supplies, it will be all over bar the shouting, I reckon."

"Well, Sir, we wish you luck in your campaign, and we will remember you kindly to the Commodore when we see him. Thank you so much for your company," said Lieutenant Dale on behalf of them both.

"It's been my pleasure, gentlemen," said Colonel Hannah; "and you can tell the Commodore that if we all survive this impending battle at Yorktown, he must look me up next time he is in Philadelphia, for he knows where I live and I shall be delighted to meet him once again."

So, bidding one another farewell, with a strong and hearty handshake, they all left the Officers' Club and plunged again into the bustling life of Philadelphia, Colonel Hannah going off to war and the young Naval Officers going to see some lady friends they had not seen since they were raw midshipmen, completely unfamiliar with the ravages of naval warfare.

In the meantime, the Commodore had a rather heavy programme of renewing old acquaintances he had last seen over three years ago, who welcomed him back into their ranks as a proven hero of the Young America. To set the seal on his daring ventures on the high seas, Congress formally thanked him and his men for their heroic missions and what they had accomplished in European waters for the American cause. From the way Paul Jones was applauded for his deeds by the Representatives of the Thirteen States, it was obvious to everyone there at the time that he was being singled out from his fellow officers as someone special in the early history of the United States Navy. Although the founding of the Navy had, of course, been a political decision, the person who had given it its earliest traditions, not in any debating chamber but by decisive action on the high seas, could quite naturally be called the Father of the Navy. And in the case of the United States Navy, that accolade fell fairly and squarely on the shoulders of none other than John Paul Jones.

This was very obvious from the manner in which he was being groomed for future command, for, a few days after receiving the grateful thanks of the American people, through the mouthpiece of Congress, the Commodore was called before Mr. Robert Morris, the Agent of Marine. This office had superseded the previous Marine Committee and the now defunct Board of Admiralty. Mr. Morris was not only a strong supporter of John Paul Jones but he was also one of the shrewdest and most capable politicians in America at the time; so when they met in his office on this occasion, the purpose of which was to lay down the blueprint for the future United States Navy after the war was over, they had much to talk about. Indeed, many of the results of those deliberations between Paul Jones and his political superior are still evident today, particularly the code laid down for officers, who, by virtue of their training and professionalism, form the backbone of the Service.

Proudly entering Mr. Robert Morris's office, the Commodore, on saluting his political superior, said "Good afternoon, Sir, I believe you want to see me to discuss organisational methods, and my future role in the Navy?"

"Indeed I do, Commodore; as we have a few important subjects to discuss, sit down and relax. Do you wish a glass of wine?"

Being very careful in his drinking habits, the Commodore said, "That's most kind of you, but just make it a small one."

"Well, I have some fine French claret here, which I will give you, to remind you of the glorious time you had in that country," said the Agent of Marine.

"Yes, Mr. Morris, I think in many ways I left my heart there, particularly in Paris," said Paul Jones, as he slowly sipped from his glass.

"Now, Commodore," said Mr. Morris, "now that I have had time to read your comprehensive report, based on your experiences both on the USS *Ranger* and the USS *Bon Homme Richard*, and your very sound recommendations for our future Navy, I must thank you for putting so much serious and fruitful thought into it, for as a plan for action it will certainly be something for us to get our teeth into."

"Thank you very much, Sir," said a beaming Paul Jones. "I am so pleased to hear that all I have said in that report has not fallen on deaf ears."

"Not in the least, Commodore, on the contrary! But, very important though the report may be, we will leave it to the end as we have more immediate things to discuss concerning yourself, now that you are back in our midst."

"Very good, Sir. As always, I am at your command," said the Commodore, anxious to hear what Mr. Morris had to say to him.

"Well, you know that since you left for the European theatre we have been building a seventy-four-gun man-of-war in Portsmouth, New Hampshire, called the USS *America*?"

"Yes, I have heard about it, Sir, but apart from that there is very little I know about it," replied Paul Jones.

"Well, the bad news, Commodore, is that Congress has ordered me to get it launched as quickly as possible, so that it is fully equipped to go to sea by the end of the year."

"Do you think that's possible, Sir?" enquired the Commodore.

"In my estimation, with the right individual in charge of the final stages of construction, launching and making it fully seaworthy, it can be done. For the good news, Commodore, is that Congress has unanimously elected you to take it over."

"This will indeed be an honour, Sir, to take over the first man o' war called after this young nation of ours," replied Paul Jones, delighted by the new challenge set before him, as he was the sort of individual who saw a venture of this nature as yet another test of his capabilities.

Mr. Morris went on, "I wanted to promote you to Rear-Admiral, so that it could be your flagship in any subsequent task force you lead, but I am afraid it fell through because of the opposition of certain factions who claim you are their junior in service."

"Sir, if you don't mind my saying so, a man should be judged on ability and not on length of service," said a slightly annoyed Paul Jones.

"Commodore, I fully agree with you; for, if you don't mind my saying so, you have done so much to put the United States Navy on the map and, in so doing, you have achieved international fame on both sides of the Atlantic. You have proved yourself, whereas many of the others are nonentities, hardly known beyond their own ship," said the frustrated Agent of Marine.

"Well, Sir, I will just have to prove my worth to you even further, when we get the USS *America* launched," said a reluctant Paul Jones.

"You see, Commodore, jealousy and inter-State factions have been among the causes of weakness of our infant Navy. An example of that was the furore caused when you were appointed Commodore in charge of the *Bon Homme Richard* Task Force. However, leave your promotion in my capable hands, for, once this war is over and we get down to re-organising the peacetime Navy, there are many of those dead-beat captains who will undoubtedly get the heave-ho," said Mr. Morris, being a man who knew where he was going and what would be best for the Navy in the years that lay ahead.

"Funny you should mention my appointment as Task Force Commander and the fuss it caused, Sir; for as soon as my appointment came through in Paris, it was the first thing I mentioned to Dr. Benjamin Franklin."

"Just ignore their petty jealousies, Commodore; you have done something very positive for the cause and can hold your head high, for you have worked very hard for everything you have achieved, something some of our other captains have never done; they are there purely through family connections."

"Indeed, Sir—thank you."

"Now, Commodore, since I am the mouthpiece of the Navy in Congress," continued Mr. Morris, "can I ask your advice as to what future role you see for the USS *America* once it is fully operational?"

"Well, Sir, if the war is still on when it is fully completed I am quite naturally at your disposal and shall go anywhere you wish to send me," said the Commodore, only too willing to serve his country whatever the circumstances might be.

"That's fully understood, Commodore, but assuming the war is over, which is highly probable the way things are going, to judge by my latest report from Yorktown, what then?"

"Well, Sir, assuming the war is over and we achieve a satisfactory peace settlement, there would be nothing dearer to my heart than to lead a squadron into Mediterranean waters, with the USS *America* as my flagship."

"What particularly attracts you to that area, may I ask?" enquired a probing Mr. Morris.

"One thing, Sir: the release of American sailors who are being held prisoner after being captured by the Barbary pirates in North Africa."

"Well, you are well worth listening to, Commodore, for your attempt to capture the Earl of Selkirk when you were on the USS *Ranger* certainly paid off, in that the British Government thereafter started releasing American sailors from their jails. But how would you approach this one?"

"Oh, this would be a much bigger and more complex operation, Sir. The first thing we would have to do would be to expand that fine body of men the United States Marine Corps. Once this was achieved and the men were fully trained for such a mission, they could then storm such places as Tripoli and have the prisoners released."

"That's a brilliant idea, Commodore Paul Jones. Just leave that one with me and I will do something positive to try to have your ideas put into effect," said the Agent for Marine who was delighted with the sound and practical suggestions just put to him.

"I am afraid time is running short, Commodore," said Mr. Morris, "as I have a rather important meeting to attend in Congress. But there are one or two interesting points you raised in your report which we briefly discussed when you came into my office, that I would like to take up with you now."

"Yes, Sir. Well, the first we must bear in mind is that what we discuss now, if it is eventually made naval policy, won't bear fruit immediately but will probably be put into effect when many of us here are dead and gone."

"Good!" said the Agent for Marine; "for a person who has fore-sight, and plans ahead, is not only interested in his own immediate prospects but may be termed something of a statesman, if I can use that word loosely; so fire away!"

"Well, Sir, the first thing I would like to see drawn up for the future of the United States Navy is a code laying down how we select officers and what we expect of them. First; they should be educated gentlemen, who are given a sound training not only in seamanship but, as time passes, a thorough grounding in the traditions of the Service. They should possess the moral fibre which will distinguish them from ordinary crew members and at the same time inspire the same quality of grit and determination in those under their com-mand."

As Mr. Morris's secretary was hurriedly writing down all these main points, the Agent of Marine said, "So far, so good, Commo-dore; please do continue."

"Every officer should be aware of his responsibilities for the safe handling of his ship and the welfare of the crews under his com-mand. He should be concerned for their hygiene, food, accommoda-tion, and general welfare," said Paul Jones, checking through his list to see that he missed nothing out. The Agent of Marine then said, "I see you have something here about 'floating academies.'"

"Yes, Sir. As we begin expanding our Navy further, I think that it is imperative to have floating academies for our future midshipmen, so that they can be thoroughly tested in their capabilities and put their theory into practice before joining a full-time fighting ship."

"These are very sound ideas, Commodore, but what's this I see about a full-time Academy? I assume it is something different from the floating ones you just mentioned?"

"Yes, Sir, for with our large coastline and the developing world sit-uation, in which I am convinced this country will play a leading part one day, it is imperative that we have a strong, organised and efficient Navy. For without a strong Navy, Sir,—Alas, America! May I continue, Sir?"

"Most certainly do!" replied Mr. Morris, whose secretary was working at full speed to keep up with Paul Jones's idea for the future Navy.

"Well, Sir, this is looking very much to the future, but I think that the time will come when we shall have to build a full-time Naval Academy to satisfy the above objectives. And one final point: to get the highest quality of officer material, future midshipmen should be chosen on ability and not through nepotism. Although it is very difficult to eradicate nepotism in any organisation, we can always try. For example, if the interviewing board thinks that a candiciate is not likely to fulfil the criteria of the code I have mentioned, he should be rejected, even although his father is a prominent politician."

"Commodore, I wholeheartedly agree with everything you say, for this is one of the problems of the present Navy of which I am only too well aware, as you are also; and I will do everything in my power to solve it," said Mr. Morris.

"Well, Sir, if you can get some of these ideas of mine implemented, we shall be going a long way to getting our Navy on a sound footing."

"I most certainly will do that, Commodore, and I must thank you sincerely for supplying me with such constructive suggestions. I will go to work on them as soon as possible," said Mr. Morris, as he made his way to his important meeting in Congress.

Paul Jones, having left for safe keeping in the hands of his favourite and trustworthy officer Lieutenant Richard Dale, the golden sword presented to him by King Louis XVI of France, made his way up country to Portsmouth, New Hampshire, to get the USS *America* ready for launching. When he arrived there he organised things in his usual efficient manner, for, with his past achievements under his belt, he was in a position now where anything he said was listened to and taken seriously. Even though he encountered one or two obstacles, he eventually had the USS *America* launched and made seaworthy, to the great delight of Congress. However, by the time it was ready to go to sea in 1782, the War of Independence was over; for, when Admiral de Grasse with his French High Seas Fleet overcame the British Royal Navy in Chesapeake Bay, this cut off supplies, and Lord Cornwallis surrendered to General Washington at Yorktown. In the circumstances prevailing at the time, the newly independent nation sold the USS *America* to France—and once again Paul Jones was a sailor without a ship. Nevertheless, his fame had spread so far internationally that Catherine the Great of Russia, of all people, wished him to become her Admiral-in-Command of the Black Sea Fleet in Russia's war with Turkey.

Having given the American Navy its earliest traditions, for which history now recognises him as its Father, Paul Jones was still keen on adventure. Therefore, in order to obtain greater experience in different tactics, which he hoped to take back to the U.S.A., he willingly accepted this challenge of serving Catherine the Great. To serve her, however, was very different from serving the young democracy of America, for, apart from other things, she was one of the greatest despots the world has ever known.

CHAPTER 9

CATHERINE THE GREAT OF RUSSIA

Mr. Thomas Jefferson	American Representative in Paris; Later Third President of The U.S.A. (1801–1809)
Catherine the Great	Empress of All Russia (1726–1796)
Tsar Peter III	Served on Russian Throne for a few months.
Mr. Charles Cameron	Prominent Scottish Architect
Admiral Samuel Greig	Founder of the Russian Navy
Field Marshall Potemkin	Supreme Commander, All Russian Forces
Nassau-Siegan	French Adventurer
General Suvorov	Famous for driving Napoleon out of Russia.
Napoleon	Emperor of France (1804–1815)

Having received his appointment, through the good offices of Mr. Thomas Jefferson, the American Representative in France, it was an eager Paul Jones on the one hand and a rather apprehensive one on the other who embarked on another milestone in his stormy and adventurous career. As it was quite the accepted thing, during the

18th century, to transfer one's loyalty to another country, if one's own country was not at war, the Admiral, as he now was in the Imperial Navy of Catherine the Great, wished to use his appointment to extend his experience so that when he had completed his task in the Black Sea he could return to his country of adoption able to offer the fruits of his experience to the United States Navy, which he wished to put on a sound footing. His apprehension arose at the thought of meeting and serving Catherine herself, as he had heard so much about her as a despotic ruler and a lady whom it was very difficult to satisfy sexually.

With the blessing of the young American nation, Admiral Paul Jones made his way to Russia, going through the Gulf of Finland and experiencing severe and bitter weather conditions. On arrival in St. Petersburg in 1788 he booked in at a very reasonable hotel, before going to meet the Empress of All Russia to discuss his new appointment in detail now that he was one of her Admirals. Having roughed it in the past he was quite happy to settle temporarily in a cosy little inn before proceeding south to the Black Sea to take up his new command. And more than comfortable it was, for he struck up a friendship with the owner, a Mr. John Brown, who was a first-class host. Mr. Brown, who had come from Yorkshire in England and served in the Imperial Navy as Chef to the Commander-in-Chief of Catherine's Baltic Fleet, had married a local girl and settled down in St. Petersburg. A tall man, with greying hair, Brown was a tremendous help to the Admiral, for, being in the Navy and speaking Russian like a native, he knew his way around not only in Russia generally but, more importantly from Paul Jones's point of view, in St. Petersburg. To the Admiral's great satisfaction there was a striking resemblance between Brown here and Hannah in Philadelphia, for he knew everybody who mattered in this great city.

Having been shown his room and given a sumptuous meal, on meeting Mr. Brown in the lounge of his hotel the Admiral said to him, "How do you like it in St. Petersburg, Mr. Brown?"

"Well, Sir, you know what they say in the Navy: any old port in a storm!" said Brown humorously, as he poured himself and the Admiral a refreshment.

"Oh, I know what you mean, Mr. Brown, as I have the same outlook on life myself," said the Admiral, as he warmed his hands in front of the fire.

"No, the real reason I settled down here, Sir, is that I married a local girl; unfortunately I cannot introduce you to her as she is out of town for a few days visiting her parents."

"How do you find the Russians then, Mr. Brown, may I ask?"

"The ordinary Russians, Sir, are the salt of the earth, exceptionally nice people; but the one you are going to work for and her hangers-on need a lot of watching –if you don't mind my saying so, Sir," said Brown, wondering how the Admiral would react, being one of her flag officers.

"So you are saying, Mr. Brown, that I should be wary of some of the people in authority?" enquired the Admiral.

"Sir, being a flag officer, you don't mind my talking to you like this?" enquired Brown.

"Not in the least, Mr. Brown, for you are a tremendous asset to me in that you are bilingual and I am not. I am here to learn as much as I can from people like you. Take it from me, whatever you say will not go any further, for I appreciate all this that you are telling me. You know what they say, Mr. Brown: to be forewarned is to be fore-armed!" said the Admiral, who was obviously keen to know what was going on in the social and political world of St. Petersburg.

"Well, where do you want me to start then, Sir?" said a much more relaxed Mr. Brown, who now realised that he could confide in the Admiral quite freely without any official repercussions.

"At the top of the house," said the Admiral with a broad smile on his face, only too eager to hear if what all the other countries of Europe were saying about Catherine was true.

"Good, Sir, I am glad you mentioned the Empress. For a start, she is not a Russian but a German princess who married into the House of Romanov."

"Well, I am learning again," said the Admiral, "for I always thought she was Russian, through and through."

"No, Sir, far from it, for you will find the Russians very genuine people indeed. She's an interloper, who married Peter III and had him quietly strangled, away back in 1762. Since then she has ruled Russia with a rod of iron."

"So she is one to watch, then?" enquired the Admiral.

"One to watch, Sir! I'd say that again! However, although I don't consider myself a prophet, I can see the House of Romanov collapsing one day, although it won't happen in my lifetime," said Brown, now openly showing his dislike for the Empress and her courtiers.

"Why do you think that, Mr. Brown?" enquired a curious Admiral.

"Well, Sir, the peasants will stand serfdom for so long, but take it from me their patience will eventually snap, and when it does there will be one God Almighty revolution. I know, Sir, for being married to a country Russian girl I know what makes them tick and they will only tolerate so much, the more enlightened they become," said Mr. Brown, as he poured his guest another drink.

With a twinkle in his eye, the Admiral then asked the question which had been on his mind for a long time: "Is it really true what they say about her sex life, Mr. Brown?"

"You take it from me, Sir—and you have been around—all the seamen in the world could not satisfy her sexual desires," replied Brown.

"I knew she was bad, but is she really as bad as all that?" asked the Admiral, who was more than eager to find out at first hand all about his new Commander-in-Chief.

"Yes, Sir, you see, her lover Field Marshall Potemkin, who will be your overall boss and one to watch, has really gone past it now. So she just picks on any young guardsman she fancies."

"Is it as simple as that then, Mr. Brown?" enquired the Admiral, who was fast gaining knowledge of the Empress, whom he would have to meet the following morning.

"No, it is not quite as simple as that, Sir, for this is what happens if she fancies any particular guardsman. Here I am thinking of one who was my assistant, a John Smart to name. On leaving the sea, he ended up in the Royal Household. One day her eye caught Smart, who is a very virile youth, and the next thing he was given a thorough medical examination for fitness and being well-endowed."

Interrupting, the Admiral said, "This can't be true, is it?"

"Oh yes, Sir, and I am not finished yet. Once he was passed by the medical authorities, he then had to sleep with one of her young matrons of honour and, having satisfied her that he was fully competent, he then slept with Catherine herself," said Brown to the smiling Admiral.

Laughing, the Admiral said, "I bet you Smart was the happiest guard in the Palace!"

"Well, Sir, he was very happy with the matron of honour but he could not satisfy the Empress. So he only lasted two nights and left a physical wreck. Believe me, Sir, she goes through men as water goes through the scuppers on a ship."

"Goodness me, Mr. Brown, I heard stories about her in Europe but I did not know she was as bad as that. So thanks for putting me in the picture so that I know with whom I shall be dealing," said the Admiral.

"That's a pleasure, Sir. Take it from me, as an old sailor who has been around, every word of it is true."

After being briefed by Brown on what went on in court circles, the Admiral retired for the night, for he had a very important appointment at the Royal Palace the following morning.

In his brand new Russian Naval uniform, which had been specially made for him in St. Petersburg, it was a rather cautious John Paul Jones who presented himself before Catherine the Great to be briefed on his role as her Admiral in charge of the Black Sea Fleet. On meeting him she said, "Good morning to you, Admiral Paul Jones. So you have arrived at last!"

Bowing his head slightly, he said to the sixty-year-old monarch, who was far from beautiful, "Yes, Your Majesty, I have made it at last and I am now at your service, Ma'am."

"Well, Admiral, as I have received some excellent reports from my Ambassador in France, it is only to be hoped that you will live up to your good name," said the Empress, as she looked him over from head to foot.

"Yes, Your Majesty, as I have not yet received an injury so far, I will endeavour to live up to my reputation," said the Admiral proudly.

"You're Scots, I believe, are you not, my Admiral?" asked the enquiring Catherine, as she read through his past history, which she had in her hands.

"That is perfectly true, Your Majesty," said Paul Jones, with an aura of experience surrounding him, which was obvious at this stage to the Empress. She went on, "Yes, the founder of our Imperial Navy is a Scot also, Admiral Samuel Greig to name. He is at present Commander-in-Chief of my Baltic Fleet. And the architect who designed the royal palace, a Mr. Cameron by name, was a Scot—what is it in your race, being such a small country, that makes you contribute so many things to humanity?" asked an enquiring Empress.

"Well, Your Majesty, that's a very good question you have asked and one which it is quite difficult to answer. But if I may say so, Ma'am, it's probably a combination of things," said the Admiral.

"For example?" enquired a probing Catherine.

"Well, Your Majesty, it's probably our quest for knowledge built on a sound educational system and independence of character which—although we are very proud of our homeland—enables us to assimilate into any country we go to, becoming part of that community very easily," replied the Admiral, as he relaxed in his plush easy-chair alongside Catherine.

Glancing over the documents she had in front of her, she continued, "I see you made quite a name for yourself in the American Navy during the War of Independence."

"Yes, Ma'am, I did my little bit for that marvellous country, which, along with your own, will probably be a major power in the world one day," said John Paul Jones, choosing his words very carefully so as not to upset the Empress.

She went on, "This revolution, in which, from what I read here, you played a prominent part—do you ever think it will spread?"

Here the Admiral, remembering the conversation he had had the previous night with Mr. John Brown on this very subject, had to be very diplomatic and say, "Well, Your Majesty, that again is very difficult to answer, so I think we shall probably have to leave that to the future."

"Yes, I think that is a very sensible outlook to have, Admiral, as none of us knows what the future has to hold for us," said the Empress, ordering her lady-in-waiting to get the butler to serve some refreshments.

When refreshments had been served, the Empress said, "Admiral, as you are here to serve in my Black Sea Fleet we may as well discuss that matter."

"Very good, Your Majesty, just you fire ahead, as I am at your command," said Paul Jones, as he listened to her attentively.

She continued: "The problem, as you already know, is posed by the Turks. What I want you to do with your Squadron is to drive them out of the Liman, which is the very shallow water between the mouth of the Dnieper and the Black Sea."

They both glanced over maps of the battle area in question. Having had a good look at what he was likely to encounter, the Admiral then said, "Your Majesty, you will appreciate that looking at maps is one thing, for I have grasped the theory of what you want already; but carrying out your wishes is another. So, with your permission, Ma'am, when I arrive there I will appraise the whole situation before the battle commences."

"Yes, I am just giving you a rough outline of what my objectives are, for my overall Commander of Land and Sea Forces, Field Marshall Potemkin, will fully brief you when you arrive down there." Catherine handed to her lady-in-waiting all the maps and documents she had.

"Very good, Your Majesty; and, thanking you for such a pleasant and interesting audience, I will now make my way down to the Black Sea," said Admiral Paul Jones, who kissed hands before being escorted out of the royal chamber.

As he made his way down to the estuary of the Dneiper, Admiral Paul Jones thought of his audience with Catherine the Great. Considering all he had heard about her previously, he found her to be quite reasonable. When he compared her with his Mademoiselle Thérèse, however, it was like comparing night and day. As far as he was concerned she could keep her virile young guardsmen, for he had no intention of, nor desire for knowing her intimately enough to have an affair with her. For him, his mission to Russia would be purely professional, at least until the impending battle had been victoriously concluded.

Field Marshall Potemkin, who had been personally exonerated from the failure of the first battle of the Lima, received John Paul Jones at his Headquarters to discuss tactics for the second battle. But as plans developed, Admiral Paul Jones began to realise he was the only professional among amateurs. To begin with, there was an overabundance of senior officers, all-scheming behind one another's backs in order to wrest power by currying favour with Potemkin. When the Field Marshall addressed his Commanders collectively on pre-battle plans, they all presented different views, all of which were very much at variance with those of Paul Jones. When he was asked his views by Potemkin he replied, "Sir, am I correct in saying that the Turkish ships have a much deeper draught than ours?"

"That's quite correct, Admiral," replied the Field Marshall, who then went on to say, "Why do you ask that question?"

"Well, Sir, our ships are practically flat-bottomed. Because of the shallowness of the Liman, why should we go out into the deep waters to challenge the enemy?" said Admiral Paul Jones, showing his true colours as a competent naval commander. With all eyes firmly fixed on the new Commander of the Black Sea Fleet, Potemkin went on to say, "Well, Admiral, what do you recommend then?"

"Well, Sir, may I humbly suggest that the obvious thing to do is to draw their ships from the deep waters of the Liman into the shallower ones. With their deeper draught, there is a good chance that we can ground and capture them relatively easily," said a confident Admiral Paul Jones.

The Field Marshall, realising that the Admiral was a true professional, conceded to his plans, to the amazement of the other senior officers present, for he was really losing face as regards strategy. But, not to be beaten, he said "What if we fail to pin them down and they begin to retreat to the Black Sea?"

"Well, Sir, this is where General Suvorov's shore battery, at the mouth of the Liman just before it joins the Black Sea, can open up with their guns and let the Turks have everything they have to offer," replied the Admiral.

When General Suvorov nodded in agreement with the Admiral's suggestion, they finally agreed on this policy. But it could be seen by the looks the Admiral was getting that jealousy was creeping in among those present.

On his flagship, the *Vladimir*, the Admiral, with a dozen ships and a flotilla of roughly the same number, under the command of Nassau-Siegen, waited in readiness for the Turks by forming an arc-like battle line stretching across the Liman, as far as possible. The first part of the Admiral's plan paid off, for the Turks, falling for the bait, formed a straight line of battle, with a similar number of ships. The Admiral's idea of using a nutcracker plan on the enemy seemed to be beginning to take effect when the battle commenced, for two Turkish ships, one of which was the flagship, ran aground to the north side of the Liman. But contrary to the Admiral's orders, Nassau-Siegen deployed his whole flotilla of twelve ships to attack the two stranded vessels, leaving the rest of the Russian fleet exposed to the oncoming Turks. The Admiral tried to stop him but to no avail. He then came to the conclusion that he had another jealous individual under his command, like Captain Landias on the USS *Alliance* off Flamborough Head. Even allowing for this lunatic the Admiral had in his midst, the second part of his plan paid off where the Liman joined the Black Sea. It was here that the gun battery was to play a decisive role, for they annihilated the Turkish fleet when they opened fire. The Turks lost practically all their ships in the debacle, with loss of life being very high. On the Russian side, casualties, and loss of both ships and men, was minimal.

When the battle was over, the Admiral realised he was not only a professional among a band of amateurs but also amidst a band of jealous characters into the bargain. For some odd reason, Nassau-Siegen got all the praise and the Admiral got a minor award. This was probably due to the fact that Potemkin thought the Admiral too big for his boots, and the fact that Potemkin was a good friend of Nassau-Siegen. Furthermore, it would have looked very bad in St. Petersburg if it were known that the Admiral bettered Potemkin in battle tactics. However, the facts were there for all to see, that it was Admiral Paul Jones's strategy in luring the Turks into the shallower Liman in the first instance that won the day. From this, a ferocious row ensued, with Nassau-Siegen having to apologise to the Admiral for his conduct. But the outcome was that the Admiral lost favour with Potemkin, who returned him to St. Petersburg, on the pretence of joining the Baltic Fleet in the impending war against Sweden. There was one individual, however, who fully appreciated the talented Admiral's tactics, and that was General Suvarov, who was later to go on and prove himself an excellent commander in driving Napoleon out of Russia.

After the Battle of the Liman, there were certain people in high places scheming for the Admiral's downfall because of professional jealousy. This came about one day when a young girl, who had visited him in his lodgings in St. Petersburg, ran out into the streets crying that she had been raped. When confronted by the police on the matter, Admiral Paul Jones emphatically denied it. He quite openly told the police that the girl was in point of fact in his house, but although she made amorous offers as she had done in the past, he told her not to be so stupid as she was under-age. This did not satisfy the police authorities, however, and they preferred charges against him. When this news broke in St. Petersburg the Admiral was shunned by all who knew him, with the exception of one or two very close friends.

As the Admiral's conscience was quite clear on the matter, he now realised there was a plot underfoot to disgrace him. And he could only put it down to the jealousy he had encountered whilst serving with the Black Sea Fleet, his professional approach to naval warfare being too much for some of the power-seeking charlatans he served alongside, particularly Nassau-Siegen. Had it been in the American Navy this individual would have been court-martialled for deliberately ignoring the Admiral's orders in battle.

However, as he was a very close friend of Potemkin's there was very little Paul Jones could have done about it, being very much an outsider. So, to clear him name, he confided in the French Ambassador and told him that, in no circumstances, would he ever have considered having sex with any female against her will. It was the sort of thing he would never have tolerated from anyone serving under his command, as it was something he personally abhorred. The Ambassador, who knew him well and had implicit faith in what he was saying, also smelled a rat and put the matter into the hands of a competent lawyer. The lawyer pursued the case vigorously and, when he had a witness who had seen the girl in question walk out of the Admiral's lodgings very calmly and meander casually down the street without a care in the world, he knew there must be something suspicious in the air, and openly challenged the girl's mother. The girl's mother, who was a lady of the night, broke down under interrogation and admitted she had been paid to put her daughter up to it by some prominent individual, so as to bring disgrace on the Admiral.

Once the lawyer had collated all the evidence at his disposal, the charges against Paul Jones were eventually dropped. But the furore created by the story in government circles ruined the Admiral's prospects of any further appointments in Catherine's Imperial Navy, to the great satisfaction of his opponents. This scandal played into the hands of Nassau-Siegen, who was appointed to the Baltic Fleet. Nevertheless it had become obvious to the Admiral that Nassau-Siegen was the character behind the plot.

So with this cloud over his head, and rumour rife in St. Petersburg that he had raped a young girl, although there were no formal charges against him, the story lingered on. In view of what happened to him in Russia and the manner in which he was treated, by what could only be called a pack of wolves, from the Empress herself downwards, this was indeed a sad anti-climax to an otherwise brilliant naval career; for, although his strategy and tactics routed the Turks in the Battle of the Liman, this success was not recognised where it mattered, in the Court of Catherine the Great.

With the combination of all these incidents, it was a sad and disillusioned John Paul Jones who departed from Russia in 1789.

CHAPTER 10

RETURN TO FRANCE; DEATH IN PARIS; THE UNITED STATES NAVAL ACADEMY, ANNAPOLIS

| Mr. Theodore Roosevelt | 26th President of the USA (1901–1909) |
| Mr. Woodrow Wilson | 28th President of the USA (1913–1921) |

Whilst in the service of Catherine the Great, John Paul Jones, because of the weather, caught pneumonia. And it was a far from fit man who returned to Paris from Russia, for when he arrived back he appeared to be drained out. Despite his early age of forty-two, his health was obviously on the wane. The manner in which he had left the service of the Empress did very little to boost his spirits, and this, coupled with his failing health, left him a sad and forlorn individual. However, he managed to regain some of his old vitality on arrival in the city that he loved, and managed to secure very comfortable accommodation for himself into the bargain. However, it was a changed Paris which saw his return, for the Revolution was at its height. This was very much against his sentiments, for although he had played a prominent role in revolutionary America, he had been very happy in France—the pinnacle of his aristocratic connections—under the monarchy of Louis XVI.

Once fully settled in, he endeavoured to make contact with some of his old social connections, but to little avail. For the aristocracy had either fled Paris or gone to the guillotine. But he was determined to track down his old flame, Mademoiselle Thérèse, whom he had last seen on board the USS *Ariel* and to enquire about his offspring. So, going into one of the salons he used to frequent, he located two fellow countrymen who were what one may call soldiers of fortune—a Mr. David Ravenscroft and Mr. David Hattan whom he had known from his earlier and much happier times in France. Having lived in Paris for some considerable time they could speak the language better than many natives, and were of the type who could freely mix with aristocratic ladies and still survive the Revolution. So, on his meeting with Ravenscroft there was no formality, as they were old bosom friends.

Going up to Mr. Ravenscroft Paul Jones said, "Good afternoon, David, so nice to see you after all these years. I am so glad to see you still managing to keep your head in Paris these days."

Ravenscroft, who immediately noticed how much his friend had failed since they had last met over ten years ago, was very diplomatic when he shook Paul Jones's hand warmly and said, "John, my friend, so good to see you after all these years, and how have you been keeping, comrade?"

"Well, David, as you've probably heard, I have been in Russia since I saw you last, and since I've returned I am not feeling one hundred per cent, but I will probably improve as time goes on," said Paul Jones, realising he was not the same zestful individual that Ravenscroft had known away back in the late 1770s.

"Yes, John, we have just been getting rather garbled reports of that war between Russia and Turkey in the Black Sea area. You must tell me all about it," said Ravenscroft, who was now well aware that his old social friend was not his usual sparkling self.

"David, I could talk for hours of my rather sad experiences there. But, first things first—whatever happened to Mademoiselle Thérèse, that old flame of mine?" Paul Jones enquired rather anxiously.

"Well, John, it's good you asked me that question, for Thérèse escaped the country on the eve of the Revolution, for she saw the writing on the wall. The rebels are knocking the aristocracy off like flies these days and they are fleeing Paris fast—those who can escape the guillotine," said Ravenscroft, who noticed the concern in the eyes of his friend.

"Did she go on her own, then, David?" he enquired rather excitedly, realising his friend knew everything that was happening among society in Paris.

"Oh no, John, she took her young son John with her. He must be about ten years now, and a beautiful and intelligent boy he is."

Paul Jones's eyes lit up on hearing this news and he said, "David, you must tell me more about him."

"Well, John, he is an exceptionally bright, well-mannered boy and, having gone to one of the most exclusive schools in Paris, he can speak English as fluently as he can French. Why are you so concerned about him anyway?" enquired Ravenscroft, not knowing of the intimate relationship that had existed between the boy's mother and Paul Jones.

"Well, David," explained John excitedly, "that's one son I know of anyway!"

Snapping his fingers and shaking his head, Ravenscroft said, "The penny has just dropped now, for although I hardly spoke to his mother I got on well with young John; we used to have long conversations in the street. I often wondered when he used to say, 'My father's a famous Scottish sailor, and when I grow up I am going to be a sailor as well'—but I never realised what the boy was on about! So you're the culprit then, you old Romeo!" said Ravenscroft, shaking his hand warmly for having produced such a fine son.

Paul Jones's mind went back to the romantic times he had had in Paris at the peak of his fame, particularly the last night he had spent on the USS *Ariel* with Thérèse. Remembering her parting words, he said, "This is marvellous information you have given me, David. It's injected new life into me, in that it gives me something to look forward to when I return to Philadelphia; you really have made my day."

Who should come sauntering in off the street but David Hattan! On seeing Paul Jones in the company of his friend, Hattan came up and, openly embracing him, said, "John, my old friend, how pleased I am to see you. Where did you blow in from after all these years?"

"Well, David, since I last entertained you before I departed for America, so many things have happened that I don't know where to start," said Paul Jones, obviously delighted to be back with two stalwart friends whom he could trust.

"I heard briefly about your escapades with Catherine the Great. Is it true what they say about her, John?" asked Hattan with a smile on his face.

"Yes, David, every word they say about her is perfectly true, but I am not guilty of having an affair with her—not that I would have wanted any for she is nothing but an ugly, despotic old ruler, with very loose morals," said Paul Jones, whose face showed that he was far from being an admirer of the Empress after his escapade in Russia.

With that, Revenscroft interrupted and said, "But you won the battle of Liman for her, didn't you?"

"Yes, David, I planned it and carried it out, in circumstances that would have driven you mad. I won in the end, tragically only picking up a minor award for it," said Paul Jones, who did everything in his power to conceal the bitterness within him.

"Why was that then?" asked Ravenscroft, as Hattan sat listening attentively to what was being said.

"Well, David, you would have to have been there to believe what happened, for I never experienced such a shambles in my life. The whole chain of command and organisation was chaotic, from Potemkin downwards. To start with, he was only there by virtue of the fact that he was Catherine's long-time lover, and, with few exceptions, he was surrounded by inept opportunist clowns," replied a very disgruntled Paul Jones.

The next question came from Hattan, who said, "On the whole, how did you find the Russians?"

"The ironical thing, David, is that the Russians were first-class people, whom I would have with me at any time, particularly such fine types as Suvorov; but the outside foreigners that were there were purely chancing their hand."

"That's good, so you found the ordinary Russian people all right?"

Thinking about what John Brown had told him in his hotel the night before he met Catherine the Great, Paul Jones went on, "Now that we have had a revolution in both America and France, this may spread throughout Europe; then it will hit Russia like a bolt out of the blue. For the whole régime, from Catherine downward, is corrupt to the eyeballs, and when the peasants eventually revolt they will purge the existing régime with a vengeance."

"You may have a lot of truth in what you re saying, for I think this revolution will catch on like the plague and sweep throughout Europe," said Hattan philosophically.

"Well, I must say that I have seen a tremendous change in France since I returned, gentlemen," said Paul Jones sadly, remembering the old Paris of the late 1770s.

"Not to worry!" said Ravenscroft. "I think we have the resilience to survive any form of social and political revolution." For they all came from a country that not even the Romans could conquer!

"Aye, you're right there, David, and I am sorry that I cannot stay longer with you both and continue this interesting discussion, but I am not feeling up to scratch today and think I will make my way back to my lodgings. But thank you both for a most enjoyable get-together, and particularly for that valuable information you gave me about Mademoiselle Thérèse and her son," said a rather tired Paul Jones.

"That's a pleasure, John," said Ravenscroft, who went on to say, "When you get better, do not be frightened to call in and see us, for we will be looking forward to seeing you so that we can relive the happy times we had in the past."

So, bidding them both farewell, Paul Jones, with his back slightly stooped, rather unsteadily made his way out of the salon and into the bustling thoroughfare. Once he had left their company Ravenscroft turned to his friend Hattan and said, "You know, David, John is far from well, for he is just a shadow of the robust individual he was when at the peak of his naval career in 1780."

"Yes, David," replied his friend Hattan, "I did not want to say anything when he was with us, not wishing to upset him, but I have never seen such a change in a man in my life before."

"But you must remember he has come through hell on the high seas, whereas we have been living it up in Paris," said Ravenscroft, who appeared to be very much concerned about Paul Jones's health.

"Yes, David, I think that pneumonia he caught while in the service of Catherine the Great is just beginning to tell now, so let's hope he recovers quickly so that he is fully fit to return to America, for that's where his heart really lies," said Hattan, who was just as concerned about his friend's health as was Ravenscroft.

Paul Jones's health, far from recovering, gradually deteriorated until he was eventually housebound. His condition got worse, until, on the 13th July 1792, one of his staff who looked after him in his final illness found him dead, as he lay, fully dressed, across his bed with both feet on the floor. The American naval hero of the War of

Independence had passed on, at the age of forty-five years. Ironically, it was not the might of the Royal Navy, or the Turkish Navy for that matter, which brought him to an early grave. No! It was the severity of the icy climatic conditions he encountered whilst in the service of Catherine the Great.

When news of his death spread around official circles in France and ultimately in America, there was a deep sense of shock at his passing away at such an early age. To those who knew him intimately in his final years his death came as no great surprise, for they could see him going downhill fast. Even though France was in the grip of the Revolution, the authorities found time to give him a funeral farewell befitting a naval hero. Those supervising his funeral arrangements, however, had tremendous foresight in that they had his body pickled in alcohol, in anticipation of the United States Government having his body returned to America one day.

❦   ❦   ❦

Over one hundred and ten years later the occupant of the White House, President Theodore Roosevelt, one of the greats in the history of that exalted office, wished to expand the United States Navy. So, one day, he called in his Secretary of the Navy and said, "Mr. Secretary, can you remember my discussing with you our need to expand the Navy?"

"Indeed I can, Mr. President, and I hope to put your plans into effect very shortly," said the Secretary of the Navy.

"Well, I think you will agree with me that, since the wars in Cuba and the Philippines, the United States global commitments have become such that we shall need a sound Navy to meet them all," said the statesmanlike President.

"Yes, Mr. President, ship construction is well underway, and if my estimations are correct, everything is on schedule," said the Secretary as he listened attentively to the Commander-in-Chief of the Armed Services.

"Well, Mr. Secretary," continued the President, "I don't only want to expand the Navy but I want to make it into the largest and most powerful Navy in the world one day."

"So, from what you say, Mr. President, this will mean further ship procurement and more enlisted blue-jackets?" said his Secretary of the Navy, who was beginning to realise the added responsibilities being placed on his shoulders.

"Not only that, Mr. Secretary, but we will need to train many more additional officers, both in the Navy and the Marines," said the President, looking like what he was—a man of vision.

"So, from what you say, Mr. President, we will need to expand the Naval Academy at Annapolis also?"

"So correct, Mr. Secretary, and I am giving you further instructions that will put the icing on the cake for that great Institution. I also want the person who gave our Navy its earliest traditions to be back there," said the determined and forthright President, who had had his baptism in warfare on the battlefields of Cuba in 1898. Looking aghast, the Secretary of the Navy said, "You want John Paul Jones back there, Mr. President?"

"That is correct, Mr. Secretary."

"But if you'll forgive my saying so, Mr. President, he is buried in Paris," said the somewhat amazed Secretary.

"I know that only too well, Mr. Secretary, but as his body is preserved I want you to liaise with the State Department, who will in turn get in touch with our Ambassador in Paris, so that we can have his body brought back to the place where he rightly belongs, which is the Naval Academy."

"Well, Mr. President, Sir, I really appreciate your splendid idea, and I will get my staff working on it as soon as I return to the Department of the Navy."

"And one final thing, Mr. Secretary: when his body is located, I want it returned to the United States with all the naval pomp and ceremony befitting the great man. So that's up to your Department to plan and organise; and I want to be fully informed all the way along the line, so that I can give the Presidential address at the re-interment ceremony."

"Mr. President, I shall act on your orders immediately I leave the White House," said the Secretary, who had a lot of work ahead of him but was very proud to be embarking on it, for what a morale booster it would be for the cadets at the Naval Academy to have their hero in their midst!

On Presidential orders, communication between Washington and Paris was swift in both directions. After many endeavours the excavations proved successful, and the preserved mortal remains of the United States Navy's greatest hero were located. The body, having been preserved in alcohol, was as fresh as the day he died. This enabled an autopsy to be carried out in Paris so that the cause of death could be determined.

The body was placed in a new lead-lined coffin which was, again, filled with alcohol and finally sealed. A full military service was conducted in Paris before it made its solemn journey across the Atlantic, which he had sailed so often. Both the American and French Governments were represented, along with the U.S. Navy, the U.S. Marines, and detachments of the French Armed Services.

When the memorial service was completed, with full naval ceremonial, the mahogany coffin travelled overland to the port of Cherbourg. From this famous port, so familiar to modern-day passengers on the *QE2*, the body of John Paul Jones was escorted back to America by warships of the United States Navy, a voyage which took about a fortnight. On entering home waters it was escorted by additional warships which, on passing the USS *Brooklyn* which was bearing his body, fired a salute of fifteen guns in honour of their dead hero who was now arriving home.

When the body eventually arrived back at the Naval Academy it was placed in a temporary vault until something more elaborate could be built. Before it was placed in this vault there was a very moving naval and religious ceremony, attended by many dignitaries from the President downwards. And it was a very proud President Roosevelt, as Commander-in-Chief of the Armed Services, who addressed this dignified gathering at the re-interment of John Paul Jones on 24th April, 1906.

The President's words probably summed up our naval hero better than those of any historian, when he said to the assembled crowd:

> I feel that the place of all others of which the memorial of the dead hero will most surely be a living force, is here in the United States Naval Academy, Annapolis, where year by year we turn out midshipmen who are to be officers in the future Navy, among whose founders the dead man stands first. Moreover, future officers who live within these walls will find in the career of the man whose life we this day celebrate, not merely a subject of admiration and respect but an object lesson to be taken to their innermost hearts. Every officer in our Navy should know by heart the deeds of John Paul Jones. Every officer in our Navy should feel in each fibre of his being the eager desire to emulate the energy, the professional capacity, the indomitable determination and the dauntless scorn of death, which marked John Paul Jones above his fellows.

Seven years were to elapse before his final resting place was completed and formally opened by President Woodrow Wilson in 1913. The tomb, which is now a national shrine, is made of marble and is modelled on the same lines as that of Napoleon. At each of the four bottom corners there are sculptured dolphins signifying peace. Round the crypt, which is large and circular, the walls contain all the honours that were bestowed upon him. Right in the centre, overlooking the sarcophagus, in a glass case, is the gold-hilted sword which was given to him by King Louis XVI of France; for, being a family of integrity, the descendants of Lieutenant Richard Dale, to whom he had entrusted it for safe-keeping, presented it to the Academy, prior to World War II.

"Come hell or high water," the preserved mortal remains of the gardener's barefooted boy came home at last to his adopted country, which, in the brashness of his youth, he had loved at first sight. It was not for him to be buried in Philadelphia, the first port from which he sailed on the USS *Alfred*; nor in that other sacred place of interment which also contains many heroes, Arlington National Cemetery. No! The Administration of the day, guided by the President, decided that there was only one place, reserved for him and him alone—the crypt in the cathedral of the Navy, the United States Naval Academy, Annapolis.

As a final resting place, this is an appropriate setting for the one who had advocated the construction of such a fine Institution many years before it was eventually founded. Since then, the same Academy has produced many illustrious naval and marine officers, and will no doubt continue to do so in the uncharted years that lie ahead. Here, present and future midshipmen will not only follow the traditions of their predecessors but will endeavour to excel the man who, by his courageous and gallant example on the high seas in the infancy of their Service, was the keel on which the United States Navy was built.

Like good sailors from all nations of the world, who have departed this life before or after him, he now rests in peace, awaiting a glorious, heavenly resurrection. Until that day arrives for mankind, when the curtain of human history is drawn, John Paul Jones is diligently guarded by members of that crack fighting corps of which he would have been so proud—the United States Marines.

ABOUT THE AUTHOR

WALLACE BRUCE was born on Vatersay, the Isle of Barra, Western-Isles, Scotland. He lectured in Social Studies at Springburn College, Glasgow. The research for his historical novel *John Paul Jones: Father of the United States Navy* took him to the Solway Firth, Whitehaven, Flamborough Head, The Texel, Harvard, and the United States Naval Academy, Annapolis. To understand what it might have been like under sail in the 18th century he underwent a grueling, yet enjoyable course on the sail training ship *Winston Churchill*, and visited the Flagship *HMS Victory*, to see how these graceful ships functioned. Armed with this knowledge, the author has been able to bring his novel alive, with his detailed and colourful descriptions of the naval battles and life afloat. One can sense the tension, the turmoil, and the might of the sea.

Wallace Bruce lives in Roy Bridge, near Fort William, Inverness-shire, in Scotland.

0-595-24232-4

Lightning Source UK Ltd.
Milton Keynes UK

171815UK00001B/25/A